SEE HOW THEY HIDE

Also by Allison Brennan

Quinn & Costa Thrillers

The Third to Die
Tell No Lies
The Wrong Victim
Seven Girls Gone
The Missing Witness

Regan Merritt Series

The Sorority Murder
Don't Open the Door

Angelhart Investigations

You'll Never Find Me

For additional books by Allison Brennan,
visit her website, allisonbrennan.com.

SEE HOW THEY HIDE

ALLISON BRENNAN

MIRA

MIRA™

ISBN-13: 978-0-7783-6844-1

Recycling programs for this product may not exist in your area.

See How They Hide

For questions and comments about the quality of this book, please contact us at CustomerService@Harlequin.com.

Mira
22 Adelaide St. West, 41st Floor
Toronto, Ontario M5H 4E3, Canada
MIRABooks.com

Printed in U.S.A.

For my grandpa Karl Hoffman (1906–1983),
who built a little cabin in the woods.

I miss you, Grandpa, and our cabin.

"You can keep as quiet as you like,
but one of these days somebody is going to find you."

—Haruki Murakami, *1Q84*

PROLOGUE

The wind howled and whistled through the trees late that winter night in the tiny town of South Fork, Colorado, blowing loose snow across roads and fields, creating mountains and valleys. If the wind stilled and the clouds lifted, by morning the town and trees would sparkle in the sunlight. Jesse could hardly wait to get out and take the sled to town, talk to people face-to-face instead of on his computer screen. He was naturally a social person, but his job kept him glued to his computer most of the day—and his vocation kept him glued to the computer most of the night.

At midnight, Jesse shut down his computer and stretched. He was done.

He hoped once Rina was out, Thalia could relax. They couldn't do this forever. *He* couldn't do it forever. At the beginning, he was all in. Now? He had doubts there was anyone left who wanted to be saved. Each one was harder than the last.

They all needed to de-stress.

He glanced down at the dog bed in the corner where Banjo, his eight-year-old Saint Bernard, looked at him with tired brown eyes.

"Five minutes," Jesse said. "You know you need to go, and if you go now, I'll be able to sleep in."

As if understanding what he said, Banjo sighed dramatically as only large dogs could and slowly got to his feet. Jesse ruffled his neck and said, "Really, you're going to complain about a little cold with that nice fur coat you wear?"

He grabbed his warm jacket off the hook by the door and put it on.

Jesse had inherited the cabin from his grandfather and over the years he'd installed better insulation, a more efficient woodstove, updated the kitchen, and enclosed the porch. This helped keep the heat inside and prevented snow and mud from being tracked into the house. In the summer, Jesse removed two walls so he could enjoy the fresh air. As his little sister said, he was much handier than the stereotypical computer geek.

The porch also kept the worst of the chill off him when Banjo did his business.

Jesse stood just inside the doorway, his hands stuffed into his pockets, as Banjo lumbered to a section of pine trees to the right of the house, his big, wide paws sure-footed in the snow. Jesse lost sight of his dog, then counted to one hundred. Banjo wouldn't wander, but sometimes even familiar smells distracted him, or a rabbit hopping through the snowbanks.

When time was up, he called, "Banjo! Come, Banjo!"

It was another thirty seconds before Banjo came out of the trees. Finally. Jesse hadn't wanted to put on his boots and go after the dog in the icy cold.

"You have the fur coat, not me," Jesse said as Banjo walked by him and shook his fur while he licked his lips. Great, Jesse thought. It wouldn't be the first time Banjo found himself a midnight snack in the woods. "You'd better not have eaten anything that will make you puke."

Banjo ignored him and went back to his dog bed, where he heaved another sigh as he settled himself down.

Jesse locked up, double-checked the windows, stoked the stove—it would be out by morning, but it didn't take long to heat up the place, and he had ample wood stacked in the grate.

He'd just started up the wide ladder to his loft when he saw a light outside the large picture window. As he turned to look, the light went out. It hadn't come from the highway, which was so far from his house that he couldn't hear or see traffic, and his driveway wasn't plowed, so no one could drive in, unless riding a snowmobile. He hadn't heard any vehicle at all. His closest neighbor was a good half-mile hike down the drive, on the plot of land where the highway met their private road. The widow, Mrs. Chastain, was in her seventies, and wouldn't be out this late. If she needed help, she would call him. While cell service was spotty, the phone lines were buried and rarely, if ever, went out.

Might be nothing. But his racing heart told him he shouldn't assume anything.

He was glad he'd already turned off the lights in the house, so no one outside would be able to see him move about through the windows. He backed off the ladder and headed to the closet next to the front door. He had a shotgun, which should be enough of a threat if someone was up to no good. He never had trouble here, but considering his night work, he was always alert.

Thalia's paranoia had rubbed off on him.

He looked out the small window embedded in the heavy front door. No vehicle, large or small. No flashlight bobbing among the trees. Nothing out of the ordinary.

He checked the lock again; it was bolted closed.

He passed his office and glanced inside; Banjo was asleep on his bed, unmindful of Jesse's rising fear. He loved Banjo, but maybe he should have opted for a more security-conscious German shepherd.

Jesse crossed through the kitchen to the side door. A large window looked out. He checked the lock. Secure. A durable lock led to the enclosed porch, but the porch itself had a flimsy bolt that he used only to prevent the wind from pushing open the door. There was nothing of value on the porch, and theft was rare in Rio Grande County.

Faint security lighting at each corner of his cabin illuminated the grounds for ten feet. Thalia had been wanting him to install an elaborate security system, but even if he did, he was well outside of town, so what would be the purpose? It would take at least fifteen minutes for the police to make it here, and they wouldn't be able to use his driveway in the winter.

At first, Jesse didn't see anything that stood out. He was about to turn away from the window when something caught his eye.

Footprints.

There were two distinct trails of footprints in the snow just inside the circle of light. They led from the grove of trees to the right and continued past his house. They hadn't been there when he let Banjo out earlier. He could still see Banjo's paw prints, though the wind had partly covered them.

These footprints were fresh. The wind hadn't had time to conceal them.

Heart thudding in his chest, he racked his shotgun. It took him two tries because his hands were shaking. It was nearly one in the morning, below thirty degrees, and two people were walking around his house.

Destroy your computer.

The thought came to him suddenly. There was only one reason someone might be here with ill intent: information.

He ran to his computer and hesitated. If he destroyed it now, all his work for the last two months would be gone. Thalia depended on him—and he would fail her. But more people would be in danger if he didn't destroy the data, so he really had no other choice.

As he was about to fire at his computer, he heard a gunshot. Then another. And another.

He aimed his shotgun for the doorway, taking a quick glance to his right to make sure that Banjo wasn't in the line of fire.

Banjo hadn't budged. But his chest moved up and down as he slumbered. Was he drugged?

Jesse remembered when Banjo came in he'd been licking his lips. He wasn't a guard dog; if he'd encountered a person outside, he wouldn't bark. He rarely even barked at wild animals.

Someone had drugged his dog.

There was no time—he couldn't let anyone access his computer. He turned his shotgun to the hard drive and pressed the trigger. Plastic and metal exploded; a piece of shrapnel—a twisted metal chunk from the inside of his computer—flew out and cut his face. He barely registered the stinging pain as he turned the shotgun back toward the door in self-defense.

A man and a woman stood there. Before he could rack it again, the man fired a pistol, hitting him in his shoulder. His shotgun sagged in his limp arm. As he struggled to straighten it, the man shot him again, hitting his biceps, and Jesse's weapon fell to the floor.

The woman stared at the computer. "That is unfortunate," she said, "but you know what we want."

"It's all gone," Jesse said, gritting his teeth against the pain. He put his right hand over the shoulder wound, trying to press down to stop the bleeding.

"The information is in your head. You will tell us everything we want to know."

"Never."

She smiled, but there was no pleasure in her expression. It was a smile of evil.

"Yes, Jesse, you will sing like a bird. Evan, how long do you think it'll take?"

Evan, a tall, skinny man wearing a knit cap and parka, said in a deep voice, "Twenty minutes, give or take."

The woman said, "Set the timer. I don't think it'll take twenty minutes."

Evan looked at his watch, pressed a button.

Then the woman turned her attention to his dog.

He couldn't stop the cry that escaped. He wanted to be brave. For Thalia, for Rina, for all the others.

But he wasn't.

"Don't touch him," Jesse said, his voice quaking in fear and anger.

"No," she said, stepping toward him, "it won't take me more than ten. And then we wait. Thalia will be here soon."

MONDAY

1

Ashland, Oregon

Kara Quinn savored the hot coffee as Ashland detective Ken Kinder drove them to the apartment where the victim, Jane Merrifield, had lived.

"You are my savior," she said. She needed the caffeine jolt after the early morning flight from DC; it was a bonus that it tasted rich and delicious. "I like your sheriff, but his coffee is disgusting."

Ken patted a large thermos sticking out of the center console of his sedan. "My wife takes care of me. I'm happy to share."

She glanced over at the beautiful small campus filled with grassy areas and mature trees. Southern Oregon University bordered Siskiyou Boulevard and had been built up and into the base of the mountains, the tops of which couldn't be seen through the fog.

She'd never gone to college, instead attending the LA Police Academy right after getting her GED. And while she'd been undercover at several colleges over the years, she'd never had the urge to attend. Still, it was a lovely campus. Maybe she could talk to Matt and they could find a case that would necessitate her going undercover at a university again. That might be fun, especially if it was a place like this.

Though *not* SOU. After all, she was investigating a homicide. A highly unusual double homicide where one victim was in Virginia and one was in Oregon. Hence, the FBI involvement. She was both surprised and pleased at the positive reception she and her partner, Michael Harris, had received when they walked into the Jackson County Sheriff's Department in Medford. They were happy to have the extra help.

"It's not the first time a college student has died," Ken said after a moment of silence as they both drank his wife's coffee. "I had a case a few years back where a girl was killed by her boyfriend, and another where two roommates got into an argument while drinking and one pushed the other off a three-story balcony. While no less tragic, they're straightforward and easy to solve. But this case...the more we learn, the less we know."

Early last Sunday morning, eight days ago, two people had been murdered at the same time in the same manner: Robert Benson, a married forty-seven-year-old antique store owner in rural Weems, Virginia, and twenty-one-year-old single college senior Jane Merrifield in Ashland, Oregon. Nothing seemed to connect the two victims, and no one would have thought to look at the cases together, except for two facts: both victims had their throats slit and the killers had littered the bodies with hundreds of dried red poppies.

Killers, because they died within the same one-hour window and there was no conceivable way one person could have committed both crimes.

Because of the unusual death scene, Dr. Catherine Jones, a

forensic psychiatrist who worked with the Mobile Response Team, had been brought in to consult on the Benson homicide. Catherine scoured the NCIC database for like crimes, and on Wednesday the murder of Jane Merrifield popped up. Jane's body had been found at a nearby park early Sunday morning. All the key forensic details matched.

That's when Catherine asked the MRT unit to coordinate the two investigations. Catherine was working closely with the FBI crime lab at Quantico, focusing on the psychology behind the flowers and looking at similar crimes. So far, she had next to nothing. Though the science was way over Kara's head, she knew that at a minimum, the lab could identify the region where the poppies were grown.

But the oddest fact in a series of odd facts was that, when Denver PD went to inform Jane's family of her death, no family could be found. The address listed on her college emergency form belonged to someone who had never heard of the Merrifields.

"Thanks for taking me to Jane's apartment," Kara said. She would have preferred to go alone, but since they were working on a task force and wanted to maintain the already good relationship local law enforcement had with their own FBI office, playing nice went with the job.

"We went through her place, but maybe you'll see something we missed. There was no sign of violence—we don't believe she was taken from her apartment. Her roommate and the roommate's boyfriend were at his apartment all night. When they returned, they assumed that Jane was at work. Didn't suspect anything until police came to the apartment Sunday morning."

"I read your reports—everyone you talked to said Jane was polite, friendly, quiet."

"*Nice* was the word everyone used. Her roommate, Ashley, has lived with her since the beginning of the term, but Jane has had the apartment since she started college three and a half years ago. That's why we really want to talk to Riley Pierce. She knew Jane since she was a freshman."

Riley Pierce was studying abroad in France, which included an internship at an art museum. She and Jane had lived together for three years.

"I've left a couple of messages," Ken continued. "She might not know anything of value for our investigation, but Ashley said Riley and Jane were best friends, and Ashley is subletting the apartment from Riley."

"Do you want me to get my team on it?" Kara asked. "The FBI has some cool resources, like access to the American Embassy and things like that. Maybe getting an official visit from a bigwig telling her to call you will help."

Ken grinned. "I like the way you put it. I think Agent Tucker is working on that."

"I'll follow up, make sure it's a priority," Kara said. "Riley might know how to reach Jane's family."

Kara messaged Ryder Kim, their team analyst and Expert-of-all-Things, and asked him to follow up on Riley Pierce, mentioning that the local FBI agent may have already started the process.

Jane and Ashley lived in an off-campus apartment a mile south of campus. Ken pulled into the small parking lot behind a sixteen-unit building. Dozens of bikes were locked on racks along the backside of the apartment. The bottom units had patios, while the upstairs units had wide balconies. All doors faced the rear.

"Ashley Grant, twenty-one, junior," Ken said as he approached the ground floor apartment marked 1B. "She was upset when we first talked to her, didn't have much information about Jane, other than her work and school schedule." He knocked and took a step back. Flowers blooming in colorful ceramic pots framed each side of the door and a cheerful sunflower sign proclaimed "Welcome!" under the Judas hole.

The local police had done a good job vetting Ashley and her boyfriend, David Martinelli. Ashley was originally from Reno, David a fifth-year senior from Portland. Both had part-time jobs—Ashley in the admissions office on campus, David at the mall in Medford. Neither had criminal records.

Police had also talked to every neighbor in the building. The last person to have seen her was her upstairs neighbor, who briefly spoke to Jane when she returned from the grocery store at 6:15 Saturday night.

She was dead six hours later.

Ken had called ahead and Ashley, expecting them, opened the door almost immediately. "Did you find the person who killed Jane?" she asked, though her voice suggested she had little hope for answers. "I haven't heard anything on the news, but..." She shrugged.

"We are investigating every lead," Ken said. "Ashley, this is Kara Quinn with the FBI. We have a few follow-up questions, as I said on the phone."

Ashley opened the door wider for them to enter. "Everyone is kinda on edge," she said. "Ashland is totally safe. I've never known anyone who was...well, *murdered.* It doesn't happen here, you know? It's hard to wrap my mind around it. Now we never go anywhere alone, and my boyfriend is staying over every night. Until we know what's going on, he's going to just move in, you know?"

I know, Kara thought sarcastically.

"Caution is wise," Ken said, "but I don't think you have anything to worry about, Ashley."

The apartment was small but neat. A wide counter with four stools separated a narrow kitchen from the living area. The living/dining combo room had overflowing bookshelves, a bean bag chair, two love seats covered with an array of colorful pillows, and a television mounted to the wall. Doors to the right and left went to the two bedrooms.

Kara confirmed what they already knew from Ken's first interview with Jane's roommate. Ashley had nothing else to add and seemed genuine in all her responses.

Kara said, "We need to look at Jane's room again."

"Right. Sure." She motioned to the door closest to the kitchen.

Kara walked to the threshold of Jane's room and opened the door. Before entering, she let her eyes sweep slowly across the room. There was a lot a cop could tell about a victim by observing their personal space. Most people didn't think to clean up a mess or hide things they didn't want others to find. Most people expected to come home every night.

Jane's bedroom was sparse. Kara didn't have a lot of stuff, but Jane's room seemed almost sterile.

A twin bed—neatly made. A dresser. Desk and chair. Single bookshelf filled with books. *Neatly* shelved books, perfectly lined up. None with titles Kara recognized, except a Bible on the top shelf. No flourishes anywhere.

Nothing super personal, like pictures of friends and family or sticky notes with reminders. Two motivational posters decorated one wall, but they could have hung in any classroom or doctor's office. One, a mountain with a hiker on top and a Booker T. Washington quote: "You measure the size of the accomplishment by the obstacles you had to overcome to reach your goals." The other, a sunset over an ocean and a quote attributed to Christopher Columbus: "You can never cross the ocean until you have the courage to lose sight of the shore."

They were pretty pictures, but did the quotes mean anything to Jane? Kara would normally dismiss such signs, yet they were the only two decorations on the wall, framed, side by side, each perfectly aligned.

Kara walked around the room. The posters could be seen from the bed and the desk chair. Sleeping or working, Jane would see the words, the images.

They meant something to Jane Merrifield. Could they help Kara find her killer?

From behind her, Ken said, "Our people went through here, but there wasn't much to find."

"She was twenty-one," Kara said. "No concert tickets tucked into the mirror frame, no pictures of friends tacked to the wall, no mementoes or knickknacks." Kara pulled a book from the shelf. The cover didn't speak to her, but it looked like *Little House on the Prairie* for adults, with a woman in old-time garb gazing wistfully at a dry field.

Not something Kara thought a young adult would read. The other books were similar. The small print on the back cover indicated *inspirational romance.*

Okay, Kara thought. A nice, tidy, sweet, religious young adult. Who would want her dead?

"She lived here for three and a half years," Kara continued. "Accumulated next to nothing. Do you have kids?"

"Three. Two girls and a boy. I see where you're going and I agree—for a college student, this is unusual. But I don't know that it's suspicious."

"Do you know if she went to church? She has a Bible and some other religious books."

"Ashley said Jane didn't go to church, but if she did without her roommate's knowledge, it wasn't often. I have an officer going around to the churches in the area and asking about her, but so far no one has recognized her."

Kara opened the dresser drawers. Clothes neatly folded. Nothing that shouldn't be here. No papers or sex toys or hidden photographs.

Closet, the same. She didn't have a lot of clothes, but what she had were hung neatly by type of garment. A single warm jacket. Two sweaters. Four shirts. Two nice slacks. Two dresses. Four pairs of shoes lined neatly on the floor. The top shelf had more books and a small black suitcase. Nothing out of place, except that there wasn't much here.

Desk, the same. Except...

Kara pulled out a small box from the bottom desk drawer and opened it. It was a jewelry box without jewelry, but this was where Jane stored everything personal.

"We didn't miss that," Ken said, sounding defensive even though Kara hadn't said anything. "I assumed they were reminders of friends or family, but there are no names or phone numbers to verify. We took photos of the contents, assuming her next of kin would want it."

"I'm trying to get a sense of Jane. All this—" she waved her arm around the room "—says something. And *this*—" she put the box down on the desk "—also says something."

What, she wasn't quite sure, but she'd figure it out.

The box held several photos, letters, and a wooden bird. Beautiful, detailed craftsmanship—the wings had individual feathers carved, the definition in the veins visible even though the carving fit in the palm of her hand.

Most of the pictures were of Jane and a girl with dark red hair who Ken said was her former roommate, Riley Pierce. The only photo of Jane with someone else featured a teenage boy. Jane herself was not more than sixteen in the picture. The boy had dark curly hair and pale eyes. Their heads tilted toward each other. Both were smiling. The background was a forest, but it could have been here in Oregon, back where she grew up in Colorado, or any number of other places.

Kara flipped the picture over—no names or dates. The photo had been taken by an instant camera, the colors faded, the edges bent as if the thick picture had been in a pocket for a long time.

"Does this place look familiar?" she asked Ken, holding the photo out to him.

"Those are pine trees, but I couldn't say where it was taken."

"I'd like to take the box, if you don't mind. Maybe our forensic shrink can glean something from this."

He nodded. "The sheriff said to give you anything you need."

As Kara was putting everything back in, she felt something slick against the side, wedged into the box seam. She pulled it up. Pressed between two sheets of thin plastic was a preserved red poppy, practically invisible against the dark wood of the box.

Okay, this is creepy, Kara thought.

There was nothing to indicate why Jane had the poppy preserved, what it meant, who had given it to her. But it was in the box, and her body was found covered with hundreds of red poppies.

Definitely creepy.

Ken frowned. "Honestly, I can't tell you whether that was in the box or not when we first came in here."

"It was wedged down the side, see?" She put it back. She couldn't even see it unless she angled the box just right in the light. "I'm going to take a video of the room for our shrink."

"I'll wait outside." He closed the door behind him.

Kara took pictures of the room, the bookshelf, then a three-sixty video.

Jane Merrifield didn't have a large footprint. She didn't leave much behind. Did the boy in the picture kill her? Maybe an ex-boyfriend? Someone else? A stranger?

According to Ken's interview with Ashley, Jane was a homebody. She went to class, worked at a local bakery three mornings a week, and spent a lot of time reading.

Why did it feel like Jane Merrifield was a ghost even before she was murdered?

2

Ashland, Oregon

When Kara stepped into the living room, Ashley was sitting on the couch, her laptop on her crossed legs.

"Um, Detective Kinder went outside," Ashley said.

Kara sat across from Ashley. She put the box on the table and asked, "Have you ever seen this before?"

Ashley shrugged. "Once or twice. Jane sometimes had it on her desk—it's a pretty box. I commented on it, asked where she got it. She said a friend made it for her when she was little."

"Did she talk to you about her childhood?"

"Not really. She was an only child. She never talked about her parents, and I didn't pry. I mean, not everyone has a good relationship with their mom and dad, you know?"

Kara knew. She hadn't spoken to her parents in years.

"You know," Ashley continued, "Jane was always sort of sad even when she looked happy, if that makes sense." She shrugged.

"Do you have an example?"

She thought, then said, "I invited her to come home with me for Thanksgiving. She didn't want to, but I pushed—I knew she'd have fun, and she finally agreed. I have a huge family—aunts and uncles and lots of cousins. We play games and have tons of food and my uncle Ted always drinks too much but he's a funny drunk, and my aunt May sings Christmas carols—she has an amazing voice, and we do a scavenger hunt. It's always a blast.

"I didn't think Jane was having fun because she just sort of hung back, you know? She talked to people, but only when they talked to her first. But when we drove back here the next day, she said she had the most fun she'd ever had in her life. And...I think she meant it. It wasn't hyperbole. I kind of thought then that she had a rough childhood, you know? Like maybe her parents were mean or abusive. She told me I was lucky."

"And other than Riley Pierce, she didn't have any close friends?"

"She was friendly with everyone, but, yeah, no one she hung out with regularly. She planned to move to France when she graduated. I don't think she wanted to."

"Why?"

"She loves it here. Said she never wanted to leave, but that she promised Riley that after they graduated, they'd both live in France. They were really close, like sisters."

Kara pulled out the pressed poppy. "Have you seen this before?"

Ashley tilted her head. "That's a poppy—they're everywhere."

"It's a red poppy."

"I mean, I've seen them growing, but I haven't seen *that* poppy."

"Did Jane ever talk to you about flowers?"

She shrugged. "I don't think so."

The police had withheld the information about the red poppies, and Ashley showed no sign that the flower held any significance for her. But it was important to the killer. Kara now realized it was also important to the victims.

Kara put the pressed poppy back in the box, closed it, and thanked Ashley for her time. She joined Ken outside. He was standing next to his sedan in the thick fog. A light, misty rain had started to fall.

"All good?" Ken asked.

"Yeah."

"Something wrong?"

She shook her head. "Just turning things around in my head. Bakery next?"

"They're closed Mondays, open at five a.m. tomorrow."

She groaned. "I guess there's no way to convince the owner to talk to us today?"

"Sure, but the staff is who you want, the people who worked with Jane."

"Okay, tomorrow I'll be up bright and early." The police had already talked to Jane's co-workers, so the follow-up could wait until tomorrow. She held up the box. "I need to overnight this to my team."

"I'll take you to FedEx."

She climbed into the passenger seat and texted her team.

A second search of Jane Merrifield's room uncovered a red poppy pressed between two sheets of plastic, wedged in a handmade keepsake box. I'm going to overnight the box and contents because I think this is important, but don't know why. Attaching pictures.

She sent the message and relevant photos, leaned back, and closed her eyes.

Definitely not a coincidence that Jane had a preserved poppy and the killer covered her body with poppies.

Her skin prickled and she had the feeling she was being watched. She opened her eyes, looked out the passenger window. A young woman, college-aged, was sitting on a short stone wall, looking at her. When Kara caught her eye, the girl didn't avert her gaze, but stared at the unmarked sedan as Ken pulled onto Siskiyou Boulevard. Kara looked over her shoulder and the girl stood and walked in the opposite direction.

"Stop," Kara said.

Ken glanced in the rearview mirror, then pulled over. "What's wrong? Forget something?"

"One sec." She opened Jane's box and pulled out the photo of Jane and the girl Ashley had identified as Riley Pierce.

"I think I just saw Riley." Kara got out of the car, and walked briskly down the street, but didn't see her. She stopped where the girl had been sitting. There was no sign of her. Three young men riding bikes on the opposite side of the road. Someone smoking pot on their balcony in the apartment above Ashley's.

Kara looked directly across the street. Riley had a clear view of not only Ashley and Jane's apartment, but the lot where Ken had parked. She'd been watching them.

Ken backed up his cruiser until he reached her. "You saw Riley Pierce?"

"I'm not positive, but it looked like her. She's gone now. Wait here for a sec, okay?"

Ken agreed, though he seemed both confused and irritated.

Kara ran across the street and knocked on Ashley's door. She answered, surprised to see Kara again. "Hi?" she said cautiously.

"Have you seen or spoken to Riley Pierce since Jane died?"

She shook her head. "No."

"She hasn't called or texted or emailed? Have you seen her around town?"

"She lives in France. She wasn't my friend—I only met her once."

"If she contacts you, call me, day or night, okay?"

"Sure," she said in a tone that suggested she thought Kara was asking for the impossible.

Kara walked back to Ken and got into his car. "We need to find Riley Pierce."

3

Ashland, Oregon

Why, why, why did you come back?

Riley had been safe in France, far from anyone who would do her harm. Yet, she'd returned to Ashland because Jane was dead.

If she had been here, Jane would still be alive. Riley may have been paranoid, but it kept them safe. Jane was too trusting, too kind, and now she was dead. Guilt filled her, drowning her with grief. She'd left, now Jane was gone.

Riley had to stop thinking about it. The what-ifs, the guilt, the regrets. The present was all that mattered. One day at a time. Pushing forward because looking back would shatter her.

Remembering the past only brought sorrow and rage. Thinking about what could have been created a whirlpool of doubt and regret. The future was uncertain, so thinking about what might happen would only bring anxiety.

Especially when you must be extra careful so they never find you.

Stay quiet, stay humble, stay free. That was the only way to survive.

Jane was dead and Riley had to accept it, move forward. But in the back of her mind she knew that somehow, someway, her mother was responsible. Her mother had found Jane.

If she had found Jane, did that mean she knew Riley was alive?

No. Impossible.

Riley had been dead for nearly four years, so why now? She hadn't even been in the country for the last eight months! There was no way her mother knew she was alive. No possible way.

For half a minute she thought about telling the police why Jane had been killed, but they wouldn't believe her. Her story sounded so outrageous they might think that she was guilty of murder, or that she made up the story for attention.

Even if they believed her, even if she could convince them of the truth, they couldn't help because she didn't know who *specifically* came here to lure Jane to her death. She couldn't tell the police where her mother lived or how to find her.

The Rocky Mountains was a big area to search.

She knew how that conversation would go.

"My mother wanted Jane dead, but she didn't kill Jane herself because she never leaves home."

"Where can we find her?"

"Well, I'm not exactly sure. Somewhere in Colorado, in the mountains, but I don't have an address. I can't even take you there because I left in the middle of the night. There were tall trees, big rocks, and miles of land before I even saw civilization."

If only she'd gotten here earlier, she could have grabbed the box before the police. Everything had just become a lot more complicated.

Oblivious to the increasing rain, Riley walked along the fence of the sports training field, not even gloating that she'd slipped away from the cop who spotted her. Just the *idea* of talking to the police panicked her.

After all, she'd grown up believing that the police were the enemy, that they would imprison her without cause, because she was from Havenwood. The stories her mother told...it didn't matter that now Riley knew they were twisted lies with half-truths, that even now Riley didn't know what was real and what her mother made up. Nineteen years of constant fear of the outside world was hard to break.

Riley knew Ashland better than most anyone. When she and Jane first moved here, she'd made it her mission to learn every street, path, fence, and building within a half-mile radius of their apartment, plus every inch of the campus. If they had to disappear, Riley could make it happen.

Jane handled the fear differently. She became a homebody, read books, learned to cook, took care of their apartment. Riley didn't fault her. Jane was a year younger and she'd always been more...*delicate.* Sensitive. It was Riley's job to protect her, to watch for threats, to create escape plans.

Tears burned but didn't fall. Dammit, dammit, dammit! Out of everyone from Havenwood, Jane was the best, brightest light. The darkness hadn't extinguished her soul.

Riley had failed her.

It didn't matter that Jane had urged her to take the opportunity in France. Initially, Riley hadn't even considered applying for the study abroad internship at a museum where she could study all the great artists and have the time and the freedom to draw. But Jane supported her, pushed her, encouraged her.

"Find peace, Riley. I'm okay because of you. I want you to find the peace I have found."

She should have stayed and protected the girl she thought of as a sister.

Riley had never told Jane that she hadn't found peace, even halfway across the world. Havenwood was always in the background of everything she did, said, thought. No matter how hard she pushed the memories away, they were there, lurking beneath the surface, returning in her dreams, dominating her nightmares.

She had escaped three and a half years ago and felt as if she were still trapped. Not all of Havenwood was bad. There was good...there was bad...there was light...and there was a deep, deep darkness that came from her mother's twisted beliefs.

Months after moving to France, Riley accepted that she hadn't left Ashland because she was running from Jane, or the claustrophobia of a small college town, or even from her family... She'd been running from herself.

You can never run away from who you are.

Riley realized that she was soaked through as the rain continued to fall. She found a tree to sit under and leaned against the trunk, staring at the empty practice field that marked the southern boundary of campus.

Jane was dead and Riley wanted vengeance. There was no justice in the world, but she could taste vengeance, feel the retribution she would dole out on those who killed an innocent.

Did Thalia know? If they found Jane, could they find everyone?

Grief ate at her as she considered her options, the quiet of the wet, foggy field wrapping around her, giving her a momentary feeling of overwhelming—and welcome—solitude.

Her first thought: run back to France. Grieve for Jane there, in safety.

The cowardly option.

Guilt and responsibility. Jane wasn't the only person at risk. If Thalia didn't know that Jane was dead, Riley had to tell her and find a way to warn the others.

There were two people who knew how to reach Thalia. Jesse, and she'd already left him an encoded note on the private online message board he maintained. She didn't know when he'd check it, but if he had, he hadn't yet reached out to her. She didn't know where he lived, only that it was somewhere in Colorado.

And Chris. Riley knew where Chris lived.

She pulled out her smartphone and made a flight reservation to Albuquerque under her second name. He would help. He might be the only person who *could* help. And she wanted to tell him about Jane in person. She sent him a quick, vague message over WhatsApp.

Watch your back. See you soon.

Leaving Ashland felt like she was abandoning her best, her *only* friend, yet again. But she had to protect the others.

Far too many people had died in her short life. And because her mother thought she was dead, Riley might be the only person who could stop this.

Taking a last, long look at the field, Riley pulled the hood of her jacket over her head and briskly walked back to her rental car—which she'd rented under the name Riley Prince, her second identity.

It came in handy to have multiple identities when you didn't really know who you were.

Or who you wanted to be.

4

Weems, Virginia

FBI special agent in charge Matt Costa quickly dealt with necessary paperwork sitting in his new office in the basement of the FBI Academy, where the Behavioral Sciences team had originally been housed.

They'd moved last month from the cramped conference room at national headquarters where they had been assigned after the formation of the Mobile Response Team a year ago. While it was much better to have this large suite of offices where everyone had their own private space surrounding a central bullpen, there were no windows and Kara called it the "dungeon."

He picked up his ringing phone. "Costa."

"It's Kara. I'm sending a package."

"I got your message."

"The old roommate? The one in France that no one has spoken to? I'm almost positive I saw her outside Jane's apartment. She disappeared fast when I went to question her. I had my eyes off her for less than a minute. I suspect she slipped between a couple of apartment buildings, but I can't be certain. It was foggy."

"How positive that it was Pierce?"

She hesitated. "Eighty percent. I'd just seen her picture, but I only got a passing glance on the street. Detective Kinder is following up."

"We can find out if she used her passport," Matt said.

Ryder buzzed Matt. "Agent Stewart is on the line."

"Thanks, Ryder. Tell him one minute." To Kara he said, "You also found a red poppy in Merrifield's room?"

"Preserved between plastic sheets. Was there anything like this with Benson's belongings?"

"Not that we found. Sloane and I are going to talk to his widow again this afternoon. We'll ask her. Keep me updated—I have another call."

"Roger that," she said lightly and hung up.

Matt switched to Agent George Stewart who worked out of the Denver field office. "Hi, George, what did you find?"

"Nothing. Absolutely nothing," George said. "The girl doesn't exist."

After Denver PD couldn't locate Jane Merrifield or her family, the FBI looked deeper into her background.

George continued, "Jane Merrifield did not graduate from Cherry Creek High School as stated in her college admission package. The only Jane Merrifield in the entire school district is a seven-year-old first grader.

"I double-checked the residence—nothing. I considered transposed numbers and checked every house that could have been hers—nothing. There are nine Joseph Merrifields in the greater Denver area, none who've heard of twenty-one-year-old Jane. There are only two Bridget Merrifields in the area—one who is ninety, one who is seventy-four.

"We checked every school district, including the graduation year before and after what's listed. We can't find one person at *any* high school in the area, public or private, who knows or recognizes Jane Merrifield's picture. We ran her prints—nothing. My guess? She's not from Denver and her name isn't Jane Merrifield."

Matt absorbed what George was saying. "Okay," he said slowly, "what about legal cases? Name changes? Sealed files?"

"We need a legal name to get any sealed files. There's nothing listing Jane Merrifield. I considered maybe a witness protection gig, but the US Marshals said they don't have anyone in the program with that name or description. I'm still working on a couple of angles, but I don't see them going anywhere. If they do, I'll let you know."

"Thanks, George. Keep the file open. We're looking to interview Merrifield's first college roommate, and if we can get more information from her, I'll send it to you to follow up."

"Want to know my gut?"

"Shoot."

"She has a damn good fake identity. Someone with major skills created it. Find that person, you'll find out who Jane Merrifield really is."

Matt agreed. Before he left to reinterview Robert Benson's widow, he relayed to Ryder what he learned from George.

"Talk to Cybercrimes, they might have a person of interest, someone who can pull something like this off. Robert Benson was an established business owner, but we have nothing on him before he moved to Weems. Maybe his widow knows, maybe she doesn't, but two people with no backgrounds, killed on the same day in the same way, is not a coincidence."

Agent Sloane Wagner was a good fit for the Mobile Response Team, Matt thought as they walked up to the Benson house early Monday afternoon.

Last year, Sloane had taken an undercover assignment for Matt and done an exemplary job under difficult circumstances. She'd earned Matt's respect with her professionalism and intelligence, and after consulting with his own boss, Tony Greer, he'd extended her an offer to join his team. Sloane was not only smart and disciplined after twelve years in the Marines, but also commanded respect among those who worked with her.

Evelyn Benson answered the door. Robert's widow was a tall, slender woman a few years older than her dead husband. Her long gray hair was neatly braided down her back. Her crystal clear blue eyes were intelligent and questioning, and her face was devoid of make-up. She seemed to have aged in the week since Matt spoke to her.

"Agent... Costa," she said after a beat, as if she'd forgotten his name.

"Mrs. Benson. Thank you for making time to speak with us again."

"Do you know...who killed..." Her voice trailed off as if she didn't want to know the answer. She touched the simple gold cross hanging around her neck.

"May we come in?" Matt asked.

"Oh...yes. Of course." She opened the door wider and Matt and Sloane stepped in. They'd been there before—the house was comfortable, clean, and cluttered with antique furniture, walls covered with elaborate wallpaper, and tables topped with doilies and delicate lamps. A house that Matt could see an elderly couple living in, not the middle-aged Bensons.

"Can I... Would you like coffee? Tea?"

"We're fine, thank you," Matt said. He motioned to the dining room off the entry. "Can we sit and talk for a few minutes?" No matter how many times he'd interviewed survivors, it was never easy.

Mrs. Benson nodded and sat on the edge of one of the chairs, as if ready to jump up and bolt at any moment.

The house was immaculate and too warm for comfort, even against the outside cold. Though technically spring, Virginia was still in the throes of winter, snow slowly melting under trees and flowers not ready to bloom.

"How are you holding up, Mrs. Benson?" Sloane asked gently.

Evelyn shook her head. "I wake up and think Robert is in the kitchen. He always rose first, would make coffee, feed the chickens, collect their eggs. He loved mornings. It's why—I didn't think twice when he wasn't in bed Sunday morning."

She took a deep breath. "I miss Robert. I never thought I'd marry. But he walked into church one Sunday and I just knew. These have been the happiest ten years of my life." Her voice cracked at the end. "I wish I knew why someone would hurt him. Robert was the kindest man I have ever known. He never raised his voice, he treated me like...like I was precious, like I was a gift. He told me that once, that I was a gift from God who gave him a new life."

Now the tears came and she brushed them away. "People from church, from town, come by every day, bring me food, talk. I listen, shoo them away after a while. I can only take people in small doses. I see the pity. I don't want pity. I want Robert back."

She steadied herself, looked directly at Matt with a damp, steady gaze. "You said you had questions."

"We know this is a difficult time, but it's important," Matt said. "You've been married for ten years, correct?"

She nodded. "Ten years last December."

"And you met a year before that?"

"Yes. I honestly don't think there was more than a day or two that we didn't see each other after we first met. We knew."

"Where is Robert from originally? Does he have family?"

"He was born in Colorado, but he told me he had a difficult childhood and didn't have any family."

Colorado. It was a tenuous link between Jane Merrifield and Robert Benson, but it was a link.

"Do you know where in Colorado?" Matt asked.

She shook her head. "He never told me."

"What did he do for a living before he came here?"

"He was an accountant."

"Do you know who he worked for?"

"Why is this important?" she asked.

"Your husband had no known enemies," Matt said. "Everyone we've spoken with had only good things to say, confirmed that you and Robert had a good marriage. So we need to look to the time before he came to town."

"Pastor Henry said it was a random crime. Someone passing through town, someone who likes...likes to..." She couldn't say it, but Matt knew what she meant.

Someone who likes to kill.

Matt told Evelyn the truth. "There was a similar murder on the West Coast. A young woman was killed in the same manner as your husband. Do you know or have you heard of Jane Merrifield?"

Evelyn stared at him, confused, shook her head.

"Jane is twenty-one, a college student at Southern Oregon University in Ashland," Matt said.

"I don't know her."

"Can I show you her picture? You might know her under a different name."

Evelyn nodded, and Sloane took a photo of Jane from her folder. It was a picture her roommate, Ashley, had provided, not a forensic photo. Jane was smiling, happy, alive.

Evelyn reached out, but stopped short of touching it. "She's dead, too?"

"Yes, ma'am."

"She's so young. I've never seen her before, but I'll pray for her soul. She was killed like Robert?"

"Yes. We're trying to find any connection between the two victims." He paused. "Jane is from Colorado."

Evelyn looked confused.

"It's the only commonality between them," Sloane said.

"Robert never talked about his past, and he never mentioned this girl. Like I said, Robert had a difficult life—he didn't talk about it. He said his life began when he met me, and he has never said or done anything to make me think he was anything but what he showed himself to be—a kind, generous man who treated every person with respect."

"Would you mind if we went through his personal effects?"

She didn't want to let them; Matt could see it in her eyes. He waited. He could get a warrant, but her cooperation would make everything easier.

Evelyn nodded once. "Where would you like to begin?" Her voice was weary, resigned.

"Did he have an office? A room or desk or dresser you didn't use?"

"He did all his work in his office in the store," she said. "Home was our sanctuary. We didn't work here."

"Would you mind if I look through his office at the store? And you can show Sloane his personal space?"

She rose, retrieved a key from a hook by the door, handed it to Matt. "I haven't been in since… I'm not ready. If you don't mind."

He took the key. "Thank you." He said to Sloane, "I won't be long."

Sloane walked Matt to the door and said out of Evelyn's earshot, "Could Jane be his daughter?"

"It's a thought," he said. "See what you can learn from her. I'll call Jim, have him expedite DNA testing. It should be easy enough to prove or disprove. Text or call if you need me."

Sloane closed the door behind him, turned back to Evelyn. "My boss didn't want to impose, but I would sure love a cup of whatever you have."

Evelyn seemed to relax before her eyes. Sloane knew women

like her. She needed to be a hostess in her home, but more, she needed something to do with her hands.

Sloane followed Evelyn to the kitchen where she immediately put a teakettle on. The kitchen appliances had been updated, but the cabinets and counters were old and well cared for.

"You have a lovely home," Sloane said as Evelyn brought out teacups, sugar, honey, lemon, and poured cream in a creamer. She brought out a jar of a variety of tea bags.

"Thank you. The house has been in my family for generations, but I never felt—well, Robert really made it a home for me." She said quietly, "I miss him."

"I know this is difficult for you," Sloane said. "We're going to try to make it as easy as possible, but that doesn't mean it'll be easy, especially losing someone you love to violence."

Evelyn stared at the stove, waiting for the kettle. "Robert was kind, as I said, but he was also quiet. He never talked about his past. Some of my friends at church were worried that he was a con artist or a thief or was running from the law."

She didn't say anything for a long minute, then the kettle whistled and she brought it to the table. She poured hot water into first Sloane's cup and then her own, then placed the pot on a trivet. She selected a bag, and started steeping. Sloane did the same, added a few drops of honey, and waited for Evelyn to speak in her own time, her own way.

"Before we married," Evelyn continued, "Robert told me Pastor Henry asked him several pointed questions. I've known Henry since I was little, and I'm sure he had noble intentions.

"Robert didn't want to talk about his life before he moved here, he said it was the past and I was his future. But he said I deserved to know he wasn't a criminal and had never been married. He told me he hadn't been physically abused, but that the emotional abuse was almost unbearable. He didn't go into details, and what he said hurt him to say, so I didn't push. I suspect he may have been involved in a bad relationship. Abuse isn't always man to woman, parent to child."

"True," Sloane said, sipping her tea. "And he didn't talk about who was abusive? How long it went on?"

"No. I told him I didn't need to know, that I trusted him. For ten years, he never did anything to cause me to doubt him."

"In hindsight, looking back to the days before his murder, can you think of anything Robert said or did that was out of character? Was he quieter than usual? Receive a call that upset him? A letter?"

Evelyn shook her head. "Saturday we attended a wedding for my best friend's daughter. It was lovely. We were home by eight in the evening, relaxed by the fire with a glass of wine, as was our habit, and were in bed by ten. Sunday, we attend church and open the antique store at noon. When he wasn't in bed when I woke at five thirty, I assumed he was taking care of the chickens—he loves those chickens. I didn't—I didn't realize anything was wrong until he didn't come in for breakfast."

Evelyn first checked the barn and then the store; when she didn't find Robert, and his car was still there, she'd called the police and they came out immediately. Such was a town like Weems, where everyone knew everyone. The responding officer looked around and found Robert dead—throat slit, hands bound, body covered with red poppies—in the woods behind the barn. The coroner determined he'd been killed between two and four in the morning.

There was no sign of forced entry. No sign of disturbance in the house, barn, or store. Evelyn hadn't woken up, didn't hear any vehicles or voices.

Robert Benson had left his house quietly and been violently murdered.

The team's theory was that Robert had received a threat or warning in the days leading up to his death and left to meet his killer because he didn't want harm to come to his wife. The second theory was that he heard something outside and went to investigate.

Their investigation indicated that the marriage was solid and there was no financial motive. Robert kept the books and the FBI forensic auditor determined they were in order. Robert had brought nothing to the marriage, so if it was the other way around and Evelyn was murdered, they may have looked to a financial motive. Evelyn owned the property and Robert had helped her expand what had been a small antique store into a more successful, profitable business.

No struggle, few forensic clues. Blunt force trauma to the back of the head, but no external injuries, other than the slit throat. The coroner surmised that the victim had been attacked from behind, bound, and had his throat slit while prone.

The flowers held the most potential for evidence, which the FBI lab was still processing. They determined that the poppies were likely grown in a greenhouse, but the roots and petals were undergoing further testing. They hoped to narrow down the region based on plant DNA and might be able to identify fertilizer or pesticides that could be traced.

Robert Benson's fingerprints hadn't popped in any criminal database. Didn't mean he wasn't guilty of something, but so far they had no idea where he'd lived or what he'd done before showing up in Weems eleven years ago.

With the near-identical murder of Jane Merrifield, they had shifted gears, looking for commonalities. But they were still no closer to answers.

"Evelyn," Sloane said, "if you think of anything, no matter how small—a name, a place, a memory Robert shared with you—even a good memory, about a time or event before he met you—please call. You have Matt's number and my number. We want to find who did this to your family."

"I will," she said.

"If you don't mind, may I look through Robert's personal things?"

Evelyn led Sloane upstairs. Their bedroom was modest in size, all the furniture well-made antiques. The room was timeless—Evelyn, at fifty-four, acted older than her age, and her decor mimicked that.

Who were you, Robert Benson? Where did you come from? What were you running from?

Who killed you?

Evelyn watched from the doorway and didn't say anything as Sloane slowly turned and observed the room.

Sloane suspected that Robert Benson had been hiding a secret. Were answers hidden in this room?

She ignored Evelyn's sad eyes as the woman watched her from the doorway. The widow didn't have to tell her what side of the bed her husband slept on: the left side closest to the window had a historical romance novel on the nightstand, a pair of delicate reading glasses, an antique clock, and a glass flowered lamp. The right side had another glass lamp, but this in a solid green; a digital alarm, and a nonfiction World War II story—an older book that Sloane had read when it first came out called *Unbroken*.

She crossed to Robert's side of the bed and opened his nightstand drawer. Inside was a Bible, box of tissues, coins, aspirin, an unused notepad, pencil, and a nearly complete crossword puzzle magazine.

On the short dresser were many figurines and a long lace doily. On the tall dresser was a framed photo of Robert and Evelyn on their wedding day, and a candid picture of them outdoors, Evelyn laughing and Robert smiling. Next to the frame was a man's wallet.

Sloane opened the wallet. A Virginia driver's license for Robert Benson. A business credit card. A photo of Evelyn. Sixty-three dollars in cash.

And a single dried red poppy.

Sloane didn't touch the flower. She said, "May I take Robert's wallet? We'll return it."

"Why?" she asked.

"There's a dried flower in here. I want to discuss it with my superiors."

"A flower?" Evelyn frowned. "Why would anyone care about a flower?"

"Do red poppies hold any significance to you or Robert?"

She blinked, shook her head, then paused.

"You thought of something?" Sloane pushed.

"Once," Evelyn said, "years ago, the year after we were married, we drove down to Richmond for my niece's graduation party. It was Memorial Day weekend and I wanted to leave flowers on my parents' graves, so on our way home we stopped. There were red poppies on so many of the graves it surprised me. Robert was solemn. He said they were flowers of remembrance for military service—for fallen soldiers—but they had a darker meaning for some."

"What kind of darker meaning?" Sloane asked. Catherine Jones, the team's forensic psychiatrist, had explained the symbolism of red poppies, but no one had yet figured out why that specific flower was left with the bodies. Catherine believed it was as a sign of remembrance—that the killers were using the red poppies in a twisted way to tell the victim that they remembered a slight or grievance, or as a sign that they would remember the victim after death.

"He didn't say," Evelyn said. "Not specifically. He put his arm around me and said the flowers were a symbol of dark times. Do you think that means anything? Why would he have a red poppy in his wallet?"

"I don't know. But we'll find out."

5

Weems, Virginia

As Matt drove with Sloane to the Bensons' church, he explained that he hadn't uncovered anything of interest in Robert's office, then listened to Sloane as she reported what she learned when searching their bedroom. The wallet was secured in an evidence bag, but Sloane showed him pictures she took of the dried poppy.

"How long do you think it was inside the wallet?" Matt asked. "Wouldn't a flower fall apart over time?"

"Yes," Sloane said. "It was slid into a slot with nothing else, and seemed to be pressed into the leather, as if it had been there for some time—I didn't touch it because it would have crumbled."

"The lab should be able to narrow it down," he said.

"I don't think Evelyn knows anything else," Sloane said. "I *do* think she recognizes that the lack of a background is suspicious, but she never questioned him. She trusted him implicitly."

"Let's talk to Catherine, then their pastor," Matt said.

He pulled over a block away from the church and called Catherine.

"Hi, Catherine, you're on the phone with Sloane and me," Matt said. "Did you get the pictures of the red poppies found here and in Oregon?"

"Yes," Catherine said.

"And what do you think?"

Catherine didn't speak at first, but that was her way, and had been even back fifteen years ago when they went through the FBI academy together. She wanted to be precise.

"Clearly, the poppies—specifically *red* poppies—are important to both the killers and the victims. This suggests that the motive is more personal than I initially thought. That, coupled with what we've learned over the last week—that the backgrounds of Ms. Merrifield and Mr. Benson are murky at best, and possibly fraudulent—I wouldn't be surprised if the victims also knew each other."

"Even with the large age difference?" Matt asked.

"Your call to run a paternity test was smart," Catherine said, "and we should have the results tomorrow. They are the same blood type—A positive—but that doesn't mean much because nearly forty percent of the population has that blood type. Jim has called in a forensic anthropologist from Georgetown to examine Mr. Benson's remains to determine if we can learn anything more about him.

"We need motive," Catherine continued. "I can suggest a half dozen theories, but without a victim profile, they're just theories. If Benson and Merrifield have a shared or common background, that helps narrow our investigation."

"And if they don't?" Matt said.

"It also tells us something." She paused. "These murders aren't random. The victims were *specifically* targeted. There are multiple people involved, at least two killed Robert Benson based on the evidence, and one or more in Oregon."

"They coordinated the killings," Matt said. "Maybe to prevent the victims from hearing about the other murder? Except, there is no indication that Benson and Merrifield knew how to contact each other."

Sloane spoke up. "If they knew each other, they may have memorized contact information to avoid their connection being discovered."

"Possible," Catherine said. "Though so far, no phone or email records indicate they have communicated. Matt, are you on your way back to Quantico?"

"We're going to talk to the Bensons' pastor first," Matt said. "Should be back in a couple hours."

He ended the call and drove the additional block to the church.

Matt and Sloane had met the pastor at the Benson house when they first spoke with Evelyn. Henry Duncan was a tall, broad man with large calloused hands. He was in his late seventies and had a full head of shaggy white hair that reminded Matt of Albert Einstein.

"Agent Costa, Agent Wagner," Henry said. He motioned for them to sit in comfortable chairs and took a seat across from them behind his desk. The office was simple and uncluttered—chairs, desk, cross, books. The only personal items, other than a worn, personalized Bible that sat on the desk, were two framed photographs side by side on the wall between two narrow windows. One of a much younger Henry on his wedding day at least fifty years ago, and the other of Henry about ten years ago with his wife, who sat in a wheelchair, and dozens of people of all sizes surrounding them—likely his family.

Henry saw Matt looking at the photos and smiled. "My wife, Eloise, died the year after that picture was taken. It was the last time she was with all our children, grandchildren, and at the time two great-grandchildren. Since, I've been blessed with one more grandchild and two more great-grandchildren."

"Lucky man," Matt said.

"I am. You are here about the Bensons."

Matt nodded. "We spoke again with Mrs. Benson and went through Robert's personal items. We have some follow-up questions for you."

"I haven't thought of anything I neglected to tell you," he said.

"Evelyn mentioned that you had a conversation with Robert before they married," Matt said. "Did he tell you anything about his past, before he settled here in Weems?"

Henry leaned back, steepled his fingers, and looked directly at Matt. "He spoke to me as his pastor," Henry said. "While I am not under the same restrictions as a Catholic priest, I take personal counsel extremely seriously."

"I respect that," Matt said, "but our forensic psychiatrist believes that Robert's murder wasn't a random act of violence, but directly related to his past. I'm looking for information about where he's from, if he mentioned friends or family from his past. There are more than two killers out there—a pair killed Robert Benson, and a pair killed a college girl in Oregon on the same night."

Henry frowned.

Matt continued, "Evelyn said he was from Colorado and may have been abused as a child or while in a relationship. She didn't have details, said she didn't want them."

"I see," Henry said. He paused again, but Matt didn't get the impression that he planned to lie. He seemed to be searching for a way to share information without revealing a confidence, or weighing, perhaps, what was relevant and important.

"Evelyn's information is correct. Robert shared more with me, but not much. I had been concerned that Robert wasn't the good Christian he seemed to be. A stranger in a small town, involved with a small-town woman who was several years older than he was, no family left in the area. We talked many times, and by his actions, not only his words, I learned to trust him. He loved God, and he loved Evelyn, in that order. I've known Evelyn's family all my life, and her father didn't manage the store well. When he died, she quickly became overwhelmed, almost to the verge of having to sell and lose her livelihood—the business and the house—when Robert came into her life. He'd told me he had been an accountant."

"Did you see his license? Was he licensed to practice in Virginia?"

"I never asked."

They knew he wasn't licensed under the name Robert Benson. But you didn't need to be a certified accountant to run your own business.

Henry continued, "Within a year, Evelyn was no longer on the verge of losing her property, and within two years the store was in the black. He worked hard. He was kind and soft-spoken. Yes, he had secrets. He told me as much." Henry paused. "As far as I know, he lived in Colorado before he came here, but I don't know if he was raised there. He had been in an abusive relationship with a woman he wasn't married to, but had been in the relationship for more than a decade. He left because, in his words, he was worried about losing his soul. That was all he said about it. I told him to tell Evelyn, and as far as I know he did, but he may have been vague about the details."

"Was he was physically abused?"

"I was under the impression the abuse was emotional. And while I felt there was more to it than that, I didn't press him."

"Do you know the name of the woman he had been with?" Matt asked.

Henry shook his head. "I would tell you if I knew, but he never said."

Matt stood, thanked Henry for his time, and asked, "Would

you object if I or someone from my team attended Mr. Benson's memorial on Wednesday?"

"Of course you may. It's at four in the afternoon. I expect a full house."

In the car, Sloane asked Matt, "Do you think that the killers are going to show up?"

"It's always a possibility. In this case? I doubt it. A stranger would stand out in this town. But I need to cover all the bases."

Halfway back to Quantico, Ryder called.

"The Santa Fe County sheriff in New Mexico just posted an alert," Ryder said. "Male in his early thirties found dead off a hiking trail outside Santa Fe. He's been dead for a while, and they found several red poppies under his body."

6

Ashland, Oregon

Kara was in a crabby mood.

It was late Monday afternoon and she was hungry, frustrated, and had spent the last two hours listening to the task force go over everything they already knew.

She needed to be working in the field, looking for Riley Pierce, not sitting in a conference room. But she was stuck here because her idea to stake out the bakery and Ashley's apartment had been nixed.

She had the feeling that Detective Ken Kinder didn't believe she'd seen Riley. He didn't outright *say* it, but he was skeptical, and suggested that because Kara had found the box with her picture, she may have mistaken another girl with red hair for Riley.

It was *possible*, Kara supposed, but she was *almost* certain it was Riley.

They hadn't received a response to Ryder's request for flight information yet. It wasn't like he could just press a couple of buttons and *voila!* confirm Riley Pierce had flown in from France this week. There was a *process*, and while they didn't need a warrant, it still took time.

So she had to wait. Fortunately, Matt leaned toward her assessment, and had Riley Pierce—who did have a passport—flagged. If she checked into any flight in the US, she would be detained for questioning. She wasn't considered a suspect in Jane's murder, just a person of interest.

Unless, of course, they found out that she was in the country at the time of the murder.

The question that had been bugging Kara—and honestly, everyone else—was how did the killer convince Jane to meet with him?

No sign of disturbance at her apartment. She hadn't left a note for her roommate about where she was going. No common drugs in her system, though they were sending samples to the state lab for more thorough testing. She was found two miles from her home in Lithia Park, which was closed at night—not that the "sunrise to sunset" hours kept people out of the park when it was dark. She had her cell phone on her, but her last text was in response to her roommate who said she would be home in the morning because she was staying at David's. Jane sent a thumbs-up emoji and the response: I'll bring you the oopses from Nana's! Nana's was the bakery where Jane worked mornings, five to nine, three days a week. The "oopses" were imperfect pastries that the owner let staff take when their shift was over.

Police had talked to everyone at the bakery; the owner was concerned when Jane didn't show up without a call because "not once" had she missed a day of work in three years.

The task force had already run everyone who worked at the bakery, interviewed them about customers who may have paid Jane too much attention, talked to fired employees. They'd spoken with professors and classmates and neighbors. She wasn't a member of any clubs.

Jane hadn't been sexually assaulted. She hadn't been tortured. There were no defensive wounds. Either she'd gone willingly with someone she trusted who killed her, or she'd been surprised and the killer—without hesitation—had slit her throat.

There had been two killers at the Benson homicide based on footprint evidence; he also had no defensive wounds and hadn't alerted his wife that anything was wrong. He, too, left his home voluntarily, either because he didn't perceive a threat or because he was trying to protect his wife.

But Jane had no one to protect. Or did she? Had she known Riley was in town or coming to town?

It was enough to give Kara a splitting headache. The case, and the lack of food.

"Earth to Detective Quinn."

She jumped, looked around the table. Her partner, Michael, had spoken and he looked at her with mild humor.

"Sorry. Thinking."

"You can go to the hotel and catch a few winks," he said. "It's been a long day."

"That's okay." She smiled tightly at the assembled group. The sheriff, the DA, Detective Kinder, the deputy coroner, a uniformed cop who worked with Kinder, and Agent Tucker from the local FBI office. "Did I miss something?"

"Ryder just confirmed that Riley Pierce flew into the States yesterday," Michael said. "Her passport was used at the De Gaulle Airport, transfer at JFK to Seattle, landed late last night. No rental car, but she could have taken a bus from Seattle to Ashland. We're checking terminals. Which would put her getting in sometime this morning to early afternoon."

"Do we know when she bought the ticket?"

"Wednesday—the same day Detective Kinder left her a message."

Why hadn't she stopped at the station? Called Kinder and let him know she was in town?

"Janice requested Pierce's files from the university, we should have them first thing in the morning."

"That's great," Kara said, and meant it.

The DA, a petite woman with a slight accent that Kara couldn't place, said, "It took a bit of coaxing, they don't like to share information, but as I pointed out, I *could* get a warrant, and they were saving both of us time and headache."

"We had no doubt you'd get it," Michael said with a charming smile.

He had been flirting with Janice Kwan since they arrived. It wasn't obvious, but Kara knew Michael. Janice was definitely his type—he liked women in power who also looked very feminine. Maybe the contrast between power and sweetness? She didn't know, but he was frustrated that their team traveled so much he didn't have time to cultivate a relationship where he lived. He didn't talk about it much, but when he did, she felt for him. Michael wanted a family. He didn't have a good family growing up, so wanted to make his own.

The conversation shifted to reviewing interviews and updating data, and Kara tuned everyone out. Truth was, she *was* exhausted, but if she went to the hotel, she wouldn't be able to sleep.

She didn't sleep much as a matter of course, but the last two days had been a whirlwind, and then there was the not-so-little life-changing decision to make an offer on a house in Alexandria, Virginia. She'd sold her condo in Santa Monica, and the same day she received the substantial money in her bank account, Matt had taken her through the neighborhood and said, "This feels like you."

He was right.

It was a small house on a large odd-shaped lot with a view of the Potomac River from the front porch because of a protected park across the road. It was both private—a rare half acre lot in the area—and in the middle of everything, walking distance to restaurants and a corner grocery store. That he understood her, that he didn't pressure her to move in with him, meant everything to her.

But putting an offer on the property was a major step. She was content to live in the dorms at Quantico, where she'd been staying since November. They were busy and in the field a lot, so it wasn't like she was stuck there.

Still...having her own place with her own things would be nice. Plus, more privacy.

So all the stuff going on in her personal life, coupled with this case that she'd been working practically around the clock for the last few days, had her unusually out of sorts.

She kept going back to Jane Merrifield's life. No boyfriend, a lot of friends but no one close, a simple, sterile room that just didn't say college girl to Kara.

Kara couldn't get rid of the tickle in the back of her head, that there was something very strange going on. Maybe it was the poppies that creeped her out.

The only real commonality—other than the connection to Colorado that Matt and Sloane had uncovered today—was that both Jane and Benson were spiritual. Though Jane didn't regularly attend church, she had a well-worn Bible and religious books on her shelves. But that might not mean anything. A lot of people went to church or believed in a higher power. A lot of people contemplated spiritual questions.

In the larger context, what mattered was why these two people—with minimal connections, whose paths didn't appear to have crossed, who didn't seem to know each other—were killed in the same manner on the same day.

She sensed everyone was wrapping up, so she said, "I'd like to see where Jane's body was found."

Ken said, "We already collected evidence and released the area."

"All evidence has been sent to Quantico," FBI Agent Tucker added. "What do you hope to find?"

Kara had been on several task forces in the past. Sometimes, they worked. More eyes reviewing evidence, exploring different angles, getting the job done faster to save lives.

But sometimes, they failed. It shouldn't matter why she wanted to see the crime scene. Like Jane's room, she wanted a better sense of the crime, the victim, the killer. How could she explain that she simply wanted to stand in the spot where Jane Merrifield was killed and *absorb* the area? It made no sense, even to her.

"I don't expect to find anything," Kara said.

Michael, ever the diplomat, said, "Let's stop there on our way to the hotel. We need to check in, and I'm hungry."

She smiled gratefully at her partner. "Good idea."

"Hold that thought," Michael said when his phone vibrated. "Can you give me a second?" He stepped out and Kara wondered what was going on.

She didn't have to wait long. Less than two minutes later, Michael returned. "That was my boss. Another body has turned up, high probability it was our killers."

"Where?" the sheriff asked.

"New Mexico."

"Are you sure you don't want to go to the hotel and catch a nap?" Michael asked as he parked near Lithia Park in Ashland.

"Do I really look that bad?" Kara said, half joking.

"You look tired and you didn't sleep on the plane."

"Thanks for your concern, but nothing food won't fix. First—" she gestured at the trail that led to the crime scene "—let's just see what's here."

They walked in silence for a minute, then Michael said, "The local police did a good job. I don't think they missed anything."

"Maybe not here," she said, though she couldn't help but think about the keepsake box she'd found in Jane's drawer. "They didn't notice the poppy in Jane's room." They'd found the box, cataloged it, but hadn't considered it significant. Maybe it wasn't.

Kara thought it was.

The sky was gray and the forecast indicated rain overnight and into tomorrow, but for now the fog had mostly lifted and the drizzle turned to damp air. Lithia Park was a hundred-acre narrow wooded area with grassy knolls, trails, sports courts, and a playground. It began downtown right off main street, and ended near the Ashland Creek trailhead in the mountains that bordered the town to the west.

There were several access points into the park, very few security cameras. They didn't have to hike far to where Jane's body had been discovered behind the Butler Bandshell, a small outdoor amphitheater surrounded by trees and fronted by gently sloping lawn.

Today, there was a group of young kids running around while the adults supervising them sat on a blanket and talked. Four college-aged men tossed a Frisbee, the smell of weed thick as Kara passed them. Other people jogged or hiked in pairs on the path west of the field as it meandered up into the mountains. But the cement stage, covered by a slanted metal roof, was empty.

Kara stared at it. "Why did she come here?"

"She knew her killer," Michael said.

"Yeah, that's what I was thinking, but still—late on a Saturday night, no message, no text. She lives two miles from here."

"The center of downtown is just down the path with bars, restaurants, theaters, a late-night coffee shop."

"But she told her roommate she was staying in, and during the first interview, Ashley told Ken that Jane didn't drink much and didn't use recreational drugs. She had no boyfriend, no close friends outside of Riley Pierce."

"Devil's advocate," Michael said. "Say Riley Pierce is involved. Why lure Jane away from the apartment? Why kill her here?"

"First, if Riley is involved, it would be easy to lure Jane out, if we believe Ashley that they were close. But we know she was still in France when Jane was killed. Doesn't mean she's not involved in some way. But killing her here... It wasn't on the stage, which would be bold and theatrical. They killed her behind the stage, where she wasn't found until morning. To hide her? To delay discovery to give them a chance to get out of town? Some psychological or personal reason? All of the above?"

"Benson was lured out, as well," Michael reminded her. "No sign of forced entry, no struggle, no defensive wounds. Though his hands were bound and Jane's weren't."

"I could see him not fighting back to protect his wife, but who was Jane protecting? And fighting back is instinct. You don't want to die. Even if you don't fight back hard, there should be something, an involuntary action, like putting your arms up to stop a blow."

"There were no other marks on their bodies, other than faint marks on Benson's wrists from the rope," Michael said. "Jane was petite, one person could have killed her."

"Surprise attack from behind," Kara said. "Jane may not have even seen her killer."

"No evidence under their nails, no skin or fiber. Instinct," Michael said, "would have you grabbing the arm, hands of someone coming from behind. The crime scene investigators concluded Benson's throat was slit while he was lying on the ground. He would have seen his killers."

"Quick and efficient." Autopsy showed no hesitation, just one deep cut under the jawline. Both victims bled out where they were killed. Who stood there and took it? Or, in Benson's case, lay down and allowed it?

Kara walked behind the stage. She immediately saw where

Jane's body had been found, and not just because she had studied the crime scene photos.

The area was narrow, wide enough for at least two people to walk side by side. Trees provided a canopy, as well as privacy—or a hiding place.

Jane had been killed just behind the east side of the stage where there was a slightly wider spot of well-packed earth, possibly for performers to wait before they came onstage. The police had cleaned up the area and removed the crime scene tape. But Kara pictured it as Jane had been found: on her back, arms and feet outstretched—clearly staged—throat slit. Hundreds of red poppies covering her body, littering the ground. Three hundred forty individual flowers had been collected—enough to fill a small garbage bag.

Local police had scoured the area for evidence, but there was next to nothing. Plus, no security cameras. Though technically the park was closed at night, the amphitheater was open if there was an event. There hadn't been anything scheduled late Saturday when Jane was killed.

There was privacy here. The slope, the trees, the structure set far back from the road, out of sight of the parking lot. But there were dozens of other private places someone could have lured Jane. Why *here*? Was the location important to Jane...or to her killer?

But more important than why, at least to Kara, was *how.*

How did they lure Jane out to a place where she was alone and vulnerable? Did she come here alone? Or did someone pick her up?

They hadn't found any witness who said they saw Jane leaving her apartment on Saturday night, so either scenario would work. There was no evidence on her person that she had been dragged across the field from the parking lot. No bruises, marks, scratches, abrasions. She hadn't been bound and no evidence of being gagged.

She came here of her own free will, Kara decided. *With* someone she didn't fear, or to *meet* someone she didn't fear.

Or perhaps...a bait and switch? She *thought* she was meeting a specific person, but instead she met her killer. "Okay," she said. "Any brilliant conclusions?"

"Not really, and it doesn't matter."

"What are you thinking?"

"She either trusted the person who killed her, or she came here to meet someone she trusted. Either way, her killer knows her well. And based on what we've learned from her roommate and colleagues, she had no close friends at all—outside of Riley Pierce, who was in France at the time of the murder."

"The killer could have stalked her and learned her habits."

Maybe, Kara thought, but that didn't explain why Jane would walk two miles from her apartment to meet someone.

There was something here that Kara wasn't seeing. Maybe not at the crime scene, but something else. Kara couldn't wrap her head around Jane's psychology, about why she had made the decision to leave her apartment on Saturday night. It wasn't logical. But, as she knew from the team shrink, it might not be logical to them, but it would be logical to the victim.

Maybe she couldn't process the information because she was tired, hungry, and crabby.

"Let's go," she said.

"You're still thinking."

"Yep. I'm missing something. But if you can find a place with a good cheeseburger? Maybe I'll figure it out."

7

Santa Fe, New Mexico

Chris's house was dark, though it was too late for him to be working and too early for him to be sleeping. His small Jeep sat in the carport. Riley parked the rental car behind it and turned off the ignition.

Her heart pounded in her chest as she considered what she might find inside. What if he had been exposed?

If they had found Chris, was Thalia also in danger?

Why did she care? Thalia had used her, manipulated her, convinced her to go along with her plan. And when Riley had finally had enough, when she broke, Thalia was furious.

"Without you helping me in Havenwood, more people will die. You're selfish, Riley. I'm so disappointed in you."

Selfish. Maybe, but so what? Didn't she deserve to be free? Or was she still required to pay for the mistakes of her past?

Riley closed her eyes. Chris had always been kind to her, always seemed to understand her when Thalia didn't. Still, she was scared. Not that Chris would do anything to her, but of what might happen when Thalia found out that Jane was dead. That Thalia might blame her.

And Thalia might be right. After all, Riley had run away. Not only from Havenwood, but from Jane. No matter how many times Riley told herself she was going *to* France, she was really running *from* her past.

The memories were there, even when she ignored them. Memories had weight, and they weighed her down. She'd tried to tell Thalia how she felt, but the words were never enough. She had never forgiven herself.

Silence was sometimes a crime.

Ultimately, Riley was Calliope's daughter, and Thalia hated Calliope. No surprise that the hate bled out to encompass Riley. The sins of the mother...sins of the daughter.

Riley breathed deeply, opened her eyes, and stared at Chris's house, willing him to open the door and smile at her. She watched for signs of life, found none. She should go in.

She couldn't move.

Chris understood better than Thalia, as much as the quiet man could. He'd helped her, provided shelter and money and worked with Jesse to establish her new identity. Riley had wanted to stay here, in Chris's remote, beautiful home in the mountains about Sante Fe, and she thought Chris would have agreed.

Thalia said no.

"Chris is a way station, and I still need to get people out, even without your help. You're dead, right? If anyone finds out you're alive, it will jeopardize all of us."

"Just do it," Riley mumbled to herself and opened the car door. The cold made her shiver. She pulled her jacket tight, lowered her cap over her ears, and stared. Willed Chris to turn on the lights, open the door, smile his warm, rare smile.

The dark house felt empty. That didn't mean Chris was in trouble. It just meant he wasn't home. He could be helping Thalia with another rescue, or taking someone to their new home. Or they heard that Jane was dead and were warning the others.

But Riley couldn't shake the feeling that everyone she loved was in danger.

She approached the silent house. It wasn't completely dark, she realized as she neared; night-lights in the kitchen and bedrooms cast faint glows. After walking around the house and determining that all was still, Riley retrieved the key from under a small statue near the kitchen door and let herself in.

The house felt...empty. Unused. Clean and tidy, but a scent of dust that she didn't expect, and a chill because the heat had been turned low, as if Chris had been gone for some time.

Riley didn't turn on any lights. Hell, she didn't even know if she should be here, feeling like she was violating his privacy in the worst way.

Yet, she'd known Chris her entire life. Trusted him even more than Thalia, who was blood. Chris was the calm, cool, reasonable adult whenever she and Thalia had clashed. She hadn't seen him in three and a half years, but that didn't matter—she hadn't seen him in half a decade before she escaped, and it wasn't weird. He was like the big brother she never had and always wanted.

"Chris," she tried to call out, but her voice was a whisper. "Chris, it's Riley."

Silence. No one was here.

Riley walked to the guest room where there were two double beds. She and Jane had been here for two weeks before they went to Ashland. It had been the first time she'd felt safe since before her grandmother died, but now as she sat on one of the beds and looked around the spare room, she'd never felt more alone—which was saying something. Her plan was dependent on Chris's help, and Chris wasn't here. She should wait for him, but time was ticking. She didn't know when he'd be home. It could be days...weeks. When Thalia said jump, he said how high. It had always been that way. Riley didn't know why he trusted her so much when she could be such a bitch. But he did.

They knew things they never told her. They had suffered things she hadn't suffered.

In pain came understanding.

That Riley understood far too well.

She needed a place to sleep, at least for tonight. The last five days, since she learned Jane had been killed, had been a whirlwind. Packing up in France, getting a last-minute ticket that cost a small fortune. Sleeping on planes, in airports, and even in the rental car last night. Riley needed a bed, a good meal, a shower. Maybe Chris would be home in the morning.

She could wait until morning.

Peace in her decision settled over her and Riley realized she was starving. She hadn't eaten all day, and it had caught up with her.

The refrigerator was nearly empty, confirming her theory that Chris was on a rescue or relocation trip with Thalia. Fortunately, the pantry and freezer were well stocked. She cooked up rotini pasta and added frozen broccoli halfway through, drained everything, and tossed it with olive oil and seasonings. The process of cooking calmed her.

She ate in the dark, the small bulb above the stove providing the only light. Then she cleaned the dishes and put everything away.

Her stomach was still unsettled.

Something was wrong. She had sensed it the minute she arrived, but had avoided looking for answers, holding on to false hope that Chris's return was imminent.

At midnight, she couldn't avoid it anymore.

One of the rules Riley lived by—everyone who escaped Havenwood lived by—was no social media. She had a smartphone with full privacy settings, which didn't mean much because if someone was determined, they could find a way in. But even with all the protections, she was doubly careful. No social media. No internet searches. A work email she used only on her museum computer. No email on her phone, but she could log in to her account with a private web browser. Every single time, she would change her password and log out.

But Chris wasn't here, and that was unusual, so Riley logged into his computer as a guest and searched news sites. Immediately, her blood ran cold at an article posted this morning.

Monday, March 31
Body found by hikers off the Atalaya Trail identified as local teacher Chris Crossman

Chris couldn't be dead. Not Chris. She read on.

Friday morning, three students from St. John's College were hiking on the Atalaya Trail when they spotted the remains of thirty-two-year-old Chris Crossman, identified today by the Office of the Medical Investigator.

Santa Fe police are working with the county sheriff's office to investigate Crossman's death, which has been ruled a homicide. The OMI said cause of death was a fatal knife wound to his throat, though time of death is indeterminate.

Crossman, a substitute high school math teacher, has been a resident of Santa Fe, New Mexico, for ten years. He hadn't been reported missing and had no scheduled classes this week. The last time anyone saw him was Friday afternoon, a week before his body was discovered, when he finished a two-week teaching assignment at the main high school.

Respected by his colleagues and students, Crossman was described as studious and reserved. The principal, Meredith Anderson, said he was a model teacher who also tutored low-achieving students free of charge. She said he enjoyed hiking the Atalaya Mountain anytime the weather permitted.

Riley ran to the bathroom and vomited violently, until everything she'd eaten was gone. She drank water from the faucet and threw up again. Now the tears came, tears and sobs she couldn't stop. She wanted to scream, but her throat still burned from getting sick.

When she was certain there was nothing left in her stomach, Riley lay on the cool tile floor and waited until the room stopped spinning. Waited until she could stand without falling.

Thirty minutes later, she was steady enough to return to the computer and read everything she could find on Chris's murder.

But there was little else except that Chris was killed in the same way as Jane.

That was no coincidence.

Riley couldn't stay here. Would the police connect the two murders? Eventually. Had the police already searched Chris's house? His body had only been identified this morning, but they'd come here soon, looking for evidence, wouldn't they?

Like Jane, someone had lured Chris out of his house, into the woods, and killed him.

If the police had searched the place, they hadn't made a mess. What would they think of Chris? Of his simple life? Would they even care about his death?

They'd never solve it. Even if Riley told them what she thought happened, who she thought had killed him, she had no proof, no evidence.

She knew next to nothing about how the police did anything. They had no television, no access to news in Havenwood. Everything she knew she'd learned in the last three years—or from years of her mother telling her that the police and everyone else in authority "Outside," meaning beyond Havenwood, weren't to be trusted.

But if she couldn't stay here, where *could* she go? She needed to find Thalia, tell her what was happening.

She froze as a terrifying thought hit her.

Her mother had found Jane and Chris. Did her mother also know that Riley was alive?

Riley had an overwhelming urge to run, go back to France, hide for the rest of her life.

But if she was right and her mother was responsible for Jane's and Chris's murders, that meant others were in danger. Could she leave when everyone she had rescued was in jeopardy?

The only way to stop Calliope was to expose Havenwood. But if she exposed Havenwood, innocent people would die. It was a no-win situation and Riley wanted to scream.

She *could* warn those who she and Thalia had already rescued, but she had to first find Thalia.

She hadn't spoken to her aunt in three and a half years.

Riley stared at the computer screen, willing answers to come to her.

To find Thalia meant reaching out to someone who hated her.

But Andrew owed her his life. He would help her because he was honorable.

Honor trumped hate.

She cleaned up her mess, cleared the browser history, then filled her backpack with necessities. She knew where Chris kept cash, so she grabbed a couple thousand dollars.

Riley took one long, final look around Chris's house, remembering his life, trying to honor him and all that he'd done to help the people of Havenwood. Fruitlessly, she wished he were alive, that he would walk through the door and say it had all been a misunderstanding, tell her this entire nightmare was in her head.

But he didn't and it wasn't. So she left.

TUESDAY

8

Santa Fe, New Mexico

Sloane Wagner and Jim Esteban flew to Santa Fe first thing Tuesday morning, picked up a rental car, and drove straight to Chris Crossman's remote home in the hills east of St. John's College.

Before this case, Sloane hadn't partnered solo with Jim. She liked everyone on the team, but hadn't had a chance to get to know the former director of the Dallas Crime Lab who was the MRT's forensic and crime scene expert. Jim was the oldest member of the team at fifty-three, and had three young grandchildren he was happy to talk about when he wasn't talking about crime or baseball, his two favorite subjects.

Crossman's small but modern two-bedroom adobe-style home was built at the top of a steep, narrow driveway off a winding two-lane mountain road. The other houses in the area were larger, also set back from the road. When Sloane looked up the cost of housing in the area, she was surprised most sold for well over a million. Crossman's house was estimated at nine hundred thousand dollars, which seemed pricey for a substitute teacher, though they were still running a full background on the victim. Perhaps he had family money or left a lucrative career. One of Sloane's friends from high school had written a software program that he sold for millions when he was twenty-three.

The police didn't know much about Crossman. His prints were in the system only because he was required to submit them to teach. Still, his body was in bad shape from decomposition and animal activity after five to seven days of exposure. Hikers had discovered the body Friday morning, and it wasn't until Monday afternoon that the connection between Crossman and the other two victims had been identified.

Wind and animals had dispersed all but a few dozen red poppies from the area. But the few they found were unusual for the region, especially in late March when the weather was still cold and spring hadn't yet caught on.

Crossman was thirty-two and bought the house with cash ten years ago for less than half of what it was now worth. He was a substitute math and science teacher at the high school. The school had offered him a full-time position, but he declined. He was considered quiet, private, and smart. He had no friends at the school, and his two closest neighbors—they shared a driveway and got their mail at the same location—only knew him to say hello.

No one knew where he'd lived before moving to Santa Fe, but the sheriff's department had requested his employee records from the school district. The last time anyone had seen Crossman was a week ago Friday, when he substituted for a teacher on vacation. He hadn't returned any messages the school left the last week.

The chances that he was killed at around the same time as the first two victims was high. At least within twenty-four hours of Merrifield and Benson.

"Nice place," Jim said as they entered. "All up-to-date and comfortable. Private."

She agreed. "It is nice, but I grew up with three brothers. It's a little too quiet for me."

"Didn't you grow up in the middle of nowhere?"

"Outside Bozeman, not exactly nowhere." She smiled. "We have a working ranch, lots of people around all the time. Roosters made sure we were up before the sun."

"Must be nice up there, except for the natural alarm clocks."

"I miss it," she said, feeling nostalgic. She had used up all her vacation time to spend Christmas and New Year's with her family. It was good to be home, and she had doubts about accepting Matt's offer to join the Mobile Response Team. Yet she'd only been asked to commit for two years. If it didn't work out for whatever reason, he promised she could transfer to the Helena office.

She respected her boss Matt and liked the entire team. Everyone had welcomed her into the fold without much of a hiccup, even though she was a rookie—albeit an older rookie, since she had been in the Marines for twelve years and had turned thirty-five on Christmas Eve.

"Where do you want to start?" she asked Jim.

"I'll take the bedrooms. You take the living room and den. We'll meet in the kitchen."

Jim walked to the back of the house where the bedrooms were located, and she stood in the center of the living room and did a three-sixty, getting a feel of the place.

Yes, private. Yes, comfortable with a central great room that encompassed the living, dining, and kitchen area. Yet, the house felt sterile. Crossman was a tidy person who valued a few nice things. No clutter, no photos, no knickknacks or collectibles. The generic art complemented the Southwestern theme of the house, and the well-made furniture was neutral in color and style.

She walked into the den, which was three steps down from the living room and separated by a low wall. It was a nice space with a view of trees through a large picture window and a small tiled patio off sliding glass doors.

She looked at his books—he didn't have many, and no fiction, but the tomes he shelved were pristine and ran toward history, science, and how to teach math. No framed diploma, no photos, nothing personal. They wouldn't have even known what he looked like except his driver's license photo showing light black skin, golden brown eyes, and a serious expression. Crossman's license stated he was six feet tall and one hundred eighty pounds. That was confirmed by the ME.

His desk drawers weren't locked. Inside were immaculate files—banking statements, bills, time card copies, notes from teaching.

Sloane went through the folders thoroughly, but there was nothing that stood out as suspicious. Except his birth certificate.

He was born in Denver, Colorado.

"Jim," she called out.

He stepped into the threshold of the bedroom. "The guy has nothing. His room is sparser than a priest's. I'm going to check the guest room."

She held up his birth certificate. "He was born in Colorado."

"Text Matt. He'll want to know right away."

She took a picture of the document and said, "His computer is still here, the police didn't take it. It's password protected, but it could have useful information."

"They didn't take the computer?"

She shook her head, sent the image of Crossman's birth certificate to Matt and Ryder.

Jim frowned. "Okay, we'll call Matt when we're done, ask what he wants us to do with it, but my guess is he'll have us box it up and ship it to Quantico."

He stepped into the guest room at the end of the hall, and Sloane started going through the kitchen cabinets. Everything was neat and organized. The pantry was well stocked, nearly every shelf full of boxes and cans of food. She took photos.

She looked in the garbage and frowned. There was an empty pasta box and frozen veggie bag. That was all that was in there. His last meal? She made a mental note to check the autopsy report, and took a digital picture to remind herself.

Jim called out, "Sloane, you have to check this out."

She stepped into the second bedroom. It was as large as Crossman's room, with two double beds separated by a wide nightstand, almost like a hotel room. A desk and chair, bookshelf with popular fiction, and a television—there was no other TV in the house.

Jim was standing in the walk-in closet. "There are a lot of clothes in here, none appear to be worn—some still have the price tags. Men's, women's, different sizes. He practically has a mini department store. Shoes, too—all high-quality, practical shoes. Loafers, sneakers, hiking boots. Drawers of undergarments, still in the packaging. No kids' clothing—I don't know what that would mean if there were. I don't know what *this* means. And look—on the top shelf there are *nine* identical suitcases. Check out the bathroom, tell me what you think."

She walked into the attached bathroom. At first, she smelled heavy cleanser, as if someone had just cleaned. The space was, again, well organized with two sinks, a shower without soap residue, fresh towels hanging on the wall. She opened the small hamper and wrinkled her nose. Someone had used a towel to clean up vomit. She didn't know how long ago. She closed it.

Next, she opened the linen closet and said, "Whoa."

"Yeah," Jim called out from the bedroom closet. "See what I mean?"

Inside the linen closet were bins of personal hygiene products, all labeled. Toothbrushes, toothpaste, travel-size containers of shampoo and conditioner, combs, brushes, basic makeup supplies, razors, deodorant, and more. The top shelf had a half dozen empty toiletry bags.

She stepped into the room. "Maybe he donates items to a homeless shelter or a church," she said. "His tax records are in his desk. I can look through them, see if there's a corresponding donation."

"Maybe," Jim said, though he didn't sound like he agreed with her first thought. And Sloane dismissed it, as well. If he were to donate, why put the items away here? If he ordered them, wouldn't he keep them boxed up for easier transport?

"The desk is locked—see if you can open it," Jim said. "I'm going to photograph everything else."

Why would the bedroom desk be locked, but not his office? Maybe so his guests couldn't access it?

Sloane got down on all fours and looked under the desk. No booby traps or anything unusual. While on her knees, she retrieved her pocketknife and quickly popped the lock.

She opened the single drawer. Inside was a metal lockbox. She took it out, set it on the desk, and inspected the lock. There was both a four-number combination lock and a keyhole.

"We can open it at the station," Jim said.

"Give me a minute." While she studied the lock she said, "I think someone was here. There were used towels in the hamper, a couple things in the nearly empty trash."

"Maybe, or maybe he just didn't get around to taking it out. We'll talk to the locals, the neighbors. I'm going to call Matt, tell him what we've found." He stepped out.

Sloane could break the lock, but Jim might frown on that—the box *was* evidence.

Instead of trying to guess a four-digit combination, she took out her pocketknife again and, using the smallest tool, carefully inserted it into the lock.

Click.

She opened the box and stared.

There were eighteen unsealed bank envelopes filled with cash. She opened one and slid out the stack, counted. Twenty hundred-dollar bills. All the envelopes appeared to contain the same amount.

$36,000 in cash. In a barely secure lockbox.

But the money didn't surprise her half as much as the other item: a manila envelope filled with laminated red poppies.

9

Ashland, Oregon

Kara and Michael had just finished eating the free hotel breakfast when Matt called her. "You with Michael?"

"Yep," she said as she licked syrup off her fingers.

"Can you both talk?"

"One sec." Kara wiped her hands and motioned for Michael to follow her down the hall. She used her room card key to open the door of the currently unoccupied business center. She closed the door behind them and put Matt on speaker. "Okay, go."

"Check your email. Jim and Sloane found some strange items at Crossman's house in Santa Fe. New clothing and shoes, both male and female, in multiple sizes. Nine identical suitcases. Thirty-six thousand in cash, but more interesting, Crossman had a stack of laminated red poppies that look exactly like the poppy you found in Merrifield's apartment."

"Theories?" Kara asked.

"I'm on my way to meet with Catherine to discuss this new information. I'm at a loss. Crossman and Merrifield must have known each other at one time, or they have a common acquaintance. Crossman was also born in Denver."

"Related?"

"Unlikely, not impossible," Matt said. "I've asked Quantico to run DNA. We're still waiting on the paternity test for Benson and Merrifield, should have it today. Prepare to head to Denver when you wrap up things in Ashland. Ryder will set up a conference call this afternoon, sometime between three and six eastern time. If you get something hot let Ryder know and he'll juggle."

"You know I live for meetings, especially over Zoom," Kara said, rolling her eyes at Michael. He playfully hit her.

"Be careful, both of you. I don't know what the hell is going on, but Crossman had secrets. Sloane thinks someone may have been in the house since his murder, so we're sending over our Albuquerque Evidence Response Team to do a deep forensic dive. Prints, hairs, fibers, the works. Read the email, look at the pictures. If you have anything to add, contact me."

Matt ended the call. Kara immediately pulled up her email and Michael did the same. Kara scrolled through the photos. The laminated poppies looked exactly like the one she'd found at Jane's. But there was something else familiar in the closet, though she couldn't quite put her finger on it. "I need to go back to Jane's," she told Michael.

"After the bakery?"

"Sure."

"What are you thinking?" he asked as they walked to their car.

"They know each other, but I can't figure out the how. They're all from Denver, but they're not the same age. They all have very small footprints, no social media, living not so much off-the-grid as very private. Maybe they witnessed the same crime...or they're related some way and their family is bad news?" She shrugged. "Benson has been in Weems for nearly eleven years. Crossman in New Mexico for ten. Jane in Ashland for three and a half years. But so far, we don't know where any of them came from, and none of them have family that anyone knows about. They were all killed by the same group of people working together the same weekend." Kara paused, then said, "Riley Pierce knows what's going on. She knows what connects these people. She might even know what the poppies mean. We find her, we'll have some answers, if not all the answers."

Michael didn't argue with her.

They didn't learn anything new about Jane at the bakery, only confirmed the information Ashland PD had. However, while Michael looked through Jane's employment records, Kara talked to the owner about Riley Pierce. Lani, a middle-aged grandmotherly type, definitely had a lot to say.

"You want to know about Riley? She moved to France. *Internship.*" Lani pursed her lips.

What did the tone mean? Kara wondered. "You've met her?"

"Yes. Jane has worked for me for—well, over three years. I hired her temporarily during the holiday crunch when she was a freshman. She knew baking, clearly she'd learned in the home. She was intuitive about it—I had to teach her to follow my recipes, but let her experiment sometimes. Anyway, she was a joy to work with, and she's one of the few I trusted in the kitchen without me supervising."

"So you knew Jane well."

"I thought I did, but the police asked a lot of questions I couldn't answer. I know she wasn't close to her family and didn't talk about them at all, not even to say negative things. I tried to get her to open up, but she would just smile and shake her head, say she didn't think about the past. She very much looked forward. Serene. That's a good word for her."

"And Riley?"

"The opposite of serene," Lani said with a scowl. "I didn't know her well, but where Jane always had a smile and kind word, I don't think I saw Riley smile once. I know they were best friends—once, Jane said they grew up together and Riley was like a sister. Maybe there's more to the girl, but I never saw it."

"You didn't like her."

"I didn't know her," she said.

"But you knew her enough to recognize she and Jane were opposites."

Lani nodded. "Riley was moody. Not even moody, because that would imply she was happy at times, and she wasn't. She had this dark aura about her, always seemed a bit on the agitated side. For example, we have a Christmas party every year for staff and family. I had to talk Jane into coming. I knew she didn't like crowds, but I said it would be fun and casual. I insisted she bring Riley, since they were roommates. The entire time, Riley stood by the door, watching everyone like a hawk. Completely unapproachable. Jane came the next year without her."

"Has Riley been back since moving to France?"

"No, and I'm sure Jane would have said something if she had. And Ashley? She's a sweetheart. Comes in every once in a while, friendly, sociable. She was good for Jane."

And Riley wasn't sociable, Kara thought but didn't say. Kara didn't hold it against Riley, it wasn't a crime to be grumpy. Good thing, otherwise Kara would be guilty. But the impression helped.

Lani sighed and sorrow returned to her face. "I can't believe someone killed her. Jane was an angel, truly. The world is a lesser place without her in it."

By the time they left, it was raining again. Kara took it in stride. She'd gone to high school in a small town outside Spokane, Washington; she knew about rain and cold and drizzle.

She'd always prefer the near-perfect Los Angeles weather, but she didn't hate the rain.

Michael, on the other hand, opened his umbrella with a frown and covered them both on the short walk to the car. Kara would have teased him, but it wasn't fun teasing Michael about his fastidiousness. He took his personal grooming very seriously. But his impeccable wardrobe was fair game. He'd earned the nickname GQ.

They drove to Ashley's apartment. Kara knew from Kinder that Ashley didn't have classes on Tuesdays. It was after nine, so Kara had no problem waking her if she was still sleeping.

When Ashley answered the door she was in pajama bottoms and a tank top, her hair a mess, and a mug of coffee in her hand. "Hi," she said with a yawn. "What time is it?"

"Nine ten," Kara said. "This is my partner, FBI Agent Michael Harris. I'm sorry to just stop by, but I wanted to look at one more thing in Jane's room. Is that okay?"

"Um, sure?" She opened the door wider and Michael and Kara walked in. The smell of marijuana was strong.

A young man was slouched on the couch in sweats and no shirt. A bong was on the table in front of him and he made no move to hide it. Why would he? Marijuana was legal in Oregon. Kara didn't much like it, though. Everyone she knew who smoked pot regularly had little motivation to do much of anything.

"We can show ourselves," Kara said and motioned toward Jane's door.

Michael followed her in, closed the door. "Let's make this quick."

She stood in the middle of the room, looked around. Then she pulled up the photos from the email, scrolled through them, and walked over to Jane's closet. What had seemed so familiar to her?

Shoes...clothes...

The suitcase.

She pulled Jane's suitcase off the top shelf and brought it over to her bed. She studied the photo of Chris Crossman's closet and the row of identical suitcases stacked side by side on the shelf above the clothes.

Jane's was the same style suitcase. It looked identical.

"What do you think?" she asked Michael.

He looked from the photo to the suitcase, nodded. "It's the same. But devil's advocate—it's a common brand."

"Yes, but both owners are dead."

She took pictures of Jane's suitcase, then searched it. There was only one thing inside—a toiletry kit. It looked identical to the kits in Crossman's linen closet. Inside the kit was half-used shampoo and conditioner—same brand that Crossman had—and an extra toothbrush and pink razor.

There was also an envelope that looked exactly like the ones that held Crossman's cash.

Kara carefully opened it. Inside were three one-hundred-dollar bills.

"I think it's conclusive," she said and showed them to Michael.

"Call Matt, tell him what we found, take pictures, and then we'll bring everything with us."

Chris Crossman had given Jane this suitcase. And Jane had likely stayed at his house, at least for a short time. What *that* meant, however, she had no idea.

10

Quantico, Virginia

Ryder set up the video conference in Matt's office, then left to take a call from Denver that he had been waiting for. Matt would have preferred Ryder on the conference call—his insight was valuable, and he was the go-to guy for information—but getting answers from Colorado was a priority.

Catherine came in and sat next to Matt so they would both be on-screen during the call. He finished bringing the rest of the team into the secure chat—Jim and Sloane in a conference room at the Santa Fe police station, and Kara and Michael in the business center of their hotel, which Michael had secured for the next hour.

As soon as everyone gave their thumbs-up that they could hear, Matt said, "You all read each other's reports, so we can save time. Catherine has been fine-tuning her profile, and Ryder's on a call with the Denver field office, so he may have more information in a few minutes. Zack Heller is analyzing Crossman's finances to determine why he has so much cash. Jim, we'll start with you and Sloane. Did you learn anything new from Crossman's colleagues?"

"Not much," Jim said. "But I thought it interesting that, just like Kara learned from Jane's colleagues at the bakery, no one knew anything about his past. He never talked about family or where he was from. His employment records are thin—social security number, degree in mathematics from University of Colorado at Denver, teaching credentials from the state of New Mexico. His emergency contact is his next-door neighbors, a married couple who don't live here full-time. They asked Crossman to keep an eye on their place when they're gone—they split their time between Los Angeles and Santa Fe. Ryder has the documentation, so he's going to verify the degree, see if he can find anyone who knew Crossman while he was at college."

"Any new sightings of Riley Pierce?" Matt asked Kara and Michael.

"No," Michael said. "Ashland is a small town, barely twenty thousand residents, half of which are college kids. The police have been looking for her."

"Ryder confirmed she doesn't have a driver's license issued in Oregon or Colorado in the name Riley Pierce," Matt said, "so she'd likely be using her passport to travel. But she hasn't boarded a plane in the last twenty-four hours. We're working on bus stations and trains, but that takes a bit longer. She could have taken a series of local buses, or had someone pick her up."

Kara looked like she disagreed. "Kara?" he said. "You have a different opinion?"

"We already know that the three victims have nearly nonexistent backgrounds, and Crossman had access to a lot of cash," she said. "We can't dismiss the idea that Riley might have another identity. Maybe she rented a car under another name."

"Good point, but until we get another sighting or name to

check, it'll be hard to pin her down. She has a passport issued in Denver when she was nineteen, three and a half years ago. That coincides with what we know about Jane, who allegedly lived in Denver at the same time."

"Maybe we can look for women who bought a ticket out of Portland, Medford, or Seattle within the last forty-eight hours?" Kara suggested.

"That would be labor intensive, but Ryder might have some shortcuts, or he can call in one of the techs," Matt said. "Write it up for him with clear parameters."

Kara nodded, and then Matt said, "Catherine's profile hasn't changed, but it's been refined. We still believe that the victims were known to the killers, that these weren't random murders. Based on forensics, Crossman may have been killed the day before Benson and Merrifield, up until the same time window—early Sunday morning. If before, we're looking for three to four individuals coordinating. If he was killed at the same time, we're looking at four or more people involved." He turned to Catherine. "Floor is yours, Catherine."

She cleared her throat and said, "While Matt's correct and I haven't changed the base profile, we have more information now. But the more we know, the more questions I have.

"One of the important things we've learned is that all three victims have a connection to Colorado, two confirmed in Denver. This is not a coincidence. But at this point, they are no relation to each other. Right before this call, I received the paternity test, and Benson and Merrifield are not related by blood.

"However," Catherine continued, "the three of them either knew each other or have a common connection. They could have once lived on the same street or in the same small town, been at the same store at the same time, any number of things. But they *are* connected. The killers are highly organized. The leader—and there will be one person in charge—is highly intelligent and instills loyalty and discipline among his or her killers.

"Red poppies have traditionally been a symbol of mourning, loss, or grief, generally reserved for the military. There are other interpretations, and during Sloane's interview with Mrs. Benson, she stated that her husband saw them not as a sign of comfort, but of a dark purpose. Yet, he kept a dried poppy in his wallet. I'll add, however, that I don't believe the poppy was in his wallet for long—it hadn't crumbled as a dried flower would without protection. I sent it to the lab and they'll have a more accurate timeline, but I'm thinking days, not more than a week. The poppy meant something to him. They also mean something to Jane Merrifield and Chris Crossman."

Jim said, "Crossman had an envelope of laminated poppies that match the one Kara found in Merrifield's apartment. All of them are on their way to the lab for analysis, but I'm working off the assumption that Merrifield's came from Crossman. There was nothing like that at Benson's?"

Matt shook his head. "We didn't find a laminated poppy. However, we didn't do a deep search. I don't know that it will be necessary, but if it is I'll reach out to Benson's widow."

"Though I'll await confirmation, I agree," Catherine said. "Kara's discovery that the suitcase in Merrifield's apartment and the money envelope match those found at Crossman's, tells us that Jane was likely at Crossman's house at some point. This is a clear, personal connection between two of the three victims." She cleared her throat before continuing. "Matt reached out to Mrs. Benson, and she stated that her husband didn't have a similar suitcase, at least she had never seen him with one. That doesn't mean he didn't have one in the year before they married, just that he didn't bring it to her house."

"One of the things I've been thinking," Jim said, "what if Crossman was like the underground railroad, taking in people who needed help, giving them supplies, cash, sending them on their way?"

"His house is set up that way, isn't it?" Catherine concurred.

"And you may be right, except if that's the case, what's the motive? We know that Robert Benson had an emotionally abusive partner. If Jane had an abusive boyfriend, that would be a connection. How did they know about Crossman? Did they find him on their own, or did someone introduce them? The victims could also have been on the run because of a criminal reason—maybe they witnessed a crime, feared for their life and don't trust the authorities."

"You're thinking," Kara said, "that maybe these people had a run-in with the criminal justice system in Colorado and went to Crossman to get new identities? Either because they committed a crime or witnessed a crime? Crossman ran his own personal WITSEC program?"

"I hadn't thought of it that way," Catherine said with a half smile, "but yes, that's plausible. Until we know more, it's really just conjecture. Still, Crossman was a way station, at least for Jane Merrifield and—very likely—her former roommate, Riley Pierce, since interviews have indicated they knew each other before college. Kara, you seem to have a grasp on the girls. Thoughts?"

"According to Jane's boss, Jane and Riley had been childhood friends and went to college together," Kara said. "Everyone we spoke to said they were very close, but that Jane was the friendly one and Riley was standoffish and brooding. Neither of them talked about their childhood in any detail.

"My big question, which I wrote in my report, is how and why did Jane go off with her killer? Either she left her apartment with someone she knew and walked or was driven to the park nearly two miles away, or she voluntarily met with someone there. No defensive wounds, no sign that she was restrained or fought back. Ditto for Crossman. I can't believe that they stayed still and let someone slit their throats. Benson was restrained, but he didn't have defensive wounds either."

"It's a valid point," Catherine said. "I have said from the beginning that they knew their killer, and the forensics support that theory."

"But even if you know someone, you don't just let them kill you," Kara said. "So what if each scene has two killers—one who lures the victim to a private location. Maybe says, 'Don't tell anyone, this is between you and me,' and then when they arrive, they're talking and the killer comes up behind them and slits their throat. Or, in Benson's case, tied his hands."

Kara frowned, and Matt understood her frustration. The victims had no defensive wounds at all, and because they weren't drugged, it stood out. As if they were resigned to die.

"That is a logical theory," Catherine said. "And it lends credence to the idea that even if the victims didn't know each other personally, they all knew their killer. I agree that Riley will have more information. She traveled across the globe to Ashland, yet didn't contact law enforcement. She could be in danger, and she may know why. She also may understand the meaning of the poppies."

Kara's shift in focus toward Riley Pierce was warranted, but it was nice to have Catherine back it. "She could have gone into hiding," Matt suggested. "After finding out what happened to Jane, she was scared and disappeared."

"But she didn't return to France," Catherine said. "She hasn't used her passport."

Sloane spoke up. "Could she have been lured to the States? Perhaps the killers used Jane's murder to bring her back. She might already be dead."

Catherine considered that, nodded. "Yes, that's possible. I fear there is a list of targets. That these people will continue down the list until they're done, and then it's over. They aren't spree killers or serial killers, not in the traditional sense. There is no escalation, no cooling off period. The murders themselves are quick and efficient. The flowers… I'm having a harder time nailing down their purpose. I thought I knew—I thought it was either as a sign of remembrance or forgiveness, possibly remorse.

"Now?" She shook her head. "Now I think it means something completely different. But I have no idea what."

Ryder burst into Matt's office, stopped halfway in. "I'm sorry," he said quickly. "But I found something important."

"You have the floor," Matt told him.

Ryder looked a bit sheepish at having interrupted the meeting, but Matt motioned him to sit and said, "You were talking with Agent Stewart in Denver?"

"Him, others," Ryder said. He pulled out his tablet and brought up a set of notes. "It was Crossman's birth certificate that made me believe we're dealing with an organized criminal group of some sort. It's a real document, issued from the State of Colorado, with an authentic seal. But it's false. Not fake, but we confirmed with the hospital administration that Chris Crossman was not born at St. Matthews Hospital on that date. Agent Stewart went to the county office and there is birth data for both Benson and Merrifield at St. Matthews Hospital."

Catherine frowned. "So they were all born at the same hospital, years apart? There could be a motive here, though I'm not seeing it."

Ryder shook his head. "No, I'm saying the birth certificates are falsified, that someone inserted the birth information digitally into the system, so the county issued official, certified birth certificates."

"Is that even possible?" Catherine asked.

"Yes," Ryder said, "for an extremely skilled hacker who has deep knowledge of the Colorado systems."

"I spoke with the US Marshals when we couldn't confirm Jane Merrifield's identification," Matt said. "None of our victims are in Witness Protection or known to any other agencies. None of their fingerprints have popped either. And while the Marshals are capable of creating false identification, there is a record."

"It's a hacker," Ryder insisted. "I've reviewed all government-issued documentation that we have on all the victims, and Agent Stewart helped with the field work. Crossman had a Colorado driver's license when he moved to Santa Fe ten years ago when he used that *legal* ID and his birth certificate to obtain a New Mexico license."

"He was a certified teacher," Catherine said. "He graduated from college, he received his credentials—he had to take the test, be verified."

"He may have taken the certification test," Ryder said. "I'm still verifying that. But according to the school district where he substituted, they never followed up to confirm his college degree from University of Colorado Denver. I asked Agent Stewart to contact the university directly for proof of his attendance.

"If it was one oddity, it would be interesting but not suspicious," Ryder continued. "While we have yet to find any official documentation on Robert Benson, his social security number was issued in Colorado. Crossman and Merrifield have documentation from Colorado, but it's incorrect or false. Merrifield's home residence is wrong. The high school listed on her college records said she never attended. The local police and Agent Stewart haven't found any individual in Denver who personally knew Jane Merrifield. Crossman has a suspicious birth certificate and no record that he was born at the hospital listed. And while Mrs. Benson said that her husband had lived in Colorado, we can find no records on him. She's looking for his birth certificate now, said she saw it once before they married, but it's not in their important papers. We have more to go through, but he never had a driver's license in Colorado."

"What about social security numbers?" Catherine asked. "False documentation is difficult but not impossible. False social security numbers are much more difficult."

"Merrifield's was issued over three years ago—the same month she applied to SOU. And Crossman's was issued ten years ago, before he bought the house in New Mexico."

One person not having a social as a child was possible, Matt thought. Some parents didn't apply when they were born, and after birth there was a longer process. But two was definitely unusual.

"What about Benson?" Matt asked.

"His was issued eleven years ago in Colorado, shortly before he turned up in Weems," Ryder said. "To get a social security number as an adult, you have to submit your birth certificate and a second document proving identity. Plus, you have to show up at the SSA in person and explain why you don't have a number. There will be a log, and I've requested the information, but they're telling me it'll take weeks to retrieve the data."

"Write up exactly what you need and I'll get Tony to flex his muscle," Matt said, speaking of the assistant director in charge of their team.

"Already done," Ryder said. "I have a theory, though."

He looked a little sheepish, but Matt nodded, urged him to continue.

"Someone with incredible skill to cover their tracks hacked into multiple systems to insert falsified information for these people. Their licenses are real, their birth certificates are real. They are real people—but they were not born under those names at St. Matthew's. This is well above my abilities, but I'd like permission to talk to the cybercrimes team at the lab. They might have some ideas about who could be behind this."

"Do it," Matt said. "This is the first solid lead we have. Does anyone have questions?"

"Ryder," Kara said, "when you and Agent Stewart follow up with the agencies in Colorado, can you add Riley Pierce to your list?"

"Sure."

Matt saw where Kara was going with this. "You think she's also living on false identification."

"Yep," Kara said. "Riley and Jane knew each other before college. They were roommates for three years until Riley took an internship in France. It reasons that Riley at a minimum knows more about Jane's past than we do, and could have her own false identity."

Ryder nodded, jotted down the information, turned to Matt. "If you don't need me for anything else, I'd like to get started on this."

"Go," Matt said.

After Ryder stepped out, Matt said, "Catherine, what do you think?"

"That Ryder is one of the smartest people I know."

Matt smiled and nodded his agreement. He said, "Do you think these people wanted to disappear?"

"It makes sense from what we know, though with the time differences, I am less inclined to believe they witnessed or were involved in a singular event that prompted them to change their identities," Catherine said. "What's also clear is that Crossman was central to the organization."

Sloane said, "Even if Crossman didn't graduate from college in math, he was known to be a gifted substitute teacher. I don't have documentation of his computer skills, but his colleagues all said he was their go-to guy to help with computer problems."

He could be like Ryder, naturally gifted in electronics without advanced training, Matt thought. Or he could have superior skills.

"You're suggesting," Catherine said, "that Crossman may have created these identities."

"It's possible," Sloane said. "His computer is on its way to the lab here at Quantico. If there's anything there, they'll find it."

"It's one more piece," Catherine said, "but we need the information from Colorado. There should be a trail leading to when and where they were created. If, as Ryder said, an individual has to go in person to the SSA, those records could be vital. The victimology is important to every case, but here, it's critical. Why were these three people targeted? What do the poppies mean to the victims and to the killer? Is Riley Pierce a threat or in danger?"

"Catherine," Jim asked, "are these killers a threat to others? Meaning, other than their specific targets, which you earlier said were premeditated and well planned, are they a threat to, say, someone who might stop them from achieving their goals?"

Catherine thought on that. She rarely spoke without thinking through what she wanted to say. "I can't give a definitive answer, but based on their methodology and detailed planning, I think they will avoid indiscriminate violence. They don't want to be caught. This isn't a killer who has remorse for his actions. They are intelligent, especially the organizer. That individual would understand if they kill wantonly, they will have more eyes on them, more law enforcement involved. They don't want that."

"Excuse me a second," Jim said and stepped off camera.

"Then why the theatrics?" Kara asked.

"Theatrics?" Catherine asked.

"Yeah. Leaving the bodies where they'll easily be found. The flowers. It's bold. It feels like a statement."

"It may well be a statement," Catherine said, "but also consider how quickly the murders happened. No one heard anything. No scream. No fight. No defensive wounds. There was far more time and care taken in planning the murders than the act itself, which was quick and efficient."

Kara leaned back, thought. Michael said, "Matt, you want us in Colorado?"

"You read my mind," Matt said. "Are you wrapped up there?"

"There's nothing we can do that the local team can't," Michael said. "They have a task force, and they're following through on each piece of evidence. This afternoon we received Riley Pierce's college file, which includes her family's address in Denver. We can help Agent Stewart follow up. And if anything breaks here, or they locate Riley, they'll call us."

Matt agreed. "Ryder will have tickets for both of you out of Medford tomorrow morning. Probably early, so get a good night's sleep. Sloane, you and Jim need to meet the Evidence Response Team from the Albuquerque office at Crossman's place tomorrow morning. Anything they learn, you learn."

Jim came back in view. "We got something else. Sloane noticed food in the trash—pasta and frozen broccoli. The ME just got back to me about Crossman's stomach contents. His last meal was four to six hours before his death, and it wasn't pasta. He ate stew—beef, potatoes, carrots, onions—along with red wine. Suggests dinner. Doesn't mean he didn't have the pasta earlier, but the trash was empty except for those items."

"You think someone came in after he was killed," Matt said. "The killer?"

"Possibly, but why clean up? Nothing else was out of place. They still don't have a clear TOD because of the temperature and animal activity, but they have an entomologist from the university coming in to analyze insects and larvae, so they should be able to narrow it down. However you slice it, my professional opinion is that Chris Crossman died at most twenty-four hours before Merrifield and Benson."

Matt asked, "Do you think that's how the killers found Benson and Merrifield? That maybe Crossman had their locations? A full day would be enough time to travel from New Mexico to Oregon and Virginia."

"Possible, but we didn't find anything in the house. Might be in his computer, or the killers took the information, or they tortured him—though there is no evidence of physical torture. If Crossman was involved in creating the false identities, then it's plausible he was killed first."

Matt wrapped up the video chat. He said to Catherine, "I've never had a case like this."

"Neither have I. Kara is correct that Riley Pierce is a person of interest."

Matt rose, paced his office. "Do you think she's a threat?"

"I couldn't say, but I would be cautious," Catherine said. "She was informed of Jane's death, but never contacted the police. She was seen near Jane's apartment, but ran from law enforcement. She might be scared if she knows who the killers are, but then why would she have left France? If she thought there was a threat against her here, why not stay across the Atlantic?"

"I need to be in the field," Matt said, "but there's too much to do here. The lab hasn't given me the results on the poppies, and they should know more by now."

"I'll follow up first thing in the morning," she said. "But some tests take time, not because they're dragging their feet. You've been working this case nonstop for more than a week, Matt. Come to the house for dinner. Chris made his famous steak chili and homemade corn bread. And Lizzie would love to see you."

Matt had been friends with Catherine and her husband, Chris, since Catherine and Matt went through the FBI Academy together fifteen years ago. He'd been the best man at their wedding and was Lizzie's godfather. Their friendship had ups and downs over the years, and the last two years had been particularly rocky for many reasons. But they were working through it and they'd always worked well together.

Matt couldn't help but think that Catherine would never have invited him if Kara were in town. Catherine and Kara did not get along, even before Catherine found out that Matt and Kara had a personal relationship. Over the last few months they had developed a manageable working relationship, but the tension was constant, and it bothered Matt that Catherine always seemed to be waiting for Kara to make a mistake that could be used to push her off the team.

"Do you have other plans?" Catherine asked pointedly.

"All right, I'll be there."

Catherine smiled warmly, pulled out her phone. "I'll text

Chris and let him know. It will benefit both of us to put this all aside for the evening and come back fresh in the morning."

Maybe that's what Matt needed—a break.

"I have to talk to Ryder, then I'll head down there." Catherine and Chris lived in Stafford, about thirty minutes south of Quantico. Matt lived in the opposite direction, but he had an overnight bag and would stay in the Quantico dorms. They were in the midst of a partial hiring freeze and could only train enough agents for replacement. There was a whole wing of vacant dorm rooms. Kara had been living in one for the last several months—when she wasn't at his place.

Matt found Ryder in his large cubicle talking on the phone. He waited until the analyst was done, then said, "I'm going to leave in a few minutes. Any news?"

"Balls are in motion, but it's near end of business in Colorado so nothing will happen until tomorrow. I have Michael and Kara on a flight first thing in the morning, and Agent Stewart will meet with them when they arrive."

"Good. Now, go home."

"I will. I'll be late tomorrow—I have a meeting at headquarters with the head of Cybercrimes. They might have something for us. They've been tracking a hacker in Colorado, but that's all I know right now. They were very interested in what we had."

"Be careful with them," Matt warned. "Cybercrimes likes to play games, and if this hacker is connected to these murders—either because he helped the victims or maybe turned on them—then we need to know everything they know."

"Understood, sir."

Ryder left and Matt shook his head. *Sir.* He'd tried for the last year to break Ryder from that habit, and sometimes it worked—but more often than not, it didn't.

He finished work so he could go to Catherine's with a clear conscience. He considered calling Kara, but she and Michael were working, and his call would be personal. Instead, he sent her a text message.

Wish you were here. Heading to dinner at Chris & Catherine's. Call when you're settled in for the night. XO.

He missed her. But work came first and Kara would be upset with him if he wanted to casually chat when she was in the field.

Matt hadn't realized how much he'd needed a night off.

He and Chris sat in the heated sunroom with a glass of whiskey and a college basketball game on in the background. At one time he would never have missed March Madness; now, it was April and he didn't even know who had made the final four until they turned on the television.

"Dinner was great, buddy. Thanks," Matt said. "I know it's cliché, but Lizzie has grown too fast. I can't believe she's twelve. Wow. She's an amazing kid." He sipped his drink. "I need to get down to Miami and visit my brother and his family. I've only seen the new kid twice, but she's a cutie."

Matt's brother, Dante, was a doctor like Chris, though Dante was a pediatrician and Chris a pediatric surgeon. He had been married for ten years and had three young kids. Matt wouldn't be surprised if they had more.

"Did you take Kara down to visit?"

"Not yet."

"You seemed serious about her."

Chris had met Kara a couple of times, but they hadn't really socialized.

"I am."

"Then why not introduce her to your brother?"

"I wanted her to come down for Christmas, since we both had the time off. She went to visit her grandmother in Washington."

"And?"

"And that's it. I told you, Kara and I are taking this one day at a time. Her family isn't like mine or yours. She doesn't expect anything to last."

"Then introducing her to your happily married brother and sister-in-law will show her there's another way."

"I'm not going to push her. She's buying a house, so she's putting down roots. She needs her space and privacy. I'm okay with that."

Chris didn't say anything.

"I am." Mostly, but he didn't say that.

He loved Kara and would have been ecstatic if she'd moved in with him. But, she valued her own space and it was a big step for her to sell her condo in California and buy a house here. She probably would have been content living in the dorms at Quantico indefinitely.

"Okay."

"What's with the third degree?" But he knew, and didn't wait for Chris to answer. "Catherine. You know Catherine has problems with Kara. It's an off-limits subject with her now, and I can make it off-limits with you, too."

He didn't know why this conversation irritated him, but it did.

"Catherine recognizes that her feelings toward Kara are partly because of your past relationship with Beth," Chris said. "She's working on that. And I don't hold the same views about Kara's abilities—I trust your judgment there. You wouldn't have her on your team if she wasn't among the best at her job."

"Thank you," Matt said, lifting his glass in a mock toast. "I appreciate your approval."

"But," Chris said, ignoring his sarcasm, "while your job has always been important to you, so is family. Kara doesn't seem to have the same foundation, or desire to make one. I don't want you giving up those dreams."

"I haven't."

"Matt—you're one of my closest friends, and I've never seen you committed to one woman before. I'm glad you found someone, but I don't want to see you hurt."

Matt didn't know how this conversation became so personal,

and he was about to completely change the subject when his phone vibrated. It was Kara. He bit back a smile and said to Chris, "I have to take this."

"Feel free to use my office."

Matt answered the phone as he walked down the hall to Chris's home office. "Hey," he said, then closed the door. "What's up?"

"Michael says we have to get a good night's sleep because we have to be up at *three thirty* in the morning. It's seven here. I can't sleep at seven."

He smiled. "Nothing good on television?"

"I wouldn't know. I might go down the street to the pub—we had an amazing dinner there."

"What did you have?"

"Steak smothered in mushrooms so perfectly cooked it was orgasmic."

"Wish I were there."

"Me, too," she said. His heartstrings tugged. "How was your dinner with Catherine and family?"

That she said it without sarcasm was a feat. "Good. I'm still here. Chris and I were having a glass of whiskey."

"I didn't mean to interrupt."

"You didn't. I miss you. I'm glad you called."

She didn't say anything for a beat.

"Kara?" he prompted.

"I just heard back from my Realtor," she said.

"And?"

"I'm one of three offers, and the seller is looking at them on Saturday. She wanted to know if I was willing to go up, and I said no. If I don't get it, I don't get it."

Matt frowned. Kara sounded so...nonchalant.

"What?" Kara said when he didn't immediately speak. "You think I should go into huge debt just for a house? I'm happy living at Quantico."

"You want to live in a dorm for the next couple years?"

"I had a lot of equity in my condo, and my living expenses are low. I put what is a fair offer for that house and I have the plus of a large down payment and pre-approval for a loan and a fast close. It's what I offered, and I'm not desperate. If it doesn't work out, it wasn't meant to be and I'll find something else."

"I thought you loved the house."

"I do. But I try not to get too attached to things. It's just a house."

Chris was right about one thing. Where Kara was concerned, Matt's heart was on the line.

"By the way," Kara said, "Ryder seemed frustrated when I talked to him earlier. Everything okay?"

"He's working with multiple agencies and jurisdictions. I would have lost it days ago. But he has a lead from Cybercrimes and I'm hoping we have more by the time you land in Denver tomorrow."

"Good. Okay, you get back to your bestie and I'm going to channel surf until I get tired."

"I *really* wish I were there. You wouldn't need television."

She laughed, and his heart lifted. "It won't be long. I mean, if I do get this house, we're going to have a *lot* of work to do."

"I didn't think it needed that much work."

She laughed harder, and then he realized what she meant.

"Aww, you got me. Yes, every room needs to be given a lot of personal attention."

"I can't wait," she said.

"I love you."

"Ditto." She ended the call.

Kara rarely said *I love you*, but she showed it. That was what mattered. And Matt didn't care. Most of the time.

He definitely wished she was here.

11

Fort Collins, Colorado

Riley didn't know where Thalia lived. She probably moved frequently, staying nowhere long, always on the move. Or maybe she lived in a remote cabin far from anyone, just like they'd grown up, hidden from the world.

With Chris dead, the only other person who knew how to reach Thalia was Jesse. He hadn't responded to her post on the message board, but she tried not to read too much into that. He probably hadn't seen it yet. In a day, two maybe, he'd respond. Or maybe he read it and reached out directly to Thalia, because he was loyal to her, not to Riley.

But she didn't *know*, and she had to know that Thalia was safe, that she had a plan. Two people Riley loved were dead. They had to make sure everyone else they'd rescued was safe.

Riley sat in her rental car on the quiet semi-suburban street in Fort Collins, Colorado, where she could see the home of

Donovan and Andrew. Donovan had come home from work shortly after five, but Andrew, a veterinary assistant, was still out and it was already seven.

So she waited.

Donovan would slam the door in her face. She wouldn't blame him.

After all, his brother was dead because of her. He hadn't forgiven her, and honestly? She hadn't forgiven herself.

But she pushed the guilt and pain deep down because it would do her no good. Apologies, even though she was so desperately sorry for what happened, would never bring James back.

It was Andrew she needed to talk to. Once Andrew found out that Jane and Chris were dead, he would help. He wouldn't be happy to see her, but he would take her to Jesse so they could warn Thalia.

She also needed to warn Andrew that he and Donovan might be next. They should disappear for a while until she and Thalia could do something.

She had no idea what they *could* do, other than creating all new identities for the others and urging them to relocate. To create a new life yet again.

Riley closed her eyes, remembering how she'd begged Thalia to take her all those years ago.

"You're eleven," Thalia had said. "I can't have you slowing me down."

"Please," Riley begged. "You don't know how mean my mother is."

"I've dealt with her cruelty far longer than you." Thalia put her hand on Riley's shoulder. "You are strong and brave. Stay strong. I need you here, my eyes and ears. Someday, it'll be your turn. Just not now."

Riley had a hard time forgiving Thalia for rescuing others before her. Yet, without Riley in Havenwood, Thalia wouldn't have been able to do any of it. Alone, Thalia couldn't have saved even one person. Every time Riley brought another person to the hidden sanctuary high in the mountains above Havenwood, Riley thought Thalia would take her, too. But always, Thalia said no.

"You need to stay."

"Now's not the time."

"I need you in Havenwood."

"If you leave, Calliope will never stop looking for you."

So finally, Riley gave Thalia no choice. She faked her own death so her mother would never look for her.

There were truths that Thalia didn't know, because Thalia hadn't lived in Havenwood for years. When Thalia left, everything changed. And finally, Riley couldn't take it. When she brought Jane to Thalia that summer night, Riley was prepared to leave on her own. She would disappear...or die.

Because death was better than living with evil.

The sound of a passing truck jerked Riley out of her memories.

The truck pulled into Andrew's driveway. Andrew exited the vehicle and entered through the side door. She slowly counted to one hundred, then approached the house.

Andrew had once been a friend, a compatriot. Someone Riley had confided in, shared with, trusted.

As much as she trusted anyone.

That was a long time ago.

She knocked on the front door. The house might have been small, but it felt like a home. Thriving plants on the porch surrounded two chairs where Donovan and Andrew could watch the sunrise on a clear morning. A quiet street in a quiet neighborhood.

A life they'd built together from the ashes of hell, and Riley was going to shatter it.

Donovan answered. He stared in disbelief.

"What are you doing here?" he said through clenched teeth, his face reddening.

"I need to talk to you and Andrew."

"You of *all people* should never have come."

He was right, so she remained silent. But she didn't leave.

Andrew appeared in the doorway, surprise and worry on his dark face. "Come in," he said.

"No!" Donovan said. "We're going to have to leave now, you know that, Riley? Don't you? We have a life here. You destroy everything you touch. I don't want to leave!" His voice cracked.

Andrew put a hand on Donovan's arm to quiet him.

"We need to talk," Riley said. "It's important."

Andrew nodded and Riley brushed past Donovan. The living room was warm and comfortable. Simple, not cluttered. Homey with two love seats, a small television on the wall, a colorful rug on the hardwood floor. The dining room to the left had an old table that sat four and a hutch displaying a collection of mismatched china that was so charming Riley almost cried.

She buried the tears deep in the well. Her eyes burned, but they remained dry.

Deep breath. Be calm. Stay in control. No fear.

She turned to face the two men.

"Jane and Chris were murdered."

Andrew looked stricken, and Donovan put his hand to his mouth with a gasp.

"How?" Andrew asked.

"They were lured out of their homes and their throats were slit." Blunt, to the point. Because how else could she tell them? "I don't know how they were found, how they fell into a trap, but they're dead. The police called me about Jane."

"What did you tell them?"

"I didn't talk to anyone. I wasn't in the country."

"Of course you weren't," Donovan said in disgust. "You ran far away—"

Again, Andrew silenced his partner with a calming hand.

Riley cleared her throat. "I have an internship at a museum in France. The police left a message and I came as soon as I could. And, um, I went to see Chris, but he'd also been killed. Around the same time as Jane, within days."

"This is..." Donovan threw up his hands. "This is *the worst* thing that could happen. What if they know where we are? We have to go, Andrew! Tonight, *right now*!"

"We don't know anything yet," Andrew said calmly, though the news had obviously shaken him.

"I need to talk to Jesse," Riley said. "He's the only one who knows how to reach Thalia." She didn't state the obvious: *Now that Chris is dead.* "I posted on the message board as soon as I heard about Jane, but he hasn't responded. I tried again yesterday, nothing. I don't know if his network is down or he's being cautious or if he's working on a rescue with Thalia, but I need to talk to him. You know where he lives."

When Andrew and Donovan were first rescued, Andrew was seriously ill. He almost didn't make it out of the mountains he was so weak, and they stayed with Jesse for several weeks until Andrew regained his health.

She looked at Andrew, not Donovan.

"Thalia saved your life," Riley said quietly. "Help me save her."

He nodded. "I'll take you."

"No!" Donovan shouted, fists clenched.

Andrew said to Riley, "Give me a couple minutes, okay?"

She nodded. "I have a rental car. It's a gray Nissan."

"We'll need my truck, it has four-wheel drive. Jesse lives off the beaten path. It'll take about five hours."

Donovan looked near tears and Riley felt like shit that she had come here and screwed up their lives. After everything they'd been through, they didn't deserve it.

What choice did she have? There were more people at risk if she walked away, ignored the murders, didn't warn Thalia. They knew it, too. While Donovan might be able to turn his back on the people left behind, Andrew couldn't. Riley had counted on his honor and loyalty.

She stepped onto the front porch, pulling her jacket closed

against the cold, and walked to the rental to grab her backpack, then back to Andrew's truck to wait.

Twenty minutes later, Andrew came out carrying an overnight bag. Donovan wasn't with him.

"We'll drive to Denver and get a room. It's a four-hour drive from there, and I don't want to drive in the snow."

"The sky's pretty clear," Riley said. "I can help drive since it's late."

"Trust me," he said, "it'll be snowing within an hour."

She pushed her guilt aside. "We can leave first thing in the morning. I'll sleep in my car—I don't want to cause problems with Donovan."

"No," was all he said.

"I'm sorry." She *was* sorry, but how many times would she feel like she had to apologize because she was Calliope's daughter? How long would she have guilt for things she hadn't even done?

Andrew unlocked the truck, took her bag and put it behind the passenger seat along with his. Then he walked around to the driver's side, got in, turned the ignition.

"Riley," he began, then sighed and rubbed his face.

She'd practically grown up with Andrew. She'd confided in him. He was the big brother she'd always wanted. But so much had happened and she knew, deep down, that he partly blamed her for all the bad things that happened in Havenwood. Not because of what she did, but because of her mother. She tried to understand why some people couldn't separate her from Calliope.

Because sometimes, she went along with the insanity thinking she could change her mother. But you can't change people, especially someone who thinks they are never wrong.

"I'll take you to Jesse, make sure he's okay, and that's it. I never want to see you again. I'm sorry," he said quickly. "That came out worse than I wanted. This isn't about you. I've always cared for you, Riley. I don't blame you for anything you did or didn't do, and I will always be grateful to you for getting Donovan and me out of that hellhole. It's Havenwood and the twisted people who live there. Seeing you brings it all back."

She knew how Andrew felt. Because *being* her was just as bad. "I don't blame you and Donovan for hating me."

"I don't hate you, Riley. Donovan—his emotions are still raw when it comes to his brother. But I can't look at you and not see her."

She knew he was talking about her mother. She nodded, understanding, even if deep down she didn't. Not really.

I'm not my mother! Riley told herself.

Yet, she was alone. She lived in the world, but no one really saw her. No one could understand what it was like to be in her shoes. Nor would they want to try.

"We've done everything possible to forget Havenwood. I don't want to lose what I have now, what Donovan and I have built together," Andrew said. "You of all people should understand that."

She was Calliope's daughter, a pariah. Anyone who came into her life was in danger. Calliope might believe she was dead and gone, but that wouldn't matter to those who had lived there for so long, like Andrew.

Maybe Thalia had been right and Riley should have stayed for the greater good. If she had sacrificed herself for others, Calliope would never have sent people out to hunt those who escaped.

Thalia had never wanted her to leave. And Andrew believed the same.

She had been selfish three and a half years ago when she faked her death and walked away with Jane. But she didn't regret it, even if that meant she would be alone for the rest of her life.

"You'll never have to see me again," Riley said.

Andrew backed out of the driveway and headed south toward the interstate.

12

Havenwood
Seventeen Years Ago

Calliope kissed her beautiful girl on the top of her glorious red head and laughed. "Oh, Riley, it's a beautiful day!"

She swung her daughter around in the meadow, laughing at the fit of giggles coming from the five-year-old.

They collapsed in the meadow and looked up at the clear blue sky. Riley asked questions. Always, lots of questions! Calliope knew that was normal for a young child, but some questions she didn't want to answer. She didn't want to explain why she never went with Daddy Robert and the others when they sold their crafts. Why she never went to town to buy goods they couldn't grow or make here in their valley.

Some things couldn't be explained to a child.

To avoid more questions, Calliope said, "Can you keep a secret?"

Riley sat up, crossed her legs, and nodded her head up and down vigorously. "Tell me, Mommy."

"No one knows yet except your daddies," Calliope said. "You're going to have a little brother or sister."

Calliope put Riley's little hand on her stomach. "There's a baby inside." Her best estimate was that she was four months along. Naked, she could see the small bump. Soon, she wouldn't be able to keep it a secret. She planned to announce her pregnancy at community dinner next week when everyone was back in Havenwood. She was always nervous when they were spread out, her nights filled with bad dreams thinking about everything that could go wrong outside Havenwood. Craft fairs and hunting trips and supply runs—they were all dangerous. She needed everyone under the same sky so she could be at peace.

"Really?" Riley said, eyes wide. "A baby?" She smiled. "Can I hold him? Can I feed him? I'll share my dolls if she's a girl, I promise!" She crossed her heart.

"You'll make a wonderful big sister. Now, find your basket, we'd better head back so we can make pies."

Riley carried a small basket and Calliope had a larger one. They'd gone to collect early apples from the orchard. Though the apples weren't quite ready for harvest, with a little sugar and butter, and her mother's delicious piecrusts, the tart apples would be perfect for pie.

September and early October were the busiest times at Havenwood, as they worked long hours to harvest all the fruits before winter. They grew apples, plums, and pears. Many people didn't think fruit could grow in the Rocky Mountains, but some varieties did extremely well.

Havenwood had the orchard, a large garden, and a greenhouse. Two barns for animals, and a large enclosed chicken coop attached to a small shed they kept heated when temperatures fell consistently below freezing. The enclosure was to protect the birds from coyotes and other wild animals—years ago, they'd learned the hard way that they couldn't let the chickens roam in the valley.

Riley, an inquisitive child, kept stopping to pick flowers, telling Calliope what kind of weeds and plants she saw. Her daughter loved nature and she would grow into a kind, generous soul. Calliope and the other residents of Havenwood made sure to encourage that interest. Havenwood children were collectively schooled and Calliope put their education above all else.

Perfect, Calliope thought. A perfect home, a perfect child, a perfect life.

Havenwood had become the utopia her mother had envisioned and Calliope had cultivated.

Calliope heard a truck—then another—coming down the road from the east. It was too early for the group to return from the Labor Day craft fair in Flagstaff where they sold their crafts and specialty jams. They weren't expected back until Tuesday. Maybe they sold out on the first day and were returning? She wanted to see Robert—she missed him so much. It would be wonderful if they were home, but she didn't think that likely.

Havenwood was built in a hidden valley deep in the mountains. Occasionally they encountered campers, usually lost or who hadn't seen the private road signs that clearly marked the boundaries of Havenwood property. Never day hikers because there were no maintained trails near Havenwood, but the occasional deep woods backpackers.

Calliope didn't like strangers to know of their slice of paradise, and her mother and William too often befriended people, inviting them to camp in their valley for a night and share a meal. So far, no one had done anything to hurt them, but Calliope kept waiting for people to return, expecting hospitality in exchange for nothing. Calliope also despised listening to stories of corruption and violence outside of Havenwood. It seemed life Outside had gotten worse in the years since they founded Havenwood.

Calliope had seen enough violence as a child, before her

mother met William and they decided to move here with Calliope. She'd been nine, but the minute she stepped into the valley, she knew it was home.

She hadn't left since.

When Calliope and Riley reached the village—the grouping of homes surrounding an ancient tree around which Havenwood had grown from two families to four to now over one hundred people with a common dream—she saw that the two trucks weren't filled with strangers. Todd and Sheila were there. They'd come back to Havenwood, and for a split second Calliope was thrilled—she *knew* they would return, that they would miss utopia as soon as they lived in the filth and decay of the outside world.

Then Calliope saw they had brought others. Three large men with guns.

"Mommy, who are those men? Is that Sheila? That's Todd!"

"Shh," Calliope said sternly.

Glen ran around the back of their home and stood by her side. He took the basket from her arms and put it on the ground. "We need to get out of here," he said. "Let me take you and Riley to the house. You don't want to get upset, not with the baby. Athena can handle this."

"They have guns," Calliope whispered, her heart racing. Todd and Sheila brought strangers with guns to their home. Their *sanctuary*.

Her mother approached them, but Calliope didn't move. She couldn't. Every fear she'd had for the last twenty years since her father was murdered in front of her bubbled to the surface, all at once.

Glen said, "Please, for the baby, for Riley, come with me now." He scooped Riley up in his arms. She clutched her small basket, eyes wide, scared because she didn't know what was happening.

These people were scaring her child. They'd brought *fear* to her daughter.

"Daddy Glen? What's wrong?" Riley said, her voice shaking.

"Where's Thalia?" Calliope demanded.

"Her group is still at the lake," Glen said.

Thalia and a half dozen others were fishing and wouldn't be back until sunset. Peter and his larger group were hunting and not expected back until end of day tomorrow. They had most of the guns. Havenwood stocked up on food from April through September so they didn't have to worry about hunger during what could be harsh winters.

"Secure Riley and the rest of the children in the schoolroom," Calliope told Glen. "Get as many people and shotguns as you can. Find Anton." She detested guns, but they needed rifles to hunt deer, and shotguns to scare away wild animals. "Anton will know what to do. We need to send these people away."

"Calliope, we can't fight them. And if they go, they'll just come back, maybe with more people. Let Athena find out what they want, she'll convince them to leave."

Would her mother be able to fix this? Calliope didn't know. But Todd and Sheila wouldn't be here threatening them if they hadn't been allowed to leave in the first place. Her sanctuary had been invaded by evil.

Like the evil that killed her father.

Never.

Calliope was scared, but more than the fear, she was angry. She approached her mother. Glen tried to stop her, but she looked pointedly at him, then at Riley. "Protect her with your life," Calliope said in a low whisper, then turned away, trusting that her partner would comply.

"Mommy?" Riley said. "Mommy!"

"Shh," Glen said and walked briskly with Riley toward the schoolhouse. Calliope breathed a bit easier. She loved Glen, but he was the weakest of her men.

"We don't want trouble," Calliope heard Athena say as she neared. Worry clouded her mother's expression—a concern Calliope rarely saw in her. "I will sell you twenty percent of our harvest, and then ask that you never return."

"That's not going to work for us," Todd said with arrogant confidence. "Come now, Athena, we'll take it all, as I said, and then maybe we won't come back."

He was smiling, but it was a dark smile, a cruel, lying grin that made Calliope's blood run cold.

Todd nodded to Sheila, who started to walk toward the barn where Havenwood dried and stored the marijuana they grew in their greenhouse. The marijuana sales gave them enough money to pay property taxes, buy medicine and fuel and other goods they couldn't make or grow. Twice a year, in late spring and early fall, a small group would deliver product to a distributor. It was an arrangement they'd had for as long as Calliope could remember. Then Robert would clean the money using their craft fair business.

Without the fall sale, Havenwood would be at risk. They couldn't survive on what they made at the craft fairs. They needed the revenue from the marijuana.

"No," Calliope said. She blocked Sheila. "How can you betray us like this?"

Sheila backhanded her. "I bought into your mother's pathetic ideas for too long, Calliope. Grow the fuck up."

Athena stepped forward. "I am reasonable, but do not touch my family." She had a calm, soothing voice, though Calliope, who knew her mother well, heard the tension.

"This is how it's going to go," Todd said. "We'll fill our trucks with as much product as we can fit. Whatever is left you can keep. We'll be back in May with four trucks. Be prepared to fill them."

Calliope laughed. These people would tarnish Havenwood like this? "You are the grasshoppers and you think we are the ants?"

Sheila grinned. "Yeah, I think you are."

Calliope shook her head. "No," she whispered. "No."

"You don't have a choice," Todd said. "Who are you going to tell? The authorities? You're going to call the cops? Oh, boo-hoo, someone stole your marijuana crop. We all know you're not telling anyone. This arrangement will suit me, and you'll adjust."

Her mother had invited Todd and Sheila to live with them. Taught them how to live off the land. Treated them as family. And for two years, they *were* family...until they left in April, as soon as they could get out of the valley during the first snow-melt. They left and Athena didn't stop them. She asked why, and they said they were bored.

Now they were back, to steal from the community who had taken them in.

"Most of your men are gone this weekend," Todd said. "Can't have the testosterone and guns around to cause a fuss."

"You've been watching us," Athena said.

"Of course I have. You'll stay here by my side, Athena, just in case someone gets a foolish idea to try to stop us." To Sheila he said, "Go, I want to get out of here quickly. I'm sure someone has gone to the lake to get help, but it'll take them at least an hour to get back here."

"No!" Calliope screamed and lunged for Sheila's weapon.

The man closest to her hit her in the stomach with the stock of his rifle before she could disarm her former friend. Calliope collapsed to the dirt, unable to breathe, a horrific pain tearing through her body.

Athena rushed to her side. Sheila was about to hit Calliope again, but Athena screamed, "Don't touch her!" She squatted and held Calliope in her arms. "Darling girl, it's going to be okay. I promise."

It would never be okay. Not if Todd was allowed to leave. Calliope knew that, why didn't her mother see it? She tried to move but her stomach ached and she wanted to weep. But instead of tears, she gathered her strength and rage. She would need both.

"Watch them," Todd ordered one of the men. He looked down at Athena and Calliope with a scowl, shaking his head. He, Sheila, and the other men headed to the barn.

Calliope clutched her stomach as she watched them walk away.

"It'll be okay," Athena murmured in her ear.

"They betrayed us!"

"We'll find a solution. When everyone is back, we'll find an answer. Just stay put. I don't want anyone hurt."

"They'll come back with more people! Take everything we have! Tell others where we are and destroy Havenwood. We have to stop them."

As Calliope said it, she realized the only way to save Havenwood was to make sure the interlopers never left.

"Help me up," Calliope said. "Please, Mother, please help me."

Athena did.

"Stop," the stranger guarding them said.

"She's hurt," Athena said. "Let me take her inside to lie down."

The man looked torn, then said, "I'll follow you. No funny business."

Calliope walked with great pain, but she would do anything to protect her home.

Anything.

Her mother's house was closest, and that's where they went. Calliope mentally prepared herself for what must be done.

Havenwood had the numbers. Against five armed people, they would win. As long as someone took charge—someone like Calliope because her mother was weak. Her mother was capitulating to these evil people. Letting them walk away with everything. Condemning Havenwood to a life of fear and servitude.

As soon as Athena walked Calliope across the threshold, Calliope reached behind the door for Athena's shotgun. She used it to scare foxes away from the chickens. She'd never shot an animal with it.

Or a person.

There was a first for everything.

Calliope racked the shotgun and, without hesitation, shot the man on the path. He staggered back, raised his gun to fire, and she racked the shotgun a second time and fired again. Athena screamed.

"Calliope! Stop!"

Though she'd never killed a person before, she didn't see them as people—they were predators. Evil creatures, monsters, demons who would destroy Havenwood like the people who destroyed her family all those years ago.

The company who laid off her father because they were cutting back.

The men who beat him up one night when he was working as a security guard.

The man who killed him in front of Calliope that rainy day in February, on her eighth birthday.

"No," Calliope whispered, trying to push those awful memories far away. She hadn't thought about her father in years. What she saw. What she heard. The smell of blood. But it came back now, washing over her. Suddenly, she embraced her feelings of helplessness when she was a child and couldn't fight back.

She was no longer helpless. She had a world to save.

"Mother, they will return with more people. Don't you see? They will take everything. If we can't protect ourselves, everyone will leave because they won't be safe. We'll have nothing and no one."

"You can't—"

"They came *here*. *They* are the attackers. Why can't you see the truth?"

Calliope saw indecision and weakness in her mother's eyes.

"Mother," she said firmly, "we must protect Havenwood today, or there is no tomorrow."

Athena nodded.

The shotgun blasts had Todd and the others running back to the center of Havenwood. Todd was enraged. "What have you done?" he screamed and raised his gun.

Calliope laughed, partly hysterical, but feeling so very free. What had *she* done? What should have been done months ago when Todd and Sheila said they were leaving.

She shot at Todd, but he was too far for the buckshot to hit him.

Then she saw Anton run out of the barn with a rifle, Glen right behind him. Anton fired multiple times, hitting Todd, then one of the armed men started firing back at him. Glen fell down. Calliope didn't register his collapse, not at first.

Todd's men looked for cover, but Todd had brought them into the open. There was no cover. Sheila started to scream.

Garrett came out of his workshop, gun in hand. Calliope had never been so happy to see him. He was supposed to have gone on the hunting trip, but had broken his ankle at the beginning of the summer and couldn't handle the long trek. He was also former military. Best, Todd and Sheila didn't know about him. Garrett had joined Havenwood that summer after Robert and Athena met him at a craft fair.

Garrett looked at her across the clearing, his mouth open as if in shock. Then he fired his handgun at their attackers; one by one they dropped.

Todd's men fired back but they went down fast now that a man who knew how to shoot had come to stop them.

Calliope fell in love with Garrett in that moment.

Athena screamed at them to stop.

Silence descended across the valley as the echoes of gunfire and screams subsided.

"What have you done?" Athena asked, shaking. "What are we going to do?"

Calliope looked at the fallen.

"Bury them," Calliope whispered.

Suddenly, a cry from Annie's house pierced the quiet.

Bobby came running out. He was ten, a happy, joyful child who now had tears running down his face. "My mommy—she's bleeding."

Calliope stared at him, not quite registering what that meant. Athena ran to the child, rushed inside to help. Calliope stood where she was, then began to sway.

Garrett rushed to her. "You're bleeding. Where are you hit?"

She looked down, saw the blood pooling in the dirt at her feet. "My baby."

There were three Havenwood casualties that day. Glen, Annie, and Calliope's unborn child.

WEDNESDAY

13

Santa Fe, New Mexico

Sloane and Jim split up Wednesday morning—Jim headed to the Office of the Medical Investigator to review his findings and work through jurisdictional issues, and Sloane to Chris Crossman's house to supervise the Evidence Response Team from Albuquerque as they processed the property.

The team knew what they were doing and she didn't want to get in the way, so she stood outside and wrote up notes for her report. She was almost done when she heard a horse clomping up the driveway. A woman in her early sixties wearing jeans and a red flannel shirt with a black down vest sat atop a beautiful white-and-brown Appaloosa.

Sloane stepped off the porch and put her hand up, signaling for the rider to stop. She didn't want to contaminate Crossman's property any more than it already had been.

"Hello, ma'am," Sloane said. "Beautiful mare you have there."

"Thank you." She smiled, but her eyes showed concern as they darted toward the house.

"This is a police investigation," Sloane said. "I'm going to have to ask you to turn around."

"Is something wrong? Is Chris okay?"

"Do you know the owner?"

"Of course. I've known Chris Crossman since he moved here."

"Where do you live?"

"Up the mountain about a mile, then turn left and it's the end of the road."

"Your name?"

"Abigail Schafer."

"Ms. Schafer, I regret to inform you that Mr. Crossman was killed last weekend. I'm surprised you didn't hear about it."

She stared at Sloane in disbelief. "Chris is dead?"

"Yes, ma'am."

"I just came home yesterday," she said. "I was showing my horses in Texas. I saw the cars on the main road and came up, surprised because Chris doesn't usually have so many guests."

"You knew him well?"

"I suppose. I mean, we're not close friends—I'm very social, Chris is quite reserved. But sometimes he would come riding with me. He loved horses, was really good with them. He'd been raised with horses."

This woman could be a good source of information.

"Do you have a few minutes?" Sloane asked. "We're investigating his death and you may be able to fill in some blanks." She didn't want to be too specific, but she also didn't want to lose this potential witness.

"Anything I can do to help. Let me get down."

Abigail expertly dismounted, patted her horse, and held the

reins loosely in her hands. She pulled a bottle of water out of the saddlebag and drank. "Can you tell me what happened?"

"He was murdered on the Atalaya Trail," Sloane said.

"Oh, my God, he was murdered? That's—awful. This is a safe community. Chris hikes all the time. I ride most of these trails, often alone. I can't believe it."

Sloane asked for her identification, wrote down her name, address, and license number. Best to double-check the identity of a neighbor, especially one who showed up at the victim's house. Her ID verified her address, and she happily gave Sloane her phone number.

"You said you've known Chris since he moved here? How long ago?"

"Ten years next month. He saw me riding down on the road, came out and asked me about the horse—not Bella, here, I was training a stallion that day for a friend. I invited him to come riding—he took me up on it."

"How often did you go riding together?"

"Oh, maybe four, five times a year? He was busy, and like I said, very private. If I was in a group or teaching—I give horseback riding lessons—he didn't join. But we make plans fairly regularly. Last year I had a death in the family, and my usual caretaker couldn't come out to care for my horses. Chris stayed at my place for a week, did an amazing job looking after them. Like I said, he grew up with horses."

"Do you know where he grew up?"

"In—well, gosh, I don't think he ever told me. He said a ranch, maybe? But there must have been mountain trails, because he was a natural."

That was a start. "Do you know if he had any family? We can't find his next of kin."

"He didn't talk about his family. I can chatter on and on about mine—I raised four boys, all out of the nest now. My husband passed three years ago—Chris was so kind then. He'd come and help with the horses, but didn't fill the time with idle chatter. Let me ramble, sure, and didn't seem to mind. I liked him. I would have had him over all the time, but he wouldn't have liked that."

"Because he was private," Sloane repeated.

"Exactly."

"Did he have regular visitors? Friends that you've met?"

"Not often, but he had a girlfriend—not serious, at least I don't think so, because she didn't visit often. Maybe they were just friends. I tend to romanticize everything."

"Do you have a name?"

Abigail shook her head. "I never talked to her. Saw her a couple of times, but Chris never introduced us. I asked him once about it, and he avoided answering. I was a little irritated—I mean I wasn't being overly nosy, just asking about a woman I've seen at least a half dozen times. But I let it go."

"Can you describe her?"

"Reddish-brown hair. Very skinny. Too skinny, if you ask me. She would have been pretty if she didn't have this hardened look about her. Probably in her early thirties."

"White? Black? Asian? Hispanic?"

"White—her skin was tan from being outdoors. Being an outdoors woman myself, I can tell."

"And distinguishing characteristics? A tattoo? Her voice?"

"I never met her face-to-face. The closest I ever was...well, I came up once last year to bring Chris a gift basket as a thank-you after he watched the horses. She was here. I saw her through the doorway, but that was as close as I got. Chris didn't invite me in."

"Did you see a vehicle here that wasn't Chris's?"

"Oh. I didn't think about that. Yes, actually. A white Ford truck. I don't know anything else about it, just a Ford. My husband always drove Fords."

"Was it new? Old?"

She shrugged. "I don't know. Not really old. There was a shell on the back, I remember that."

"You wouldn't by chance remember what state the plates were from?"

She shook her head. "I didn't notice."

"That's okay," Sloane said. "You've been a big help."

"You don't think she killed him, do you?"

"We don't think anything right now. We're still retracing his steps. One more question. Other than this woman, did you ever see anyone else here?"

"No. He wasn't social, like I said. But he was a very kind person."

Kind. That word again. Robert Benson was kind. Jane Merrifield was nice. Chris Crossman was kind. All quiet. All loners. Benson was the most social with his church, but even he preferred being home alone with his wife.

"Thank you for your time. If I have additional questions, I'll call."

"This is such a tragedy," she said, shaking her head as she mounted her horse with the ease of someone half her age.

It certainly was, Sloane thought as she watched Abigail Schafer ride back down the driveway on her Appaloosa.

14

Fort Collins, Colorado

Donovan Smith didn't want to go to work; he was still so upset and angry with Andrew. Okay, upset with Andrew for leaving, and angry with Riley for showing up at the house. Deep down he knew that nothing was going to be the same.

He loved their home and community. He didn't want to leave Fort Collins. Maybe they wouldn't have to. He had to hold out hope that this was all a mistake, that it was a false alarm.

He and Andrew had built a nice life here in the six years since they escaped Havenwood. Comfortable. Happy. He liked his job at the nursery—he had a gift for working with plants. All those years tending to the Havenwood greenhouse had paid off. They didn't make a lot of money, but that was okay—they owned the house outright, thanks to Thalia and Chris, and they lived frugally. They didn't need a lot. They had no desire to travel and had simple, inexpensive tastes. They loved peace and quiet.

Peace.

Havenwood was supposed to be peaceful, but it was hell. Looking in, you wouldn't know it. You'd think, *Oh, what nice people! Just old hippies taking care of their families, living off the land.*

Looks were deceiving.

He hated Riley for bringing back the memories. He'd had nightmares last night, woke up in a cold sweat. Wished Andrew was there, but Andrew had gone with *her.*

He talked to Andrew when he was driving to work, as he and Riley were getting ready to leave for Jesse's house in South Fork, but Donovan knew better than to beg him to come home. Andrew's duty and honor wouldn't allow it, and then they'd both be upset.

So Donovan said fuck it and walked into the nursery where he worked. As usual, he was the first to arrive. Maddie, who was supposed to be here at 7:00 a.m. on the dot, was always late. They opened to the public at eight during the week, and Maddie seemed to think that was *her* arrival time.

There was a lot to do in the morning to prepare; the most important was to download and process orders from the website, as well as check the temperature of the greenhouse and the status of the drips, then weeding and trimming plants. He much preferred to do the work in the greenhouse than deal with the computer, but he started the process, then sorted the mail.

A letter, unstamped, was addressed to him. He opened it. Inside was a dried red poppy.

His heart skipped a beat.

"Thalia," he said out loud and sighed in relief.

Finally, some sanity in what was a chaotic situation. Thalia would have answers. She always did.

He picked up the flower and smiled. The enclosed note read: *9 a.m., your house.*

He could do that. He would simply tell Maddie that he wasn't feeling well and she needed to take over until Carmen and Tom arrived at ten. Wednesdays weren't busy anyway.

He waited and waited and Maddie finally came in at quarter to eight. He explained the situation, that he had a touch of food poisoning, and was going home. She grumbled about it, but he ignored her complaints and left.

He couldn't wait to see Thalia. It had been far too long. He understood the need to remain cautious, but they had been friends, and sometimes he missed Havenwood. If he were being honest, he would have returned if Calliope and her...her *minions* weren't there. Before Athena became too sick to run the community, it had been a wonderful place to live.

But it couldn't be saved now. Not after the misery and pain that had been unleashed. He would never be able to return knowing how his little brother died, knowing that while Calliope was to blame, they were all culpable—*especially* Riley.

His stomach twisted in regret. Though he had never hurt anyone, he couldn't help but feel remorse. Silence was also a crime. But until Riley arrived at his door yesterday, he had put Havenwood in the past. He didn't think about it every day. Now? He hadn't been able to stop thinking about it.

Donovan arrived home early, at eight thirty, and unlocked the door, closed it behind him. He'd make tea. He wasn't a fan, but Thalia loved tea. He put the kettle on to boil, turned, saw her.

"Donovan, you truly disappointed all of us."

A cry bubbled up in his throat and he felt rooted to the spot. All the fear, the deep, mind-numbing pain he'd lived with for so many years, froze him.

He sensed movement to his right, coming out of the back of the house. But his instincts were too late to save him.

He saw the knife right before it sliced open his throat.

15

South Fork, Colorado

Evan missed Havenwood. It had been a long four weeks.

But they were almost done with their mission. Anton and Ginger had taken care of one of the traitors up north just this morning and were waiting for the second to come home. Marcus and Karin had returned to Havenwood straight from New Mexico ten days ago in order to brief Calliope and work to locate the others.

Jesse Morrison hadn't been as forthcoming as they had hoped.

Evan didn't like being alone. He needed his family. Especially now, after being on the Outside for four weeks.

Four very, very long weeks.

But Calliope needed him in South Fork, watching Jesse Morrison's house. So he was here.

He would do anything for his family.

He drank coffee and situated himself in the drafty one-room cabin at the end of the road. It was the perfect perch to watch anyone who approached Morrison's place through his binoculars. The cabin was on Morrison's property, but it was barebones. One room, no electricity, but it had a stove and the fire he stoked kept the room toasty.

He'd only left once in the last four weeks, and that was to drive to Ashland.

It had been a nearly impossible job, but it had to be done. So he did it.

He closed his eyes, but then he pictured Jane and her big blue eyes full of surprise when she realized she was about to die.

Evan rose, shook his head to clear it. He had barely slept in the last ten days since he slit Jane's throat. When he slept, he dreamt of her. Of watching her play with the other kids, her long blond hair braided down her back, bouncing as she ran. Of her singing while picking vegetables in the greenhouse. Of how she and his nephew, Timmy, had fallen in love and were planning to have their own house at Havenwood.

Then Timmy died and Riley died and Jane ran away.

A cry escaped Evan's throat. How could Jane have abandoned the family? How could she have abandoned *him*? He was grieving for Timmy, too. He'd loved Riley like a daughter. Jane was all he had left, and she walked away. For the longest time, he believed she had wandered into the woods on purpose and died. He envisioned all the ways it could have happened. Fallen off a cliff. Starved to death. Froze to death. Been mauled by a mountain lion like Timmy.

But she died none of those ways. When Evan learned Jane had betrayed Havenwood by leaving with Thalia—the woman who had stolen from them—he was enraged. He wanted to bring her home.

He was sent to kill her, but he would have brought her back to Havenwood. Calliope would accept her back, Evan was certain. So he gave her the option.

"Come back, Jane. Come back and all is forgiven."

Tears fell down her cheeks. "No."

He slit her throat.

He'd killed a girl he loved.

It had to be done. As Calliope said, those who leave will bring pain back with them. Never forget that Todd and Sheila killed Glen, Annie, and Calliope's unborn child.

Robert deserved to die after stealing from Havenwood. Chris deserved to die for helping Thalia kidnap people from Havenwood. But Jane? Sweet Jane...

Stop thinking about her.

Once they'd learned Thalia was kidnapping Havenwood residents, Calliope sent five people she trusted the most to Jesse Morrison's remote home in South Fork. They met here, did what needed to be done, and Evan was told to stay because Thalia would be coming.

It didn't take long.

After, Anton and Ginger were sent to Virginia, and Marcus and Karin were sent to New Mexico.

And Evan was sent, alone, to Ashland.

You'll be able to go home soon, he told himself.

They were almost done. Evan had only to wait here until Anton and Ginger were done in Fort Collins. Then they would all go home. They hadn't found the others, but they had more information to work from. By the end of the summer, every traitor would be punished.

He heard a truck turn from the highway below and start up the snow-covered gravel driveway. It was probably the old woman at the bottom of the hill, but Evan did what he always did; he stepped outside on the narrow deck, picked up his binoculars, and watched.

He couldn't be seen through the trees, and he dressed to blend in with the surroundings.

It was a new white truck and it passed the old woman's house and headed straight up the road to Jesse Morrison's.

Evan was surprised when he saw Andrew get out of the driver's side. He pulled out his phone to call Anton, his heart thudding in his chest. He might have to kill Andrew by himself.

What was Andrew doing here? Did he see Anton and Ginger this morning and run away?

Evan didn't think he could have gotten here so fast. Something didn't feel right.

Then the passenger door opened and Evan almost dropped the binoculars and his phone.

Riley.

It couldn't be Riley. Riley was dead. She had drowned in the lake. Anton and Garrett had seen her go under. She never resurfaced.

They had a memorial service for her. They buried an empty casket with her favorite things. The carving of a horse that Timmy gave her. Her favorite sweater that Athena had knitted for her the winter before she died. And her artist supplies—the pencils and charcoal and paper Garrett brought in every year.

Evan had cried with Calliope. All of Havenwood wept when Calliope's daughter died.

Evan had loved Riley like a daughter. Riley and Jane, Timmy and Cal, the four musketeers had been inseparable. And they all left, one way or the other. Dead…or running.

He stared through the glass, zoomed in on her face.

It *was* Riley.

She was alive. She was here *with Andrew.*

When Evan could act, when he could finally get his head together and do something, he called Anton. At first, his friend didn't believe him.

"I swear to you, it's Riley. It's her, Anton. She's alive and she's with Andrew."

"Follow her," Anton said. "We're leaving now. I'll let you know when we're in South Fork. Don't go back to the house. If you get a chance, kill the traitor and grab Riley."

"We need to tell Calliope."

"I watched her drown, Evan. I need to see her with my own two eyes. Then I'll call Calliope."

16

South Fork, Colorado

Agent George Stewart from the Denver FBI office picked Kara and Michael up at the airport and filled them in. They were headed to South Fork, Colorado, about four hours from Denver. Ryder and the FBI cybercrime unit had a person of interest—Jesse Morrison, former Colorado State computer programmer, had quit eight years ago and moved into a family home outside the small town of South Fork. While they had no hard evidence that he was a hacker who helped create false identities, Cybercrimes had flagged him because of some suspicious online activities.

Matt wanted them to be cautious when they approached Morrison. As well as all the usual safety issues, Matt had also said, "I don't want an innocent civilian to have a reason to trash us on social media because we went in without cause."

Kara slept almost the entire drive and woke up refreshed when they pulled into the sheriff's department. She let George and Michael work through logistics while she located the bathroom—and more coffee. She was back in the car finishing the second half of the breakfast burrito she'd picked up at the airport when Michael and George came out.

As they climbed into the front of the SUV, Michael said, "The sheriff gave us the lay of the land. They're following us there for backup, but we're taking lead on the interview."

"How far?"

"About fifteen minutes," George said. "He lives off an unpaved road outside of town. Hopefully the four-wheel drive will get us up the driveway. I looked on a map—he lives half a mile from the highway."

It took nearly twenty minutes to reach the base of the long, winding packed gravel driveway that led up to Morrison's house, where two deputies met them. Snow covered most of the driveway, half of which was shaded by trees, but someone had recently driven on the narrow road. Could someone have tipped Morrison off that they were coming?

After coordinating with the deputies, George led the way up the driveway. On the right corner were four mailboxes. On the left corner was a house. Behind the house was a long driveway to the left. They headed straight up the road as it curved to the right toward Morrison's property.

Kara felt…tingly, as if it was too quiet, too still for a midweek afternoon.

George parked facing the house. A small pickup truck with large, wide wheels was in a carport. Snow had blown in and blocked the back of the vehicle. Ice was thick on the windows. No one had driven it in some time.

George, the senior agent on-site, told the deputies to go around to the side door and hold, and he would back Michael and Kara up in the front. He stayed at the base of the stairs and watched the windows, while Michael led Kara to the front door.

Kara always deferred to Michael in tactical situations. He'd been in FBI SWAT for three years, and he had extensive military experience. She'd been an LAPD detective. Completely different skill sets.

Michael rapped hard on the door and said, "FBI looking for—" He stopped as the door slowly swung open.

Kara drew her weapon.

Michael called, "Mr. Morrison? FBI."

Silence. But there was a smell Kara recognized.

So did Michael.

He motioned for her to go in to the right. Simultaneously, Michael entered and went left. They circled the main room looking for any threat. A deep chill permeated the entire cabin, as if the place hadn't been heated for weeks. A black stove in the corner of the room was cold, the fire long died out.

Michael went to the kitchen and Kara walked to the back, checking behind each door as she went. Closet. Bathroom. Office.

In the center of the office a body lay very, very dead on the floor. The windows in the room had been cracked open, which had helped minimize the putrid smell as well as partially preserve the body, but decomposition had long ago begun.

She called out to Michael, brought up her phone and compared the DMV photo of Jesse Morrison to the corpse.

She was eighty percent certain they were the same person, but she wouldn't swear to it in court.

Michael stepped in and swore under his breath. "I need to clear upstairs. Stay put."

Great, she thought as Michael left again. She got to watch the body. She stared at what was left of the computer. Someone had destroyed it.

Michael returned a minute later, had Matt on the phone. "We'll get the coroner to confirm, but I'm pretty certain it's Morrison. He was tortured."

Kara looked again at the body. She hadn't noticed immediately, but now saw that fingers were missing from his hand.

She glanced away, then saw three severed fingers sitting on the desk. She wasn't a squeamish cop, but *damn* her stomach started to churn. She focused on Michael and breathing normally.

Michael was listening to Matt, then said, "Okay—we'll wait for them." He pocketed his phone and said, "Matt's having Jim and Sloane drive up from Santa Fe. It's a three-hour drive. They're leaving now."

"So that means we're staying overnight?"

"Ryder is getting us a place," Michael said.

There were answers here, Kara knew. They just had to find them.

"No poppies," she said.

"That doesn't mean anything," Michael said. "Matt said to search the house, except for the office—we need to wait for Jim and the coroner to process the body."

George Stewart was standing on the threshold. "The sheriff just called. An anonymous caller, male, reported Morrison's death."

"When?"

"Not five minutes ago. But get this—when the sheriff listened to the call, he recognized the background noise. The caller is at a diner on the edge of town. Ten minutes from here."

17

South Fork, Colorado

Riley and Andrew sat in a diner only five miles from where Jesse Morrison lay dead in his own home.

They hadn't said more than a few words since they discovered his body. The coffee they ordered was barely touched.

When they first found Jesse, they'd run from the cabin, in a panic, as if the long-gone killer was still in the house. Then, without discussion, they went back together.

The smell of death had permeated everywhere in the cabin. They spoke quietly, out of fear or respect, or both.

"He's been dead for at least two weeks," Andrew said. "Could be longer, I don't know."

"He wouldn't betray us," Riley said. "Right? He wouldn't do that."

"He was tortured."

"How—how can you tell?"

Andrew looked at her. His eyes were bright, as if he was about to cry. "They cut off several of his fingers."

Riley's eyes went to the dog bed in the corner. "The dog… They didn't—"

"They took Banjo."

"How do you know?"

Riley followed Andrew to the kitchen. "His leash is gone—it always hung on that hook. One of his dog bowls." He opened a large cabinet, nodded. "The dog food."

"They killed him and took his dog?"

"Banjo is a Saint Bernard. Not really guard dogs, but he would have defended Jesse if he could. Maybe they—maybe they threatened the dog. I don't know if I could keep silent if someone threatened to kill my pet. Jesse loved that dog more than any person."

Tears brimmed in Riley's eyes. She would not cry.

"Everyone is in danger," she whispered. "They found Jane and Chris because of what they found here."

"Did you see the computer?"

She shook her head.

"Someone shot it. My money is on Jesse, thinking that would save him, or to protect us. Maybe he gave up only who he could remember. Or he had physical records or notes or a backup drive. I don't know. Dear Lord, I don't know what they have or who's in danger."

Now, at the diner, they were quiet. Andrew called Donovan. He didn't answer at first, then texted back that he was working and would call when he was free.

Riley wished she had someone to call, someone who cared about her. She'd had Jane, but her friend was dead. She'd had Chris, but he was dead, too.

Jesse Morrison had never been part of Havenwood. He'd helped them because Thalia paid him to do so. He created their identities, gave them backgrounds and documents. He walked everyone through what to say to get their social security card. He'd set up a message board for questions and promised to check it weekly.

No wonder he hadn't responded to Riley's thread.

Before Riley, eleven had escaped Havenwood. She didn't know how many in the last three and a half years. Thalia preferred to take people one at a time, unless they were a couple like Andrew and Donovan. But when it was Jane's turn, Riley had gone with her...

Thalia was furious. She told Riley to go back to Havenwood. That it wasn't time, there was more work to be done.

"No," Riley had insisted. "My mother thinks I'm dead."

"You can't deceive her. There's no body."

"Garrett and Anton saw me drown."

Thalia didn't believe her. But they didn't have time to argue, so she took Riley with Jane. Later, Riley had explained how she'd done it.

"I told Garrett I hated myself, my mother, Havenwood itself. She wouldn't let me leave, wouldn't let me go to the craft fairs, but she'd never be able to stop me from killing myself. I used everything at my disposal—how Timmy was dead, how Cal had disappeared, how everything had changed since Grandmother died. Garrett told her, as I knew he would, and she locked me in my room. I broke a window to get out, knowing they'd follow. Garrett and Anton were only minutes behind me. It was dusk, hard to see, and I waited until I knew Garrett could see me jump into the lake and swim away."

"That lake is freezing," Thalia said.

Even in the summer, the runoff from the snow ensured that the lake was tolerable only for a few minutes at a time.

"I've been going to the lake every day for months. Staying in the cold longer each time, building my endurance."

Thalia looked like she didn't believe her, but Riley didn't care. She said, "I made a show of it, screamed and went under again. Garrett swam out to find me, but the third time I went down, I held my breath and swam to the opposite bank. I hid in the forest all night, then crept back to Havenwood and watched."

Thalia looked at her strangely. With surprise? Respect? Disdain? Riley didn't think she'd ever know what her aunt really thought of her. But she didn't care because she was finally free.

"Calliope believes I'm dead because Garrett and Anton told her they saw me drown. I left evidence—a shoe, a torn shirt—on the far end of the lake where the river starts, where the boulders mask the sudden drop. I did it to protect you, to protect me and everyone we rescued."

Riley didn't understand why Thalia was so angry.

"I solved the problem of me leaving," Riley insisted. "If she thinks I'm dead, she won't look for me."

Thalia shook her head. "Without you on the inside, I don't know if I'll be able to save anyone else. I hope you can live with that, Riley."

Without Jesse, no one else could escape with clean identities to start a new life. Without Chris, no one would have support and training to adapt to the Outside. Anyone Thalia rescued would be on their own without protection or help.

And Calliope would never stop looking for them.

Sometimes, Riley wanted to burn the whole place down. Because Havenwood never forgot.

"They probably don't know where we live," Andrew said.

"What?" Riley asked, pushing back darker memories that threatened her already fragile state of mind.

"Donovan and me. You said Jane and Chris were killed nearly two weeks ago. So they probably don't know where I live."

"Maybe not," she said, but she didn't know for certain. "They want Thalia because she took Robert and they drained all of Havenwood's accounts. Maybe they found her… Maybe they don't care about anyone else." Riley didn't believe that.

Eleven years ago when Thalia and Robert drained the bank accounts and left Havenwood, they believed that Havenwood would implode.

It didn't. Calliope and her inner circle rebuilt the community as an open-air prison.

Andrew stared at her. "Calliope wants you."

He sounded like he was accusing her, as if this was all *her* fault. And, deep down, she wondered if it was. If somehow, her mother found out she was alive.

If Jesse had been tortured, would he have given her up?

A chill ran through Riley's body.

"We have to call it in," Andrew said after a minute. "We can't leave Jesse like that. It could be weeks—months—before anyone finds him."

"Pay phone. Burner. Something."

"Maybe," he said cautiously, "we go to the police."

"And tell them what?" she snapped.

He didn't respond.

After a long minute, he said, "For the first time in my life, I haven't been looking over my shoulder. I haven't been living in fear. When Donovan and I first escaped, I kept expecting them to show up on our doorstep. As months, then years passed, I finally felt we were free. That they didn't care that we left, that their threats and warnings were hollow. We have a good life, a quiet, peaceful life. And now...it's going to take even longer to feel like we're safe again, if I ever feel safe at all."

"You're going to stay in Fort Collins?"

"We'll go on vacation. We have some savings, we can go south, enjoy the warm weather. Florida or Arizona or something. Ride this out."

Riley nodded. It was a good plan. Except, "What about Thalia? They're looking for her, she needs our help."

If they haven't found her yet, Riley thought.

"Thalia has always been able to take care of herself."

"I need to be able to reach you."

He didn't say anything.

"You don't trust me?"

"That's not it," he said. "Riley, I don't blame you for what happened. But you *are* Calliope's daughter. She was never going to let you go. If Jesse told her you are alive, they'll keep looking for you." He reached out and touched her hand. "Go far away.

Don't follow Thalia on her crusade. It was always going to end this way. Run. Hide. Go far away, back to France. I'll call in an anonymous tip to the police so Jesse can have a proper burial. He deserved better than what happened to him. He was a good person who wanted to help because Thalia convinced him it was a just cause. Now he's dead."

Riley's bottom lip quivered, but Andrew was right. That didn't mean she was going to follow his advice. She and Thalia may have disagreed about how they handled the rescues at Havenwood. Thalia may never have forgiven Riley for leaving and not being her person on the inside. But they were family and Riley had to find a way to warn her.

If she was still alive.

Andrew put out his hand and she gave him one of her burner phones. He called the sheriff's nonemergency number. Even though it might be recorded, it wouldn't have the capabilities of the 911 center.

"I want to report a dead body." He gave Jesse's address, then ended the call before the person could ask any more questions.

"What now?" Riley asked.

"I'm going back to Fort Collins today. You can come with me, then leave in your car. If you want to stay here, I'll return the rental for you tomorrow."

Riley didn't know what to do.

Their food arrived, though neither felt much like eating. Riley picked at her french fries.

"Riley, forget Havenwood, forget Thalia. Go back to France. It's the safest place for you to be. Focus on healing."

She snorted.

"I'm serious," Andrew said. "We're never going to stop Calliope and her people. They are on their own destructive path. We don't want to be anywhere near them when everything implodes."

"Don't the others, the innocents, the *children*, deserve a chance to be free?"

"Calliope has nearly everyone brainwashed. I saw it and left six years ago. It has to be worse now. Is there anyone left who is really that innocent?"

She didn't have an answer to that. She didn't know. She'd walked away nearly four years ago and hadn't gone back.

Except, Havenwood had once been paradise. Not everyone agreed with Calliope and how she ran their village. Riley knew every person who still lived there. She loved them. Blood or not, they were family. She wanted them to have a real choice, to stay or leave. Because the way Calliope ran Havenwood, the choice was stay or die.

"I have to find Thalia," Riley said. "She needs to know what happened to Chris and Jane. Do you know where she is?"

"No," Andrew said quickly.

"You're lying," she said. "You know how to reach her."

He hesitated, then said, "Not exactly. But she comes by a couple times a year and she said once that she has a place not far from us."

Riley almost didn't hear the second half of his sentence.

She comes by a couple times a year...

Riley hadn't seen Thalia since her aunt brought her and Jane to Chris's house.

"It's a place to start," she said. "I know some of her aliases. Think about other clues."

Thalia would either live in the middle of nowhere like Jesse, or in the middle of a city where she could blend in with the masses. That didn't really narrow it down. It would be an uphill battle to find her. She needed Andrew's help, but didn't know how to convince him.

After two bites, Riley pushed her plate away. "I can't eat. I'll go back with you. Give me a minute." She put money on the table and walked to the back where the restrooms were.

She splashed icy water on her face and stared at her reflection, but didn't see herself. She saw her mother.

Andrew said she should forget Havenwood and everyone there. How could she?

How could she forget any of it?

She knew her grandmother's story and her mother's story. The truth was somewhere between them.

Her grandmother told her after the death of her first husband, when she was struggling to provide for her daughter, she met William Riley, a kind and gentle man who was also disillusioned with society. His family owned property in the mountains, and he invited her to join him and his brother's family to move there and live off the land. They created Havenwood and designed it to be a utopia. Every year more people joined them and the community grew and prospered.

They almost lost the land because of back taxes, and that's when her grandmother and William decided to grow marijuana. Robert, a new arrival to Havenwood along with his dying mother who wanted to live her last months in peace and quiet, was a math whiz. He set up their finances so they would never be at risk of losing the hundreds of acres deep in the Rocky Mountains. They had created their utopia, a community of people who worked together, played together, worshipped together. They weren't religious in the traditional sense, but they were spiritual. There were no rules, other than to be kind and contribute to the good of all.

Her grandmother rarely talked about the Day of Mourning, only that it changed the hearts of everyone. Riley only remembered snippets of the fateful day that resulted in the murder of one of her fathers and her unborn sibling.

Her mother had a different story.

Havenwood was perfect, a utopia for those who wanted a safe haven. But not everyone wanted to stay. Some people didn't like the rules. Some people didn't like the isolation. Some people didn't want to work. People left. And two of those people came back with the purpose of destroying Havenwood. They murdered Glen and Bobby's mom. Riley remembered her daddy Glen, though only vaguely. He was always happy and spent more time with her than her daddy Robert and her daddy Anton, who both had lots of jobs to do.

Eventually, Calliope convinced her mother that they couldn't bring in outsiders. That new people would destroy the fabric of their home. She would point to Todd and Sheila.

What she didn't tell Athena, and what no one knew for a long, long time, was that Calliope wasn't letting anyone leave. Oh, they made a big show of a goodbye party, but Riley learned much later that Calliope had those people killed.

There was a song Riley never heard until she escaped Havenwood. An Eagles song, about a place you could check in anytime but you could never leave. It haunted her because that was her life, and she hadn't realized how dark, how evil her mother was until that fateful day when she was eleven and she learned the truth.

The day the proverbial doors shut on Havenwood for good when Thalia and Robert left, and Calliope convinced everyone that Thalia had killed Robert and run away to avoid punishment.

It took Riley several minutes to compose herself. When she left the restroom, Andrew was standing in the small waiting area, frowning. "I can't reach Donovan. I called to talk, just to hear his voice, make sure everything is okay, and it goes to voice mail."

"When you talked to him earlier, did you tell him about Jesse?"

"No—I didn't want to do it over text. He said he'd call when he was free, but he hasn't called, and he's not answering his phone. I texted him that I was worried and to call me, but he hasn't called and now he's not even texting me back." Andrew sounded panicked.

"Do you have anyone to check on him?"

"His work. Yeah. I should have thought of that."

He ran a hand through his hair as he stepped outside. She followed. He hit a number and waited. "Maddie, it's Andrew. Is Donovan there? He's not answering his phone and it's kind of an emergency."

As Andrew spoke, Riley looked around the parking lot, getting the odd feeling that she was being watched.

A woman got out of the back seat of a black SUV with multiple antennas. A sheriff's vehicle pulled into the lot.

Riley recognized the woman. It was the cop from Oregon. Short, blonde, focused. She looked straight at Riley.

How did she find me?

"Andrew," Riley said, her voice a squeak.

"What do you mean he left this morning? Where is he?" Andrew was saying into the phone.

"Andrew, we have to go."

Riley tried to pretend she didn't see the woman, or the big black guy in a suit who got out of the passenger seat and stood behind her.

"Andrew!"

He turned to her. "Donovan left work this morning—no one knows where he is."

She started to pull him toward his truck. Why she thought she could get away from the police she didn't know, but panic drove her. Years of believing that the police were cruel. Years of brainwashing and indoctrination and Riley would rather die than talk to them.

She knew everything Calliope had told her were lies and half-truths, but the fear and panic she felt was real.

"What?" Andrew asked, going with her while looking and sounding confused. "Riley, what—"

"Riley Pierce," the woman called. "Stop."

Andrew looked confused. Riley didn't stop. Her heart was pounding, her head thudding, her body hot and cold at the same time.

She stammered, "The. Police. Run."

Andrew hadn't been raised in Havenwood. He came with his parents when he was fourteen, the year before everything began to fall apart. He didn't have Calliope as a mother. He didn't have her loyal followers constantly chirping in his ear.

Thalia had told her that her soul protected her, that deep down Riley knew what was right and just. Riley didn't believe that. If she hadn't seen the truth with her own eyes, she could have turned into her mother.

Yet now, all the lessons about the evil, unjust Outside suddenly came crashing down and Riley needed to escape. Run. Hide.

Andrew was talking, but Riley couldn't hear him through the ringing in her ears.

get away get away get away

Then he shouted, "Riley! Stop!"

She froze.

Andrew gripped her arm, pulled her to his side. "It's over," he said and turned her to face the detective.

The woman said, "I'm Detective Kara Quinn, this is my partner, FBI Agent Michael Harris. I saw you outside of Jane Merrifield's apartment. We just want to talk to you, Riley."

"No." Riley didn't know if she spoke aloud, but she shook her head back and forth.

Andrew said, "We're not armed. We haven't done anything."

"Did you call in the anonymous tip about Jesse Morrison's murder?" Kara asked pointedly.

Andrew didn't say anything.

Kara said, "We really need to talk to both of you."

"My partner—I can't reach him," Andrew said. "I think—I'm afraid something might have happened to him."

"Give us his name and address and we'll have an officer do a welfare check."

"Don't," Riley whispered. "You can't trust them."

"He's five hours away," Andrew said. "I have to do something." He cleared his throat. "Okay. I'll tell you anything you want, answer any questions, but I need to know that Donovan is safe."

★★★

Evan watched as Riley and Andrew got into the back of an SUV. They weren't handcuffed, they went willingly.

He called Anton.

"We have a problem." He explained what had happened.

"Find out where they are going, but be discreet. We're still a couple hours away."

"I took pictures. It's Riley. It's really her."

Anton didn't say anything. He was Riley's last living father. This must be painful for him. It hurt Evan, too. How could she do this to them?

"Anton," Evan said, "we have to bring her home."

Again, he didn't say anything.

"I'm not going to kill her," Evan said firmly.

"No," Anton said. "You're right. Calliope is going to be heartbroken that Riley deceived her. Deceived all of us."

"It explains a lot," Evan said. He'd been thinking about it for the last hour as he followed Riley to the diner and waited. They had many theories about how Thalia had been kidnapping the people of Havenwood over the years. One or two people almost every year. They set up traps, but never figured out how she got into their valley.

She hadn't gotten in. Riley had brought people *out* to her.

"She's been helping Thalia all along," Evan said quietly.

"We don't know that," Anton snapped.

But Evan knew. All the little questions they'd had over the years were answered if Thalia had an inside person.

"Evan," Anton said firmly when Evan didn't say anything, "we don't know what happened. But we will learn the truth. I'll be there as soon as I can. Keep watch, be safe. Calliope has lost too many people over the years. We owe it to her to come home in one piece."

18

Quantico, Virginia

Matt listened to Michael relay the situation in South Fork, then said, "I'll be in Denver tonight. I want Catherine to listen in to the interview with Mr. Gardner and Ms. Pierce. They are not suspects, but they *are* persons of interest. I want her in Kara's ear."

"Roger that."

"Have you heard back from Fort Collins PD about the partner?" Matt asked.

"They're en route to his house."

"Let me know as soon as you do. Where do this Gardner and—what's his partner's name?"

"Donovan Smith," Michael responded.

"Where do they fit in?"

"Gardner made the anonymous call. He already told us that he and Riley Pierce went to the house to check on Jesse, who he claims is a friend of his. They found him dead, left the scene, went to a diner and called it in. They ordered food, but according to the waitress neither ate more than a few bites. So far, the evidence at the cabin supports his statement. If one or both of them killed Jesse Morrison, it was weeks ago."

Ryder popped his head into Matt's office. "You need to leave for the airport in ten minutes, and Dr. Jones is here."

"Tell Kara to hold off until Ryder can set up the feed with Catherine," Matt said.

"Roger that," Michael said.

Matt ended the call and grabbed his go-bag out of his office closet. He always had an overnight bag packed in case he needed to leave in a hurry.

Ryder set Catherine up in their unit's secure communications room. A large monitor would allow her to view the video feed of the interrogation, and she would be able to talk to Kara through their comm system. Matt really hoped Kara didn't shut her earpiece off. He knew she didn't like people directing her questioning—and Kara was good in the box—but in a case like this where they had no idea what was going on, a psychiatrist with Catherine's experience was invaluable.

Catherine looked up from her notes, took off her reading glasses. "What's Jim's ETA to the crime scene?"

"Two hours and change," Matt said. "It'll be dark by the time they get there, but the sheriff's department is bringing in a forensics team to support Jim and provide equipment." It would take two days and two drivers to transport the forensic RV to South Fork, so Matt made the call not to use the vehicle and rely on the local crime lab and facilities.

"Michael said that he didn't see any poppies on the scene," Catherine said, "and the victim appeared to have been dead for some time, so at this point I'm comfortable calling him the first victim."

"Jim will confirm, but I agree."

"Is the only connective thread tying Jesse Morrison to our victims the false identities?" Catherine asked.

"That, and the fact that Riley Pierce, Jane Merrifield's former roommate, was one of the people who discovered the body this afternoon." Matt filled her in on the timeline Michael had provided. "Neither Riley nor Andrew have a record, but we suspect Pierce's identity is false."

Ryder cleared his throat. "Andrew Gardner has a social security number issued six years ago. An educated guess is that his is also a false identity. We're still working on confirming the other information he provided. His employer, Fort Collins Veterinary, confirmed he's worked as a vet assistant there for just over five years. His partner, Donovan Smith, has worked for a local nursery for the same length of time. They bought their house for cash and have no mortgage. Agent Heller is looking into that purchase. So far we haven't found anything on either of them prior to the move to Fort Collins."

Matt asked Catherine, "What do you think is going on here?"

"I don't feel comfortable even guessing at this point. How confident are you that Ms. Pierce and Mr. Gardner will cooperate?"

"Gardner appears to want to cooperate, but he's agitated right now."

"Because of his partner?"

"He hasn't heard from Smith in hours. His panic is telling me he knows about the other murders and is worried that Smith may be in danger."

"I think," Catherine said, carefully, "that one of the initial questions we need to ask is if they fear they are in danger, why didn't they go to the authorities? That tells me they know the motive of these crimes and don't want to bring in law enforcement."

"Are you thinking they might be guilty of a crime themselves?"

"It's a consideration," Catherine said. "But the victims and,

I'll say potential victims, are demographically different—age, gender, race. A religious married white man, an interracial gay couple, two white female college students, a black math teacher. What do they have in common other than the fact that they all live or lived in Colorado?"

"It's a place to start," Matt said. "We don't have much else at this point."

"Matt, you have to leave," Ryder said. "Your driver is at the entrance."

"I don't need a driver."

"If you want to make your plane, you do." Ryder handed him his bag and herded him to the door.

"Call or text any new information," Matt said as he walked out.

His cell phone rang as he climbed into the back of the sedan waiting for him. It was a sergeant with the Fort Collins Police Department. "Is this Agent Mathias Costa?" he said.

"Yes, this is Matt Costa."

The driver pulled away from the curb before Matt shut his door. He juggled the phone and pulled the door closed.

"I went with two officers to Mr. Smith's house. When no one answered the door, we inspected the property and through the rear windows spotted a body on the kitchen floor, giving us probable cause to enter for a welfare check. The individual was deceased and we identified him by DMV photo as one of the homeowners, Mr. Donovan Smith. Someone slit his throat."

"Secure the property and don't touch the crime scene. I'll call in the FBI Evidence Response Team to process. My team is investigating four other murders we believe are connected to Smith." He should have been more diplomatic, but he feared if he didn't claim jurisdiction now he'd be battling later.

"Okay, I can do that."

"Were there flowers on or near the body?"

"Yes, sir," the officer said with surprise. "Hundreds of red poppies."

19

South Fork, Colorado

Kara watched Michael's expression as he spoke to Matt. Usually her partner had an enviable poker face, but right now she saw stress in his tight jaw.

"Matt, I don't think Gardner killed him," Michael said.

Kara raised an eyebrow. Matt didn't think that, did he? Did he have evidence they didn't have?

Michael continued after listening. "Gardner was forthcoming, showed receipts from a gas station that he was a hundred miles from Fort Collins when Donovan left the nursery, telling his co-worker that he was going home because of food poisoning. Gardner seems genuinely concerned and very agitated." He listened, relaxed, and said, "Okay. Call when you land." He pocketed his phone and told Kara, "Matt's on his way to Denver."

"The boyfriend is dead?"

"Yes. Same MO, except his body was found in his house, not outside. It appears they were waiting for him."

She glanced at the closed door. "We need to tell Andrew."

"Now that it's just us," Michael said, "how do we approach these two?"

She'd been thinking about that for the last hour. "Did you see the look on Riley's face when she first saw us?"

"She wanted to run. Guilt?"

"Fear. Deep fear."

"I didn't notice," Michael said. "I was more concerned about whether one or both of them had a weapon."

"Andrew grabbed her so she couldn't run. I'm wondering if when she saw me the other day in Ashland her running was also out of fear. I didn't get as good a look at her face then."

"Most people who run from the cops have something to hide," Michael said.

"Maybe, but..." Kara couldn't quite articulate what she had thought when Riley first recognized her. "She was scared of us, or maybe authority in general. It was deep, not fleeting." She shrugged, wishing she had the words to explain. "Anyway, I don't think Andrew Gardner planned to run. He was surprised to see us, but quickly admitted he was the anonymous caller."

Michael said, "When he finds out his boyfriend is dead he's going to be a mess."

"We can't let him walk away," Kara said.

"No one thinks he's guilty. He was more than a hundred miles away when Smith was leaving work."

"Technically, we know at least three people are involved," Kara said, "so we can hold him on obstruction of justice, at least overnight."

Michael frowned, so Kara continued, "Look, I don't think he's involved either. His reaction is justifiable and his concern authentic. But we could use his actions to hold him if we need to—he potentially contaminated a crime scene."

"That's weak."

She shrugged. "Maybe, but they have answers, and we need

them to talk. Consider that as soon as Riley heard about Jane's murder, she hopped on a plane from France to Oregon but didn't talk to the police. Then she shows up here, where another friend of hers has been murdered. Maybe she's investigating on her own, intending to take justice into her own hands—I don't know. But she came here, with Andrew, a step ahead of us."

"She could be involved," Michael said.

"Do you honestly believe that?" Kara didn't, but maybe she should consider it, based on Riley's actions. Still, she didn't get the homicidal vibe from her.

"We won't know until we start asking questions."

"I don't think she's going to talk unless we have more information to use with her," Kara said. "Whether she's scared of us, or just doesn't like cops, or a criminal, I don't know. If we can get information out of Andrew, then we can use that with Riley."

Michael agreed. "Take the lead. And put the earpiece in."

Kara sighed, but did as Michael instructed. He carefully pinned the mic on her shirt.

She turned it on. "Testing, testing, one-two-three-four."

"You're coming through loud and clear," Ryder said. "We have the video feed working in Pierce's interrogation room."

"Switch over to Andrew Gardner's room. We're talking to him first."

Catherine's voice came through her ear. "Why?"

Kara really hated explaining herself, especially to Catherine. She and Michael were lead, and they should be free to do what they knew was best without some shrink second-guessing them.

But, she put a smile in her voice and said, "Once he finds out that the love of his life has been murdered, he'll tell us everything he knows. Riley isn't going to talk until we can tell her something she doesn't think we know."

"Based on what?"

"My gut."

She heard Catherine sigh and Kara rolled her eyes.

"All right," Catherine said, "Ryder has the video on in Mr. Gardner's room. I can see him. He looks upset, but he could be involved, so be careful how you approach him with questions. I'll give you direction."

"I'm looking forward to it," Kara said with barely veiled sarcasm.

Michael shook his head slightly, urging her to cool it. Always trying to keep the peace.

Kara walked into the room. "Mr. Gardner? I'm Detective Kara Quinn, this is Special Agent Michael Harris, with the FBI. We met at the diner. Thank you for waiting."

"Did you talk to Donovan? Is he okay?"

Kara sat directly across from Andrew; Michael sat to her right.

Death notifications always sucked. And it was usually best to do it quick.

"We regret to inform you that Donovan Smith was found dead in your house. I'm deeply sorry for your loss."

He stared at her, his chest hitched, his eyes glazed. "I knew. I knew when he didn't call me back. He *always* calls back. I knew something was wrong. Oh, God. I never should have left him. I should have insisted he come with us. What happened? Tell me. Please. Tell me the truth."

Michael said, "Officers went to the house for a welfare check and entered when they saw a body on the floor in the kitchen. His throat was cut. All physical evidence points to a quick death. I don't believe he suffered, if that helps."

Andrew drew in a sharp breath.

"Donovan... He fought back. He's a big guy, strong. He must have fought back. There has to be evidence—"

"There were no signs of struggle. The Fort Collins Police Department is there now, but they're holding the scene until the FBI Evidence Response Team arrives. We'll process the scene and have a better understanding of exactly what happened."

"I need to go—to be with him." He put a hand to his mouth and shut his eyes.

"You wouldn't be allowed into the house tonight," Kara said. "We believe that Donovan's murder is connected to three other homicides. We were here to talk to Jesse Morrison because we traced the three dead people to him."

His eyes shot open. "Three? Donovan is the third, right?"

"No. He's the fourth."

His voice was a whisper. "Who?"

Kara heard Catherine's voice in her ear. "Find out what he knows first."

She didn't need Catherine to tell her that. Kara said, "You knew about the murders, didn't you?"

"I—" He stopped, collected himself. "Riley came to our house last night and told us that Jane and Chris had been killed. I—Donovan and I—knew them. And we—" Again, he stopped, cleared his throat.

"Jane Merrifield and Chris Crossman?" Kara asked to clarify.

"I didn't know their new last names."

Bingo. New names.

"But you knew who Riley was talking about when she said Jane and Chris."

"Yes."

"Let me tell you what we know," Kara said.

"No," Catherine said in her ear. Kara ignored her.

"We know that Jane Merrifield and Chris Crossman are false identities created by Jesse Morrison. We also know that Riley Pierce is a false identity. They don't exist, except on paper. Do you know their real identities?"

He nodded.

"You're not Andrew Gardner, are you?"

He shook his head.

"Do you want to explain to us why you have a false identity?"

"I—can't."

"Then we'll have a problem. Because lying on federal forms, to the social security administration, accessory to felony hacking—these are all crimes."

"You don't understand."

"Explain it to me."

"Tell me. First tell me—who's the other victim? You said three before Donny—Donovan." His voice cracked.

"Kara," Catherine warned in her ear.

"Robert Benson," Kara said.

A sharp intake of breath told her that Andrew knew exactly who Benson was.

"Robert?" His voice squeaked. "A fifty-ish white man?"

"You know him," she said bluntly.

He nodded.

"How?"

He shook his head.

"You need to tell us the truth about what you know," Kara said.

"Your partner was murdered," Michael added. "Three people you know—four, including Jesse Morrison—are dead. You know who's responsible."

Andrew didn't say anything for a long minute, then he laughed, but it was a twisted, pained laugh. "I was going to say that if I told you, they'd kill me. But they're already killing us. I'm as good as dead." His voice cracked.

"If there is a threat to your life," Michael said, "we can protect you."

Andrew shook his head. "No, you really can't."

Kara saw the fear in his expression as well as hearing the resignation in his voice. "Andrew," she asked softly, "who killed your friends and your lover?"

He took a deep breath, slowly let it out, composing himself. "I can't tell you specifically *who* killed Donovan. I don't know. But I know why. Because we left."

"A gang?" Michael said, and Kara shook her head. It wasn't a gang—not with such a wide range of demographics represented. Men, women, gay, straight, black, white—not a gang. Maybe like a gang.

"A cult?" Kara offered.

Andrew shrugged. "I don't know what to call Havenwood."

Kara's heart raced. This was it. They were close to answers. "What's Havenwood?" she asked.

"You might call it a commune or a cult, but it's not. Well, it wasn't. Not at first. It was heaven on earth…until it became hell." He took a deep breath. "I—I need a bathroom. And water. Please."

Michael rose. "Five-minute break," he said and escorted Andrew down the hall.

In her ear, Catherine said, "Why do you always have to openly defy me?"

"Are you my mother?"

She shouldn't have said that. This was being recorded, and that sounded downright juvenile.

"It would have been better to find out what he knew specifically, before sharing any information he didn't have."

Kara ignored her comment and instead asked, "Have you ever heard of Havenwood?"

"No."

"Do you think it's a place? A town?"

Ryder said, "I'm running it."

Of course he was.

"Ryder," Catherine said, "set up a call with AD Montero as soon as possible."

"Who's that?" Kara asked.

"Tonight, if he can do it, or first thing in the morning. A call is fine, but face-to-face is best."

"Yes, ma'am," Ryder said.

Kara waited. Waited. "And?" Kara said, growing increasingly irritated. "Who's AD Montero?"

"Dean Montero is the assistant director of Quantico," Catherine explained with another sigh. "He's an expert on cults in the US. He'll be an invaluable resource if Havenwood is a commune. He could already know something about it."

Why did everything have to be so difficult with Catherine? No one else on the team made Kara feel inferior. They were a *team*, a unit, working together toward a common goal. In fact, Catherine treated Sloane with more respect than she did Kara, and Sloane was a rookie.

Originally, Kara thought it was because Catherine was highly educated, a forensic psychiatrist with years of college and experience, and Kara entered the police academy out of high school. Kara had street smarts, not book smarts. But over the last year, Kara realized that while her initial instincts were partly right, mostly it was about Matt: Catherine didn't approve of their relationship. She pulled the "I've been Matt's friend for fifteen years" card and didn't think Kara was good enough. And though she had toned down her animosity after the lecture she'd given Kara last summer, her silent disapproval was deafening.

Michael came back in the room. "Where's Andrew?" Kara asked.

"He was sick in the bathroom. A deputy will escort him back here in a few minutes."

"Catherine is calling in a cult expert."

"Dean Montero? I'd like to be in on that call."

"Hear that Catherine?" Kara said. "So would I."

Silence, but Kara knew Catherine was fuming. Good. She should have suggested it. She was the shrink, but Kara and Michael were in the field and they needed to be privy to all information. The insight could be helpful.

They heard running down the hall, a shout for a medic. Michael and Kara ran from the room and toward the commotion. Michael said, "I'm a certified EMT, what happened?"

"Mr. Gardner cut himself."

Michael pushed through; Kara watched from behind him. Andrew Gardner lay on the tile floor, deep cuts in both forearms, from his wrist up almost to the inside of his elbow. Two cops were kneeling next to him trying to put pressure on the wounds. He bled profusely and was trying to fight them, but grew weak from loss of blood.

Michael shouted, "Towels, shirts, whatever you have. Get pressure on the wounds. Ambulance ETA?"

"Ten minutes."

Michael grabbed everything the deputies shoved at him and wrapped Andrew's arms tightly. "Everyone out except you—" he pointed to the deputy holding Andrew's other arm "—and my partner."

Kara stepped inside the door as the other officers went into the hall.

"Hold on, Andrew," Michael ordered. "Stay with me. You don't want to do this."

"Let me go," Andrew said, his voice weak. "Let me die."

"No," Michael said firmly. "Not on my watch."

Andrew's skin was ashen, and his blood seeped bright red through the towels. Kara wished Michael hadn't asked her to stay—she was good in a crisis, but watching their witness bleed to death was making her squirm. Had he tried to kill himself because his partner was dead? Or because he didn't want to talk about Havenwood?

By the time the paramedics arrived, Andrew had lost consciousness, but he was still alive and Michael thought they'd stopped the flow of blood.

Michael moved aside as the paramedics took over. "He needs to be on suicide watch," Michael told them. To the deputy he said, "And we need a guard on the room 24/7."

"I'll talk to the sheriff," the deputy told Michael.

After Andrew was wheeled out of the room, the deputy offered Michael the locker room to clean up. As Michael passed Kara, he said, "I want to talk to Montero before we question Riley Pierce, so however Ryder or Catherine can get him on the line, do it."

"Yes, boss," she said.

He gave her an odd look.

She smiled. "You channel a good Matt Costa. He would be so proud."

Michael just shook his head, but he had a half smile on his face as he followed the deputy down the hall.

Good. She needed to lighten his mood a bit. It had been an all-around shitty day.

She pulled out her phone and called Ryder. "Michael wants to talk to this Montero guy ASAP. One of our witnesses tried to off himself, and I don't know that he's going to make it."

20

Havenwood
Fourteen Years Ago

William sat on the boulder that looked like a grizzly bear and surveyed the valley that he once loved, but had grown to despise.

Something had changed over the last few years and Athena either didn't see it or, more likely, didn't want to see it.

For more than two decades he had done good work here. They grew their own food. Raised their chickens. Provided for the families that had once made Havenwood great. There had been such joy here when his brother's family had started Havenwood with him and Athena. It was hard work, and the first two winters had been particularly difficult, but they'd built something they were proud of. Athena, who was so good with people, brought more families in, then added to his own by giving birth to Thalia, his precious daughter, who would be eighteen this summer.

There were many changes. His brother died, then his sister-in-law left with their only child to make a fresh start. They were in Australia now, on a ranch, but he hadn't heard from her in years. More people came, and some left. He had raised his stepdaughter and his daughter, but they were so very different. Calliope refused to leave…and Thalia had dreams bigger than the valley.

He'd always thought Thalia would go to college—she was such a smart young woman. He and Athena had never gone, and Thalia should have the choice about whether to stay here or leave, spread her wings.

Before the Day of Mourning, Thalia had talked about studying wildlife biology. She had met a forest ranger on one of her hikes—she used to hike for miles, much to Athena's worry. She thought she might want to be a ranger, to protect the land and animals in the Rocky Mountains. Or just to bring the knowledge home to Havenwood.

But Athena had begun to discourage their daughter, saying she needed her here to help run Havenwood. William knew why—Calliope had quietly taken over. She'd changed everything. Slowly, but William saw it. Athena refused to admit it.

Calliope was her daughter, after all. The daughter she had always felt she'd failed as a child.

"I was not a good mother when Calliope was little," Athena told him shortly after she found out she was pregnant with Thalia. "My husband—he was a difficult man. Angry at everyone. At me. At the world. When he lost his job, it was everyone's fault but his. When he couldn't find work, it was everyone's fault but his. But he had one saving grace—he loved Calliope. He never hit her. She was his angel, his princess. He wanted to give her the world."

"He hit you." William touched her cheek gently.

She kissed his hand. "I should have left. I'll never forgive myself for not leaving, but I'd convinced myself that it wasn't often, that when he found work again it would get better, that he didn't hit our daughter, so it was okay."

"It is never okay," William said.

"I know that now. I know that because of you." She kissed him, put her head on his shoulder. "He wanted more for us than he had growing up, and he made some bad decisions." She paused. "I wish you were Calliope's father. She needs your gentle soul to temper her fears."

"What happened?" She'd never told him more than her husband had been killed. She had never wanted to talk about it.

"My husband went to work for bad people," Athena said. "He messed up. They killed him right in front of Calliope. If I hadn't found you, if we hadn't found Havenwood, I don't know that she would have survived. She found her peace here. I hope it's enough."

"She has you, and she has me. I love her as if she is my own, as much as I love the child growing inside you now."

At the time, William believed what he said. But now, he didn't love Calliope. He feared who she had become.

Athena didn't see it, but he didn't blame her. Thalia...she saw. But she would never leave her mother. William couldn't participate anymore.

He was getting old—he was ten years older than Athena—and the winters were hard on him. Arthritis ran through his joints, brutal and painful. He would miss Athena terribly, but this was the best decision for him.

He wished she would come with him.

He'd been planning his departure for more than a year. He'd already taken care of the paperwork for Athena—he would never take Havenwood away from her. But he also would never allow Calliope to have the land. When Athena passed, it would go to Thalia. If anything happened to Thalia, or if she didn't want it, it would go to Riley. And the paperwork was clear: if Riley wasn't around or if she didn't want it, she couldn't sign it over to anyone. He feared Calliope would manipulate her daughter into giving it to her. Instead, the land would go to a group that ran summer camps for children.

And if there was no group to run it, maintain it, pay the taxes? It would go to the government to be absorbed into the National Forest.

Calliope and her people would never own Havenwood. William couldn't allow it.

"Dad, what are you doing up there?"

Thalia was looking at him from the base of the rock.

"Come on up."

She frowned, but scrambled up the back of the boulder where there were footholds that had been made over time. She sat next to him. "You shouldn't be climbing rocks."

"It's the last time."

"I don't want you to go." Her voice cracked and she leaned into him.

"I would ask you to come with me, but I know you won't leave your mother."

"Maybe we all should go."

"Do you want to?"

She didn't say anything for a long minute. "Sometimes."

"And your mom?"

"She will never leave. Even when she's sad, she's happier here than anywhere else. Last time we went to a fair, she said there were too many people, too much traffic, and you remember when someone stole one of our quilts? She was so upset."

"The world isn't perfect."

"I'm going to miss you so much. But I'll visit."

He took her hand and squeezed it. "I'm not getting any younger. You have a father who is old enough to be your grandfather."

"I don't care."

"Tucson is dry and will be much better for my arthritis. I'll meet you at the Tucson Craft Fair next summer."

"That's nearly a year from now."

"And if you want to leave," he said, "I'll take you home with me. You can apply to the university there. And you can always come back."

"People who leave never come back," Thalia said. "The world corrupts them."

"There's a lot of bad in the world, that is true. But there is also good. You're part of the good, sweetheart. Your mother and you have given me a family when I never thought I would have anyone."

They sat there in silence for an hour, then Thalia helped him climb down from the rock. They walked slowly back to the village.

Calliope waited at the gate for William.

No one was allowed to leave Havenwood. They just didn't realize it yet. Some had tried; Calliope had stopped them. Until she could convince her mother that no one should leave, she would have to do it this way.

It was her mother's fault that William would die.

She heard the old truck rattle up the steep slope several minutes before she saw it. He stopped because she hadn't opened the gate. He put the truck into Park and rolled down his window.

"Calliope. I didn't expect you here."

"I just wanted to say goodbye. I know I wasn't very supportive of your decision, but I understand."

"Thank you for that. Can you get the gate for me?"

"Sure."

Calliope unlocked the gate, but pretended to struggle with the bolt, which often got stuck.

William got out to help. He grunted, but slid it back, then pushed the gate open.

"Goodbye, Calliope."

She reached out to hug him. He accepted her embrace.

She pulled a butcher knife from the deep pocket of her dress. "No one leaves," she said as she slid the blade into his gut, all the way to the hilt.

He fell to his knees as the life drained from his eyes. He stared at her in disbelief. It was the same expression her father had all those years ago when he was shot and killed.

She turned, suddenly disturbed by the scene. Confused. Not knowing if she had done the right thing.

But it *had* to be done. If William left, others would follow.

Anton came out of the trees. "He made me do it," she said as tears fell down her cheeks.

"No one leaves," he said softly, repeating her words. "We'll take care of it. Clean yourself up, I'll see you at home."

21

South Fork, Colorado
Present Day

Kara and Michael sat side by side at a computer terminal in the sheriff's office. Ryder had set up a video chat with Catherine and the cult expert.

Catherine introduced the man, practically gushing, Kara thought.

"Assistant director of Quantico, Dean Montero, is the FBI's foremost expert on cults and cult psychology. He has traveled the country training FBI offices and local law enforcement on not only cults, but the psychology of domestic terrorism.

"Dean," Catherine said, "this is senior special agent Michael Harris. He's SWAT and search and rescue certified, and acts as our tactical expert in the field. And LAPD detective Kara Quinn is temporarily assigned to our unit."

Kara immediately felt out of the loop. Catherine damn well

knew that Kara's assignment was no longer "temporary"—it was permanent, though because of FBI rules and bureaucratic hoops, she was *technically* still employed by the Los Angeles Police Department. Catherine's tone grated, but Kara kept her face impassive. She couldn't let Catherine's little digs get to her. If she was being honest with herself, it worked because she did feel, at times, less qualified than the rest of her squad.

"Michael, Kara, good to meet you," Dean said. "Catherine has filled me in on the case, and I'm here to assist in any way I can."

Michael said, "We're about to interview Riley Pierce, a twenty-two-year-old college student who may have been born into and grown up in a cult."

"Havenwood," Dean said. "As I told Catherine, it's not on our radar. No one in the FBI has heard of it, though we might know of it by a different name."

"Our other witness attempted suicide after giving us basic information about the cult—"

"Yes, I watched the recording of your interview with him."

"His partner was murdered," Michael said. "In hindsight, should we have handled the questioning differently?"

"You couldn't have known his mindset, and you weren't aggressive or hostile. You gave him information, asked for information in return. It was a good interview."

"Should we have held back the information regarding his partner's murder?" Michael asked, still anguished about what happened.

Dean shook his head. "He had a right to know, and I don't think he would have said anything of value to the investigation until he had confirmation one way or the other," Dean said. "Don't let his attempted suicide weigh on your conscience."

Kara had intended to remain silent, but she wanted Dean's "expert" opinion. Though she didn't much care for so-called "experts" since often they had never worked in the field, she knew very little about cults.

"In your opinion," Kara asked, "do you think that Andrew

Gardner attempted to kill himself because of grief, or because of fear?"

"You mean fear of the cult?"

"Fear of talking *about* the cult. As if by speaking, he was going to be struck down by lightning."

"'The first rule of fight club is you don't talk about fight club,'" Dean quoted.

Kara grinned. She couldn't help herself—it was exactly what she'd been thinking.

Dean continued, "It's difficult for me to determine his motivation at this point, not without more information about Havenwood as well as Mr. Gardner's psychology. However, there are some basic psychological commonalities among those who have escaped this culture."

He sipped water and continued, "Former cult members are often skittish, nervous, worried about retribution. They are quiet, introverted, and often isolate themselves alone or with a few close friends or family. They rarely share their experience in the cult, even if there was no violence. There are many reasons for this—sometimes, because they are embarrassed that they were drawn into what they now see as bad for them. Sometimes, because they feel foolish for joining the group in the first place. Sometimes, because they had a disquieting experience. Often, there is a financial motive, as they may have turned over their life savings to a cult and blame themselves for being manipulated. All this depends on the type of cult—did the cult cater to a deep value, such as religion? Or a political or moral view, such as survivalists or environmental protection? There are many different types of cults, and based on the limited information Andrew shared, I don't have a sense yet of what Havenwood is."

He looked down and shuffled some papers, then said, "Andrew was clearly fearful of the cult and believed they have the capability to kill, which tells me that during his time there, he saw violence, either as a witness or a participant. He absolutely believes that members of Havenwood killed the people you named, which suggests he knows an extensive amount about the cult and what they have done and are capable of doing. He lived there for a minimum of two years, and likely much longer."

Kara absorbed everything Dean said. He had a calm, melodious voice and a command of his subject, without sounding like it was his word or the highway.

"I didn't get a sense of what type of cult Andrew was talking about," Kara said, "whether they had an agenda or not. But he wasn't faking his fear."

"I concur," Dean said. "I don't think we can know the cult purpose at this point, not without more information. But people who are scared—as opposed to being embarrassed because they lost their life savings or that they were manipulated into a sexual relationship or to do something that goes against their values—it's generally that they were threatened and have reason to believe that the cult will live up to their threats. Andrew Gardner has witnessed violence."

Michael asked, "How do we entice Riley to talk to us? She might not know what information she has, but she may know who is in charge, where they are located, what crimes the cult has committed. She's acting both belligerent and scared. We didn't threaten her, chase her, or arrest her, and she's not under suspicion of murder. We know she was out of the country when the first four victims—including Morrison—were killed. She could walk out, but she hasn't nor has she asked for a lawyer."

"She might still walk out," Dean said, "but she's not going to trust the system, which means I doubt she'll ask for a lawyer. She might be fearful of authority because the cult taught her not to trust outsiders. Or she's fearful because she knows that she's committed a crime by obtaining a false identity. Or, she's done worse. But if she has the same foundation as Andrew, she is more fearful of the cult than of you."

Dean paused, steepled his fingers under his chin as if thinking.

Kara didn't know if it was authentic, or if he knew he looked like a kindly, intellectual college professor when he did it.

"I would suggest that you be calm, firm, nonthreatening," he continued. "I imagine, though this is based on my experience, not because I have interviewed Ms. Pierce, that threats won't work. She'll close up, feel isolated and alone. Being firm, clear, open, will likely elicit the most information. You'll want to find out how she came to be in the cult, whether she grew up there, whether her family is still there, why specifically she is afraid. It won't all come out at once."

Catherine said, "We'll have a video and mic so we can hear everything, and will provide guidance as the interview progresses. Michael, this time, you'll wear the earpiece so I know we won't be ignored."

Kara bristled, but didn't take the bait.

Michael didn't say anything, and Kara was a bit irritated that he didn't stand up for her. He knew as well as she did that Catherine's micromanaging of interviews was counterproductive. If she wanted to be in an interview, she should join them in the field.

But Kara bit her tongue.

Dean said, "I'd also suggest that you find a natural stopping point. If she's talking, let her talk. But if she clams up and firm but gentle prodding doesn't get her to open up, give her a break. It's getting late anyway. What are your plans for housing her? I don't think it's wise to keep her in a cell, but if you let her go, she'll never come back on her own."

"I'll take her into protective custody," Kara said. "There's another female agent here, so between Agent Wagner and myself, we can keep her overnight in our hotel."

She could see Catherine didn't like that idea, but before she could object, Dean said, "A good plan. I'll observe the interview and do some research. I may come out to Colorado if I feel I can be of assistance."

Great, she thought sarcastically.

They ended the call and Michael said, "Hey, I know you're mad."

"Me? How can you tell?" She smiled tightly.

Michael squeezed her hand. "I don't like the earpiece either, but I pick my fights."

"I don't like her in my head yammering when I'm thinking. I know how to interview people. I don't mind these—" she waved her hand at the computer "—briefings. They help, give me information to better approach a witness or suspect. But constantly second-guessing me? Nope. Not going to do it." She raised an eyebrow. "I'll bet you twenty she doesn't say one word to you."

"I'll take that bet," Michael said. "She won't be able to help herself."

Kara laughed. He was right. She handed him a twenty-dollar bill. "Thanks, partner. I needed that."

22

South Fork, Colorado

Riley felt like a zombie.

She'd been sitting in a conference room with comfortable chairs, so it wasn't all bad. A couple hours ago, someone had brought her a sandwich and water, which she ate mostly out of habit. She was allowed to go to the bathroom, she wasn't in handcuffs, and they hadn't arrested her. One of the officers even brought her some paper and pens when she asked. She would have preferred pencils, but he couldn't find any. Still, the pens kept her mind occupied as she doodled on the notepad.

She'd thought about walking out to see what they would do, but Outside scared her more than the police right now. She didn't know what Andrew might tell them about her. She also wanted to know what the police knew about Havenwood and Jane's murder.

She didn't think they knew about Thalia, and Jesse was her

only link to Thalia. He could have something in his house to help track her aunt down, but if that were the case, then Havenwood would now have that information. Andrew and Donovan would run at the first opportunity. For all she knew, they'd already let Andrew leave and he was back in Fort Collins with Donovan, packing to disappear. She felt…stuck.

It was after six when the detective she'd seen in Ashland—Kara—came into the conference room with the large black FBI agent. She suppressed the jolt of panic and forced herself to breathe evenly.

It was hard to overcome a lifetime of indoctrination, but she was making progress.

Kara had probing blue eyes, sharp and focused, like she really seemed to *see* Riley. It unnerved her.

Riley turned to the other cop, but averted her eyes when she saw blood on his white shirt.

"Riley," he said, "I'm Agent Harris, but you can call me Michael. We want you to be as comfortable as possible."

Informal. To get her to trust them.

She couldn't trust anyone. But she needed to know what they knew.

They sat down across from her.

"Riley," Kara said, looking her straight in the eye, "your friend Andrew tried to kill himself. We just got word from the hospital that he's stable, but in critical condition. He lost a lot of blood."

She stared in disbelief. Andrew? "Are you sure he did it to himself?" Could Calliope's people have infiltrated the police station? Were they here, waiting for her to walk out?

Michael's face was solemn. "He was alone in the bathroom and slit both arms from here to here." He demonstrated by drawing a line with his finger from his wrist to the inside of his elbow. "Andrew told me to let him die. We did everything possible to stop the bleeding. I really hope he makes it."

He sounded sincere.

Kara said, "He learned that his partner, Donovan Smith, had been killed. In the same way as your friend Jane. He told us about Havenwood."

Riley stared, unblinking, shocked. Donovan was dead. Andrew talked about Havenwood? She shook her head. None of this could be happening.

"He told us that Havenwood is like a cult," Kara said. "That he escaped, you escaped, the others. He also said that someone in the cult is hunting you down. We want to stop them. I think you do, too."

Talking about Havenwood was forbidden. Thalia had beat that mantra into their heads after the escape.

"Never utter the word Havenwood. *It doesn't exist. You were born today. You didn't exist before now. Understand? You are no one except who you make yourself to be. If you say a word, if Calliope thinks someone Outside is going to invade and shut down Havenwood, she will kill everyone there and they will be happy to die for her."*

They didn't talk, but they didn't forget. For three years Riley and Jane lived together in Ashland and not once did they mention Havenwood or anyone who lived there, even when they were alone together. And the rare moments they talked about a good memory, it was vague, a feeling more than a clear conversation.

"I miss fresh eggs every morning."

"Remember the swim contest? That was so much fun."

"Let's go horseback riding—I miss it."

Because like everything in the world, there was yin and yang. Darkness and light. Evil and good. Havenwood was no different.

"We can protect you," Michael said.

Riley almost laughed. Protect her? Maybe. But when they learned the truth about Havenwood, would they want to? The things Calliope had done, things Riley did with her. And, mostly, what Riley didn't do. They would see her as an aberration. They would burn Havenwood to the ground. It's what Calliope had always told them would happen if outsiders came in.

Not everyone at Havenwood was evil. There were children. There were people who had been lied to and manipulated. They deserved to live. All Riley could give them now was her silence. How else could she help?

"You can't," she said, her voice rough. She drank some water, cleared her throat. "You can't protect anyone from Havenwood."

"Tell us about Jane," Kara said. "You were good friends. She had a picture of you in her keepsake box. Also, a beautiful carved bird, a photo of a teenage boy, and a red poppy."

Of course Jane kept Timmy's picture and the bird he made her. The only memory she had of the first boy—the only boy—she loved.

"Why did she keep a red poppy? Do they mean something to Havenwood? Like a state flower?" Michael asked.

What could Riley do? Walk away? She felt so lost right now. Her friends were dead; Andrew had tried to kill himself. Calliope was killing everyone she had saved. She desperately wanted to stop her, but she didn't know how.

Kara said, "Riley, you've clearly been through something at Havenwood. You might think no one can help you—you might believe that running is the only answer. But Chris ran and they killed him. Jane ran and they killed her. Donovan was killed this morning. They're not going to stop. So either you sit there and remain silent. That is your right. Or you share what you know about Havenwood and let us get justice for the dead."

Riley stared at the cop. "What if you can't and everything gets worse?"

"It can't get much worse," Kara said bluntly. "They tortured your friend Jesse. They know where many of your friends are now. Help us, and we'll do everything in our power to save them. Remain silent, and one by one, they will die. I think you know that."

Riley bit her lip and whispered, "What about the innocent people at Havenwood?"

Michael said, "Kara and I have a team behind us of very smart, well-trained federal agents. We don't want anyone else to die."

Riley wanted to believe them. And maybe, deep down, she did. But mostly, she wanted information—she needed to know what they knew of Havenwood. She needed to find it. Because the only person who might be able to stop her mother was Riley herself.

"What do the red poppies mean?" Michael repeated.

"The poppies are Thalia's flower. The day she decided to leave, wild poppies had bloomed everywhere in the Havenwood valley. She said it was a sign, that we'd know she came back for us when she left a poppy for us to find."

"Who's Thalia?" Michael asked.

"Thalia was the first to leave, but promised to come back for those who wanted to escape. When she left, she told me when I found a poppy under my pillow, to go to my grandmother's grave and she'd take me away." But she'd lied. She had left poppies for Riley, but only to help others escape. Thalia needed her on the inside. Now Riley hated the sight of the stupid flowers. "It became a kind of...well, I guess a form of communication. Whenever Thalia needed to talk to someone, she'd leave a red poppy with a note so we'd know it was her."

The two cops exchanged glances again, and Riley knew they weren't telling her something.

"What?" she asked, her stomach churning uneasily. Something was very wrong.

Kara didn't answer her question directly. "There was a stack of laminated poppies in Chris Crossman's house, the same kind we found in Jane's box. It seemed odd."

Riley nodded. "Everyone passed through Chris's house. He

would give us money, clothes, new identification, a background—just in case we needed it. Jesse created the identities, but Chris had them for us. He gave us a laminated poppy to remember where we came from, and to use if we needed to communicate."

"Tell me more about Jane," Kara said. "You and Jane left Havenwood together, correct?"

Riley nodded. "Jane was the best of all of us. She never let anything kill her spirit. She had an inner light that they couldn't destroy, until they killed her."

"Who are they?" Michael asked.

She shrugged. Who would Calliope send out to kill? Who did she trust enough to hunt down those fortunate enough to get out?

"I could guess, but I don't know."

"Start with this," Kara said. "Where is Havenwood?"

"I don't know."

"Do you mean it moves around? They relocated after you left?"

"No. I mean, I don't know. I never left Havenwood until I was nineteen, and I've never been back. It's somewhere in the Rocky Mountains, but I don't know where or how to get there. I was born there and left in the middle of the night." Riley paused, then said, "Andrew knows because he came to Havenwood in his teens. But the only road into the valley is monitored. They know when people are coming."

"Someone must know how to get there."

"Thalia."

"What's her full name?"

Riley shrugged. "I don't know what name she uses. We only had first names at Havenwood."

Kara glanced at Michael, as if they were silently communicating. Then Kara said, "Riley, I'm going to tell you what we know, and we need your help to fill in the holes. You may not know how to give directions to Havenwood, but you *can* help us find it and put an end to this."

"I doubt it."

"Jane wasn't the only person who died ten days ago."

Riley squeezed back tears. She didn't think she had any left inside her, but suddenly, this was all so overwhelming.

"I know. Chris Crossman. After I saw you in Ashland, I went to Chris because he knows how to contact Thalia. They needed to know about Jane and I thought we could come up with a plan…but he wasn't at his house, and I read online that he had been killed. I knew then that we were all in danger."

Michael asked, "Do you know the other people who escaped?"

"I know everyone who left before me." She didn't know how much to tell them. Should she give them names? Should she explain the process?

"The more you tell us, the more we can help," Kara said. "If you hold back, you're not going to help anyone."

Riley wanted to believe her. Maybe she was grasping at straws, but Andrew's suicide attempt had really rattled her, almost as much as finding Jesse dead.

"I identified people in Havenwood who were ready to leave," Riley said. "I brought them to the meeting spot, then Thalia took them to Chris, who gave them new identities and helped find them jobs, homes, anything they needed. He gave Jane and me money for our apartment and more than enough to live on. But I don't know where anyone else is. I'd only been to Chris's house, and the only reason I knew where Andrew and Donovan lived is because Chris told me."

"So," Kara said, "you stayed behind in Havenwood after Thalia left in order to help others escape."

Riley nodded.

"For how long?"

"Eight years."

"And no one there suspected you?" Kara asked.

She didn't believe her. "I'm not lying."

"I didn't say you were," Kara said, "but you helped people escape for eight years and no one thought it was you."

"Calliope is my mother."

"Calliope?" Michael said.

They didn't know. Riley almost stopped talking. If they didn't know about her mother, they didn't know anything.

Yet, somehow, now that she'd started, she wanted to share. Where did she start?

"Yes. Calliope is my mom, the leader of Havenwood ever since my grandmother died. No one would suspect that I'd help anyone leave. Thalia knew that—that's why she made me stay behind."

Kara's eyes narrowed as if she wanted to ask more questions, then Michael said, "How many people did you help?"

"Eleven people escaped in total," Riley said without hesitating. "Thalia and Robert were the first, they left on their own, but I knew. I helped nine after they left. Including Chris."

"Jane and Chris were not the only people killed," Kara said. "When we mentioned Robert Benson, Andrew became agitated. And you just mentioned Robert. Who is he?"

Riley blinked rapidly. "Robert?" Her voice sounded like a squeak.

"Robert Benson was killed in the same manner as Jane and Chris. He has no background until he moved to Virginia eleven years ago."

Riley swallowed uneasily, drank more water. "Do you have a picture?"

Kara pulled up her phone and a moment later showed Riley a photo. It was Robert. He was smiling and stood next to a woman who had kind eyes.

Riley took the phone and stared at the photo. "He…he looks happy."

"By all accounts, he and his wife had a good life, a good marriage." Kara took the phone back. "You know him."

"He was one of my fathers."

"One of your fathers? Like a priest? Or your dad?"

"A father. A leader. I mean, he could have been my biological dad, but we don't care about that at Havenwood. I don't know who my dad was. My mother had many companions. Marriage is an unnecessary societal creation. All the men wanted to make my mother happy. Robert left eleven years ago, with Thalia. And everything changed."

How could she explain?

"Havenwood wasn't always a prison. It used to be a wonderful place to live. My grandmother told me of all the violence and hate and greed and rush rush rush of society. My grandfather was killed and left her with a daughter to raise." Riley paused. She had wondered over the last few years how much of what she had been told—by her grandmother, her mother, Thalia—was true, and what were lies.

"Anyway," Riley continued, "she wanted a better life. Free of all unnecessary conventions. My grandmother had wonderful stories of how Havenwood started with two families, then four families, then more, who shared everything and worked together in cooperation and love." Riley had often wished she had been born in her grandmother's time, so she could have seen the best of Havenwood.

"And from all the stories, Havenwood was utopia. But like all utopias, it wasn't real. Jane—" Riley closed her eyes. "Jane was my best friend. She had this faith I've never seen before. Havenwood is spiritual, not religious. There's a difference," she insisted, looking from Kara to Michael.

"There is," Michael concurred.

"Jane had a Bible. She was never without it. She said once that all people sinned. That it was hard not to, but if you loved God, you could keep the commandments. I didn't understand then, and while now I know what she meant, it's bullshit. Because Jane is dead, and she was the best person I knew. But I'm alive. What's fair in that?"

"You know," Kara said conversationally, "my parents were con artists. They had me do things for their cons when I was growing up. When I was younger, I didn't understand. When I got older, I knew what we were doing was wrong, but I did it anyway because I didn't know better and I had no one to talk to. When I was a teenager, I wanted a better life. I didn't want to cheat people anymore. My father was arrested and sent to prison, then my mother hooked up with an asshole boyfriend. I sabotaged one of their scams. Ended up living with my grandmother—one of those good people like Jane. She turned me around. You were raised in a world where you didn't know better, and even when you did, you were young and didn't see a way out."

"But Jane never did anything wrong. She just said no and walked away. I should have, too."

"Riley, I'm not a religious person," Kara said, "but there's this idea of forgiveness that I buy into. Starting with yourself. We need your help. If there is anyone else out there who left Havenwood, they are now targets. You can help save them." Softly, Kara said, "Riley, if you were the one who died and Jane was sitting here right now, what would she do?"

Riley felt a weight lift from her. It was as if the answer was there all along, but Riley couldn't see it until now. In that moment, she felt Jane's hand on her shoulder and a peace came over her.

"My mother has run Havenwood ever since my grandmother died eleven years ago. And our imperfect but peaceful little society completely fell apart."

23

Havenwood
Eleven Years Ago

"Grandma, I want to go to the fair," Riley whined. "I'm twelve." Not quite. Two more months. But she had explored every inch of the valley they lived in, climbed every climbable tree, crossed every creek, found every trail that had been forged.

But wherever she went, however high she climbed, all she saw was more trees. Sometimes, she felt they were the only people in the world.

Only certain people took their goods to the fairs. They spent all winter creating beautiful things—quilts and sweaters, carvings and paintings, jams and jellies. Riley wasn't good at sewing, she cut herself every time she tried to carve wood, and she didn't like to spend time in the kitchen. But she could draw, and her grandma said she had real talent. She drew everything she saw, and things she imagined. She wasn't so good at painting, but for the first time the council picked her small charcoal drawings to sell at the fair, and she wanted to go and see who bought them.

She wouldn't talk to anyone—people scared her. She'd never left Havenwood because her mother had told her about all the evil outside the valley. But she wanted to see more, to see what she had read about.

Her mother always said no. When Riley was a little girl, bad people tried to kill everyone at Havenwood. Riley still remembered her daddy Glen that day he told her to stay in the schoolhouse with Jane and the other children. He had been so scared, but he went out to help her mother and grandmother. He died, but he helped save Havenwood. That meant he was brave and strong. And no one had tried again! It had been *forever.* So why was her mother still scared?

Her grandma was an elder, and people listened to her. So if she could convince Grandma that she would be good and not talk to any strangers and do everything Daddy Robert said, then Grandma could tell her mother to let her go.

Riley had it all thought out.

She and her grandma were walking down an overgrown trail on the far side of Havenwood. Riley wasn't allowed this far on her own, but she was with her grandma, so it was okay.

Grandma was quiet. She had been quiet a lot lately, ever since she was sick last winter. Riley didn't want to think of her grandma as *old.* But Athena was the oldest person in Havenwood and that scared Riley. Old people could die. Young people could die, too, like when Peter fell from the roof of the barn three years ago. Or when Jennifer ate berries she wasn't supposed to. Or the time Tom and Robert went to hunt a bear who had killed one of their horses, and Tom was attacked. Or when her mother was pregnant and lost her baby when the bad people came to steal from Havenwood.

"Grandma, if you talk to Mommy, she'll listen."

"Quiet, Riley," her grandmother said.

She bit her lip. She didn't want to be quiet. She loved time alone with her grandma. They used to always have time alone to explore and collect blackberries and her grandma would watch her draw and said she never got tired of it.

But they hadn't had time alone as much as they used to.

After several minutes (it was only ninety seconds, but it felt like an hour), Riley said, "Where are we going? I'm not supposed to go this far past the south creek."

Grandma didn't answer. Riley frowned and followed. She ran ahead, then came back and walked with her grandma. Something was wrong.

"Grandma, you look sad."

Her grandma sighed, stopped walking and looked at her. "Riley, you are the reason I made Havenwood."

"Silly, I wasn't born when you moved here."

Her grandma smiled, but it was a sad smile, and that sadness made Riley sad. Her grandma was *never* sad. She was always full of joy.

"I'm an old fool," she said quietly and turned into a small opening.

Riley hadn't been in this meadow *for years*. She and the other children had been told that there was an old mine here, and they would fall into it and die and no one would ever find them.

She stood on the edge of the meadow because she was scared of falling into a rotted mine shaft.

Her grandmother walked into the middle.

"No, Grandma! Stop! It's dangerous."

She didn't listen to Riley, and Riley wondered if she should run back to the village and get Daddy Robert to help her.

"Stay, Riley," her grandma said as if she could read her mind. Maybe she could. Or maybe Riley spoke out loud and didn't realize it.

The meadow terrified Riley, but it was beautiful, covered

with wildflowers. Every color imaginable, but dominated by red poppies. Nothing this beautiful could be bad, right?

Her grandmother stood in the middle of the meadow, and the scene was so beautiful, Riley had to draw it.

Riley sat on a rock, pulled her sketch pad and pencil from her satchel, and rapidly started to sketch her grandmother. She worked fast, her hand almost with a mind of its own. She wished she had colored pencils with her, but she hadn't brought them. Only a snack and her pad and two regular pencils.

She brought her grandmother to life on the page. The flowers, the field, and she hoped to remember the colors so she could add them later.

She didn't think she'd ever forget.

When she looked up again, her grandmother was on her knees. Oh, no! Had she fallen? Was she hurt?

"Grandma!" Forgetting the fear of a mine she had never seen, she ran to the middle of the field as fast as she could until she reached her grandma. She squatted next to her. "Are you okay? Do you need Jasmine?" Jasmine was their doctor. She knew everything about the human body and would know what's wrong.

"No," her grandmother said, and that's when Riley saw tears on her face.

"Are you hurt? Do you need water?"

She was staring at the dirt. Riley turned and it took a minute, but then she realized what her grandmother had been doing.

She'd pulled up flowers and dug a hole. In the hole was a stick. No...not a stick. It was a bone. Two. Three. It looked like a hand. But it couldn't be a hand. It had to be an animal.

"What's that?"

"Oh, Riley, I am a fool. We need to leave. Do not tell anyone—not *anyone*—what you have seen or where we went."

Riley didn't sleep well that night. She wanted to talk to her grandmother and find out what made her sad and why she was keeping secrets.

It was still dark when Riley finally got out of bed. She didn't know what time it was, but the homes across the valley were quiet. Though late spring, it was cold at night, and Riley slipped into her warm boots and pulled her heavy coat around her pajamas.

She knew which stairs creaked and avoided them without thought. Her house was quiet and warm, the embers in the potbellied stove still smoldering. She would go to her grandmother's cottage—it wasn't far, and she wasn't scared of the dark. Besides, each house had a light in the window, and each path was marked with lights. They were like tiny stars on earth, guiding her.

She stopped when she saw that there were more lights on in her grandmother's small house than there should be. And voices. They weren't shouting but they were angry.

Curious, but cautious, Riley walked along the trees to avoid being seen as she neared the house. She couldn't see through the curtains, but as she stood under her grandmother's window, she heard her voice.

"I'm leaving. You can't talk me out of it."

"They *will* listen to you, Mom!"

It was Aunt Thalia.

"Not anymore, darling girl. Your sister has turned enough souls to her. I just want to go. William tried to tell me...but I was more in love with my dream than I was with your father."

"I will stand with you. I won't let you face Calliope alone."

"It's not just Calliope. It's Calliope's partners. And others. Too many to fight, and I'm old and tired."

"We can't let her get away with murder."

Riley gasped, then covered her mouth.

"I'll walk away at the fair. No need to make a scene."

"Mother—you're not the only one who feels uncomfortable with the fact that we haven't heard from people. If everyone knows that Calliope has killed our *family*—they won't stand with her. We can banish Calliope and anyone who helped her. I think we have enough people to do the right thing."

"But do you have violence in your heart? Would you kill another human being? Because they will take a life. They have done it before, it's easy for them."

"I have Robert on my side."

Father? Riley didn't understand everything they were talking about, but her daddy Robert had been as quiet and distant as her grandma the last few months.

"He has control over the money," Aunt Thalia said. "We take control and tell everyone what you found, and she'll leave. She's weak."

"Do not underestimate your sister. She will never leave Havenwood. She never has."

"My *half* sister. If what you tell me is true, I will prove that she killed my father and all the others we thought left Havenwood."

"The field of poppies is littered with their souls."

"Mother, think on it. Everyone here respects you. Everyone, even the people Calliope thinks are on her side, they love and respect you more than anyone else."

"I'm tired, Thalia. So very tired."

A hand clamped down on Riley's mouth and held her tight.

"Naughty little girls eavesdrop."

It was Daddy Anton. She tried to kick, but she smelled something sickly sweet and suddenly was floating...and the world slipped away.

When Riley woke, she didn't know what time it was. She felt sick to her stomach and could barely move her limbs. She heard crying downstairs.

Slowly, every step making her body ache, she went down the stairs to a roomful of people. Her mother had tears in her eyes, but she wasn't crying. Daddy Anton had his arms around her shoulders as she spoke.

"Athena, my mother, passed peacefully in her sleep last night. She hasn't been well since the virus she caught last winter. We will have the funeral on Saturday. Fear not, as Athena will be one with nature. As she was in life, she will be in death."

Riley started to cry. "Grandma?"

"Oh, baby," Calliope purred. "You shouldn't be up. You've been so sick."

Her daddy Anton caught her as she swayed on the stairs and would have fallen. "I'm sorry, Riley. We didn't tell you because you were delirious with fever."

"No, no—I don't remember. Where's Grandma?"

She sobbed in Anton's arms. Her head was a jumble of dreams and nightmares, and she didn't know what was real and what wasn't. This had to be a nightmare. Grandma wasn't dead.

Two days later Riley was still so weak from whatever illness she had that her mother didn't want her to go to the funeral. But Riley insisted, and Robert carried her the entire way to the church. They called it church, but it wasn't like a traditional religion, as her grandmother had explained. It was the spiritual center of Havenwood where people could go to pray or think, dream or hope, think about their place in the world and how they could best serve Havenwood and their brothers and sisters who chose to give up all to live there.

Riley didn't want to believe that her grandmother was dead, but her body was on display, in a casket that the carpenters had made specially for her, with flowers carved into the sides. Everyone walked up and spoke to her, in a moment of privacy, leaving behind something they thought she would like. Mostly flowers. A carved bird from Timmy. A quilted square from Jane.

Riley was the last to approach her grandmother. She shuffled, felt sick, and Robert picked her up and carried her.

She stared down at the person she loved above all others, even above her mother and all her fathers. Riley didn't know what they'd done to her grandmother's body, but she didn't look herself. She wore her favorite dress, the color of the midday sky, with tiny yellow and white daisies. As silent tears fell, Riley reached into her pocket and pulled out the last drawing she'd made, of her grandmother among the wildflowers. She put it next to her grandma's hand.

Robert stared at it. "Where did you draw that picture?"

She buried her face into his shoulder. "I promised Grandma I'd never tell."

A few days later, Riley was feeling better, but her head was still fuzzy. She no longer remembered standing under her grandmother's window and hearing Aunt Thalia and Grandma talk. She had odd dreams, and some nightmares, and she slept hours during the day and longer at night. One recurring nightmare had her waking in a sweat. It was about her fathers, all of them but Robert, holding her picture of grandma in the meadow.

"She knows."

And then Riley would wake and cry and the nightmare would slip away.

She'd slept through most of three days after burying her grandmother, and awoke at dinner that third night feeling hungry for the first time in...how long? A week?

A commotion outside caught her attention. She opened her window—the fresh air felt amazing to her, and she breathed deeply.

Her bedroom looked down into one of their many gardens. Her mother was standing in the middle, hysterical. "She killed Robert. She killed him as certain as I stand here!"

Robert? Her father, dead? How could that be? Who had killed him?

"We'll find Thalia, bring her back," another of her fathers said. "Lock down Havenwood until we return."

Four men and two women left and Riley felt ill again. She heard things...odd things...over the next few weeks. Her aunt Thalia had killed Robert and taken all the money that ran

Havenwood. Riley didn't want to believe it, but why would her mother lie?

It wasn't until two months later, on Riley's twelfth birthday, that Riley found a note hidden in her room and learned the truth.

Thalia and Robert had left together and didn't take her with them.

> Dearest Riley:
>
> I'm sorry to leave you behind, but I was in danger. Robert found the meadow you drew; he knows the truth. He, too, is in danger because of it. Don't say a word. He is alive and free. One day, I'll return for you. When you find the red poppy, go to your grandmother's grave at dawn the next morning. I will be there.
>
> Thalia

Enclosed in the note was a dried red poppy.

But it was months later when the snow cleared before Riley found a red poppy on her bed. She stayed up all night, ran to her grandma's grave before the sun came up. She had a bag packed and she couldn't wait to leave. She missed her daddy Robert so much.

Thalia came to her an hour later. She looked at her bag and said, "No, not you, not now. Rilcy, I need you here helping me. My eyes and ears. You are the only one who knows who we can trust, those who will leave and not return. Starting with Chris. Give him this letter. And in the fall, I'll return for him."

"I miss Daddy Robert. Please, Aunt Thalia! I want to go. I miss Grandma. Nothing is the same."

"Do you know what happened to Grandma?"

Riley bit her lip. She had uneasy feelings about that whole week, but it was still so fuzzy in her head.

"Calliope killed her," Thalia said. "And the only way you can help now is if you stay here and help me get people out."

"What about me?" She was crying. She didn't want to cry, but she couldn't stop herself.

"You're safer here for now. If I take you, I'll have to hide forever. Calliope's people will hunt me down to get you back. I can't risk it."

"Take me to Daddy Robert."

"No. You have to trust me, Riley. You're only twelve."

So Riley trusted her. For years, she trusted her until she couldn't live in Havenwood a minute longer. She faked her death and walked away and Thalia couldn't stop her.

24

Quantico, Virginia
Present Day

Assistant director of Quantico Dean Montero had started his career as a cop in San Antonio, Texas. He'd been young and idealistic, had a cop for a father, a pediatrician for a mother, a childhood filled with love, discipline, and family.

His third year on the job, he was first on-scene at a suspected domestic situation. When he arrived, he heard gunshots, called for backup, pulled on his vest, and waited.

Then he heard a wailing baby. Nothing but the crying child in the silence of that house in the north San Antonio hills.

He went inside. Against all protocol and safety regulations, he went inside that house because a baby cried.

Five people were dead. Mother, three children, and the bastard ex-husband who had killed them, then himself. The oldest boy had shielded the baby who, miraculously, was unharmed.

Dean pulled the baby from under her brother's dead body and cradled her until his own mother arrived. He didn't remember much. A cop, with hundreds of hours of training and thousands of hours on patrol, who had seen the dead, had seen violence, had dealt with killers and sexual predators and violent addicts, refused to give up the sleeping baby until his mother came to the scene and said she would personally take care of the child.

The entire scene had shaken Dean in a way he didn't understand at the time. It wasn't the most gruesome crime scene he'd witnessed, but it changed him. He left the force and went to college at twenty-one, hoping to learn something—anything—to help prevent such tragedies. He studied everything he could, graduating in four years with two degrees, in education and criminal justice, and a minor in theology. He did a one-year master's program in psychology where he wrote his thesis on cults, pulling in his experience as a cop and his studies to try to identify the types of personalities that gravitate to cults, both physical (communes) and in cyberspace, and what makes them safe or dangerous.

It was that paper that caught the attention of the FBI, who recruited him. He spent fourteen years in the field traveling all over the country identifying and exposing cults. For the last two years, he'd served as second-in-command at Quantico.

"What do you think?" Dr. Catherine Jones asked Dean after he listened to Riley Pierce's story. "Have you heard of this place?"

He shook his head. "There are communities all over the country that have a back-to-nature foundation, as Havenwood appears to have, but few rise to the level of cult. It seems quite incredible that after more than thirty years, no one has discovered it and they have never been investigated by law enforcement."

"Do you believe her?"

"Yes. What she said she believes as truth. Whether it *is* the truth, I can't say, but she wasn't attempting to deceive Quinn and Harris."

"I'm sorry that Quinn took over the interview," Catherine said. "Michael tried to steer her back to what we needed, but clearly she wasn't listening to our advice."

"She did well," Dean said. "She developed a rapport with Riley, gave her permission, in a sense, to speak freely. Is it true, about her parents?"

"Yes," Catherine said.

He sensed underlying tension between Catherine and Kara, but dismissed it. Teams that worked closely together often had members who clashed over time. With two strong personalities—like Catherine, who he had known for years and respected, and Kara, who he had yet to meet in person but now had a sense of her style—conflict was to be expected.

"I'd like to interview Riley. She has more to say, she just doesn't know it yet. Would Agent Costa object if I joined his team in Colorado?"

"Of course not," Catherine said.

He raised an eyebrow. "I don't know Matt Costa well, but I've heard he's very protective of his unit." Dean had been trying to meet with Matt about the Mobile Response Team for some time, and while he appreciated that both of their schedules were tight, they could have found a mutually agreeable time.

"Matt is a professional," Catherine said. "He'll welcome expert insight."

"Mr. Kim," Dean turned to the analyst who ran operations for the MRT. He knew Ryder Kim from the academy; he'd graduated from Quantico a little over a year ago and Dean had been one of his instructors. "Would you please give your boss a heads-up that I'm on my way? I think I can contribute to the investigation. I'd like to interview Riley Pierce first thing in the morning, alongside Detective Quinn. But I don't want to assign tasks to his team without his okay."

"Yes, sir," Ryder said.

"Would you like me to join you?" Catherine asked.

"I don't think that's necessary," Dean said, "but you will be available for a psychological profile?"

"Of course."

"What are you thinking at this point?"

Catherine hesitated just a moment.

"I don't expect a detailed profile," Dean said. "I'm looking for generalities. I understand cults, and cults can attract a variety of personality types. But a cult like the one Riley describes is highly unusual, especially that it has existed for several decades and never been on the FBI's radar. This could be because they have little public presence. Yet no one has complained, not even a report from a parent or child that their loved one was manipulated into joining and they aren't allowed to talk to them. That is the number one reason a group is put on my radar. How did the cult bring in new members? How did they vet them so that they didn't have friends and family looking for them? It's unique and interesting, and I hope Riley has answers."

"I was initially brought in because of the unusual crime scene at the Benson homicide," Catherine said. "The red poppies were a red flag, but now I think they are a taunt."

"How so?"

"Thalia, Riley's aunt, gave the poppies to the victims to remember her, as a calling card for when she visits again. While I can't ignore the possibility that she could be involved, I don't think she would rescue a dozen people over a decade, then start killing them."

"I concur," Dean said.

"While we need to look there in order to rule her out, I think—and this is a guess, which I don't like to do—that the poppies were meant *for* Thalia. To tell her that they never forgot those who left the cult."

Dean considered, nodded. "It would be logical, if Thalia was the one who found the bodies."

"Perhaps it was their way to draw her out," Catherine continued. "If what Riley said is accurate, and Thalia financially damaged Havenwood when she left, they may want her to pay for that. First, by killing those she helped, and second, by drawing her back so they can punish her."

"There could be more bodies," Dean said, "or they haven't found the others."

Catherine nodded. "Riley was young when her grandmother died. Her memories may not be clear. Plus, she's been away for nearly four years."

"That is precisely why I want to speak with her. She knows more, but it'll take time and finesse to discern the truth. I also believe she'll help us find Havenwood. Riley knows where the community is, she just doesn't know she does." Dean leaned back, thinking about everything they'd learned in the short interview. "She's an artist," he said. "I'm hoping to use that to entice her to draw a map. She might not know precisely *how* to get to Havenwood, but she should be able to recognize landmarks. At a minimum, she'll be able to draw the faces of everyone she remembers, which may help in identification."

Ryder stepped back into the room. "I have you on the first flight out in the morning, at five."

"Thank you, Ryder."

"I also let Agent Costa know you're coming. He'll meet you at the airport."

Dean thanked him again. His initial assessment was correct: Costa was very protective of his team, hence picking Dean up at the airport. Being an outsider wasn't going to be easy.

Dean wouldn't have pushed his involvement if he didn't think he could be an asset for their case. And after listening to the interview with Riley Pierce, he was positive he could help.

25

South Fork, Colorado

Sloane and Jim arrived at Jesse Morrison's house just after sunset, but the sheriff's department had brought in lights and the coroner was gracious enough not to move the body before they arrived. It had been a long day, but the cold air gave Sloane her second wind.

"I'm going to check with the coroner," Jim said. "Go talk to Michael." He gestured to where Michael was sitting in his car with the heater running.

Sloane walked over and tapped on the window, then slipped into the passenger seat.

"Hey," she said. "Jim's talking to the coroner. Where's Kara?"

"At the station with our witness."

"The girl who knew one of the victims?"

"She knew all of the victims," Michael said.

"Suspect?"

"No." Michael gave her a rundown on their interview with Riley Pierce.

"A cult?" she asked when he was done. "That was the furthest thing from my mind."

"You should listen to the interview if you're not wiped out tonight," Michael said. "And she has a lot more to say. AD Montero will be here in the morning to talk to her."

That surprised her. "From Quantico?"

"He's an expert on cults."

"I remember, but I didn't think he worked in the field."

"I've never met him," Michael said. "He wasn't at Quantico when I was at the academy."

"You don't sound like you're happy to have his help," Sloane said.

"Like you said, he hasn't been in the field for a long time," Michael said. "His quick debrief into the psychology of former cult members helped us—particularly Kara—get Riley to open up. But I don't know what he's going to be able to do here."

"Were you inside?" Sloane tilted her head toward the cabin.

Michael nodded. "Poor guy was tortured. I don't know what he gave up, but based on what Riley said, he created fake identities for people who escaped. Someone shot his computer, don't know if it was him or whoever killed him. But it makes sense that he gave up some of the people—Riley confirmed that Robert Benson, Jane Merrifield, Chris Crossman, and the newest victim, Donovan Smith, were all cult members who left. Jesse Morrison was hired help."

"Do you know if there are other former cult members out there? Or do you think Riley and Andrew are the last still alive?" Sloane asked Michael.

"Riley gave us a list of names—first names only, because they didn't use last names at Havenwood—of people she helped Thalia get out of the cult. But she doesn't know who left over the last three and a half years. She didn't explicitly say, but implied that she hadn't spoken to Thalia—her aunt—since she escaped."

"There could be more victims out there," Sloane said. "Or maybe the cult wasn't able to find them."

Michael shrugged. "What I don't understand is how a large group of people can conspire to kill people they've lived with, worked with, for years."

"Cult psychology is not my strength," Sloane said. "But we were both in the military."

"The military is not a cult," Michael said sharply.

"No, of course not. That's not what I was getting at. People who were never in the military don't understand us. We follow orders because we trust our CO. Our CO works hard to build trust and respect. We have experience, education, training, and the confidence that there is a chain of command that reviews and vets information that we act on. There is a structure—a huge and sometimes unwieldy bureaucracy—but a clear structure so that we know our orders are righteous.

"Now, take away everything but our commanding officer," Sloane continued. "That's the cult leader. They've built trust and confidence. Whether that's because of religion or a common goal or belief, or any number of things, they are charismatic and have the power to lead and motivate people. Others put their faith and trust in them, but they treat that person like a demigod. They can do no wrong."

Sloane could see Michael didn't completely agree with her. But that was okay, she was still trying to wrap her mind around everything they had learned, and where to go from here. She was new to the team, and while everyone had welcomed her and didn't make her feel like a rookie, she had a steep learning curve.

"Maybe," Michael finally said. "I think of it more like the mentality of thrill killers. Where a group of people commit crimes that they would never even think of on their own."

"I can see that," Sloane concurred. "There still would need

to be a dominant personality to pull them together, convince them to abandon their morals and values."

Jim walked down the stairs of the cabin, taking off his gloves and putting them into an evidence bag as he walked. Sloane and Michael exited the warm car and approached him.

"The coroner is going to clear the den," Jim said, "then you two can go in to search. I'm joining him at the morgue—nice guy, a lot of experience, but he's never handled something like this. Michael, I'm going to take the car if you can take Sloane to the hotel with you?"

Michael nodded, then asked, "Can you tell us anything after inspecting the body?"

"Not much. Wish I had my mobile lab. Maybe we should have retrofitted an airplane instead." He didn't sound like he was joking. "Anyway, he's been dead at least two weeks, up to a month. We'll be able to narrow it down. I don't know if they opened the windows to slow decomposition, or if he had them open when he was killed. No sign that the dog was killed in the house, so I'm hoping his killers have a tiny amount of compassion and took the animal to a shelter. The sheriff's department is checking all shelters in the county and adjoining counties."

"One of our witnesses said that Morrison was very attached to the dog, a Saint Bernard. He's likely chipped," Michael said.

"Dog like that?" Jim nodded. "Yep." He looked over his shoulder as the coroner and an assistant brought the body bag out on a stretcher and rolled it over the rocky ground to the wagon. "We're not going to do the autopsy tonight, but we'll prep him and if we find anything important on his person, I'll tag you."

He left, and Michael and Sloane went into the house.

"Where do you want to start?" Sloane asked.

"You take his bedroom, I'll take the den."

"You don't need to spare me from the gore."

"I'm not. I'm the senior agent and I want to go through his papers. You figure out if he kept anything important upstairs. In my experience, people who want to hide something and don't have a safe, pick personal spaces, like an underwear drawer."

"You're the boss."

Michael grinned. "Don't tell Matt."

Sloane went upstairs to where Jesse Morrison once slept in a large, open loft. There was a small bathroom, but nothing important there. No prescription medications. No sign that a woman stayed over regularly. She did, however, find mini shampoo and conditioner bottles of the same brand that Chris Crossman had at his house. Could that mean someone who stayed with Chris also came here?

His bed was made. There was dog hair on the comforter. She smiled, though it was bittersweet. When she grew up in Montana, her golden retriever slept on her bed every night. She would love to have a dog again, but with all the traveling in this position, it wouldn't be fair to the animal.

She looked through Morrison's drawers, which had mostly male clothes, though she found two pairs of women's underwear, a pair of women's jeans, and a couple T-shirts that seemed too small for Jesse. All the items were in the bottom drawer of his dresser. Old girlfriend? Maybe.

She looked under clothes, in the nightstand, under the bed. There was no closet, only an armoire. He didn't have any formal clothes—aside from one skinny tie shoved in the back of the top drawer. Jesse Morrison lived in jeans and flannels. He had several pairs of hiking boots—all good quality shoes—and extensive outdoor gear, which would be necessary living in this climate. There were a couple books on the nightstand, nothing she'd read. A lone photo was stuck in the middle of a book shoved in the back of the nightstand drawer.

She pulled it out. It was of a dog—she presumed the missing Saint Bernard—sitting between Jesse and a woman.

Jesse appeared to be a few years younger than his current thirty-five. The woman was younger, closer to twenty-five.

The photo was faded, but she had long dark red-brown hair in a thick braid that fell over her shoulder and dark eyes. She wasn't smiling, but her arm was around the dog's neck.

Sloane looked at the back of the photo. Nothing was written on it. She sealed it in an evidence bag, marked where she'd found it on the label, and went downstairs.

Michael was still in the den, frustrated. "Either he had no papers of value, or they cleaned him out. We'll grab the computer. I doubt Quantico can salvage anything, but maybe there's a chip or two that they can pull data from."

"I didn't find much, but this photo was hidden in the middle of a book."

Michael stepped out of the den and looked at the picture. "We'll ask Riley if she knows who this woman is." He looked around. "I'll take the bedroom down here and the bathroom. You want to tackle the kitchen and living room?"

"Got it."

They didn't find much else of interest, though Sloane figured out how the killers got in—someone shot out the kitchen window and then unlocked the heavy side door. She took pictures, and then asked one of the deputies to print the entire area. They might not find anything, but there was a chance the killers had left something of themselves behind.

There was a mat with the name *Banjo*, but no dog bowls. She opened cabinets and found one that had dog biscuits and a place where there must have been a large bag of food—a few loose kernels were scattered around.

Carefully, she examined the cabinet door and saw a small amount of blood.

"Deputy?" she called to the man who was taking prints.

"Yes, ma'am?"

"Print this door, too. Where the dog food was. There's blood here—we'll need samples of that." Most likely the victim's, but after working with Jim for a short time, she knew he would want a sample of every drop of blood found where it wasn't expected.

"On it," the deputy said.

They would send the Denver ERT in to go over the cabin in greater detail, but that wouldn't happen until tomorrow, and they needed all the information they could get now, as they worked to find the killers before another body dropped.

She and Michael regrouped in the living room. Michael said, "The killer—or killers—searched the place, but not in a rage. The desk drawers in the den had been rummaged through and files appear to be missing. There could be hiding spots we haven't found. ERT will do a more thorough search of the outbuildings tomorrow." He looked around. "The guy lived frugally and Zack is going through his finances. Why would he risk himself—legally, physically—to help create fake identities? He must have gotten paid for it. Hackers can make good money."

"Who paid for it?" Sloane asked. "Thalia? The escapees from Havenwood? Where would they get the money if they lived in a cult for years?"

"According to Riley, Thalia stole from Havenwood when she left with Robert, who controlled the money. She also said that people went to Chris for supplies and help, so I suspect he had access to the accounts."

"Did they have enough money to buy multiple fake identities?" Sloane said. "How much money are we talking about? Chris Crossman paid for his house in cash, so did Andrew and Donovan. Jane and Riley had money to live in Ashland. That's a *lot* of money out there to help these people."

"Zack is working on it," Michael said. "Riley said they made their money selling handmade goods at craft fairs. Quilts, hand-carved figures, jellies and jams, things like that. If that's the case, even in a cash business, there must be some business records. But so far Zack hasn't found anything under the name 'Havenwood' and Riley doesn't know any last names. Claims no one had a last name."

"Zack's only had the info for a few hours," Sloane reminded him. She looked at Michael, really looked at him. His eyes were bloodshot. "You look beat. How long have you been going?"

"We were up at 3:30 this morning Oregon time to catch the plane, then the drive from Denver. It's been a long day." He looked at his watch. "It's after eight. Have you eaten dinner?"

She shook her head.

"We're done here. The sheriff will keep a deputy on the house until our ERT unit comes in tomorrow. I'll text Kara and Jim and see if they want to join us. I don't even know what's open around here."

As Michael pulled out his phone, his cell vibrated. "Aw, the boss." He answered. "Harris here...Yep...Okay." He ended the call. "Costa just landed. He's going to the crime scene up in Fort Collins, then tomorrow he and Dean Montero will be flying down and should be here before noon."

"Agents?" One of the deputies came down the steep driveway that went behind Jesse Morrison's cabin. "We found something odd, thought you might want to take a look."

"Odd how?" Michael said as he motioned for Sloane to follow them.

She sighed. She was hungry, but now her already late dinner would have to wait.

The deputy said, "It looks like someone has been living in a small cabin up here and got out in a hurry. According to the property maps, it's on Jesse Morrison's property. It's old, rundown, but has a working stove that's still smoldering."

The hike up the narrow, unmaintained road was difficult, especially at night with their flashlights. Sloane saw tracks that looked like an ATV. She pointed them out to Michael.

She said, "It snowed last night, these ATV tracks were made after that. But several hours ago."

"Deputy," Michael said, "does anyone live up here?"

"No. There's a road behind Mrs. Chastain's house that's closest to the highway. That leads to another house, but you can't even see it from here. All this is part of Morrison's property, which ends at the national forest about half a mile west as the crow flies."

"Did anyone check the outbuildings earlier today?"

"Not to my knowledge. We inspected the barn and storage shed, but honestly, I didn't even know this was up here until my officer found it."

They had reached the tiny cabin. A narrow but sturdy porch wrapped around the building, which was built into a grove of trees.

Michael went inside while Sloane stood at the threshold and looked out. She couldn't see much of anything in the dark, but she saw the lights surrounding Jesse Morrison's house. If she could see the lights, she imagined someone here would be able to see people approaching.

Michael came out a minute later. "I told them to seal this structure and I'll ask Denver ERT to collect evidence. Someone was staying in there. They cleaned up after themselves, but they were in a hurry. There's some trash in the garbage can and clothing was made into the bed. Even I could see hair on the pillowcase. We'll likely get prints and DNA. By the looks of it, he left in a hurry."

"When?" Sloane asked. "After you and Kara arrived—or earlier, when Andrew and Riley were here?"

Michael hesitated, then said, "Once Kara and I found the body, no one could have left—there has been a South Fork deputy on the property ever since. He would have heard an ATV. If he walked, he might have slipped away. But we can't search for a vehicle or tracks in the dark. We'll have answers tomorrow."

26

Fort Collins, Colorado

Matt read Michael's long message about the one-room cabin they had found higher up the mountain from Jesse Morrison's house, and the idea that someone—possibly someone with ill intent—had been living there until Riley and Andrew showed up. He responded with, Keep me in the loop, then pulled on latex gloves and approached the door of the small well-kept home that belonged to Andrew Gardner and Donovan Smith. Detective Richard Thompson greeted him.

"The coroner removed the body a few hours ago, and we had our crime scene investigators come in to photograph and collect evidence. But you wanted to see the place?"

"Yes, thank you for meeting me," Matt said.

"I can't believe there are three other murders just like this and we haven't heard about them."

"Virginia, New Mexico, and Oregon," Matt said. "Now Colorado."

Thompson led him to the kitchen. "What we know is the victim, Mr. Donovan Smith, arrived at work at 7:25 this morning. He works 7:30 to 3:30 Tuesday through Saturday at a local nursery in town—plants, trees, that sort of thing. Has been there for five and a half years, solid employment record. He told his colleague when she arrived shortly before eight that he wasn't feeling well and was taking the day off."

He handed Matt a sealed evidence bag. "This note and flower was found in his truck."

A red poppy. The note read *9 a.m., your house.*

Donovan was expecting Thalia. According to Riley Pierce, Thalia used the poppy as a calling card. So he came in thinking he was visiting a friend.

The detective went to talk to an officer who would be sitting on the place for the night, and Matt slowly walked the house trying to get a sense of the people who lived here. One thing was clear—there had been no struggle. Donovan had come in expecting to meet with Thalia, a woman he trusted, and was killed. Nothing outside of the kitchen had been disturbed. The detective indicated that they had fully printed and photographed the house and grounds, but would need the other homeowner to determine whether something was missing.

Was Thalia herself—the woman who allegedly helped these people escape the cult—killing them? While Matt couldn't see the motive, he wasn't ready to say no since he had no idea who the woman was. All he had was the word of a frazzled college student who had a rather bizarre and, if he was honest, unbelievable story about growing up in the middle of the Rocky Mountains, in a seemingly vibrant community—until her aunt left with her mother's lover.

There were too many holes, too many questions. He'd agreed to let Dean Montero assist, only because the man understood cults and he might have a better plan to extract information from Riley and Andrew. But the assistant director of Quantico hadn't been in the field in years, and Matt hoped he wouldn't make things more complicated than they needed to be—especially since this case was complicated enough.

Matt found nothing of interest in the main bedroom. The second bedroom was small with a double bed, desk, and dresser. It couldn't fit much else. The dresser was full of summer clothing for men. The closet, however, confirmed the men's connection to Chris Crossman.

Two suitcases identical to those found at Crossman's house were stacked on the top shelf.

Matt took them down and opened each of them. There were toiletries that matched the brands at Crossman's. He searched all the pockets and found one money envelope—empty—and a second money envelope with two thousand dollars—twenty crisp one-hundred-dollar bills.

Also in the envelope was a laminated red poppy.

He put everything in an evidence bag. The items confirmed the murders were connected, but didn't give Matt any new information.

"Agent Costa," he heard the detective call.

Carrying the evidence bag, he returned to the living room.

Thompson said, "One of my officers found a neighbor with a security camera that may have captured the killer's vehicle."

Matt followed Thompson outside, stopping to secure the evidence bag in his trunk. Donovan and Andrew lived in the middle of the block. Across the street was a wooded park; they walked three doors down to where an officer waited at the corner.

"Mrs. Rachel Williams states that when she was leaving for work this morning, she saw Mr. Smith turn onto the street and pull into his driveway. There were two cars she didn't recognize on the street, a gray Nissan Maxima that is a vehicle rented to Ms. Riley Prince." He gestured to a car near the main park entrance. "And a dark, newer model van that was parked on the other side of the Smith-Gardner property. I noticed the security system, and she will allow us to view the feed. It's automatically saved to her computer."

Riley Prince. An alias? Second identity? She would need a government-issued driver's license to rent a car. Matt sent the name and the vehicle information to Ryder to investigate, then followed Thompson to the house.

Mrs. Williams was a sixty-year-old widow who taught American history at the Fort Collins high school. She was more than happy to assist them. Her den was cramped, and Thompson said he'd wait in the living room while Mrs. Williams sat at the computer and Matt looked over her shoulder.

"My late husband set this up, taught me how to use it. My daughter keeps the software updated, but I know my way around computers. Maybe not like the younger generation, but I do just fine."

She slipped on glasses that were hanging on a chain around her neck and clicked on an icon that brought up the security feed. "This is live," she said. "See? You can see that nice officer standing out front."

The system provided a clear color feed.

"It's set up to keep three days of video from four different cameras. Any more than that and it takes too much storage. But I can download any day or segment to keep." She pulled down a menu and clicked a few commands, then the screen changed. Four boxes appeared on the large monitor, each showing a different angle from her corner home.

"You're definitely tech savvy, Mrs. Williams."

She smiled. "I teach high school juniors. I have to be on my toes. I already looked at the recording because I didn't want to tell the nice officer that I had something if I didn't." She fast-forwarded, then stopped. "See that van?"

He couldn't miss it. It showed up on the north corner of her house and he could follow it to the next camera as it turned up the street toward the Smith-Gardner home.

The only problem was he couldn't read the plates. A partial

was visible, but even if they enhanced it, he doubted they would get more than two numbers.

But it was more than they had before.

A nondescript white female was in the passenger seat. He was confident that the team at Quantico could enhance her image. The driver was unclear in the first frame, but in the second Matt identified a male, based on a thick mustache and short dark hair. He wore sunglasses. Quantico might be able to pull out more details.

"What time was this?" he asked.

She stopped the video, said, "Seven fifty-five this morning."

Local police found the note and poppy in Donovan's truck. Had the two suspects delivered the note to his place of work, then driven directly here to wait for him? Conjecture, but logical. The security system at the nursery didn't have cameras, so they couldn't confirm who'd left the note and when, but it had to have been between closing last night and Donovan's arrival this morning.

Matt asked Mrs. Williams for a copy of the recording. She handed him a thumb drive. "I took the liberty of copying all three days from my backup drive. Because they could have come by earlier, right? To check out the house?"

"Good thinking," he said.

"There's one more section." She clicked a few tabs, then showed Matt a video of the van leaving. Now he had a better view of the driver, though he still didn't have a straight-on headshot.

"Good, I'll make sure my people sharpen and enhance. We might even get a full plate."

"But this was at 12:45 this afternoon," she said, pointing to the time stamp. "They were there for nearly five hours. There's no way out of the neighborhood, except to go past my house."

The killers stayed at the house for hours. Did they expect Andrew to return? They left at about the time Riley and Andrew were at Jesse Morrison's house. That gave weight to Michael's theory that someone was staying in the remote cabin and spying on people who came to the house.

"They were a very nice couple," she said as she walked Matt to the door. "Quiet, no parties, didn't really socialize, but kind. When my husband died three years ago, Donovan brought me a tree from his nursery and planted it for me. To remember my husband. It was so thoughtful. I watch it grow and think of our wonderful life. I hope you find the people who killed him. Please let Andrew know I'm praying for him."

Matt checked into his hotel after midnight. He would only have a couple hours of sleep before he had to meet Dean Montero at the airport and hop on a small commuter plane for South Fork.

Matt read through his messages and texts, responded to everything that needed a response. Kara had taken Riley Pierce back to the hotel with her. He frowned, uncertain that was the wisest course of action. They didn't know much about her, and her story seemed...incredible. It wasn't that he disbelieved it, but cult members could be so brainwashed that they might truly believe what they said was the complete truth. Or, worse, they could be lying and putting his team at risk.

All they knew at this point was that Riley wasn't a suspect in the homicides. She'd been out of the country, which they had confirmed with the museum she worked for in France. But that didn't mean she wasn't involved in some way, or that she wasn't a threat for another reason. She had, ultimately, inserted herself in the middle of the investigation and now they were relying on her for key information.

Kara was a great cop with terrific instincts and it would take a particularly devious criminal to deceive her. But she'd been focused on Riley from the beginning, from the minute the young woman had run from her in Ashland. She suspected Riley had information, which was proven correct. And she suspected that Riley was in danger, which made Kara protective. Warranted? Was Kara putting herself at risk?

He called her, hoping he didn't wake her. She answered on the first ring.

"Hey," she said softly.

"You're not sleeping."

"If you thought I was sleeping, why did you call?"

He smiled. "How is everything down there?"

"Good. Sloane and I are doubled up at the hotel—apparently this is a big tourist area in the spring, who knew? It's friggin' freezing. But it's a nice place. We're taking turns keeping an eye out."

"For?"

"Making sure that Riley doesn't leave. I think I've convinced her that we're her best bet to stay alive and catch the people who killed her friends, but she doesn't trust anyone. Literally, no one. Not even her friend Andrew. In fact, I don't think they're friends. I guess it's like if they were soldiers who didn't personally like each other but had a common goal."

Astute, Matt thought. "The sheriff has someone sitting on Andrew Gardner's hospital room."

"Matt, I've been thinking about how they killed Donovan."

"Other than the fact that he was in his house and the others were outdoors, he was killed in the same way. Same flowers left behind."

"Yeah, same people, I get it. But that's the thing—they could have lured him into the mountains, using the red poppy as Thalia's calling card. He would have gone anywhere, probably, considering Jane left her apartment for a park two miles away. But they didn't, knowing his body would be found sooner rather than later. Someone could be watching his house."

"To know when Andrew gets home, kill him too," Matt said. He'd been thinking the same thing. "I don't think they're here now." He filled her in on what he'd learned about the van leaving hours after Donovan was killed.

"They could have sent Andrew a message, as well," Kara said.

Matt sent Detective Thompson a message to check with Andrew Gardner's employer about any unstamped letters addressed to him.

"I'll have the local cops follow up on that," Matt said. "What are you thinking?"

"If there's a note and poppy at Andrew's work, they were expecting him to return. And they only left because the person staying in that cabin on Morrison's property saw him with Riley."

"Which puts her at risk," Matt said. He was getting a bad feeling about this case. "You all need to watch each other."

"We are," Kara assured him. "You know, if they *are* watching, then they know the FBI is involved and we've connected the murders—even though there is nothing about it in the press."

"It would have happened eventually," Matt said. "The murders are too unusual."

"I guess what I'm trying to say is, you also need to be careful. If they're watching, you're now the face of the investigation."

"They don't know me from Adam," he said. "I could be anyone in law enforcement. And by your reasoning, they could be down there, watching Morrison's house. That puts you and the team in the crosshairs."

"I'm more worried about the other people Morrison created identities for," Kara said. "Maybe they couldn't find them all right away, but if Havenwood's hit squad have their full names it's just a matter of time."

"We'll find them first," Matt said, sounding more confident than he felt. "I'm going to catch a few hours' sleep. I'll see you tomorrow. Be careful. Love you."

"Love you too," she said and ended the call.

He smiled. It had taken months before Kara could say the words, and she didn't say them often, but when she did, it always made him inexplicably happy.

27

Havenwood

Calliope paced the length of the Office, waiting for the call. Back and forth, back and forth. She was so tired of *waiting, waiting, waiting* for news.

The Office was the only building in Havenwood that consistently had cell phone reception. Their computers were here, charging phones that they took when they left the sanctuary, along with their business files. Few people were allowed inside.

Her mother, Athena, had had an open-door policy. Need to call your mother? Of course! Want to read the news? Go right ahead. Want to wish your sister a happy birthday? Not a problem. It had become Grand Central until Calliope put an end to it.

Havenwood was not a part of the world; they were separate, self-sufficient, complete. Robert had set up the financial structure before he betrayed her, but she was smart. She rebuilt Havenwood. Stronger. Better. More secure.

The phone rang and she practically jumped on it. She forced herself to wait until after the second ring before she answered.

"Hello," she said calmly, though her heart was pounding.

"It's Anton."

"You're late. You said you would take care of Donovan and Andrew this morning."

"Donovan is dead. Andrew never showed."

Rage began to boil. She squeezed her fist around the phone. Control. She needed to maintain control.

"Why?" she said in a calm, authoritative voice. She was the leader of Havenwood, she reminded herself.

"We waited for several hours, suspecting he couldn't leave work immediately but would at lunch. But then Evan called. Andrew showed up at the hacker's house."

She breathed easier. "Evan dealt with him."

"He wasn't alone."

"So?" Calliope was growing increasingly annoyed. Anton wasn't usually so cryptic.

"Riley was with him."

"Who?"

"Riley."

"You are mistaken." She couldn't have misheard him. Therefore, he was wrong.

"Riley didn't drown," Anton said. "She tricked us. I was there, I saw her go under, she never came up. Garrett was there. I mourned her, we all did. But Evan took pictures. I just sent them to you."

Her daughter was dead. She'd been dead for three and a half years. She didn't leave Havenwood, she was *dead.* Riley didn't leave *her.* Riley would *never* leave her on purpose.

"Calliope," Anton said quietly. "Look at the email."

She sat at the computer and launched her email. It was slow, but eventually a picture began to load.

It was a parking lot. There were a lot of people in the photo, but her eyes immediately went to the young woman with long dark auburn hair.

A second picture loaded. It was the same woman, zoomed in.

Riley.

"My baby," she whispered.

"She was with Andrew at the hacker's house. She's now with the police."

"They arrested her?"

"We don't believe so. Evan followed them to a hotel. There are a lot of federal agents around."

"It's really her?" Calliope whispered.

"Yes, it's Riley. Evan and I are positive."

"How did this happen?" Calliope didn't want to believe that her daughter, the most important person in the world to her, had...pretended to die? Why would she have let her own mother think she was gone? She'd *cried.* For days. Weeks.

"You want her home?"

"Of course I want her home!"

"It might be difficult," Anton said. "But I will bring her to you."

She trusted him. Anton had been with her longer than any of her partners and never let her down. "What about Andrew? Is he with the police, too?"

"He tried to kill himself. He's in the hospital on suicide watch. They have a cop on him, but they won't be on him forever."

"Andrew knows far more that can damage us than Riley. He must die. If you can't get to Riley—I don't want to lose you, Anton. You or Evan or anyone else. So if she stays hiding behind the police, I may have another plan. I need to think about it, weigh our options. Call in twelve hours with a status report."

"Yes, Calliope, love."

"Thank you," she said. "You are my rock, Anton."

She hung up. Sitting on the couch, she leaned over to pet Banjo. She'd forgotten how much she'd missed having a pet until

Anton brought the dog to her last month. He was a beautiful animal. Petting his thick, lush fur calmed her like nothing else, and the last thing she wanted to do was lose her temper. Her plan was still rough around the edges, but she would figure it out.

She always did.

"Banjo, come," she said and left the Office. The dog walked at her side, loyal to her now. Reminded her how easy loyalties shifted, changed. Feed him, care for him, and he was hers.

People needed a bit more work.

She walked to the jail where Carl was on duty and asked, "Has my prisoner talked?"

"Not a word."

"Take a break. Be back in ten."

He left and Calliope unlocked the main door, then unlocked the door to the pit, and walked down the sturdy, narrow stairs to the cold basement where her traitorous sister—her *half* sister—was chained to the wall.

"Come," she commanded Banjo when he hesitated at the top.

Thalia looked up at her with pain in her eyes, which pleased Calliope. But she still wasn't broken.

Then Thalia saw the dog and a cry escaped.

"Your *hacker* deserved to die, but I am not cruel. I would never kill an innocent animal." She glared at her half sister.

"You betrayed me, Thalia. You betrayed everyone in Havenwood."

Thalia stared at her, eyes hollow but defiant. "Fuck. You."

"Everyone who betrayed Havenwood, who betrayed *me*, will be *dead*. The people you took could ruin everything we have built here! Don't you remember those who tried to destroy us? Killed Glen and my baby? Don't you remember?"

Thalia didn't say anything. She *did* remember, she just didn't want to admit that Calliope was right. That Havenwood had to be protected by any means necessary.

She glanced around the room. The waste bucket in the corner, the tray of uneaten food, the photos of the dead Calliope had printed and pinned high up on the wall, where Thalia couldn't even reach them if she was unchained.

The dog loped over to Thalia and licked her. Tears ran down Thalia's face. She should be crying. She was living her last days.

"You never understood what needed to be done to save Havenwood."

Calliope pulled a folding chair from the corner, opened it, sat down, her long dress flowing around her. Her bright red hair falling in shiny curls. She knew she was a vision. The most beautiful woman in Havenwood. But more than being beautiful, she was smart. She had seen the cracks, watched people leave, watched her mother *let* people leave. She called the dog back to her. He hesitated.

"Banjo, come," she said again, firmly.

He came, sat next to her, and she gave him a treat. Rewards worked. With dogs and people.

She pet him as she watched Thalia cry.

Without people, Havenwood was nothing. Calliope had found a way to make people stay. Most wanted to, they just needed a bit of finesse to steer them in the right direction. Rewards. Enticements. Those who couldn't be persuaded? Punishment.

They couldn't be allowed to leave and risk the sanctuary that was their home.

"I love Havenwood," Calliope explained to her sister as her fingers scratched Banjo gently behind the ears. She felt the hate and anger rolling off Thalia, and somehow, that pleased her more than her sister's tears. "I love Havenwood more than you. If it weren't for me, we would have ceased to exist long ago. If it weren't for me, everyone here would be wandering the world in search of what they lost, depressed, wishing they hadn't been so petty and selfish. I showed them a better way."

She had saved Havenwood. And what had her sister done? Betrayed her and their mother's legacy.

"People were stealing from us. Our own people, and Mother never did anything about it. They used us, used what we had, what we freely gave, and then stabbed us in the back. And still Mother turned the other cheek. What a naive woman. She had the vision but was too weak to maintain it."

"You killed her," Thalia said.

"Her fault, not mine. I wish it could have been different, Thalia," Calliope said. She rose, towering over her chained sister. "But everything you did, stealing Havenwood's money, taking Robert from me, kidnapping people in the dead of night, all of that is *nothing* compared to you turning my own daughter against me."

Thalia sucked in her breath.

"I don't know—"

Calliope backhanded her. "*You know.* Anton sent me a picture. It's Riley, my baby, and you turned her against me. That's why she faked her d-d-death." Thinking about it made Calliope's heart race. "I'm getting her back. She's *mine*."

"Riley has seen the darkness of your soul," Thalia whispered, her voice raw. "She knows who you are and what you've done. She will kill you before she submits to you."

"You thought you could deceive me, make a fool out of me. Everyone here believes you killed Robert. They believed me eleven years ago when you left with him." She stepped closer, her face close to her betrayer. "You may not have slit his throat, but his death is on you, dear sister. You have been tried and convicted. The sentence is death."

Calliope walked out of the jail, Banjo right behind her.

The final pieces of Calliope's plan began to form.

She smiled. It would work.

It had to work.

THURSDAY

28

South Fork, Colorado

Kara ordered room service for her, Sloane, and Riley. The less Riley was seen in public, the better.

Riley didn't talk much. It was like the stories she shared yesterday about the weeks surrounding her grandmother's death had drained her. She'd slept well, though, which Kara took as a sign of trust.

When Riley was in the shower, Kara poured her third cup of coffee and picked at the food remaining on her plate. She wondered what Dean Montero was going to contribute here. He'd sent her a long email outlining how he wanted to approach the interview with Riley when he arrived, that he planned to steer the conversation based on his experience, but for her to "jump in" at any point she felt was beneficial.

Kara rarely second-guessed herself, but Dean was a high-ranking fed and she was a cop—did he really want her to speak her mind? Or was she there simply to give Riley comfort because she'd developed a rapport with the young woman? Getting more information wasn't going to be easy, not because Riley didn't want to help—though Kara sensed her pulling back several times yesterday—but because there might be some things she really didn't know, or events that were twisted in her head. Kara might not be an expert on cults and brainwashing, but she understood childhood trauma.

Based on how Riley told her story, Kara suspected that she may have been drugged. Riley didn't come out and say it, but it was implied. Did Riley know or suspect that she had been drugged? Maybe not hard illegals, but something mild to induce a state of euphoria? It was just a thought she'd had that Kara wanted to explore.

Sloane brought over her own cup of coffee to the small table in the suite of rooms. "Did you read Matt's memo?"

"Yep." Matt had put together everyone's reports so they all had the same information. Ryder usually did it, but he must be swamped.

A text message came in from Michael.

On my way to interview Andrew Gardner. Let me know if you learn anything from Riley that I can use to convince him to talk.

She responded with a thumbs-up emoji.

Kara sipped her coffee and said to Sloane, "Maybe I don't understand cult mentality, but I still don't understand why none of the people who left went to the authorities. *Not one.* I understand domestic violence—and from what Riley described, she suffered some sort of abuse—and I understand how some people won't go to the authorities for any reason, but not one of the eleven Riley rescued? Not one person said, 'Hey, someone needs to stop this cult.'"

Sloane was nodding as Kara spoke, made a few notes on her phone. "Maybe AD Montero has some insight."

"Maybe," Kara said.

"Wasn't he helpful yesterday? Didn't you talk to him before interviewing Riley?"

Kara shrugged. "We didn't have a lot of time, but he had some interesting observations. I don't know why he's coming out and what he brings to the investigation, but I'll give him the benefit of the doubt."

Sloane smiled, but didn't look at her.

"Okay, maybe I won't. I don't like people coming in and messing with our team rhythm."

"I'm new, and you didn't seem to hold that against me."

"Because I'd already worked with you, I knew you were a good cop."

"I think he'll be helpful," Sloane said. "Your points are valid. It's surprising that no one has heard of this group all these years."

Riley stepped out of the bathroom. "We sold handmade goods at craft fairs, every spring and summer. Four or five fairs a year, all over the west. But after my grandmother died, only my mother's inner circle was allowed to leave. We had a small counsel, a group of people who made decisions, who appointed the Fair Committee. I didn't know why then, but now I do—the year my grandmother died, two people slipped away at one of the fairs. Just disappeared. My mother was livid. According to her, she had given them everything and they betrayed her."

"Do you know who they are?"

Riley shrugged. "Meg and Paul. They'd been there since I was little, but like I said yesterday, we didn't use last names. There was no need."

"Did your booth or products have a label? A name? Something that, maybe, we can trace?"

"Originally, it was simply Havenwood. But after my grandmother died, it became Calliope's Creations," Riley said.

"Why didn't Zack find it under Havenwood?" Kara said to Sloane.

"Every state has to be checked individually," Sloane said. "We can't get tax records without a warrant, so Zack has been contacting state offices for incorporation and nonprofit records. Older records are harder to find, especially if they haven't been digitized. But having the new name might give us another angle." Sloane got on her phone.

"How does that help?" Riley asked.

"If your mother is selling goods or services, she needs to pay taxes. Have annual filings, that sort of thing. If she hasn't, then she's in violation of major tax laws."

"Hmm." Riley looked like she was thinking about something else.

"Do you know something more?"

"We didn't make most of our money at the fairs."

"Oh?"

"Long before I was born, we had a barn dedicated to growing marijuana. That made a lot more money for Havenwood than our quilts and jams."

Michael had spoken to Andrew Gardner's doctor first thing in the morning and Andrew was stable enough to be interviewed. As he drove to the hospital, Matt called.

"Dean Montero and I just landed. I texted Kara that we'll be at the hotel in about twenty minutes. We all agree that keeping the witness in one place is safer if she is, in fact, a target. Have you talked to Gardner yet?"

"On my way," Michael said.

"His doctor cleared it?"

"Conditionally," Michael replied.

"If she or anyone else at the hospital throws up roadblocks, pull in Catherine. She speaks their language. Gardner is a material witness to homicide."

That was a stretch, but Andrew Gardner could have information that would help them. "Will do."

"Thanks for picking up the slack while I've been traveling. Ryder is already working the drug angle, and Zack has a new theory about the craft fairs. He's pulled in another analyst to help him track fairs in the country now that we have a couple names to work with. There are no LLCs with 'Havenwood' or 'Calliope' in the name, but they could be under a different umbrella."

"And," Michael interjected, "the craft fairs may have contracted with the umbrella corporation."

"Exactly. It's a long shot, but right now, other than the two witnesses who are marginally reliable, it's our best shot," Matt said. "Call me when you're done with Gardner."

The closest hospital was off a country road in nearby Del Norte, about fifteen minutes east of South Fork. It looked more like a modern office park than a hospital.

Michael pulled into a visitor space in the parking lot, then entered the main building.

He showed his badge and told the information desk that Dr. Heather Granderson was expecting him. She came out only a minute later. "Agent Harris?"

"Yes, ma'am," he said and showed his identification.

"I'm so sorry, but Mr. Gardner has taken a turn for the worse. Thirty minutes ago, a nurse found him unresponsive and we've airlifted him to a larger medical center in Colorado Springs. He was stable but unconscious when he left."

"I need to talk to the deputy who was sitting outside his room and the nurse who found him."

"The deputy left after Mr. Gardner was safely transported to the helipad, and I can answer any of your medical questions, though at this point we don't know what happened. He was monitored 24/7 under suicide watch. We have a camera in his room, and a nurse dedicated to that wing."

"Dr. Granderson, I need to speak to the nurse and view all security footage from that wing."

She looked put out, so Michael attempted charm, though he was more than irritated that the deputy hadn't contacted him immediately.

"Follow me," she said.

She used her card key to get into a secure part of the building, then turned left and led him down a long, wide brightly lit hall. Though the hospital had the slight antiseptic smell pervasive in all hospitals, it wasn't overwhelming, and the walls were decorated with framed pictures of the surrounding area.

She used her key to get into another wing, and stopped at the nurses' station. "I need Jenny Dunn."

"I'll page her," the nurse said.

"Have her meet us in Gardner's room," Michael said.

The doctor didn't like taking orders, but Michael didn't believe in coincidences. Gardner was stable last night, and Michael had talked to Granderson not more than an hour ago. Gardner had been awake and while still showing signs of depression and grief, his vitals were strong.

Something had happened to Gardner in the thirty minutes from alert to unconscious.

Granderson led Michael down the hall to where there was a round work station and three windowed rooms. The rooms were all empty, but one had clearly been in use.

Before they even walked in, Michael saw the flowers.

A bouquet of spring flowers interspersed with dozens of red poppies.

"Who brought in those flowers?" Michael demanded.

The doctor was taken aback by his harsh tone. "Agent Harris, there is—"

"I need to know right now. And no one goes into that room until a forensics team goes through it. Understood?"

She bristled, then said, "I need to contact head of security." She stepped away.

Michael pulled out his phone and called Matt, told him what little he knew, and said, "Can I pull Jim in to review Gardner's medical records and gather evidence in the room? This is fishy to me."

"I'll send Jim over as soon as he can get free, and contact the sheriff and ask what's going on with his deputy."

"Have the deputy talk to me directly," Michael said. "I have questions."

"I'll make it happen."

When Michael ended the call, Dr. Granderson approached with a young nurse and a tall, skinny man in a suit. "Agent Harris, this is Ms. Dunn, and Tom Royce, our head of security."

Royce said, "My people are downloading you a copy of all security footage from this wing."

"Thank you," Michael said. He might need footage of other parts of the hospital, but he'd wait to see what he learned from the nurse.

He turned to Dunn. "Ms. Dunn, were these blinds open so you could see into Mr. Gardner's room?"

"Yes, sir. There was a nurse at this station every minute. They can't leave unless the replacement has arrived. And the deputy was right there." She gestured to a chair that had line of sight to the main hallway and the room.

"Did the deputy step away for anything?"

"No."

"I find that hard to believe," Michael said. "I've worked stakeouts—there are always breaks, for the restroom, to get coffee, to stretch legs."

"When he had to step out he said no one was allowed into the room unless it was an emergency. And he was never gone for more than ten minutes."

"You found Mr. Gardner unresponsive at what time?"

She glanced at the doctor. "I didn't leave the station."

"I'm not saying you did," Michael replied. "You were here watching him. What made you go in to check on him? Was it routine or did something alert you that he was in trouble?"

"Earlier this morning, he complained of nausea, so we added an antiemetic to his IV. He was alert, spoke of his partner—which the psychologist on staff indicated was a good sign. Then he had his breakfast, but didn't eat much, still complained of nausea. He slept and then as I was working at the desk here—" she motioned "—I noticed his blood pressure was dropping. I went in to check on him, found him unresponsive, and contacted Dr. Granderson."

"We stabilized him," Granderson said, "but he didn't regain consciousness and his blood pressure remained dangerously low. I talked to our sister hospital in Colorado Springs and they have a full trauma team, so we sent him there."

"When did the flowers arrive?"

"Last night," Dunn said. "At the beginning of my shift. They were delivered from a local florist, Colorado Flowers and Gifts. I took them in to him when he was sleeping, put them on his bedside table."

"Was there a card?"

"Yes. I didn't read it."

Michael went into the room and looked at the flowers. It was a colorful spring mix interspersed with several red poppies. A card and envelope lay next to the flowers. Gardner had definitely opened it.

Michael pulled on gloves and picked up the card.

In memory of Donovan.
Breathe.

"Out," he told everyone as they crowded the doorway. He put the card down, took a quick picture of it, and left the room behind them. "No one goes in there, touches the flowers or anything else, until my forensics expert arrives." To the security chief, "I need security footage of whoever delivered the flowers ASAP."

"Agent Harris," Granderson began, but he cut her off.

"I believe that your patient was poisoned. That something in the flowers or the envelope was contaminated."

"I know who delivered the flowers," Dunn said. "He delivers all the time. This is usually his last stop because he lives a mile down the road."

"Name? Address?"

"Trevor Knight. I know he lives close, but I don't know exactly where."

"I'll contact his employer," Michael said.

When the security chief left to gather the information Michael wanted, he called Matt again. "I believe Gardner was poisoned. It might be airborne." He paused. "I think he knew. Gardner knew the flowers were poisoned and didn't tell anyone, maybe because he's still suicidal, I don't know. Now he's in a coma and unless we can figure out what poison was used so the doctors can reverse it, I don't know that he'll make it."

"Wait there for Jim," Matt said, "then find the delivery guy and get answers."

29

South Fork, Colorado

Kara still didn't know what to make of Dean Montero. He was in his midforties with brown hair graying at the temples and golden-brown eyes. He was Matt's height—a bit over six feet tall—but thinner, on the verge of being too thin. He wore a suit, like most feds, but his was a bit more rumpled, more a college-professor vibe. She half expected him to pull out a pipe and start puffing.

Ryder had procured the only two suites in the small hotel, plus two additional rooms for the team to use. Kara, Sloane, and Riley shared one suite; Matt and Michael the other. Sloane was keeping an eye on Riley while Matt, Dean, and Kara debriefed.

Kara went to the meeting in Matt's suite, cautious about Dean Montero. She had learned to be a bit more trusting of feds she met in the course of her job, but old wounds and all, and Kara still had a hard time trusting outside her team. They shared information and then Dean said he had some thoughts about how to approach the second interview with Riley. She was pleased that he suggested they not tell Riley at this point that someone had tried to kill Andrew at the hospital. She might think they couldn't protect her and run.

"She's exhibiting signs of repressed trauma," Dean explained, "and she believes she's vulnerable, that the people of Havenwood might find her if they suspect she's alive. If she has something tangible to grow that fear—such as our suspicion that Mr. Gardner was poisoned while under police protection—she could regress and clam up completely."

Matt looked at Kara and she nodded her agreement. "She'll bolt first chance she gets," Kara said. "I don't think she's consciously aware of it, but she's identified every way out. She hasn't asked to leave, hasn't asked for a lawyer, and she knows she's not under arrest. She feels safe here for now, but at the same time she believes her life is in danger if Havenwood knows she's alive."

"We have to go with the assumption that they know," Matt said.

"We don't want to share that information with Riley either," Dean said.

"We have to," Kara said. "She knows these people, can spot them, and they are a threat to her and others. For her own protection, she needs to know."

"Can we agree to hold back the information at least until after our initial conversation today?"

She reluctantly agreed only because she suspected Riley would attempt to bolt if she felt threatened.

"Let's see if we can pull more out of her," Dean said. "Good call, Detective, on having the interview here, rather than the police station. We want her to be comfortable. Matt, if you don't mind letting Kara and me handle the conversation alone? It'll be recorded, but I don't want to overwhelm her."

"I'll have Agent Wagner escort Riley here, then we'll leave.

Call when you're done." He texted Sloane, then looked at Kara, and she knew what he was thinking. It was sometimes amazing and always unnerving that he could read her so well. No one had ever quite understood her, until Matt.

He knew she was skeptical of Dean, and she suspected Matt was, as well. Dean wasn't part of their team. Kara gave Matt a nod, acknowledging his unspoken concerns.

"We're good here," she said. "But I'm worried about Michael."

"Why?" Matt asked with a glance toward Dean. Did he think she was going to air something confidential? Okay, maybe he didn't know her as well as she thought.

"I'm worried about *everyone*," she clarified. "Michael's in the field alone, Jim is now at the hospital alone. The killers—and we know there's more than one—only target their victims *when they are alone*. They could be capable of going after a pair, but it's easier and safer to take us out solo."

"Point taken," Matt said. "I'll have another talk with hotel security, and remind Jim and Michael to be on alert. When possible, we'll work in pairs."

Matt answered the knock on the door and Sloane walked in with Riley.

Riley wore jeans and a sweater, no makeup, her hair damp and pulled back into a ponytail. She looked younger than twenty-two and very much alone even standing in the room with four federal agents. Kara had empathy—she knew what it was like to be surrounded by people yet feel like you were on an island.

Dean smiled and introduced himself to Riley.

"We're just going to have a conversation," Dean said. "There's no need to be nervous."

Riley looked skeptically at the recording equipment. The living area of the suite had two couches and a small round table. Dean had set up the camera next to the table, and placed unopened water bottles at three of the chairs.

"This helps us protect your rights," Dean said. "We're not

going to share the recordings with anyone outside of this investigation."

Riley looked at Kara, as if wanting her assessment. "I'll be with you the whole time," Kara said. "You need to take a break, let me know and we'll take a break."

"Okay," Riley said quietly.

Riley had been worried about this conversation, but not for the reasons the police thought.

They were concerned about her mental health, about how she might feel if she talked about Havenwood. They also might be concerned that she had committed a crime. She had. Some of the crimes they might not care about. Since she'd left Havenwood she knew no one really cared much about growing marijuana. But she was pretty certain selling it in the quantities that they had was serious.

But some of her actions...she had been party to violence. To torture. To murder. It didn't matter if she hadn't killed anyone with her bare hands, she had been present and she had done nothing.

The guilt clawed in her gut and she almost ran to the bathroom to puke the breakfast she'd managed to eat. She was just as guilty as her mother. Calliope may have killed, but Riley let her. She'd been running from her guilt for years, and now she couldn't. She had to face it head-on. And if she had to go to prison, she would accept the punishment.

Would you really?

She shook her head, dismissed her conflicting thoughts, and tried to do what was right. What Jane would want her to do.

Yet, in the back of her mind she feared if she revealed the truth, everyone in Havenwood would be dead before they could be rescued.

Agent Wagner and Agent Costa left, then Dean motioned for her to sit at the table. She sat. Waited.

Kara said, "Our goal here is to learn everything we can in order to catch the people who killed your friends and keep you safe. Understand? We are on your side."

Riley nodded, but she didn't quite believe it. Would they be on her side when they learned she had let Donovan's brother die?

Would they be on her side when they found out she'd watched others be tortured by her mother's hand and said nothing?

"Are you okay?" Kara asked. "Do you need anything? I'm going to make coffee."

She shook her head. "I'm okay."

"This probably seems overwhelming to you," Dean said and sat across from Riley. He was smiling kindly. But evil rarely showed on the outside. Her mother was the most beautiful woman she'd ever seen.

Riley dismissed the thought. She needed to focus. She *wanted* to stop her mother's henchmen. She *needed* to stop her mother. She didn't know how, so maybe this was the only option.

"I'm okay," Riley said, feeling more confident. "I want to help." She said it and believed it.

"I want to talk to you about Havenwood before and after your grandmother died," Dean said, "but first, you told Kara that the community made money through selling marijuana. I'm interested in how that works. Do you know?"

"Sure. We grew it, dried it, sold it. It started with my grandmother, but that was mostly just for Havenwood. My grandma sold only enough to help pay for things we needed. Like property taxes."

"Your grandmother owned the property."

"My grandpa Will did, hundreds of acres. The entire valley we called Havenwood. Way before I was born, they almost lost it. He owed a lot of back taxes. That's why Grandma started taking Havenwood goods to craft fairs, but selling quilts and jams and wood carvings didn't earn us enough money. So she started selling marijuana and within a couple years they caught up. Then

Robert came to Havenwood and he was super smart with numbers. He made sure we never got in trouble again, because the government would love to take our property if we didn't pay."

Kara sat down with her coffee. "Robert Benson?" she asked.

Riley nodded.

"Yesterday you said Robert left with your aunt Thalia," Kara said.

"Yes. But you make it sound like they left together, to be together, and they didn't. They tried to destroy Havenwood."

She'd been so lost then. She didn't miss Thalia as much as she thought she would, but she deeply missed her daddy Robert.

"We know how hard this is for you," Dean said, "but we need to understand the dynamics of Havenwood so we can locate the compound and stop them from hurting anyone else."

"Thalia believed that if she took the money, Havenwood would implode and people would leave. Since Robert controlled the money after William left..." Riley frowned.

"William didn't leave, did he?" Kara said quietly. "You talked around it yesterday, but I think it was clear. Your grandmother found a grave and believes that someone killed William instead of letting him leave the compound."

"It wasn't a grave," Riley said quietly. "It was a graveyard. Everyone we were told left was killed and buried in that field."

"You also talked about your grandmother's death. Again, you didn't say she was killed, but you think she was, don't you?"

She squeezed her eyes closed and rubbed her temples. "I don't remember a lot from that time."

"Were you drugged?" Dean asked.

"I don't know. I was really sick for a while. Depressed—I missed my grandma so much. I didn't know until much later that Thalia believed my mother poisoned my grandmother." Riley still had a hard time wrapping her mind around it. "William is Thalia's dad. He's not my biological grandfather, who was killed when my mother was little. But he's the only grandpa I knew."

"When did Thalia and Robert leave?" Dean asked.

"We thought he was dead." She had believed her mother, until Thalia returned and told her what really happened. She wished she could have said goodbye. She had loved her daddy Robert more than any of them.

"Who? Robert?" Kara asked.

"My mother said that Thalia killed him and ran away. We had a funeral for him." Riley paused, considered what had happened eleven years ago. "Do you know how it feels when things are strange, odd, changing, but it's so slow and small that you don't realize it until all of a sudden, everything is different? That's what happened. Small changes—like my mother took over for my grandmother in running the Havenwood council. She didn't get rid of anyone on the council, but added more people—those loyal to her. The council limited who could go to the craft fair, until it was just a few people. Suddenly, the freedom and joy we had were gone. Protecting Havenwood against Thalia and outsiders became our only mission. No one new came to Havenwood. My grandmother always invited one or two families to move to Havenwood each year, but my mother put an end to that. No one Outside could be trusted."

"When you left, how many people were at Havenwood?" Dean asked.

"Ninety-six. At one point, we had over a hundred forty. But ninety-six when Jane and I left."

"Were most of the people recruited by your grandmother?"

"Yes."

"Other than you, was anyone born there?"

"Oh, sure. Jane was born there—that's one reason we were best friends." Her voice cracked and she drank more water.

"By our best estimates, Havenwood started between thirty and forty years ago, would you say that's accurate?"

Riley thought. "My mother is forty-five. She was nine when she moved there."

"That helps." Dean smiled and it was a nice smile. He made Riley feel comfortable. But Kara was watching her closely, and Riley thought she saw things maybe Riley didn't want her to see. Silly, she knew, but it was disconcerting enough that Riley averted her gaze.

Dean continued, "I noticed that you're an artist. Kara showed me your doodles from yesterday when you were waiting at the police station, and you talked about sketching your grandmother. You have an exceptional eye, a lot of natural talent." He pulled a sketch pad and box of pencils from his briefcase and slid them over to Riley. She stared at them, didn't touch.

"I was thinking," Dean said when she didn't immediately reach for the pencils, "that while we talk, you can draw. Anything you want, but I'd really love to see Havenwood as you remember it. The good and the bad."

She frowned and bit her bottom lip. She drew for herself, no one else. Not after her sketch of her grandmother in the graveyard.

"Or not," Kara said. "It's up to you."

Dean glanced at Kara and seemed irritated, but then he blanked his face and said, "Absolutely up to you."

"Did anyone teach you to draw?" Kara asked.

Riley shook her head. "We didn't have cameras or cell phones or anything like that. So I would draw things I saw. Trees, flowers, people. Sometimes with colored pencils, but usually charcoal and regular pencils. I practiced and got good."

"Did you like drawing people or things better?"

Riley shrugged. "No real preference." She stared at the sketch pad, her fingers itching to draw, but she didn't reach for the pencils.

Dean said, "Would strangers occasionally hike into Havenwood? And if so, anything memorable about those times? Anyone specific stand out?"

"When my grandma was alive, she would invite lost hikers to stay the night, have a meal, then someone would escort them out. There were no roads near us. The only way in by truck is a winding unpaved road that is unusable in the winter. So it didn't happen often, a few times. After Grandma, Calliope wasn't kind to people. She told them they were trespassing on private land. She had signs put up warning trespassers, and eventually, we didn't see hardly anyone."

"So there is a road into your valley?" Dean asked.

"You wouldn't know it was there unless you knew about it," she said. "It was gated and no one was allowed past the gate. I later found out there are cameras, and they could see who was coming and going."

"And you used that road to go to the craft fairs, or buy essential items?"

She nodded. "We had three trucks. Six people from the council would go to each fair and we'd prepare for months. When my grandmother was alive, she usually went. Some people wanted to start selling our products online, but Calliope and Anton—Anton is one of my fathers—thought it would expose us."

"Expose you how?" Dean asked.

"To people who would destroy the beauty of Havenwood. The world is corrupt, industry destroys the environment. We believe in living simply and never exposed ourselves to the Outside. My grandmother had rituals to purify our souls. Meditation and isolation, mostly. My mother...she had more."

"Like what?" Dean asked.

Riley shook her head. "I don't want to talk about it."

"That's okay," he said. "When you're ready."

Kara said, "How did Thalia know who to rescue from Havenwood? How did she know they wouldn't turn her in?"

"Me."

"I don't understand," Kara said.

"I didn't tell you the whole truth yesterday. I didn't lie—but I left things out."

Riley pulled the sketch pad to her. She opened the box of pencils and twisted one in her fingers.

Kara Quinn had a pretty, interesting face. There was depth there, hidden things. Riley started drawing.

"After Thalia and Robert left," Riley said, "Garrett took over the finances of Havenwood. Garrett replaced my daddy Glen when he died and moved into the house. Robert had trained him, so it made sense. I started listening. I was really good at making myself practically invisible. I learned quickly that my mother and the council knew that Robert had left with Thalia and taken all of our money. We had to work harder to make it up. We needed money, so we couldn't just sell stuff a few times a year anymore. And while we could grow most of our own food, and we had chickens for meat and eggs, there were expenses. We had generators that needed fuel, repairs, spices and flour for baking, shoes, things like that. Supplies for our handcrafts. So Anton expanded the marijuana farm and we were doing well.

"When Thalia returned nearly a year later, I begged her to take me with her. She said I had a job to do, that I needed to find the people who wanted to leave, and Thalia would get them out, give them new identities—starting with Chris. She couldn't take me because I was too young. I was the only person she trusted to find the right people to rescue."

"How did Thalia get past the cameras?" Kara asked. "You said there were cameras, right?"

"Only on the gate and the office—that's a separate building on the edge of the road on the north side of the valley. There were other ways out of the valley if you know where they are. Some are dangerous with steep drops, most impassable when there's snow."

"Why didn't Thalia turn Havenwood over to the authorities?" Kara asked. "Even though marijuana has been legal in Colorado for years, it's heavily regulated. Thalia could have turned them in, we could get a search warrant and find bodies. Get them not just for growing pot without a license, but for murder."

Dean winced at Kara's bluntness. "Kara, Thalia was raised at Havenwood. It's hard enough to walk away, and almost impossible for her to share with anyone, even the authorities, what was going on there."

"She believed that her mother was murdered," Kara said. She turned to Riley. "Correct? Thalia thought someone—Calliope or someone else with Calliope's blessing—killed your grandmother."

Riley didn't like the tension between Kara and Dean. She wanted to make them happy, to give them what they wanted, because they were going to find Havenwood.

Then Riley could finish what Thalia had started.

"We believed that the authorities would burn down Havenwood with us in it," Riley said quietly. "My mother and Daddy Anton told us so many stories of police violence. I know what happened at Waco. I know what happened at Ruby Ridge. Innocent people died and the police don't care."

"Which is why you ran from me the other day," Kara said.

"I knew you were trying to find out who killed Jane. I didn't even think about running, I just did it."

"It's understandable," Dean said, conciliatory. "I've researched and investigated many cults and organizations like Havenwood, and it's rare to find someone who grew up in one and willingly walked away."

"I didn't walk away," Riley said. "I escaped. And my job was to help others escape. I was never supposed to leave, but I was so lost and alone. I've always been a good swimmer, so started building endurance because the water is so cold. It took me weeks, but I was able to hold my breath for six minutes while swimming under water."

Riley told them how she faked her own death, how terrified but free she felt when her mother believed she was dead.

"I had hidden supplies weeks before," Riley said. "I hid for two days to make sure everyone believed I had drowned. The only person who knew the truth was Jane."

"That was quite a feat," Dean said.

"When you want something bad enough, you can do anything," Riley said.

"Why then?" Kara asked.

"Because Jane was next." Riley turned the page in the sketchbook. Stared at it, at the pencil and shading because it was easier to talk if she didn't have to look at Kara and Dean. "Cal was gone—I'd already helped him escape. And Timmy had died—he was attacked by a mountain lion. That left Jane and me in our group, and if Jane left I would truly be alone. I couldn't do it."

"No one should be alone," Dean said.

Riley nodded. Now it didn't matter. She still ended up alone.

"Jane met me and I took her to the meeting place on the far northern end of the valley. There's an old rotted-out cabin at the end of a steep trail. I don't know if it's on our property or not, but it's where I brought people for Thalia to get out of the mountains. I never went beyond it. So I went with Jane, and the next night Thalia was there. She was so angry with me, ordered me to go back, but I told her my mother thought I was dead and I would never return."

Riley stared at the pencil in her hand. "What if," she said quietly, "they didn't believe I drowned? What if they found my supplies and knew I faked it? What if that's why they went after everyone else, looking for me? All this is my fault."

"Nothing is your fault," Dean said. "You did what you needed to do to survive."

"Thalia warned me over and over if I walked away Calliope would search to the ends of the earth for me. That's why she didn't take me when I was little, that's why she didn't take me when I was eighteen, like she promised. That's when I came up with the idea of faking my death. I thought it had worked.

And now Jane is dead, along with Chris, Robert, Donovan, and Jesse, and I know in my heart that Thalia must be dead because she didn't warn anyone."

Her voice cracked and she fought tears.

"Listen to me," Kara said, her voice so sharp that Riley jerked her head to look at her. "I don't care what you think, the people responsible for these murders are the ones who lured them out and slit their throats. Not you."

"Okay," Riley said in a whisper. But she didn't fully believe it. She looked down at the sketch pad, made a few tweaks, then pushed the pad over to Kara. "You can have it," she said. "If you like it."

Kara stared at the paper. "It's really good," she said. "Dean is right, you have a lot of talent." She carefully tore the page out and placed it in front of her, then slid the pad back to Riley. "Keep it. If you're moved to draw anything else, do it. No pressure."

Dean said, "You know more about where Havenwood is than you realize. Think about landmarks. Unusual rock outcroppings. The types of trees. Any roads or signs you saw when you left with Jane and Thalia. Just draw what you remember. It doesn't have to make sense, but it will help us narrow down the location."

"Can we take a break?" she asked.

"Sure," Dean said. "Are you hungry? Can I get you anything?"

"No, thank you." She picked up the pad and pencils.

"One more thing," Kara said. She pulled out her phone and showed Riley a picture. "Who is this woman?"

Riley stared at it. "Thalia, a few years after she left Havenwood."

Then Riley walked into the adjoining room.

"Before you jump down my throat," Kara said, "she needed to hear that it's not her fault."

"I probably wouldn't have been so forceful, but I agree she needs to hear it and often."

"If I was as calm as you, she would think I was placating her. I have to be who I am, or she'll pick up on it in a heartbeat."

Kara reached over and shut off the video.

"She trusts you," Dean said.

"No, she doesn't trust you or me. I can tell her she isn't to blame, but that doesn't mean she believes it. There's more there, a lot more. We've barely scratched the surface."

"You sound worried."

"I don't know if Riley is right and Thalia is already dead. She could be. But why now, why not three and a half years ago? How did Calliope find a place to start looking? There are two possibilities I can think of. Either someone who left went back and spilled the details, or Thalia did. I'm leaning to someone returning."

"Maybe you understand cults better than I thought."

"No," Kara said, "I really don't. But I understand the psychology of abuse victims, and the penchant for them to return to those who hurt them."

30

Havenwood

Thalia was going to die.

Calliope and her followers had built this prison, practically a pit in the ground, after Thalia left. By the waste and the blood, she knew others had been kept here. How many people had to be broken before the rest saw the truth?

Everything her parents built had been destroyed.

Thalia desperately wanted to fix what had gone wrong with Havenwood. She'd been so close…and then her mother had died.

She had never wanted to leave the sanctuary she'd called home since she was born. Thalia was her mother's daughter—she loved nature, art, the beauty of the world around her. Her mother had a hard life, and Havenwood was her chance to be reborn. She had a framed picture she'd brought from the outside world that hung in her house Thalia's entire life. It was a picture of a sun-drenched forest with a quote by Frank Lloyd Wright: "Study nature, love nature, stay close to nature. It will never fail you."

For years they lived by that quote, and Havenwood was truly paradise. People joined them, contributed to the community in a variety of ways, wherever their talents took them. They built homes, a greenhouse, endured harsh winters like their ancestors hundreds of years before. But they were joyful and spiritual. They weren't the Amish, but they lived life as simply as they could, focused on nature and community, love and acceptance.

Thalia was much younger than Calliope, and she had once loved her sister.

Until she saw firsthand the darkness in Calliope's soul.

All utopias failed, that was human nature. Thalia had never believed in evil—until Calliope. Had her soul always been damaged, or did losing Glen and her baby break her? Thalia didn't know. But there had been signs over the years, signs Thalia was too young to understand until it was too late.

She shifted and cried out in pain. She had broken ribs, bruises, a sprained ankle, more. She was angry with herself and so very depressed. Her own arrogance and selfishness had resulted in her captivity.

She'd trusted the wrong person. After Riley left, she should have stopped trying to help. Her niece was much better at picking who would survive on the Outside than she was.

Now Calliope was killing everyone who mattered to her. For the first time, Thalia was glad their mother was dead and couldn't witness what her own daughter had become.

She jumped when she heard a key in the lock above, feared the end was near. She would be dead, and Calliope would hunt down the rest who had left and kill them like she had the others. Would Calliope kill her face-to-face? Or would she send someone else, like Anton?

The footfalls on the wooden stairs were light, barely there. Neither Anton, who was a large man, nor Calliope, who strode purposefully wherever she went.

In the dim light from the two wall sconces on either side of the staircase, Thalia saw Abby.

The girl who betrayed her.

"I'm sorry," Abby said. "I didn't want this to happen."

Thalia mustered all her strength to speak. "What did you think would happen when you came back?"

Her bottom lip trembled. "I couldn't live out there. It's awful. I didn't realize—Havenwood is so much better."

"I gave you a house. A job. Support. If it was hard, why didn't you reach out? I would have been there for you!"

She coughed, her chest battered and bruised, her body cold and sick from being in this basement for too long. The small stove in the corner took the icy chill off the windowless room, but it wasn't warm.

She might die before Calliope killed her.

"Havenwood is my home, and Calliope accepted me back."

"She killed Jesse and Chris, the two people who gave you freedom, real choices."

"I don't want choices. It's hard, Thalia. And Calliope told me that she gave everyone the choice to return, all forgiven. *They* chose death. I don't know why they would choose dying over Havenwood."

Thalia didn't believe it, but she'd never be able to convince Abby of it. Abby didn't realize that she had killed just as certainly as if she held the knife herself.

"I just wanted you to understand, Thalia," Abby said.

"I don't understand. My mother wouldn't understand."

"I miss Athena," Abby said suddenly.

"Calliope killed her," Thalia said, even knowing the girl wouldn't believe it.

Abby sighed, shook her head. "I wish things were different, I really do. I wish you would have come back like I did, accepted that Calliope has led Havenwood with vision and purpose. We're stronger, better than ever."

"It's a prison."

"No, that was a lie you told me, and I believed it. You took advantage of my grief. I'd lost my baby, didn't know how I could live here with her memory everywhere. I'm better now, and I'm never going to leave again. You out of all people should understand. That you lie about Calliope is so sad. But what I can't forgive is that you took her daughter from her. Calliope told me that Riley is *alive*, that you staged her death. I lost my baby girl, I know how it feels. You ripped Riley from the only world she ever knew."

Abby turned and walked back up the stairs. Thalia saved her breath. Abby would never see the truth.

She'd thought Abby was ready to leave. She was wrong.

After Riley left, Thalia had to change her approach to rescuing people. She lived in the mountain above the valley. She knew this land better than anyone, even better than Calliope. Her sister only knew what was within the boundaries and focused on the one road that led to the valley. But there were other ways to get to Havenwood.

Thalia watched people. Approached them when she felt it was right. The year after Riley left, Thalia had rescued a couple who Riley had already identified as being the most likely to go. It had been a success, so she was emboldened. When she learned from the couple that Abby had just lost her two-year-old daughter in a tragic accident, Thalia approached her.

Thalia had convinced Abby that a hospital was only forty minutes away, that the child could have been saved. But Calliope wouldn't allow it, lied about nearby services. A toddler with her hand nearly cut off would certainly prompt questions. Strangers would come to Havenwood. The authorities.

That couldn't happen.

But Thalia should have seen Abby's deep sorrow and deeper insecurities. She hadn't been able to make it on her own. Even with everything Thalia had given her, Abby was lost, and Havenwood beckoned.

Calliope took her back only because Abby told her everything she knew about Thalia's network.

Thalia wanted to die, before she saw another photograph go up on the wall.

31

South Fork, Colorado

Matt had created a workroom in his hotel suite. He wished Ryder were here to set everything up—the analyst seemed to pull computers, printers, and cables out of thin air.

Michael came in. "The hospital downloaded everything we need to a USB because it was too large to email." He dropped it on the desk. "The delivery guy was bribed. A woman came to him with a sob story along with twenty dollars for his 'kindness.' I went at him pretty hard, and I don't think he's involved. He's working with the sheriff's sketch artist because he had a good memory of the woman. But you need to see the video." He looked around. "Do we have a port to read this?"

"Shit," Matt muttered and looked at both computers that Ryder had the hotel send up for their use. "Oh—here." A small port on the side took the USB. Matt had grown technologically lazy because Ryder always handled computer work.

Michael took over the mouse and scrolled through a collection of MOV files until he found the one he wanted. "Hospital rooms don't generally have cameras in the room, but because Gardner was on suicide watch, we have one."

Michael pressed Play and spoke as Matt watched Andrew Gardner lie in bed on one side of the screen, and the nurses' station on the left. "Last night, the delivery driver brought the flowers to the main nurses' station, checked in, then delivered to the individual departments. You can see...here," Michael said as a young man in a uniform with a flower on the logo walked into view. He put the flowers down and chatted with the nurse for a few seconds, then he left. Michael fast-forwarded about five minutes, then stopped when the nurse rose and brought the flowers into Gardner's room. She put them on his side table. He was sleeping. She checked his vitals, made a note on his sheet, and left.

Matt asked, "Did the nurse get sick?"

"No," Michael said. He stopped the replay, went through the directory, and picked out another recording. "Gardner woke briefly at midnight and didn't seem to notice the flowers. The nurse checked him every two hours, and I confirmed that he was never alone in this wing. Here." He slowed down the video. "At three in the morning he is awake and asks for water and help getting up to use the bathroom. We don't see inside the bathroom, but the nurse waits outside the door and helps him back into bed. That's when he sees the flowers."

The nurse said something to Andrew and he nodded. She motioned to the card, and he shook his head.

"I asked the nurse about the exchange," Michael said. "She offered to read the card, and he said he would do it later, claimed he was tired. But he didn't sleep. A few minutes later, he sat up and the nurse came in. She told me he said he wanted to sit up for a few minutes. She kept an eye on him. As you can see, he stared at the flowers for a long time—twelve minutes." Michael fast-forwarded through that segment. "Then, he picks up the card, opens it. Sits there again for several minutes. And…there, you see he puts the card to his face and breathes deeply. Then he leans over, puts his face in the flowers, and breathes deeply again."

"Where are the card and the flowers?"

"Jim has them at the county crime lab, but it's a bare-bones operation. He's working on it and talking to the doctors in Colorado Springs where Gardner is now on life support."

"Poison?" Matt asked.

"Likely. Jim has some ideas based on the time frame. Gardner was nauseated for about three hours after he breathed in the flowers. He had breakfast, didn't eat much, was given more antinausea medication. He then went to sleep and it was about thirty minutes later that the monitors registered an irregular heartbeat and low blood pressure. Jim is factoring in a three- to four-hour window for the poison to exhibit symptoms."

"This video suggests he knew the flowers were poisoned and he willingly breathed in the substance."

Michael nodded. "That's my take. And the note—telling him to breathe. I think he knew exactly what he was doing and what would happen."

"He could have gotten help. He could have called us."

"He lived in a cult, Matt. They're often brainwashed. Even though he left, it's hard to overcome the training. He lost his partner, was already suicidal."

"They knew," Matt said. "They knew he tried to kill himself and they gave him the weapon to go through with it."

"Kara has developed a bond with Riley Pierce, but we need to be careful with her, too. Her mother is the leader. She's been out of it for over three years, but she's not really… I don't know how to say it. Her mannerisms, the way she talks, how she talks around things. We need to watch her and be prepared for anything."

Matt agreed with Michael's assessment. "Kara is aware that Riley may be deceptive." He gestured to the drawing Riley had done of Kara. "The girl drew that in less than twenty minutes."

Matt loved it. She had captured more than Kara's physical appearance. The way she'd shaded her eyes, you could see intelligence and compassion as well as her inner strength that Matt didn't think most artists would be able to re-create. It wasn't perfect—Kara's mouth was a bit larger than in the drawing, her hair was generally messier, the proportions of her forehead seemed off. But for a twenty-minute sketch, it was stunning.

"She's talented," Michael agreed.

"Dean thinks she can draw us a map of Havenwood. I'm skeptical. They're giving her a break. When the delivery driver is done with the sketch artist, I want Riley to look at it. I think the best chance of us finding these people is through the property and tax records, but that takes time. We also know the property is remote, but there is an unpaved road leading to the valley. The property could be surrounded by government land. The Rocky Mountains is full of plots of private property grandfathered in when the government created different national forests. Ryder is looking into it, but again, it's labor intensive and the records are not all in one database."

"They have resources," Michael said. "They traveled cross-country so must have identification to fly. I suppose they could have driven to Virginia and Oregon, but that doesn't seem realistic."

"Which means they're not as isolated or remote as Riley thinks—or told us." Matt walked over to the minibar and made himself another single-cup coffee. If Ryder were here, there'd be a pot of strong coffee and snacks—both healthy and junk food. Matt should have had him fly out with Dean Montero. He felt like he was missing his right hand.

"The craft fairs probably required a business license or ID," Michael said. "Someone—several someones—are in the system. We'll find them."

"In time to save the others?" Matt wondered out loud.

With the assistance of Cybercrimes, Ryder and Zack were

going over all files related to Jesse Morrison. Their IT people didn't think they would be able to salvage the computer, but now that they'd determined that all the false birth certificates had been "issued" from the same hospital in Denver, they were backtracking to find other potential false identities. It was a laborious process that required the time and assistance of the hospital. Ryder was also working with the Social Security Administration because all the false numbers were granted from the same office. Again, it was time-consuming and they wouldn't have the information for days, if not weeks.

Matt tried not to be frustrated. Complex cases like this were filled with days of action, then days where the investigation appeared to stop. What they needed took time to mine. But it wasn't Matt's job, and that made him antsy. If he tried to get in the middle of it, he'd slow everyone down. They were stuck in the tiny town of South Fork investigating Jesse Morrison's murder and the poisoning of Andrew Gardner until Matt decided there was nothing more they could do here.

Not for the first time, he thought, *What do we do with Riley Pierce?*

He could arrest her for the crimes they had on her, including two fake IDs, false passport, and social security number. She would be granted a lawyer, but he might counsel her not to speak to them, or delay further interviews. Right now she seemed to be forthcoming. So he didn't want to pull that card, and Dean Montero had agreed. He hoped not to find out what happened if they disagreed on something, because Montero technically outranked him.

He and Michael sat at the makeshift worktable and wrote up reports, reviewed evidence, and coordinated with the four agents sent from the Denver office to collect evidence at Morrison's house and the outbuilding where they suspected one of Havenwood's people had been hiding for the last several weeks. After a couple of hours he felt that he had accomplished something.

Matt looked at his watch and said, "Michael, I need food and air. Want to join me?"

"George and I are meeting with the Denver agents at the Morrison house in thirty. I'll get something on my way back."

"Let me know if there's anything new."

Matt left and walked down the hall to the suite Kara and Sloane shared with their witness. He opened the door to find Kara alone. "I was going to get some food. Where is everyone?"

"Riley is sleeping—at least pretending to—Sloane is at the lab with Jim, and Dean went to check into his room and talk to his boss. Who is his boss?"

"The director of Quantico, but I suspect he's answering to Tony on this case." Tony Greer was the assistant director who oversaw Matt's team. "I'm getting lunch, you want me to bring you back something?"

"Actually, how about if Riley and I join you? I think she needs to get out. She feels like she's under a microscope right now. Give us five minutes?"

"Sure," Matt said. When Kara got up from the couch, Matt kissed her. Quick, easy. "I've missed you."

She raised an eyebrow, but smiled. "No hanky-panky while we're working."

"We've been working on this case for almost two weeks," he said. "I *really* miss you. We both have some vacation time coming. When this is over, let's take a long weekend and go someplace where we don't have to do anything. Maybe we can head to Florida and you can meet my brother."

"Table that conversation," Kara said, looking suddenly panicked. "Let's catch these killers first."

"You're scared."

"Am not."

"Are too." He squeezed her hand. "Dante doesn't bite. Neither does Veronica. They're both mad that I didn't bring you down for Christmas."

"I told you, I wanted time with my grams. She's not getting any younger."

"And that's fine." He thought about what Chris Jones said after dinner the other night. "I should have gone with you to Washington, then we could have gone to Miami together. I was being selfish."

"You weren't, and we'll talk later." Kara walked into the adjoining room and Matt let it drop.

Five minutes later, Kara came out with Riley, who was dressed in new jeans and a sweatshirt that he was certain he'd seen in the gift shop downstairs.

"She didn't have anything clean to wear," Kara said, "so I'm expensing this outfit."

He didn't explain to her that she couldn't do that, but he'd figure something out.

"We'll go to the restaurant in the lobby," Matt said. If it was just him, he'd be going out, but he didn't want to put Riley into a potentially compromising situation. One of the killers had been in town last night, and could very well still be here. If they knew about Andrew, they likely knew about Riley.

The hotel had a three-story main building with guest doors facing the interior, and individual cabins that lined the property. The lobby boasted a stone fireplace mounted with a giant moose head, a bar running down one side, and a cafe on the other. It was still ski season, and Matt didn't know how Ryder was able to find these accommodations on such short notice.

Though it hadn't snowed while they'd been here, they were expecting snow tonight and into the morning. Matt hoped they could get out of here tomorrow. He didn't see what more they could do here, once they finished clearing Morrison's house. Jim and Sloane could stay to continue investigating Morrison and processing any evidence, and the location was also close enough to Santa Fe that Jim could coordinate with the Albuquerque office on the Crossman crime scene.

But Matt would have to figure out what to do with Riley.

They ordered and while waiting for their food, Riley leaned back in the chair and began to draw in her sketch pad. She seemed to relax when she had a pencil in her hand.

After a few minutes, Matt said, "You're very talented, Riley. The picture you drew of Kara really captured her essence, especially her eyes. You studied art in college?"

"Art and Art History," she said without looking up. "I didn't know there were so many different styles and mediums. At the museum where I interned, every day when I'm done I walk around and find something new, even in paintings I've seen a dozen times."

"What are your plans for when the internship is over?" Matt asked.

Her face clouded, but she still didn't look at him. "I wanted Jane to move to France with me. She didn't want to. So I don't know what I would have done. I might have gone back to Ashland, though I didn't fit into the whole college scene. I don't know what's going to happen anymore."

She sounded defeatist. Matt exchanged a glance with Kara.

Kara said, "You're going to stick with us until we can find you a safe place. A place where you feel like you fit."

"Maybe I'll never fit in anywhere," she mumbled. Then she said, "What about everyone else? There are others out there. Can you find them?"

"We have some leads," Matt said, "and when we get a list, we'll track them down."

Kara said, "No one had last names at Havenwood, but did you all keep your real first names when you escaped?"

Riley nodded. "Jesse gave us the last names."

"Before you left, you helped Thalia get people out. So you know some of the people who left Havenwood."

Matt saw what Kara was getting at. "Our computer experts have backtracked how Jesse created the birth records in the hospital in Denver. They're now going through more than a decade of records searching for a unique code that seems to be attached to the files Jesse created. It takes time."

"Oh. Yeah. I can give you everyone's first names, sure." Riley brightened, looked marginally optimistic. She flipped the page on her sketch pad and started writing down first names.

"That'll help us narrow the records we need to search, saving a lot of time."

"Add their age and basic description if you can," Kara said.

The food arrived and Riley nibbled as she wrote.

Matt mouthed to Kara, *Good idea.*

She grinned, popped a french fry into her mouth, then nodded toward the lobby.

Matt glanced over and saw Dean Montero walk in. He was about to go up the stairs when he spotted them in the restaurant. Surprised, he walked over. "Ryder Kim works miracles," he said and took off his coat. "He managed to get me a room on short notice, albeit a cabin." He motioned to the empty chair. "May I?"

Matt nodded. "This team wouldn't function half as well without him."

"I remember when you recruited him straight from the academy," Dean said. The waitress came over and he ordered a burger, then said, "He was the top analyst candidate in his class and several offices wanted him."

Matt knew that, of course.

Dean was watching Riley, but being directly across from her he couldn't see what she was drawing. She was focused on her work, barely glanced up when Dean came over. Kara was the only one who could clearly see the page.

Matt's phone vibrated. He looked down; it was Ryder. "Excuse me," he said and got up.

Stepping out of the restaurant and into a corner of the small lobby, where he had some privacy, he answered. "What do you have?"

"The report came in from the lab on the red poppies. I sent it to you and Jim, but in a nutshell based on water and minerals, they narrowed the region to southwestern Colorado, and northern New Mexico, in the mountains. They assure me if we get a soil sample, they can test against it. But there's one more interesting fact. The poppies have trace amounts of THC."

"Which means?"

"They were grown in soil that also grew marijuana. They could have grown side by side, or they were stored together. It's distinctive, because it's not seen in these flowers in the wild."

"That's good as far as building a case, but that still doesn't tell us where they are. We know from our witness that the group lives somewhere in the Rocky Mountains."

"Zack is making progress with the finances. He found the original LLC paperwork for Havenwood, but it closed down eleven years ago."

Around the time that the matriarch died, Matt thought.

"The LLC has a Nevada address, which is a mail drop that has also been closed for eleven years," Ryder continued. "The mail drop doesn't keep records that long, so we don't know who opened it. I sent a local agent to pull the filings—they're not online—and maybe if we cull through them we'll find something that helps. We'll have that tonight or first thing in the morning."

"Terrific."

"Nothing on Calliope Creations, but we're looking at variations. Our best lead right now is the original Havenwood paperwork. If they paid property taxes through the LLC, we might be able to trace it that way. And based on Kara's report from her interviews with Riley, the commune wasn't trying to stay off the grid when it first started. We're also in contact with several local assessors, but without the name of the payor or tract numbers, they can't help."

"Stay on it, Ryder," Matt said. "Do we need to stay here?"

"That's not my call, sir. I don't know how fast we're going to narrow down their location."

"Is there a map included in the report about the poppies?"

"Yes."

"I'll show it to our witness, maybe it'll spark a memory."

"Okay—something just came in." He paused and Matt heard the clicking of the keyboard. "The laminated poppies were not grown in the same soil as the flowers left with the bodies, and they don't have any trace of THC. They were pressed, preserved, and laminated at the same time—they can't determine when. The ERT unit found a laminating machine at Crossman's residence and they're testing it to re-create the squares. It's likely the same one."

"Thanks, Ryder." Again, it was good information for the case but didn't help them find Havenwood.

"Did Assistant Director Montero check in without a problem?"

"You are a miracle worker," he said.

Matt ended the call, walked back to the table, and glanced at the sketch pad as he sat back down.

Riley was not only writing names, but she had sketched faces of each person. He wanted to say something but she wasn't done and he didn't want to disturb her.

"Everything good?" Dean asked.

"Yes. We have lab reports to review, I'll make sure you get a copy." He'd prefer not to talk about too many details around Riley.

"This is everyone I know who left," Riley said. "I don't know anyone who left after I did. It was my job to find the people who wanted to leave, and then make it happen when Thalia told me she was coming. I don't know how she got people out after. She may not have."

She handed the sketchbook to Matt. "This is quite impressive," he said. "The sketches are very helpful."

She had listed the names of the dead, but hadn't sketched their faces.

Aside from those, there were five people on the list.

Bridget, twenty, fair skin, brown hair, green eyes. Left the year after Chris.

The sketch showed a pretty woman with a scar on her jaw line. She would be closer to thirty now.

"Do you know how Bridget got this scar?" Matt asked.

"An accident. I wasn't there. A chain broke in the barn and hit her."

The next two people left two years later, the year before Donovan and Andrew.

Tess & Greg. Tess is in her thirties, white, blonde, brown eyes. Greg is her partner, maybe forty or older, half black, dark hair and eyes.

The sketch had them together, a fuller sketch then Bridget, waist up, showing Greg much taller than Tess with his arm around her shoulders.

"They'd come to Havenwood the year before William died," Riley explained. "They were newly married and their families didn't approve of their relationship. Tess could sew anything, and Greg was a mechanic. He worked on the generators, lights, trucks, you name it. They loved Havenwood, but knew it wasn't the same after my grandmother died. Tess became pregnant and was scared because she'd had a miscarriage early in their marriage, before they came to Havenwood. Another woman, Ginger, nearly died in childbirth. Calliope wouldn't let her leave to get help. Ginger lost a lot of blood and was sick for months. I was good at eavesdropping, finding out everyone's secrets, and I went to Tess and told her I could get her out."

"Do you know if she had the baby?"

Riley shrugged.

"Do you know when she was due?"

Riley considered. "She left in June and was about four months pregnant."

"That helps a lot."

The next person was Cal, a teenager. "Cal, Jane, and I were all about the same age," Riley said. "His mother brought him to Havenwood and then she disappeared. She was very odd, moody, prone to lashing out at people. I don't know what happened to her, but I think she wandered away and got lost.

"Anyway, he was raised by my grandmother since he was eight, and when she died he sort of...well... I guess just took care of himself. He was defiant and challenged my mother and Anton especially, and he got in trouble a lot. He wanted to leave, made it known to everyone. He was an agitator and Calliope started drugging him. I mean, I don't know for certain, but he became lethargic and unmotivated. Maybe she was poisoning him.

"I got him out as soon as I could. That's when Jane learned that I was helping Thalia. She told me she wanted to leave too, but only if I went with her." Riley paused. "After Cal left, Jane's boyfriend, Timmy, was attacked by a mountain lion and died. It was awful."

The last person was a lone female, in her late twenties, named Amber. She had sad eyes and frizzy hair. She left the year after Cal, the year before Jane and Riley.

"Amber had been born in Havenwood when it was good. She watched our world fall apart and then her partner was killed in an accident and she didn't think it was an accident. I worried my mother would hurt her too, especially after she started asking about people who disappeared. A rumor went out that Thalia was helping people get out, and my mother put an end to people talking. No one was allowed to mention her name. But I'm positive she knew Thalia was responsible. Maybe not at first, but she must have figured it out after a few years. If Amber kept asking questions and pushing her, other people might also have started questioning her, and my mother couldn't have that."

"This is great information," Matt said. "I think we can find these people."

"They're not going to be in trouble for what we did, right? I would feel awful if they got in trouble," Riley said.

"As long as they aren't currently committing crimes, we don't plan to prosecute them. We'll want to talk to them, that's it. Plus, we'll offer protection. Okay?" Matt asked.

She nodded. "Okay."

Matt tore the sheet from the sketch pad and handed the pad back to Riley. "I'm going to scan this and get our people looking. Excuse me."

He left and went back upstairs. This was the first time he felt they were finally making progress.

One of these five missing people might know exactly how to get to Havenwood.

32

South Fork, Colorado

Kara wasn't surprised that as soon as Matt left, Riley went back to sketching. It was her crutch, her way of coping, and that was a positive. If Riley had this outlet, it would help her overcome the pain and grief of not only her childhood, but losing her friends.

Dean finished his burger and Kara was picking at her fries. They were good, but she wasn't all that hungry. She kept running every fact she knew around and around in her mind, twisting them to see how they all fit. She felt it was important to know *why now.* How had Calliope found the escapees? Had she been looking for them for years, or only recently? Had they caught Thalia and tortured her for information? From what Riley said, Kara didn't think her aunt would give up people she had saved. Yet pain was a powerful motivator.

Or, maybe, someone else gave them up. Someone Thalia had helped. Maybe Calliope set a trap. Lured Thalia in with a person who had a good reason to leave, and that person learned about the others. It was plausible.

Dean pushed his finished plate away and said to Riley, "You've barely eaten."

She shrugged, didn't look up from her drawing, her hand moving back and forth, up and down. It was hypnotizing.

"You need to keep up your strength," Dean said. "Can I see your sketch pad?"

Riley hesitated, and Kara sensed she didn't want to share, but then she handed it over and started eating her chicken salad.

Dean slowly flipped through the sketches. Kara glanced over. Some were very rough, as if Riley had an idea but didn't flesh it out. A few were exceptionally detailed. She drew mostly people, though she'd interspersed bits of nature around the edges, almost as if to frame the pages. Flowers, trees, bushes, small animals.

When Dean turned the page again, to what Riley had most recently been working on, Kara did a double take.

The sketch was of her and Matt sitting at the table across from each other. While drawn from Riley's perspective sitting between them, it was as if she wasn't there, as there were only two place settings. The background was rough, a few swipes and shadings of the pencil, but it was clear they were in a rustic lodge with natural lighting coming in and hitting the table.

She and Matt were looking at each other. Exchanging… something. Though they weren't touching, the picture seemed intimate—too intimate. She had a half smile on her face, Matt's expression was softer than Kara generally thought of him.

Suddenly, she didn't want anyone looking at this picture, as if someone had caught her and Matt in a private moment. This hadn't happened—she and Matt always kept their behavior professional when they were working in public. If Catherine saw this, the shit would hit the fan. Kara didn't want to deal with the fallout from that. It exhausted her just thinking about it.

But clearly Riley saw what they didn't want anyone to see.

Dean cleared his throat and turned the page. Dammit. He saw the same thing.

At the next page Dean asked, "Riley, who is this?"

He turned the pad and Riley said, "My mother."

The sketch showed a woman practically floating on the page in a gown, like an angel. Though there were only a few marks outlining the body, they could see a curvy woman, the gown flowing around her. Her face was all sharp angles, beautiful and grotesque at the same time. As if looking at her one way, you saw the beauty of her angular face, her large eyes, her high cheekbones, her lush lips. Another glance the cheeks looked sharp enough to cut, the mouth about to bite, the eyes filled with a dark ominous glow.

But there was no doubt the hair was snakes, like mythological Medusa. Long, flowing, coiling, ready to strike.

Riley had drawn her mother larger than life, beauty and cruelty leaping off the page.

Kara didn't have to be a shrink to understand the underlying emotions of how Riley perceived her mother.

"Can I have it back?" Riley asked.

Dean reluctantly handed the sketch pad back to her. "Some of those sketches may be helpful."

"Okay," she said. "Can we do this upstairs? I'm uncomfortable here. I feel like I'm in a fishbowl."

Kara looked around. The lobby was large and open with three-story ceilings, and a wall of windows on the western face of the building. Behind the windows was a deck spreading out far and wide—Kara knew from the brochure in the rooms that the deck was often used for weddings and wedding receptions. It was a nice place for that sort of thing. Not today, however, as the gray skies were darkening and it looked like the weatherman was right and they'd be getting snow tonight.

No one seemed to be paying much attention to them in the lobby. Most of the guests were coming in from an early afternoon of skiing, as wind had started to pick up, swirling the snow in the field between the lodge and the towering mountain.

Were Kara's instincts fuzzy? Had she missed something?

She glanced at Dean. He didn't act any different, his eyes on Riley.

"If it makes you more comfortable," he said.

Riley got up first, her sketchbook tucked under her arm. She started walking toward the central staircase, but Kara quickly caught up to her. "Stick with me," she said.

"Sorry, I don't mean to be trouble. I just got this...feeling."

"Like you were being watched?"

Riley nodded.

Kara definitely believed in those kinds of feelings. She steered Riley through the restaurant and lobby. When they passed the bar built into the opposite wall of the restaurant, Riley froze.

"Keep moving," Kara said firmly, practically pushing her up the stairs.

Riley stumbled. "Daddy. Anton."

Her voice was a whisper, faint and hollow and tinged with fear.

"Now," Kara said. She looked for Dean; he was still at the table reading something on his phone. What the fuck?

Her job was to protect Riley; Dean should have been behind them, he could have gone after the threat.

She followed Riley's gaze. A man in his late forties with dark hair, a thick moustache, and piercing brown eyes stared at them. He had a beer on the bar in front of him, but it was barely touched. He didn't make a move, didn't so much as flinch, when Kara stared back.

She had two options. Get Riley to safety then return; he would likely be gone. Or alert Dean and hope he could apprehend the suspect while she got Riley upstairs. The odds were slightly better for the latter option, so Kara put her fingers in her mouth and whistled loudly.

Dean immediately looked at her, confused but alert.

"Anton, bar," she shouted as she put herself between Riley and the bar and pushed her charge up the stairs.

Dean jumped up, then Kara lost sight of him as she focused on getting Riley to Matt's room. As they started on the second set of stairs she heard a commotion echoing below. She pulled out her phone and hit Matt's number. As soon as he answered she said, "Situation in the lobby, open your door!"

She didn't wait for a response, but pulled Riley around the bend and down the hall, keeping her on the inside. Kara spared a glance down into the lobby, but she couldn't see the bar from this angle.

The door at the end of the walkway opened and Matt stepped out, hand on his holstered gun, face set. Michael stepped out and ran down the hall toward Riley and Kara, then escorted them into the room.

"Riley saw Anton from Havenwood. Watch her," Kara said, then immediately turned around and ran back down the hall.

"Michael, go," she heard Matt say, "I got her."

The door closed, and Michael sprinted to catch up to her.

"He was sitting at the bar, I don't know how long," Kara said as they ran down the stairs. "I alerted Dean."

Kara glanced at the bar. The beer was there; Anton was not. She shouted at the bartender, "Don't touch that glass!" as she and Michael headed to the main door.

She didn't see Dean anywhere. Before they reached the entrance, the doors opened and two staff members were escorting Dean back into the lobby. He was unsteady on his feet and blood dripped down his face.

"Truck. Waiting out front," Dean said.

Kara and Michael ran outside. The icy cold hit her hard; she only wore a lightweight blazer to conceal her weapon. They didn't see Anton or a vehicle leaving. But to the right of the second set of doors was blood in the snow and a scuffle of footprints.

"Well, shit," Kara said and went back inside.

Michael followed. "I'll talk to security."

"Get that glass on the bar, he drank from it. We might get prints, DNA if we're lucky."

She walked over to where Dean was sitting in the lobby. He had an ice pack on his head.

"What happened?" she demanded.

"I pursued the white adult male you identified as Anton as he exited the building. Told him I was FBI and to stop. He didn't. When I opened the second set of doors, I saw a dark green Ford truck idling outside, but didn't see the suspect. I was then hit from the right. I grabbed him, but he hit me again and jumped into the truck. I couldn't pursue, but noted a female in the driver's seat and Colorado license plates. My vision was cloudy, and there was exhaust distorting the numbers. Maybe security has a good shot of the driver and plates."

"Michael's on that." She texted him the information about the truck.

She wanted to yell at Dean for not falling in step behind her when she got up. She had assumed he would. But he wasn't Matt or Michael or even Sloane, who was a rookie but would have instinctively risen as a security precaution. Dean wasn't part of their team, and she had become so confident with her team and how they worked together that it threw her off.

She wouldn't let it happen again.

"I'm sorry," Dean said, and she was surprised he apologized. He was her superior, Matt's superior, and she didn't expect an apology. She expected him to justify himself or not address it at all. "I was making notes—I should have gone with you. I thought Riley was just making an excuse for not wanting to talk about her mother."

Riley was odd, but Kara was beginning to trust her instincts.

She went back to the table and looked from that angle. Where Anton was sitting couldn't be seen from Riley's place at the table; Kara would have had a partial view of him, but she wouldn't have recognized him.

Now she would never forget his face.

She called Matt to inform him of the situation.

"Tell Dean to have the hotel medic look at him, if they have one. Otherwise he should go to the hospital." Matt sounded irritated. She didn't blame him.

"How's Riley?"

"Frozen. She's sitting on the couch, not talking."

Riley was a fighter, but seeing Anton had terrified her into inaction. Kara had practically pushed her all the way up the stairs. Whatever happened in Havenwood had deeply affected Riley. Maybe abuse, physical or psychological. Maybe another type of violence. Kara needed to find a way to shake her out of that fear, but didn't know how. Riley's response could be the difference between life or death—for Riley, or for someone on Kara's team.

"Matt," she said, keeping her eyes on the room, wondering if there was someone else from Havenwood here, watching, "Riley identified the man at the bar as Anton. If they didn't know she was alive before, they know now."

"Sloane is on her way back to help with security. George Stewart can stick with Jim and help him with whatever he needs at the Morrison house and morgue."

"Good," Kara said.

"Kara, I think you should come back to the room," he said, his voice low. "Riley responds best to you. You might be the only one to convince her to pick up her pencil and draw us Anton's face, and anyone else her mother may have sent."

"Five minutes," she said and ended the call.

33

Havenwood
Six Years Ago

Riley couldn't look Donovan in the eyes.

His little brother was dead and it was her fault.

It was late at night and she didn't think they would make it. Andrew was walking too slow and she thought he was sick. Donovan was angry and making too much noise as they walked up the steep trail that would eventually lead to the cabin where Thalia would meet them.

James was supposed to come with them tonight. But James was dead.

She glanced back when she didn't hear Donovan's thrashing anymore. The two men weren't there and she panicked. Riley backtracked and found Donovan holding Andrew upright.

"How much farther?" Donovan snapped.

"Thirty minutes. Maybe longer because we're going slow."

"He's sick. Want to beat him to make him move?"

"Don't, Donny," Andrew said. "I'm okay."

"You're not okay. We should have waited until you were better."

"We can't wait," Riley said. "If you're not there when Thalia comes, she will leave and you'll never get out."

"I'll take my chances in the mountains," Donovan said. "If Thalia can find her way out, so can I."

"Donny, we need the guide," Andrew said weakly.

"It's okay, baby," Donovan said. "I've got you."

So kind to Andrew, but he glared at Riley. "I'll never forgive you," he said. "James trusted you."

Her chest was so tight it hurt. She turned away and continued leading Donovan and Andrew up the path.

Though late July it was cold at night. She pulled her jacket close. How many times had she done this? A half dozen? Leading others to freedom, only to return to Havenwood and pretend nothing happened.

She didn't have much time. She had to be back before her mother or fathers woke up, or they would know. She had become so good at sneaking around, but her mother had recently started a sentry program in the summer—when people left—hoping to catch Thalia coming to the valley. Riley had to work around them, and so far their focus was on the road, not the trails leading out of the valley.

It took nearly an hour to reach the cabin. Thalia was already there.

"You're late," she said.

"Andrew is sick," Donovan explained. "Can we stay here for a couple days?"

"No." Then her voice softened. "It's going to be hard, but we need to hike out of here. We can camp at a place I know until Andrew feels better, but we can't stay here. Where's James?"

Donovan's face fell, then he glared at Riley. "He's dead. He's dead because of Riley."

"What happened?"

Riley couldn't speak of it, but Donovan did. "He fell into a trap. And she knew and didn't help him. She let him die."

"Calliope," Thalia said.

"No, Riley," Donovan spat.

Thalia looked at her oddly. Riley couldn't explain. Her stomach twisted and all she could hear through pounding in her ears was James crying.

"Thalia," Riley said quietly. "Please let me come with you."

Thalia pulled her out of the cabin while the two men rested. "Calliope will hunt you down and everyone will be in danger."

"But—"

"No," Thalia said. "What really happened to James?"

"I made a mistake. James paid for it. I'm so sorry."

"But Calliope doesn't know you're helping me, does she?"

"If she did, would you take me?"

"Just answer the question."

Riley shook her head. "No."

"Listen to me—if you leave, everyone you love in Havenwood will pay the price. Do you want that?"

What about me? What about the price I'm paying?

Instead, Riley shook her head again.

Satisfied, Thalia nodded. "Who's next?"

"Cal."

"I'll let you know when."

"Calliope has sentries. It's getting harder."

"You're smart," Thalia said. "You'll figure it out. I'll be back for Cal next summer, but I'll come earlier if possible, the first time the trail is safe enough. You're going to have to run back."

No thank-you, no goodbye, no hug.

Just run.

Riley ran as fast as she dared down the trail, then circled

around the valley to the southern edge, where the lake pooled. It was deep now because of the melted snow. She wanted to jump in and disappear…

But she had a job to do. Cal was next. She had to make sure he didn't do anything to get in trouble, or it would be harder to get him out.

She headed back to their village when she heard the rooster crow. She was late.

She ran, then someone grabbed her when she reached the edge of the barn. She almost screamed, but hands clamped down over her mouth.

This was it. She was going to be punished. She would be sent to the pit for weeks…months…

"Riley," a familiar voice whispered.

Cal? She turned around and he dropped his hands.

"It's you," he said with awe.

"You can't tell. Please." Her voice cracked and she was near panic. She didn't want to be punished. She didn't want anyone at Havenwood to suffer because of her actions.

There was a voice near her house, then another. Suddenly, Cal pushed her against the barn and kissed her. It was sudden and surprised her so much she couldn't have pushed him away if she wanted. The kiss continued, and at first she wanted to scream, *No, you're my best friend!* But then she remembered all the fun they had, laughing, how when Cal was twelve and she was ten they made pies with her grandma. When Cal let her cry on his shoulder after she was forced to shoot her horse. How he always seemed to be there when she needed someone to just…sit with.

"What is going on?" a male voice said and Riley jumped.

Cal stepped back and looked sheepish.

It was Evan, her mother's newest partner.

"I—I'm sorry," Cal said.

Evan frowned. "You okay Riley?"

She nodded because she couldn't speak.

"I have to tell your mother," he said.

"Please, I don't want Cal to get in trouble."

"He won't get in trouble, you're sixteen, you can make these decisions yourself. But you both broke curfew sneaking out so early in the morning. And we have a problem."

Her heart skipped a beat. They knew.

"What problem?" she asked.

"We found the traitor. But you don't have to worry about it."

Cal's hand tightened around her own. She hadn't even realized he was holding her hand.

"Come on, you need to explain your absence to Calliope and then do your chores."

He motioned for them to follow him, then turned and started walking.

Riley stared at Cal in the awakening dawn. "What's happening?"

"Nothing good. But as far as everyone is concerned, we met behind the barn at four thirty this morning."

"You're next," she whispered.

"You'll come with me."

She shook her head. "I can't."

Suddenly Calliope was in their path. Evan said something to her, and she looked at Cal and Riley. Riley froze. She knew. She had to know.

Then Calliope said, "I'll talk to you two later. For now, you're both grounded. Cal, go home. Riley, to your room. Do not leave until I say you can leave."

She nodded, dropped Cal's hand, and ran home.

By the time she got to her room she heard a commotion outside her window. She opened her curtains and stared down at the village center, where a huge redwood tree grew. Anton and Garrett were dragging a bloodied man along the path, toward the prison—the pit in the ground where Calliope punished serious offenders.

It was Brian.

We found the traitor.

Calliope thought that Brian had helped Andrew and Donovan escape, because they were friends. Brian worked with Donovan every day in the greenhouse. She picked up on a few words below, that he'd disappeared in the middle of the night and they found him on the road. Brian was sobbing.

"I didn't do anything!" he cried out.

That was the last Riley heard—or saw—Brian.

34

South Fork, Colorado
Present Day

Kara sat across from Riley, who was still unmoving on the couch.

They were alone. Matt and Michael were working with security to identify the truck Anton escaped in. With luck, they'd get the plates and maybe a witness.

To Riley she said, "You're safe here with me."

Riley didn't say anything, nor did she look at her.

Kara wasn't good at playing games. She was good at playing *parts*. She could work undercover and adopt any number of personas. But she was straightforward when dealing with suspects and witnesses. She didn't like coddling or placating or pretending that everything was going to be fine. But she had to find a way to get through to Riley.

She thought about Riley's sketches. The girl had talent, but more than talent, she observed what couldn't be easily seen. Like the sketch of Kara and Matt. She may have occasionally looked at Matt as Riley depicted, and Matt may have looked at her with that expression of...*love*. But they hadn't been staring at each other like two lovesick teenagers, not in front of Riley. Which meant she picked up on an undercurrent and put two and two together.

Riley saw a lot more than most people. Maybe because she was an artist, she saw what people didn't want to share.

Kara brought a chair over near the small couch, where she could still see the door, but also focus on Riley.

"We need to establish trust," Kara said.

Riley blinked, looked at her. "I trust you."

"When you saw Anton, you couldn't move. I pushed you up those damn stairs, and if Anton had a gun, he had the time to shoot you."

"I'm sorry."

"Okay. Good. I need you to listen to me."

"I have been."

"Listen again. I will protect you. When I can't—when I need to sleep—my team will protect you. Sloane, Michael, Matt, they're all trained to make sure you stay safe."

"Not Dean?"

Kara smiled, not surprised she had singled him out. "Him, too, but he hasn't been in the field in a long time, and he's not a part of my team. I'm not going to leave you with him, not until I trust him. He's been a good cop, has a record of helping people like you free themselves from places like Havenwood. But he's been sitting behind a desk for too long."

"Oh."

"When I say run, you run. When I say stop, you stop. If I say drop, you drop. Do you understand me?"

"Yes. I'm sorry," she said again.

"We've already established that," Kara said. "I don't do psychology well. I'm sure our team shrink will tell me I have to talk to you this way or that way and she might be right. But I think you would know if I lied. You see people as they are."

Riley didn't say anything, but looked down at the closed sketchbook she held tightly on her lap.

"I know you've grown up in an environment that is completely foreign to me," Kara said. "I lived in Los Angeles for twelve years, and I loved having people everywhere to the point that individuals disappeared in the masses. I also lived in a very small town in Washington—not as small as Havenwood, but small enough that I recognized half the people at the grocery store and knew everyone in our neighborhood by name. One thing we have in common is our grandmothers. I love my grams. She was there for me when my mother left because I was cramping her style. You loved your grandmother. Mine is still alive, and I miss her because I can't be there all the time. So I know you really miss yours."

"If she was still alive, I never would have left Havenwood."

Kara believed her. "We have a woman who is a person of interest in the attempted murder of Andrew Gardner."

Riley frowned. "You said he was okay."

"I said he was alive and in the hospital. I don't know if he's going to be okay. He tried to kill himself. I told you that yesterday. Last night, someone tried to kill him. That is the reason we transferred him. Other people didn't want to tell you because they thought you might get scared, and I agreed with them at the time. Now I think you need to know. So you can protect yourself."

Riley frowned, her bottom lip quivering.

"I need to know right now if you don't care about your life."

"Of course I care!"

"Andrew tried to kill himself. I don't know if he did it because Donovan is dead, or because he didn't want to face his past in Havenwood, and we were asking questions."

"I *don't* want to die," Riley said firmly.

"Good. I don't want you to die either. There's been too much death. I have a police sketch of the woman we suspect, and Dean saw a woman driving away with Anton. It's not your mother.

Your sketch of her is very detailed—I think I would recognize her anywhere, even without the snakes in her hair."

"I took a class in Greek and Roman mythology," Riley said. "It was fascinating. Maybe I was interested because my grandmother was Athena and named her daughters Calliope and Thalia. When I read about Medusa, I thought of my mother. Beautiful and deadly." She paused. "My mother has never left Havenwood. They moved there when she was nine, and she was terrified of the Outside. I don't think she would leave now."

Kara pulled out her phone and brought up the image Michael had sent her, the police sketch of the woman who bribed the flower delivery driver. She showed it to Riley.

Riley sucked in her breath. "Ginger," she said.

"The woman who nearly died in childbirth?"

Riley nodded. "She is loyal to my mother, she's as cruel as my mother. But why would she leave her child to come here to hurt Andrew?"

"Her child is…?"

"Molly. I guess she's eight now?"

Damn cult had children on the premises. Kara had known that, but hearing it again reminded her that there were innocents at Havenwood, and whatever they did when they found the place, they would have to take that into consideration.

She asked, "How many children were at Havenwood when you left?"

"Eighteen, I think, but we usually had one or two births a year."

"All born there?"

"Most. All the littles. No one joined Havenwood after my grandmother died. I don't see my mother allowing anyone new inside."

That meant the kids knew nothing other than life in the commune. They wouldn't trust law enforcement, and that in and of itself was problematic.

Damn damn damn.

First, they had to find the place.

"Can I look through your sketchbook again?" Kara asked. She didn't know exactly what she was looking for, but if there was anything there, they had to go over it again and again. "Would you mind if I took pictures and sent them to my team?" The more eyes the better.

Riley handed it to her.

Kara flipped to the picture of her and Matt. She loved it.

"You can have that," Riley said. "I shouldn't have drawn it, but..." Her voice trailed off.

"You're fast. You might have a future as a police sketch artist."

Riley laughed. It was the first time Kara had heard her not only laugh, but with a smile in her voice.

Kara carefully tore out the page of her and Matt. She didn't want to fold it—she might just frame it. Then she quickly took photos of all the people, plants, flowers, landscapes that were doodled.

"Are all these from Havenwood?"

"I guess. I didn't really think about it. Dean told me to draw a map, which I can't. I have no idea."

"What about the cabin where you brought people for Thalia? You said it was old and falling apart in the mountain north of Havenwood. Do you know how far?"

Riley thought, then took back the sketch pad and started to draw. Kara watched, mesmerized by her sure, light hand as the lead bled onto the paper, as she rubbed with her fingers to shade areas, bringing out light and dark, until a structure appeared, hidden among the trees.

"What's around the cabin?" Kara asked. "An unusual boulder, a creek, a path, anything that's distinctly different."

On another page Riley started drawing what at first Kara thought was a mountain, but then realized was a boulder outcropping over which water flowed. "A waterfall?" Kara asked.

"Yes. I don't know what it looks like, but I can hear it from the cabin. I think it's the waterfall that gives our valley fresh water."

"North of Havenwood."

"Yeah. But I don't know how far it is."

"How long did it take you to get from the center of Havenwood to the cabin?"

Riley thought. "At least ninety minutes. It's really hard to get up to from the valley, because there's not an easy trail, and impossible in winter."

A waterfall and cabin north of Havenwood. She spoke of a valley multiple times. They had to be able to find it. What about hikers, people who lived in the general area? County officials? Someone had to know of a group of more than a hundred people living off the grid in a southwest Colorado valley.

"Do you remember anything after you left the cabin with Thalia?"

"Not much. It was dark."

"Did you hike on a trail? Walk on a road? Did Thalia drive a vehicle?"

Riley frowned, closed her eyes. "It took longer to walk to her truck than it did to get from Havenwood to the cabin. We were mostly on a trail, but there was a narrow packed road with some ruts in it for part of the way. Thalia said it was called a fire road. I didn't know what that meant then, now I do."

Riley jumped when there was a knock on the door. Kara told her to stay and went to the door, hand on her gun. She looked out the peephole. It was Matt. She wanted to talk to him without Riley, so she said, "Stay here, okay? It's just Matt, but I need to talk to him."

Riley said, "I'm not going anywhere. I promise."

Even if she did, she wouldn't get far because the door of the adjoining room let out on this hall.

She stepped out, closed the door. "News?"

"Partial plate, partial view of the female driver, good security shot of Anton. We've put an APB out on him as a person of interest, but we don't have any actual evidence against him.

Good call on the glass—it's already on its way to the county lab to be processed."

"I emailed pictures of Riley's drawings to the team. Maybe Catherine has some insight, or Ryder can work on narrowing the region."

"Good."

"Riley ID'd the sketch of the woman who bribed the florist. Her name is Ginger. She is part of Calliope's inner circle."

"You told her about Andrew?"

"She needed to know."

"Okay." Matt shot a glance at the door. "We need to ask her some tough questions. Dean is pussyfooting around with her, but do you think she can handle it?"

"Yes," Kara said without hesitation. "I've gotten a lot out of her. She's scared, and I don't know if she'll freeze again when faced with someone from Havenwood, but right now she's willing and able to talk."

"That's good," Matt said.

They walked back into the room and Riley was sitting and sketching. Matt saw the drawing of them and picked it up. "Wow."

"Dean saw it. Didn't comment, but you know," Kara said, feeling self-conscious.

He looked at her and there was a shift in his expression, for a moment it was just them, remembering the last time they'd been together, without work, without stress.

Then Matt smiled, and Kara felt it was all going to be okay. Their relationship, even if Dean knew about it, was solid. He carefully placed the sketch back on the table, lightly brushed Kara's hand with his fingers, and turned to Riley.

"Your names are very helpful," Matt said. "I want to get all of them under protection. Would there be any problem with my agents dropping your name when we find them?"

"I—I don't see why you need to," Riley said, a hitch in her voice.

"We want them to feel comfortable and safe, but also understand that the people from Havenwood are naturally distrustful of the authorities."

"We were all party to crimes," Riley said. "Growing and selling marijuana, especially in the quantity that we did, is against the law. We all have fake identities."

"I told you before that we're not going to go after anyone for that. We'll work it out, make everyone official if we can. I have some questions for you, and it might not be comfortable. Now that we know two of Havenwood's people are in South Fork, it's important."

Riley glanced at Kara, then nodded. "Okay."

"You said that your mother has several partners. I assume you meant romantic partners."

Riley blushed and nodded.

"Is Anton one of them?"

"Yes," she said.

"I'd like to know their names, descriptions, anything you can tell me about them. Maybe you can draw them."

"Robert, Anton, and Glen were my fathers when I was born. After Glen died, Garrett came into the house. Like Anton, he was strong and he had also been in the military and he killed the people who killed my daddy Glen. I felt safe with him, and he was nice to me. Serious, and he never smiled, but he was nicer than Anton. When Robert left, Evan moved in with my mother."

Kara said, "And everyone is okay with this, um, swapping partners."

She shrugged. "Sure. I mean, I didn't really think about it when I was little, only when I was older and realized that my mom was the only person with multiple partners. I liked Evan a lot, though he was sad. His brother and wife were killed in a car accident, and he was the only family to take care of his nephew, Timmy. There was a lot of debt in the family and Evan was having a tough time. He knew Garrett and Garrett invited him to Havenwood."

So there was a way to communicate with the outside world, Kara thought. Either because Calliope's people had access to phones and computers, or because they were the only people allowed to leave.

"When you left, Anton, Evan, and Garrett were in your mother's home? And Timmy?" Matt asked.

Riley squeezed her eyes shut. "Timmy was attacked by a mountain lion and died. That was a year before I left. Evan wasn't the same after that."

"Dean asked you about a map," Matt said, "but what about something on a smaller scale. Not how to get in and out of Havenwood, but how the community is laid out. Where the houses are, the barn, the greenhouse, things like that."

Riley smiled wearily. "I can do that. It might take me a while. I try to forget."

"Whatever you can give us is fine. Why don't you work at my desk?"

Matt cleared off the tabletop, picking up the picture of him and Kara. When Riley sat and started to work with a fresh set of pencils, he pulled Kara across the room.

"I'm sorry about this," Matt said quietly, holding up the sketch.

"Don't be." She took the paper, making sure not to wrinkle it.

"I didn't think—" He struggled with what to say. "I mean, I wasn't looking at you like that, not on purpose. Discretion is important to both of us, and I know you're uncomfortable with people knowing about our relationship."

"I don't care if people know," Kara said. "I just don't think it's anyone's business." She looked at the sketch again. "She saw what's beneath the surface, because that moment in time didn't happen. But it could have."

He reached out, lightly touched his fingers to hers. "I love you," he said in a whisper so low she almost didn't hear it.

"Ditto," she said.

35

Pagosa Springs, Colorado

Evan sat in the disgusting motel and waited for Anton.

He felt sick to his stomach.

Riley had faked her death.

Why was he surprised, when he knew Jane had left? Why was he surprised, when he knew so many others had walked away? There were signs, but he didn't see them because Riley, Jane, Timmy, and Cal were best friends. Inseparable.

He closed his eyes and put his face in his hands. He knew the truth, but most people at Havenwood didn't. Calliope had convinced everyone that Thalia was akin to the boogeyman. They believed she killed Robert, who was beloved. For a time, Evan believed it as well and hated her. Then Calliope told them that Thalia and Robert had stolen all the money from their accounts and disappeared together, implying that they were romantically involved. Evan learned to hate them both for the betrayal. Not just because of the affair—he couldn't care less about that—but taking from the mouths of the children.

Havenwood suffered. For two years, they barely held it together. Athena's illness, Thalia's betrayal, Robert's theft...it was almost too much to bear.

It got better. Because they worked hard and were disciplined. Because they cared about their village and about each other. It wasn't easy, and some people complained, but they made it through. When people disappeared, Calliope said Thalia had snuck in and killed them. They had funerals for the fallen.

But Thalia hadn't killed them, she took them. They wanted to leave. Evan and Anton and a few others Calliope trusted told the others that they'd found the bodies, made sure to provide enough evidence that no one questioned their statements.

If too many people left, they couldn't manage the land, the barns, the crops. Havenwood would cease to exist.

The ideal number was one hundred thirty people. They could function with one hundred and ten. But they were down to ninety-two, and many were too young to work.

They were imploding, and Evan feared there was no fixing what was broken.

He would never leave. Havenwood had saved him and Timmy.

Timmy is dead. Jane is dead.

He had Calliope.

At least, some of the time.

Anton and Ginger walked into the motel with two bags of fast food. The greasy smell made Evan's stomach even queasier than his guilt. "The plan is in motion," Anton said. "Marcus and Karin will be here in the morning with the body."

"I don't think it's going to work," Evan said.

"It will work," Anton said. "Have faith, brother."

"There are feds all over the place. And local cops. If she comes out, she'll be surrounded."

"If they die, they die," Anton said. "We will take Riley by

any means necessary. And I have a plan to make sure there are fewer cops around to improve our odds." He clapped Evan on the back. "Eat, then sleep."

Ginger had already dug into her burger. Evan couldn't even stand the smell.

"I need to walk."

Anton looked him in the eye. "Are you okay?"

He shrugged. "Seeing Riley really shook me."

Anton nodded. "Me, too, buddy. Me, too."

36

Quantico, Virginia

Catherine wanted to go home.

It was seven at night and she had been in her office since before seven that morning. While she was used to long hours, the last two years had seen her family torn apart and put back together.

She wanted to *be* home. With her husband and daughter and a warm fire and glass of wine.

When the email came in from Kara, she almost ignored it and left. She didn't like Kara Quinn. While she reluctantly admitted Kara was a competent cop, she wasn't suited for the FBI. She was reckless and rough around the edges. She had no... *class*. Maybe *class* was the wrong word. She had no...sense of detachment. They were supposed to be observers, investigators, analysts. Kara put herself in the middle of every case, as if the plight of the victims was her plight, as if the pursuit of justice was solely *her* pursuit.

And, she had won Matt's heart.

Catherine wasn't in love with Mathias Costa, but she loved him. He was supposed to have married her sister; they were supposed to have been kin. Beth was head and shoulders a better person, a better woman, than Kara. She was beautiful, elegant, classy, intelligent. She was everything...and Matt left her. He left her and then she became the victim of a serial killer. If Matt had stayed, if he had loved Beth like Catherine wanted him to, her sister never would have been alone the night she'd been abducted.

Catherine closed her eyes. It had been nearly two years and she still hadn't accepted that her sister was dead and she was alive. She knew intellectually that Matt wasn't at fault, but she couldn't stop thinking about what might have been, what *should* have been.

One.

Two.

Three.

She opened her eyes and clicked on Kara's email.

Catherine:

I sent these to the team, but I wanted to add a message to you.

Riley sees more than most people. I think you understand that more than anyone. She sees things that aren't there, that are beneath the surface. I look at her sketches and see trees, flowers, people. But I sense that there is more—I just can't see it. I'm hoping you can.

Kara

Damn her.

Catherine wanted to hate Kara, and when she was beginning to feel comfortable and justified in her dislike of the cop,

Kara did something like *this*. Sending her an email and asking for her advice.

Catherine read the email three times looking for something passive-aggressive, something unprofessional, *anything* to show to Matt and say, "She's not good enough for you." Or, rather, "She's not good enough for the team."

But there was nothing. Kara was straightforward and to the point.

So Catherine looked through the pictures.

Riley was certainly talented. Art, in Catherine's opinion, was part talent, part instruction. Some people could pick up a pencil or paintbrush and create something beautiful, and with guidance and practice become even better. And some people, like Catherine herself, could take years of classes and still be mediocre.

Catherine had already analyzed the five pictures of individuals Riley claimed to have helped escape the confines of Havenwood. Cal, the boy who had been friends with Riley and Jane, was the clearest of all, which isn't surprising considering Riley had grown up with him and they were near the same age. The others had varying degrees of clarity, but she hoped that even though many years had passed, the sketches could help identify the missing people. Ryder was diligently working with the hospital and social security administration to obtain the current names and addresses of each person.

Her first pass through the new set of sketches was cursory to get a sense of Riley's style and the overall feeling the images conveyed. What she choose to accentuate or dismiss was interesting. Eyes were always a focal point on faces, while hair and bodies were almost incidental, clean strokes and shadows to tell you that there was a body or hair, but nothing detailed. Nature was portrayed with light and dark, the sun often playing a role in highlighting a part of the plants. Animals were technically accurate, no human traits incorporated as many artists did.

When Catherine saw Calliope, she involuntarily drew in

a deep breath. This couldn't possibly be the way the woman looked. It was an image born of imagination, eerily beautiful.

But, perhaps, Riley's version of the mythic villain Medusa *was* how her mother looked to her. Growing up with a beautiful woman who committed, perhaps, heinous crimes. A duality, a Jekyll and Hyde personality. Someone who could persuade as well as manipulate, show compassion as well as cruelty.

In Kara's earlier notes, she'd relayed that Riley had taken classes in Greek and Roman mythology, and perhaps what she had learned in college about Medusa had cemented certain personality traits, in her mind, of her mother, merging the fictional and real people into one, as a coping mechanism for Riley. She had left everything she had known...her home and her community, her friends and her family. As she learned more about the world around her, her perception of the world she left behind would shift and change.

Riley needed counseling. Had she left the cult and gone into counseling immediately, she would probably be in a better place now. Though Catherine wasn't as confident that Havenwood was a cult in the traditional sense, not as confident as Dean at any rate, there were definite signs of a collective group run by a dominant, authoritarian figure. Not a messiah personality who twisted religious messages for dark purposes, but a strong personality who exploited the individuals' need for community—or perhaps family and a simpler life.

Riley's art also showed a maturity and self-exploration of her world that could be cathartic on its own. Guided art would help more, but Riley seemed to have found something that gave her a sense of peace to help come to terms with all that had happened to her and her family—both family by blood, and the shared Havenwood community.

The second time through, Catherine looked deeper at the meanings of the images and how they were grouped. Faces were always the focal point, with sketches of nature in the background, smaller, often as a border or doodles. Incidental. Yet, there was a lot of detail when she looked closely.

Riley had been asked to draw anything that reminded her of Havenwood. Dean had wanted a map, thinking that would direct them to Havenwood, but Kara had indicated that Riley had left Havenwood at night and didn't know how to return. Catherine wasn't positive that was the truth, but she believed *Riley* didn't think she could return. She either blocked it out or deliberately avoided thinking about it to the point that she couldn't remember.

But it was in her head, somewhere. Catherine was confident she could draw the information out of Riley, but it would take time—and they might not have time.

Still, there was enough detail here in the drawings that Catherine had a thought that might get them further.

She called Ryder, even though it was well after seven in the evening. "Are you still on campus?" she asked, referring to Quantico.

"Yes."

Of course he was. If Matt was working, Ryder was working.

"I have an idea, but I'm not quite sure how to implement it. I'll be in your office in ten minutes."

As she gathered her notes, she called her husband to give him her ETA, and left.

FRIDAY

37

South Fork, Colorado

The storm blew in Thursday night and lasted until six in the morning. By nine, the city and county had cleared the main roads and by ten, the sky was blue and the skiers had left the lodge, making the lobby feel empty.

Kara needed to do something. She was antsy and being cooped up all night and morning had put her in a sour mood. They'd had breakfast in their room, then Sloane went to the gym while Kara stayed with Riley, who was still quiet and withdrawn after seeing Anton yesterday. Once Sloane returned and showered, she told Kara to take a break.

She'd walked the halls, not wanting to spend time in the gym. She was in decent shape, and she enjoyed running (outside, not on a treadmill), but doing reps with weights or watching the news while a machine moved under her wasn't her idea of fun.

When she reached the lobby, she spotted Dean having coffee in the restaurant. The only other people on the main floor—other than staff—were an elderly couple sitting next to the windows while eating breakfast.

Kara didn't want to talk to Dean. She was still irritated about yesterday afternoon and had avoided him in the evening. But they had to work together, and because Matt was working closely with multiple FBI offices to track down the five missing people, Dean had spent most of the night working with the local authorities to locate Anton and Ginger. Michael, Sloane, and Kara had rotated shifts to keep an eye on the hotel and Riley.

"Hey," she said and sat down across from Dean. He still sported a small bandage on his head.

The waitress came over and asked if she'd like anything.

"Just coffee," she said.

The waitress poured her a cup, refreshed Dean's, and left.

"I need to apologize to you again for yesterday," Dean said.

She shrugged. Maybe she shouldn't have sat down. She didn't want this conversation.

"Matt had some choice words for me, and he's right," Dean said. "I haven't been in the field for many years, spending far too much time behind a desk. Not that it's an excuse."

"I knew your background and should have asked you to flank us. But don't be surprised if I don't want you as a partner."

"I suppose I deserve that." He turned a sheet around to show her what he was reading. "Ryder has identified the five people currently still alive but missing. He's sending agents out for a welfare check and to apprise them of the situation. We're hoping one or more of them can identify the location of Havenwood. However, he's also reached out to local law enforcement throughout southwest Colorado asking if anyone has familiarity with Havenwood, by name or description."

"Great idea."

"He tried before, on a larger scale, had no bites. Now that the lab narrowed down the region, he contacted each of the local agencies personally, including the US Forest Service. But we're still looking at millions of acres. And there's no guarantee that the poppies were grown at Havenwood."

Matt walked into the restaurant, sat and said, "Tess and Greg Miller."

"The couple with the kid," Kara said.

Matt nodded. "I thought they'd be the most difficult to find, using the common name Miller, but they were the easiest. They live in Colorado Springs, have a seven-year-old daughter and five-year-old son. He works for the county in maintenance and she works from home as a seamstress. The locals did a welfare check, they are alive and well, and I'm sending Sloane and Jim out to interview them. Then they'll check on Andrew Gardner. There's nothing more Jim can do here, so if we don't have another lead, they're going back to Virginia from Colorado Springs."

"What about protection for the Millers?" Kara asked.

"I couldn't get it authorized from our end, but Jim will talk to local law enforcement, and he's also going to suggest they go on a vacation for a while. They have two little kids—I don't think it'll be difficult to convince them to leave."

"What about the other three?" Dean asked.

"We have full names and their socials, but that's it. We don't know where they are." Matt looked at his phone. "Bridget O'Malley, twenty-nine; Cal Carpenter, twenty-four; Amber Nelson, thirty-two." He looked from Dean to Kara. "We're writing a memo for law enforcement nationwide that a threat has been made on their lives and the FBI needs to speak with them. That's all we can do right now."

"I was telling Kara about the threads Ryder's pulling."

"There's more," Matt said. "Catherine suggested they scan all of Riley's drawings and our IT experts are running a program to identify the plants, flowers, and animals. We may be able to pinpoint a tighter area to explore. Riley is working on the town map. When we get that, we're going to run it against satellite images. It'll take time, but I'm a lot more confident we'll find them sooner rather than later."

He checked his watch. "I need you back on babysitting detail, Kara. Michael and I are running down a lead at a motel forty miles south of here, outside Pagosa Springs. Based on our BOLO, one of the managers called, said the sketches match two guests who checked in. They haven't checked out."

"I'm on it," Kara said, as she got up. "I'll send the map to Ryder when Riley is done."

"Thanks, Kara," Matt said.

She went upstairs and checked in with Sloane before she left for Colorado Springs. Then she went over to where Riley was still working.

The map had taken on a life of its own. It was detailed with every structure labeled in perfect tiny block print. "It's not to scale," Riley said with a frown. "I think the houses are farther apart. And the greenhouse and barn are more south..."

Kara said, "This is exactly what we need. You can tweak it all you want, but it gives us a place to start. Let me take pictures and then you can continue tweaking it."

Riley agreed. While Kara took several pictures with her phone camera, Riley asked, "Agent Costa said that he and Agent Harris found where Anton may be staying?"

"Yes. Hopefully we'll end this sooner rather than later." That they hadn't checked out didn't mean anything—they could have grabbed their things and bolted. But they could be back at any time. The room hadn't been cleaned, and that meant they could get prints and possibly more evidence tying Ginger to the poisoning of Gardner—or both of them to the murder of Donovan Smith.

The sooner they were in custody, the sooner Riley would be safe.

38

Pagosa Springs, Colorado

Matt showed his ID to the manager and said, "You spoke with the Rio Grande sheriff about two guests that matched our BOLO."

"Yep," the manager said. "A dark green Ford truck, right?"

"Yes. The last two numbers are 3-1."

"Here's the registration card, and I checked the plate myself."

Matt looked at the registration card. Ginger Ann Bellamy.

"There was a man with Ms. Bellamy?"

"Yep, but he wasn't with her when she checked in. They're supposed to register each guest, but some people don't. I seen him, though, couple of times. Big guy, tall and broad, not overweight. Dark hair, kinda long."

"I need to see their room."

He looked at a wall of keys, grabbed one labeled 119, and handed it to Matt. "Last room downstairs, far side of the first building."

"When was the last time you saw either of them?"

"They came in yesterday in the truck, about five, five thirty," the manager said.

That would put them coming here from the lodge where Riley was staying, it was about a forty-five-minute drive, and they had seen Anton at four ten in the afternoon. Matt asked, "And when did they leave?"

"An hour later. Six thirty, that I'm pretty certain about, because I had a pizza delivered and it came about the same time they left."

"They didn't check out."

"No, sir. I assumed they were going to dinner. When I left at nine, they weren't back. My night manager said he didn't see their truck all night. Not everyone checks out, but they're paid through Sunday."

"Thank you," Matt said. He held up the key. "I'll bring this back."

"Oh, and there was another guy here, too. I only seen him once leaving their room. Younger than Ms. Bellamy and the dark-haired guy, maybe early thirties? Light hair, on the short side. Maybe five-nine? Ten?"

"You're certain he was with them?"

The manager shrugged. "Couldn't say for sure, but he came out of their room when they was in there, so I assume they knew each other."

Matt left and caught up with Michael, who had walked around the exterior of the buildings. "Truck isn't here," Michael said. "There's only one entrance, no way they can exit the back, the bathroom window is too small for someone to climb through."

"Room 119. Manager said they're not here, but they could have parked elsewhere and walked in." He told Michael about the third guy.

"Logical," Michael said. "If two were in Fort Collins to kill Donovan Smith, the third was here and staying in the cabin by Morrison's house."

Matt and Michael approached the door with caution. Michael knocked loudly while Matt stood to the side, hand on his weapon.

"Ms. Bellamy, FBI."

Silence. No movement, no voices.

"Ginger Bellamy," Michael said, "we have management permission and are coming in." He nodded to Matt, who unlocked the door, then stepped aside. Michael pushed it open, and they counted to three before Matt entered and Michael covered him.

The room was empty. They quickly cleared the closet, bathroom, and under the bed—the only places a person could hide.

"Clear," Michael said.

They looked around the room. The bed was made, but rumpled. The motel only had housekeeping every three days, per the sign on the wall. So tomorrow it would have been cleaned up, sheets changed.

There were no suitcases in the closet, no clothes there or in the drawers, no toiletries in the bathroom. They weren't coming back.

But they hadn't completely cleaned out the place. Matt retrieved his evidence collection kit from the car. He and Michael put on gloves.

Prints in motel rooms were notoriously difficult to use, but Matt wanted Ginger's prints. She was the suspect in Andrew Gardner's poisoning. They could make a case for Anton attacking a federal agent, and the beer mug was at the county crime lab for processing. They might be able to get prints from it, but the condensation on the glass probably damaged them.

Michael printed the bedroom—door handle inside and out, lamps, knobs. Matt printed the bathroom—toilet handle, sink, towel rack, inside knob. There were no glasses in the room, but the garbage was still there.

Under take-out bags was a card identical to the one included with the flowers. It had been partly written on, but she'd crossed it out and tore it in two. "Bingo," he said and put the two halves into an evidence bag, sealed and labeled it.

Michael preserved the fingerprints on cards designed for the purpose, slid each card into an individual protective envelope, and put them together in their own evidence bag.

They found several wilted red poppies in the trash and on the floor, which they collected. The flowers might be the most important find—if the lab could connect these poppies with those found on the victims, that would tie Ginger and Anton to four murders.

But not Jesse Morrison. No poppies were found anywhere in his house or property.

The receipts attached to the take-out bags indicated the food was paid for with cash, but Matt sealed them anyway. They might follow up with the clerks to see if there was anything else to learn about their suspects: which one came in; if they were together or alone; was anyone else with them, such as the unknown third man; did they say anything; what was their demeanor.

"Let's send this to Quantico," Matt said. "If they can match the poppies, and coupled with Riley's statement—and Andrew's, if he regains consciousness—we should be able to get a warrant for Havenwood."

"When we find it," Michael added.

"We'll find it," Matt said with confidence. He looked again around the room and said, "I don't think they're coming back, but since they have the room paid through Sunday, we need to talk to the manager and have him contact us if he sees their truck. Call Ryder and arrange to send the evidence."

Matt and Michael took the evidence to the sheriff's office in Del Norte to ship off to Quantico, then headed back toward South Fork. The roads had been cleared and the sky was a brilliant blue, but the cold weather had created patches of ice, making the roads slick. Matt was happy to let Michael take the wheel—he'd been raised in Chicago and worked out of the Detroit office for three years; he had far more experience driving in snow than Matt, who'd been raised in Miami and spent the bulk of his FBI career in Tucson.

Ryder called and Matt put him on speaker, then said, "Did you get my message about the package coming from the motel?"

"Yes. They're expecting it and I've indicated that it's urgent. That doesn't always mean they'll jump on it."

Evidence processing could take weeks or months depending on the type and the backlog. Priority went to cases that had pending trial dates; Matt would be near the bottom of the list. But he had one thing going for him: Jim Esteban. When Jim got back to Quantico, he could process the evidence in the mobile crime lab that was stored on-site.

"Kara sent Riley's map of Havenwood," Ryder continued. "The computer unit at Quantico has uploaded it and is running it against satellite footage from last summer, which they determine will give us the best chance of identifying the area. It's going to take anywhere from a few hours to a day."

"I expected much longer."

"It's a state-of-the-art program. We also found Bridget O'Malley. She's living outside Helena, Montana, and two agents are on their way to talk to her. I briefed them and if they learn anything they'll pass it on."

"Thanks for the update. The sheriff is calling, anything else?"

"No."

Matt switched over the call. "Yes, Sheriff?"

"There's a trespasser at the Morrison house. The neighbor at the bottom of the road called it in. A dark green truck. I sent two deputies, but they're nearly an hour away. Since you just left here ten minutes ago heading toward the mountain, you're closer."

Anton and Ginger? Very possible, Matt thought.

"We'll check it out."

39

South Fork, Colorado

The fire alarm in the hotel went off and Kara knew there was no fire.

Riley jumped up, panic on her face. "There's a fire?"

Odd, Kara thought. Whenever she heard a fire alarm she assumed a malfunction or someone pulled it. Her last thought was there was an actual fire.

"I highly doubt it," Kara said. "We're going to stay put for a few minutes."

"But what if there *is* a fire? We're on the third floor, we could be trapped!"

"Stay. I'll call."

If she could hear anything through the ear-splitting *whir-whir-whir* of the alarm, she thought as she called the head of security on his cell phone.

On the fifth ring when she was almost certain she was being

sent to voice mail, he answered. "Agent Quinn," he shouted. "I'm helping evacuate the hotel."

Detective Quinn, but she didn't say it. "Is there a fire?"

"We don't know yet."

"Smoke? Flames? Gas?"

"The alarm goes off, we're required by the fire department to clear the building until they respond and give us the green light. You need to leave. I'll meet you in the lobby and escort you out."

"There's no fire," Kara said, frustrated.

"I don't know what to tell you. I don't think there is either, but there are regulations and the hotel will be fined if we don't comply."

"Call me if there is an actual fire and I'll bring Ms. Pierce out, and if the fire chief has an issue with it, he can talk to me."

She ended the call before he pushed again.

"No fire, we're going to ride this out."

Riley still looked terrified.

Kara texted her team about the situation and her decision to stay in the room. She ended it with: If there's an actual fire, jumping from the window won't kill us. Ha.

She sent it, grinned. Immediately, Matt texted back:

Agree with your decision. Keep us informed. Trespasser at Morrison's. Michael and I checking it out. Stay alert.

Kara walked over to the window and looked out to the front. There weren't a lot of guests here right now, since this hotel catered to the skiing crowd. She craned her neck and saw a half dozen or so. A few more exited as she watched. Out of the corner of her eye she saw a lone male rider in ski gear driving an ATV from the field behind the hotel to the parking lot, then lost sight of him.

She looked at the vehicles in the lot. No dark green Ford truck that she could see, but a couple of the vehicles were covered in snow. Also unlikely to be their suspects.

Someone had pulled the alarm to lure Riley out. Most likely to kill her. Maybe because she *was* Calliope's daughter, they'd bring her back to Havenwood. Kara figured sixty-forty, but neither option was good.

Her head pounded from the alarms, but they had to stop sometime.

Riley still looked worried, but she'd sat down and watched Kara pace the room. Kara went to the door and looked out the peephole. It provided a wide-angle view of the hall; no one was there.

She heard sirens and walked over to the window again. "Fire is here," she said loudly over the alarm. She didn't know if Riley heard her.

Two minutes later, blissfully, the alarms went silent. The ringing continued in her ears. She called the security chief again. "News?"

"Fire is clearing the building. I told them you were there protecting a witness. They may want to talk to you."

"Fine by me," she said and ended the call.

Five minutes later, the security chief called her back. "Agent Quinn?"

Again, she didn't correct him. "All clear?"

"We need you down here. There's a female body. She's dead."

Matt and Michael walked the perimeter of Morrison's house and saw no disturbance—and no truck. There were fresh tire marks going up and back, and the sheriff hadn't been out here this morning since the storm, so Matt was on alert.

He and Michael checked the house—no sign of a break-in and the police seal was intact. Then the barn, which was clear. They walked up the steep path to the small cabin to ensure that the intruder hadn't returned. It, too, had an unbroken police seal.

They returned to their SUV and drove back to the neighbor's house to get her statement. If Anton and Ginger had been here, he didn't see any sign of them now.

Matt parked on the edge of the two-lane highway in front of the neighbor's home. From here, they couldn't even see Morrison's place, but Mrs. Chastain would be able to see any vehicle going up Morrison's drive.

They walked up to the door and Michael knocked. Matt stayed two feet behind him and looked around the yard. The house was set back from the road and the snowplows had piled hills of the powdery white in front of the fencing. There were no cars, but they were off the main highway and there was no ski access from this area based on the maps he'd studied.

No one came to the door. Matt heard a television inside. Michael said, "She's a seventy-nine-year-old widow. Maybe she's hard of hearing."

Michael pounded on the door. "Mrs. Chastain? It's the FBI. You called."

They waited and almost walked away to check out the property when the door opened. The woman was tiny with white hair and a hunched back. "Hello?" she said loudly.

Michael and Matt both showed their IDs. "Ma'am, you called about a trespasser?"

"Trespasser?"

"Yes," Michael said. "Did you call about seeing a dark green pickup truck?"

"Nooo," she said slowly. "I didn't call anyone today. My granddaughter called me this morning, I'm going to be a great-grandma again!"

"So you did not call the sheriff's station?" Matt said.

"Nooo, I did not. I've seen them around the last couple days, talked to a nice deputy, but I didn't talk to them today, I assure you. Is there a problem?"

"No, ma'am, sorry to bother you," Matt said quickly and

walked away. He pulled out his phone and called Kara. "Something's going on, be on alert. We were sent on a false alarm to Morrison's house. We're coming back to the hotel, ETA twenty minutes."

"We have a dead body here. Someone dumped her out on the deck either right before or right after they set off the fire alarm."

"Is everyone okay?"

"Yep, everyone but the dead person."

Kara wasn't going to leave Riley alone in the room, and she didn't want her to go outside and see the body. She brought her downstairs as she called Dean, hanging up when she saw him standing in the lobby. "Have you inspected the body? Do you know what's going on?" she asked him.

"I was waiting for you."

Kara turned to the security chief. "Who's with the body?"

"My two men."

"Stay here with Riley. Don't let her out of your sight," Kara said to the security chief. Turning to Riley, who looked shell-shocked, she added, "Hey, it's going to be okay. Just hang here, stick with Mr. Young, okay? Matt and Michael are on their way back."

Riley nodded, but Kara didn't think that she heard her. She was staring out the window.

Kara followed her gaze. She couldn't see the body from here, but Young's two security guys were standing on the far edge of the deck.

She said to Young, "No one goes in or out of this lobby until the sheriff gets here, understood?"

"Yes, ma'am."

Kara and Dean went out the double doors to the deck. There were two sets of footprints leading from the door to the edge of the deck, as far from the hotel as you could get while still staying on the platform. There, at the top of stairs that went down into the field, was a body. Kara didn't need to approach the body to know that someone from Havenwood had dumped her here—poppies littered the scene like large drops of blood. They had been scattered not only on the body, but down the stairs, as if marking a trail.

Dean asked the men, "Who found her?"

"I did," the tall, younger guy said. "I thought it was an animal, and then..." He gulped. "I haven't left since. I called my partner, he informed Chief Young, then came out here to stand with me."

Kara stared at the dead woman. She wore jeans and a flannel shirt, well-worn black sneakers. No jacket. Her dark red hair was damp and matted, from snow and blood. Her throat had been slit like the others, but there were bruises both old and new on her face; her wrist appeared to be broken. The blood was dry; she hadn't been killed here.

Kara knew exactly who she was. She recognized her from Riley's sketches and the photo in Jesse Morrison's bedroom.

"It's Thalia," she told Dean.

She was about to go back inside to call Matt when Dean said, "There's a note."

She looked again at the body. Dean was correct; a white envelope stuck out of the breast pocket, partly covered by Thalia's long hair.

Kara shouldn't disturb the crime scene, but when she saw that FBI had been written in bold letters, she said fuck it, took a picture with her phone, pulled on gloves she had in her back pocket, and yanked the paper out. Dean didn't say a word.

The envelope wasn't sealed. She opened it.

We will exchange your agent for Riley in 24 hours. Wait for our instructions.

Kara ran into the lodge, pulling her phone out to call Matt. Who had they grabbed? Sloane? Jim?

"Kara," Dean called out, following her.

Matt didn't answer. She called Michael.

On the fourth ring, he answered. "Michael, the body at the lodge is Thalia. There's a note that they have an agent. Is everyone accounted for? Matt's not answering his phone."

"He's here in the car with me talking to Ryder. We're five minutes from the hotel."

"I'm calling Jim and Sloane. We'll be in the lobby waiting for you." She ended the call and started toward the doors. She called Jim. He answered almost immediately.

"Yep?"

"You safe?"

"Yes, Sloane and I just pulled up in front of the Miller house. What's wrong?"

"I don't know. They're playing fucking games with us right now. But I have a bad feeling. Be careful. Where's Agent Stewart, from Denver?"

"I don't know."

"Find him, tell him to do a head count of all his agents who were working on the Morrison place."

"What's going on Kara?"

"Those bastards dumped Thalia's body at the hotel and left a note that they have one of our agents. Dean's with me, Matt's with Michael and I just talked to them. You and Sloane are safe. So either it's a false alarm to screw with us, or they took one of Stewart's people."

"I'm on it," Jim said and ended the call.

Matt asked Michael, "What was that?"

"Kara said Thalia's body was left at the hotel with a note that they have a federal agent. She's checking with Jim and Sloane."

Matt relayed the information to Ryder and told him to check on the status of everyone in the field and get back to him.

Michael turned into the hotel parking lot. There were people milling about outside, and two fire trucks were still there.

Suddenly, they were rammed hard from behind, forcing their

car into a parked vehicle. The air bags went off and slammed Matt in the face, the powder making him cough and his eyes burn.

But immediately he knew this wasn't an accident. This was a setup.

His phone had fallen to the floor, and he couldn't see anything at first. Then he heard gunfire and thought for sure that he and Michael were dead.

Matt reached for his gun at the same time as a hammer came down and smashed his passenger door window. He was grabbed by two sets of rough hands as a van pulled up and he was pushed inside. He heard more gunfire and feared for Michael. He fought back, but his defense was short-lived when they hit him on the back of the head and he fell stunned to the floor of the van. His hands were tied behind him and he felt someone grab his gun from his holster. They were moving fast.

The entire abduction took less than one minute.

40

South Fork, Colorado

"This is bullshit!" Kara exclaimed as she paced the small room.

Riley was sitting quietly in the corner. She had wanted to go to the adjoining room to lie down, but Kara said no. They needed Riley here—Kara didn't want to spare an agent to sit with her, and Riley might have information they needed to find Matt.

Michael and Dean were sitting at the table; Tony and Catherine were on the other end of a video chat.

Michael looked like shit. He was cut up from the accident and he probably had a concussion. They hadn't been shooting to kill him, at least Michael said they weren't, but one of the bullets had grazed his bicep and he had a bandage around his arm. He refused to sit down.

Matt was gone and they had few leads.

The dark green truck that Anton and Ginger had been seen

in last night had been used to ram the FBI's vehicle. It had been left behind and the sheriff's department was combing through it for evidence. The van that matched the description of the one outside Donovan Smith's house had pulled alongside the FBI vehicle, but the security cameras weren't in range of the actual abduction. Based on all the angles they could find, five people had been involved when they thought they were only dealing with three. Another truck sped off after the van, and they suspected that truck was involved as well—and based on the feeds, it had been in the parking lot all morning. Someone had been watching them.

Five people were in South Fork watching, waiting for an opportunity to grab, or kill, Riley.

When the fire alarm didn't work, did they already know they were going to take an agent? It didn't matter who. They had divided the team by making the false call of trespassers. Were they just waiting for agents to show up, knowing they would after the body was found?

It could have been any of them. But it was Matt.

"Where are we with the satellite maps?" Kara asked. "All the sketches and pictures? Why can't we narrow this place down?"

"Ryder is working on it," Tony assured her. "We are doing everything we can to find Havenwood, but there is no evidence that they took Matt there."

"Where else would they go? This is a group that has been off the grid for decades. I don't think they have a bunch of places around the country to hang out."

Dean said, "I agree with Detective Quinn."

Kara was surprised. She had taken out her anger on him earlier when she felt stuck. He'd offered to stay with Riley so she could coordinate with Michael, but she said no because she didn't trust him. That was unfair, she realized now. He was a trained FBI agent and while he was no longer a field agent, he wasn't completely incompetent. He could protect Riley in a hotel room.

But Riley was her responsibility—it was the last order Matt had given her, and if Kara lost her…well, she wasn't going to.

Dean continued, "While it isn't logical that they would take a federal agent to their sanctuary, it's the only place that they feel safe and secure. They may not have thought it through, or they may not realize we have resources to find them. They must know we'll have people out in full-force looking for our agent, but they are also confident that they are well hidden and won't be found. Once they determine they aren't being followed, they will head directly there. It's home, it's safety, it's security.

"Also," he said, "they said twenty-four hours. Why twenty-four and not twelve? Six? Immediately? This tells me they have a plan. They will want to trade Matt in a place they can control, where they feel they won't be apprehended. Or, they have a plan to grab Riley within the twenty-four hours because our attention will be divided."

"Where does that leave Matt?" Kara asked. "And why didn't they tell us *how* they were going to communicate the demands? They don't have his phone, that was found in the car."

"They know you are in South Fork. They'll likely communicate through the hotel, or the sheriff, or call Denver FBI," Tony said. "We will be ready to trace any call."

"They won't contact us from Havenwood," Michael said. "Even though they've been off the grid for years, several of them come and go and they'll have some idea that we'd be able to trace any call they make. They also can't think that we'd trade a civilian even for an FBI agent. I don't see their plan."

Michael was their tactical expert. He was always a rock in every situation. Kara had never seen him this stressed. He'd disabled a bomb she held, he'd rescued her from a sinking ship, but right now he seemed lost. Because he had been with Matt during the abduction? She couldn't lose Michael's strength. She needed it more than ever.

Dean said, "There are several points we need to consider.

First, our disadvantage—that until recently this cult was unknown to us—is diminishing because we have Riley who has helped us understand their mentality and provided information on how to find them. We will locate them, and I don't think they have the capacity to understand how quickly we can do so. To our advantage is that they have been off the grid for decades. They may not have a detailed plan. I concur with Kara's original theory that they expected to grab Riley during the fire alarm. Yet, they acted quickly enough to kidnap an agent they knew was returning from the Morrison property because they'd made that call. We also now believe they were staking out the building for the last two days."

Kara saw Riley shiver. She wasn't in the mood to console anyone right now. Riley was alive; she would stay alive.

Catherine spoke up for the first time. "They may think that law enforcement will trade for one of their own, and they showed the lengths they are willing to go through the murder of now six people."

Dean nodded. "They'll be prepared for a trap, so whatever they tell us when they call, it won't be what they actually plan to do."

Catherine said, "I concur. No negotiating without proof of life."

Kara's stomach twisted into a knot. How could Catherine be so calm? She was Matt's *friend*. His longest friend in the FBI.

Maybe you're the one who needs to get a grip.

She had to focus. Matt as colleague, not lover. Matt as cop, not the man she loved.

She walked over to the table and stood behind Michael, put her hand on his shoulder. He was tense, and she should have been less angry and more focused during the meeting. Recognizing that, recognizing her own weakness, made her stronger.

"Okay," Kara said, forcing herself to be calm. "What's the plan while we wait for contact? How far along is Ryder and the cyber team in finding Havenwood? If we believe that Matt is there, then we need a plan to retrieve him."

"Ryder is confident he'll find it," Tony said. "It's the timing that is problematic. They're running the program through multiple systems and they're optimistic it'll be only a few hours. Once we locate Havenwood, Michael and the Denver SWAT leader will coordinate a tactical plan. Kara, I read your report about the potential number of children on-site. The safety of the children is our number one priority. We want to find and extract Matt and then arrest those responsible with minimal casualties. This will come down to a negotiation. Therefore, I'm putting ranking agent Dean Montero in temporary command of the MRT. Dean is a trained hostage negotiator and cult expert. Is everyone clear on that?"

"Yes, sir," Michael said. Kara didn't say anything.

"As soon as we locate Havenwood, I'll call in." Tony was about to sign off when he said, "Ryder has something."

Ryder popped onto the screen. He was in the FBI lab at Quantico.

He looked like he hadn't slept in days. Circles under his eyes, his face unusually pale, and something Kara had never seen before: Ryder was unshaven. He hadn't shaved in at least two days.

"Hey," she said as if no one else was in the room or on the screen. "We're going to find him, Ryder."

He nodded, somber. "The cybercrime unit and I have broken through the security of the message board that Jesse Morrison ran. We've located the last two individuals Riley Pierce identified—Cal is going by Cal Stone, a different name than what his false identity is under. He's working on a ranch in West Texas. Amber died of a drug overdose last year. We have agents investigating her death, and interviewing Mr. Stone."

Kara shot a glance at Riley, who was sitting on the opposite side of the room. She looked almost catatonic.

"Partially good news," Dean said. "We can get Cal Stone into protective custody."

"We also identified an unknown female who goes by Abby," Ryder said. "She posted on the message board that she was struggling. Thalia had rescued her eighteen months ago, but we haven't found information as to where she landed. We've contacted the hospital and SSA to find a female called Abby or Abigail who falls under the same parameters we identified in how Morrison hacked the system, but won't have an answer until tomorrow or Monday. Abby reached out to Morrison several times at the beginning and he gave her advice. Then nothing until February. She said she needed help. He said he'd reach out privately. I don't know how he did that, but it was on March 2nd, more than four weeks ago."

Catherine said, "Which is in the window of TOD Jim established for Morrison. He could have called or texted her. Denver has his phone records and will confirm either way."

Ryder said, "We also noted an IP address that accessed the message board twice a week which doesn't match Morrison's. It's a private IP, and it'll take time to track, but I believe that was Thalia checking the board. She has done so regularly for years, since it was first set up. The last time she checked was March 4th."

Kara ran through everything they knew. It was April 4; Merrifield, Crossman, and Benson were killed nearly two weeks ago; Jim had figured that Morrison was killed two weeks before them, give or take a few days.

Michael said, "Morrison gave Abby his address and then she killed him? Tortured and killed him? Why?"

A faint voice behind them said, "She went back."

Everyone turned to her.

Dean said, "Riley, please explain."

"I knew Abby would never be able to live on her own. She was dependent on the community. I never would have rescued her."

"Do you think she set this up?"

Riley shook her head. "I don't know how Thalia rescued people after I left. She could get in and out of the valley—it's how we communicated. She'd leave a red poppy with a day and time, and I would meet her. She was a ghost. So I think she must have watched, picked Abby for some reason, and Abby went with her. Then Abby became lonely and scared and went back to Havenwood. Begged them to forgive her. As penance, they made her reveal everything she knew about Thalia's operation. They used Abby and the message board to find Jesse, and Thalia walked into the trap." Her voice cracked, but she didn't break down.

"It's logical," Dean said. "Cult members, even when they leave, often have feelings of deep sorrow, low self-esteem, lack of drive, fear of the unknown. Returning to a place they know, even if it's dangerous or imperfect, is preferable to isolation and loneliness."

"Any word about the satellite program?" Kara asked. She knew Ryder would tell them as soon as he knew, but she couldn't help but ask.

"We're using every available computer. As soon as I know, you all will know."

"Thank you," she said.

Tony signed off, and Kara texted Ryder.

I'll find him. I promise.

Ryder had been with Matt and the MRT from the beginning. The first hire. Ryder was the backbone of the team. He anticipated the needs of everyone. He set up their logistical operations. He was the go-to person for everything research related. But Kara had known, from the beginning, that Ryder's topmost loyalty was to Matt and Matt alone. Of course he was loyal to the FBI and their team, but Ryder had a deep respect and admiration for his boss. This had to be hurting him as much as her. Especially since he was there, not here.

Michael shut the laptop and rubbed his eyes. Dean said, "The sheriff is transporting Thalia's body to Colorado Springs, where Jim will assist in the autopsy. They have better facilities than this county. If there is any evidence on the body, they'll know tonight."

Dean left the room and Kara said to Michael, "Are you really okay?"

Michael stared at her, his eyes rimmed red. "Dammit, Kara, I should have been able to stop this."

"If you tried, they would have killed you. But they hit you from behind then fired multiple bullets to pin you down."

"I don't care!"

"I do. Matt wouldn't want you dead trying to save him. Neither do I." She hugged him tight; he held on as if he were drowning. "We'll find him, Michael. This is in no way your fault."

41

Unknown Location, Colorado

Matt was in and out of consciousness, but based on how his body felt, the twilight, and the sense of elevation, he figured they'd been on the road for four hours. He couldn't see his watch because his hands were bound behind him.

He did an assessment of his injuries and didn't think anything was broken. He definitely had a concussion—his head pounded and when he moved he became dizzy. He might have a cracked rib, and felt bruises everywhere.

He was cold, but it could be worse.

Thirty minutes after he was taken, the van pulled over. He heard another vehicle drive up behind them and stop. Voices were muffled, but there were at least four people. They took him from the van and put him in the back of a truck with a camper shell. That's when they blindfolded and shackled him. But they also provided him with a sleeping bag and blankets. It took him a while as they bounced over rough terrain, but he managed to lie on a blanket to keep the metal floor from making him too cold, and the sleeping bag was thick enough to provide some heat, especially since he wasn't dressed for the cold. He had on slacks and a button-down shirt with his lined FBI jacket.

Matt had to maintain his strength as best he could. He stretched as much as possible even though his wrists and ankles were chained. He listened for any identifying sounds, but heard little over the roar of the motor.

A change in terrain and speed told him they were approaching their destination. The truck kicked into four-wheel drive and bucked as it rolled over uneven, snow-topped terrain. He was tossed from side to side and at one point slid all the way to the front of the truck bed as they went down a steep incline.

Just when he thought he was going to puke, the ride smoothed out and he forced himself to breathe steadily.

Then they stopped.

The engine shut off.

He smelled wood smoke and fresh snow and something absolutely delicious cooking that made him hungry, even through his nausea. Voices, low and indistinct, murmured as if a crowd had formed. He tried to make out individual words, but it was a low din and his ears were still ringing from the long drive.

A moment later, the back of the camper shell opened. Two pairs of hands pulled him out and he fell to the ground. The shackles were removed from his ankles and he was pulled to stand. His knees buckled, but two people held him upright.

No one spoke directly to him, but he heard voices here and there.

It was near dark and the night was getting colder. The scent of damp pine overwhelming. He was forced to walk and snow slipped into his shoes, making him shiver.

About two hundred steps later, they stopped walking. He was pushed to his knees. He didn't have the strength to try to rise.

"What have you done?" a female voice said.

"We did exactly what you said, Calliope. They had Riley too well guarded. So we grabbed one of theirs."

"You brought him *here*? No!"

They'd taken him to Havenwood?

"They can't track him. He's blindfolded. We'll keep him in the prison until they make the exchange."

"Whose idea was it to bring him here? To our home?"

Silence.

"No one wants to admit to their failure? I trusted you, all of you, and you bring a federal agent to Havenwood?"

"We'll take him back," a new voice said quietly, a man who had been with them but hadn't spoken much.

"Too late for that," Calliope said. "Put him in the prison. I'll figure it out. But not one of you is welcome in my house tonight."

Silence fell around them, then someone said, "Well, shit. Don't look at me like that, Evan. You agreed."

"No, I didn't," Evan, the soft-spoken man, said. "I just didn't object because you wouldn't have listened."

"Riley has messed me up," the other man said. "She's alive. I just can't believe it." Mumbling, then the same man said, "It was a good plan. But we should have lit the place on fire for real, then she couldn't have stayed inside. Marcus, help me take him to the pit."

Matt was hauled up and half dragged a hundred feet. A door was opened and he smelled blood and vomit and death.

They took him downstairs into a room as cold as the outdoors.

"Anton, we need to restart this fire. If he freezes to death that's not going to get Riley back."

"Calliope isn't going to let him leave," Anton said. "But yeah, start the fire while I secure him."

Matt's hands were unchained, then reattached to a metal rod along the wall. He heard Marcus about ten feet away putting wood into a stove and crumbling paper. A minute later a faint warmth started to fill the small space.

Then without another word, they left.

Matt lost track of time, and may have fallen asleep or, more likely, passed out, but the room was almost warm when he heard the lock above him click. A minute later, two people walked down the stairs.

"Take off his blindfold," Calliope said.

The blindfold was removed and Matt blinked rapidly. His vision was blurry, and there was only a dim light in the room and the glow from the fireplace. There were pictures tacked to the walls, but they were blurry and he couldn't make them out.

He turned to Calliope. Even though his vision was unclear, he recognized her. She was one of the most beautiful women he'd ever seen. Thick and bright red hair cascaded in curls down her back. Her face was smooth and fresh, unlined, with high cheekbones and large round blue eyes. She wore no makeup and had no blemishes. She was tall—nearly as tall as Matt—and curvy in a flowing dress with a white wool cape over her shoulders. She smiled. "I apologize for the treatment. My decision to put you in our prison was rash because your visit was unexpected."

"You had a federal agent kidnapped," he said.

As if he didn't speak, she continued, "I have had time to think things through, and if you behave yourself, you may join the community for dinner. Anton will find you clean clothes and you can wash up. You have thirty minutes."

"You're not going to let me live," he said.

She didn't respond. "You can obey, have a meal, and sleep in a bed—or you can be difficult and rot in this prison all night. It makes no difference to me."

Here, he was trapped. Out there, he might have a chance to escape.

"Very well, I will accept your generous offer."

She smiled. "I am truly glad for that. Anton, see to him. Oh, and, Agent Costa? One step out of line, and you'll be on your knees. Don't test me."

Anton unshackled Matt and pushed him up the stairs. They walked across the small village. It was freezing here, and he wasn't dressed for the weather. But he went where Anton led him.

The village was...pretty. Pinpoint lights in the trees, ground lighting that rose above the snow. Small cabins that lined the path, some that were built up on the hill. It was a charming, quaint camp.

But he saw no one. He heard faint music, the clanking of dishes, the quiet clucks of chickens. He smelled hay and fresh snow and food.

His stomach growled.

But everyone was inside their cabins. No one watched as Anton brought Matt to the two-story house on the edge of a wide-open square with a huge ancient tree in the center. Benches had been built all around, as if they had meetings or plays here.

Anton brought him upstairs. "There is a washroom where you can clean up, clothing in the dresser. Someone will fetch you in fifteen minutes. I expect you clean and dressed for Calliope, or I will take you back to the pit."

Anton left. The lock clicked in the door.

He was still a prisoner.

Matt listened and when he heard Anton go back downstairs, he thoroughly searched the room for anything he could use as a weapon.

The double bed was solid wood, hand carved. No screws or bolts. Beautiful craftsmanship, he thought. A dresser and rocking chair were the only other pieces of furniture. Again, handmade with no sharp edges, metal, or loose parts. He inspected every inch. He could remove a drawer, but it would be unwieldy to use, other than to maybe hit someone over the head as they were coming into the room. There was men's clothing in the drawers—a handmade sweater, loose-fitting drawstring pants, underwear, thermals. He closed the drawer without changing.

Two sconces were bolted into the wall on either side of the lone window. He could break the glass and possibly use it as a weapon, but that would be dangerous for him as well with no guarantee that he'd be able to escape.

Especially since he had no idea where he was.

The bathroom had only a wash basin and toilet. They had running water here, which was pretty amazing considering they were in the middle of nowhere. They must have a well—likely, he thought, if the property had been partly developed when Athena and her husband moved here. But to support the entire town of more than a hundred people? Did they have an engineer in their midst? Or learn to do it themselves?

On a built-in ledge there was a flimsy travel toothbrush, tiny toothpaste, small bar of homemade soap, and hand towel. No mirror.

He washed his hands and face, wincing at the bolts of pain from cuts on his scalp. The water he rinsed off was pink, and as he dabbed the cuts, the cloth became covered in splotches of red, but nothing appeared to be bleeding heavily. He ran wet fingers through his hair, bit back a cry when they ran over a large bump on the back of his skull.

He could fight, but it wouldn't be pretty, and a large man like Anton would take him down really quick in his current condition.

Matt could escape, but it was night and the temperatures would be in the twenties. Even though no snow was expected, he would freeze to death in these clothes. And he knew from Riley that there were cameras covering at least part of the property. He had no idea where they were or which direction to go. It would practically be suicide to walk into the mountains at night.

His only real option was to play along. Wait this out. His

team would have a plan. They would find him—or he would try to escape.

Because there was no doubt in his mind that Calliope would never let him leave Havenwood alive.

Evan washed up, then sat in his room staring at the wall but not seeing anything. Calliope had told him to rest because he looked tired; he was tired. He'd only had a couple hours sleep each night over the last five weeks. Because of the dreams.

He had hoped being back in Havenwood would make him feel better. Havenwood was worth protecting. It was worth saving. Anyone who left was a risk to them.

Not Jane. Jane was a risk to no one. She was going to college and living a good life. It's what you would have wanted for Timmy if he hadn't been mauled to death.

He loved Calliope and loved Havenwood. He'd missed this place something fierce when he was Outside. All he could think about was coming home, taking care of his responsibilities. He had convinced himself that once he was back, all these doubts and pains would disappear.

Now that he was home, he realized they would never go away.

He had killed a bright star. He was hollow and empty inside.

Anton came to his door. "Evan?"

"Yes."

He entered. "Calliope said you might be sleeping, but since you're not, come to community dinner."

"I'm really tired, Anton."

"I'll bring you a plate. I need you fresh tomorrow, so try to sleep."

"Thank you."

Anton left and Evan rose. When he heard the others head out, he, too, left. He walked down past the barn, past the greenhouse, to the small pasture behind the horse corral, where a row of crosses marked the dead.

Seventeen crosses for the people who had died over the thirty-six-year history of Havenwood. Many old, like Athena. Many young, like Timmy.

But more than seventeen people were dead. The others were buried far from here, in a field that bloomed with wildflowers every spring.

He knelt beside Timmy's grave and silent tears fell to the earth.

Twenty minutes later, Matt was seated next to Calliope, who was at the head of one of three long tables, and across from Anton. It seemed that everyone in Havenwood was at dinner tonight. By Matt's count, there were about ninety people, and at least twenty were under eighteen. There could be more—if Calliope had patrols, for example. Anton was here, but Evan was not. Matt overheard someone talking to Garrett. Riley had told Kara that Garrett had replaced her father who had been killed.

Garrett had been in the military. He had training. Matt couldn't let his guard down.

People spoke quietly, politely. Food was brought out. Baskets of bread, plates of fresh vegetables, and tureens of what turned out to be beef stew—what Matt had smelled when he first arrived. His stomach churned in anticipation—he hadn't eaten since breakfast.

Calliope explained, "We have family dinners once a week. A way for the community to bond. We've done it my entire life. Generally, we have the dinners on Saturday, but moved it up in anticipation of you, our guest."

Matt said, "I'm not a guest—I'm a prisoner."

She stared at him with hard eyes, even though she was smiling. "You can be a prisoner. Is that what you want?"

"No, ma'am."

"Of course not. And you're smart enough to know that if you walk away, you'll be lost and die of exposure. You have no weapon, though you may think you can fight." She leaned close to him and said quietly, "I put you in the prison so you'd know that it is there. If you go back, the fire will have died out. And I will not relight it."

He believed her.

Calliope motioned for Anton to dish up a bowl for Matt. He noticed that everyone had forks and spoons, no knives. He could do damage with a fork, but not enough to escape. If he could sneak one out, he would, but it wouldn't be worth getting caught.

Everyone appeared to be in good health. No one looked him directly in the eye, other than Calliope and a few of the people sitting at her end of the table. The kids were curious, and whispered among themselves. One young woman glanced at him with trepidation, then averted her eyes when he looked at her. Did she know something he didn't?

"Eat," Calliope said, staring at Matt.

He scooped up stew with his spoon, ate. It was delicious, and he said as much.

"We have a cooperative that works," Calliope said with a wide smile. "Everyone does what they love and what they're good at. We have a team, led by Gracie and Paul, who are in charge of our weekly family dinners. They could run a top restaurant Outside—" she flicked her wrist to indicate the rest of the world "—but providing and serving community is far more satisfying. We grow all our vegetables here, in a greenhouse. We raise our own livestock and poultry. To pay for anything we can't produce ourselves—tools, gasoline for the generators—we sell crafted goods we make.

"Some people, including people in your government, don't want anyone to be self-sufficient. They want us to be dependent. We have all shunned such dependency."

"But they are dependent on you," Matt said, taking a bite of bread. It was the best bread he'd ever tasted. A woman walked over and put another bread bowl in front of Calliope. The woman was missing her pinky finger. An accident?

"We are dependent on each other, and we support each other."

"And if someone wants to leave, decides they want to try something new, you let them leave?"

"Why would anyone want to leave?"

He shrugged. "They're sick and need medical attention. They become bored with a simple lifestyle. They want to travel, meet new people."

Calliope frowned. She tapped her spoon to her glass and the chatting stopped. "Does anyone want to leave Havenwood?" she asked the group.

"No, Calliope," the group said in unison. Okay, that was super creepy, Matt thought.

She smiled benevolently at the room, then turned to Matt. "There you go."

He leaned toward her and said quietly so no one other than the few people at their end of the table could hear, "Don't lie to me, Calliope. You don't let people leave. They are trapped here. They might not see it, but they are. And when people do leave—when your sister gets them out—you hunt them down and kill them. Do these people know that?"

Her face reddened with anger, and she stood. The entire community put their utensils down and faced her.

"What is the punishment for betrayal?" she asked the group.

"Death," the group answered in unison.

Calliope's smile wasn't warm or inviting when she sat back down. It was cruel and twisted. It was the Medusa that Riley had drawn. "Everyone here," she said in a low voice, "knows exactly what the rules are and what is expected of them. They came here willingly, they stay willingly."

"Because they want to live."

"They want to live *here*. Havenwood is paradise. Those who leave are agitators who want to destroy what we have. Make no mistake, Mathias Costa. Everyone understands what's at stake. And everyone here is willing to defend it."

A chill ran down Matt's spine as he looked out to the sea of faces and realized that if the FBI came in full force, there would be casualties.

He would do everything in his power to avoid that.

SATURDAY

42

South Fork, Colorado

Kara jumped on her phone when it rang, even though it was after midnight. It was Jim.

"Hey, kiddo, how you doing?"

"Eh," she said. She wasn't going to lie to Jim, and he wouldn't believe her if she did.

"I have something. Not sure where it fits, but it could help. We just finished the autopsy of Thalia's body. A couple of things. First, she was tortured, poor woman. Broken ribs, fingers, badly beaten, cracked skull. Some bruises were more than a week old. Her prints and blood were in Jesse Morrison's house. Thalia's blood was found at the threshold of the main entrance, plus some trace hair. I looked back at photos and my notes from the crime scene, and my guess—no way to confirm, but the evidence points here—is that she was grabbed at Morrison's house sometime after his murder."

"They waited for her. Expected her. You saw Ryder's report on the message board?"

"Yes, I factored that in. So my guess is that whoever killed Thalia waited for her to come. Based on the pattern of bruises, what's healed, bones that started knitting together—she was first attacked approximately three weeks ago. Morrison was likely a week dead when she arrived, and they were waiting for her."

"The sheriff's department has taken what we learned from the message board and is talking to business owners in the area, showing them the sketches Riley created. We know at least one person stayed in the old cabin, but we need an ID."

"Good," Jim said.

"I'll ask the sheriff's department to expand the search into the mountains if you think we might find something—though it's been a month, so any evidence is likely buried in feet of snow."

"Agreed. I don't know that it would be a good use of our time and resources right now."

"Is that it?"

"No," Jim said. "I would have emailed you that. Sorry. I'm distracted. First, Sloane will be leaving for South Fork before dawn. I'm staying here to finish processing evidence, and Andrew Gardner has made a turn for the better. He came out of the coma, but they have him under sedation. They identified the substance he was poisoned with and there are long-term complications, but now that he's responding to treatment, he should be out of the woods. I'll talk to him as soon as possible."

"The sooner the better. Riley said he came to Havenwood as a teenager. He might know how to get there, at least give us more than we have now."

"I know, kid. I've read all the reports," Jim said. "Second, more about the autopsy. There are several things, and the coroner won't have his report until Monday. Thalia was kept in a cold, dank room, likely a basement with dirt floors, for an extended period of time.

"But here's the main point. She had been dead for two to six hours prior to the body dump. I could be more precise, but the cold slowed decomp, and I believe she had a lower core body temperature when she was killed, so I'm comfortable saying two to four hours. We're running more tests and could narrow it further. You already knew she wasn't killed at the lodge. She was wrapped in burlap for transport. My guess is two bags, one over her head, the other over her legs, and tied in the middle. The burlap had previously been used to store or transport marijuana. You find the burlap, I'll match it."

How that would help them find Matt, she didn't know, but at least they could tie these bastards to another murder. "Okay," she said, not knowing what else to say.

"I've also extracted blood and hair samples from the body that don't belong to the victim. I'm sending them to Quantico for DNA analysis. That's more important once we have a suspect. I can tell you that the hair samples are from three different people."

"That's really good. Lock them up, throw away the key." *When we find them,* she thought.

"And one more thing. During her last weeks of life, she breathed in wood smoke regularly, possibly from a potbellied stove like we saw in Morrison's house. The wood was infected by a fungus, specifically a type of mushroom, and we were able to narrow it down. It wouldn't be dangerous to healthy people, but because she breathed it in through the woodsmoke over a long period of time—weeks—and she was weak from being restrained, she became sick and developed a blood infection. It would have killed her without immediate treatment. But we know exactly where this fungus has been found. It's a very specific region of southwest Colorado. Quantico is already running it with the satellite search. We'll find him, Kara. I promise you, we'll find Matt."

★ ★ ★

Michael planned to relieve Kara at 2:00 a.m. so she could sleep for a couple of hours, but she doubted she would. She was looking at the picture Riley had drawn of her and Matt and wondering how she had found herself in this situation. How she had grown so close to someone that the idea of losing him made her near paralyzed with fear.

Part of it was because she was stuck. She couldn't *do* anything right now. She couldn't go out and ask questions, look for clues, knock on doors. Inaction was not in her DNA. She did much better when she had something to do, people to interrogate. Sitting on her ass made her think of what-ifs and would haves.

Plus, she'd received a voice mail from her Realtor. The seller had accepted her offer. She had a house.

But that house meant nothing if Matt wasn't around. She realized that, while she loved what she did on the Mobile Response Team, she didn't know if she would continue if someone else was in charge.

Matt was the heart of the MRT.

Riley came out of the bedroom. She sat next to Kara on the couch. Kara put the sketch down.

"I'm so sorry about everything," Riley said.

"What is your fault? Your mother? Her minions? Their decisions?" She was snippy, but lack of sleep did that to her.

"I knew my mother was capable of cruelty. I didn't think she would target anyone outside Havenwood. She's changed. I thought she would never bring a stranger to Havenwood. It is so out of her character. She's desperate. She knows I'm alive and she wants me back."

Kara let out a long breath. "She's not getting away with this. No one can kidnap an FBI agent and walk away."

"My mother believes she's invincible. That she can do anything she wants because she has some sort of…mandate from the people of Havenwood. She thinks of herself as a goddess, a benefactor. She is beautiful—I mean, objectively beautiful. She can be cruel, but justifies everything she does and you end up siding with her because it makes sense when she talks. It's only later that you think, wait, it doesn't make sense, it's mean, it's cruel."

Riley paused, then she looked directly at Kara. "I will trade myself for Matt."

"No one will let you do that."

"It's the only way to get him back."

"Matt is resourceful and smart. So is our entire team."

"She's sneaky. She's not going to give him up. She has a plan and it's probably twisted." Riley bit her lip.

"What?"

"When I was twelve, after my grandmother died, after Thalia and Robert left, my mother cracked down on people. She started rationing food as punishment. I created a stash of food because no one should be hungry, especially as a punishment. But I was reckless. I told people about it. Not everyone, but when someone got in trouble, I made sure they knew where to go. A few years later my mother found out. She set a trap—she had a pit dug, so the next person who went for food would fall. It was Donovan's brother. He fell ten feet, but that didn't kill him. She let him starve to death in the pit. When we heard his cries at night, we didn't know they were human cries." Riley was crying now. "No one knew what happened to James. And then... my mother told me. That bad boys and girls will be punished."

"That's sadistic," Kara said.

"It's important. It's why Donovan hated me and blamed me for so much that happened at Havenwood. Because I never told my mother that it was me, that I was hiding food. She knew, or I think she did, but I never stood up to her. She had a plan and it worked perfectly. She used me and an innocent boy to show she was in charge. Her plan was sick and twisted, but it worked. And then..."

"What?" Kara pushed.

"The night I took Donovan and Andrew to Thalia, she blamed another resident. She had Brian dragged into the pit. A prison. I never saw him again. It was me, and I remained silent, and Brian is dead."

"That is on your mother and her people, not on you."

"It's on me," Riley said. "I let Brian die. I could have stood up and said, 'No, Mother, it's me!' But I didn't. I remained silent. She has a plan for Matt. I don't know what it is, but if she brought him to Havenwood, she will never let him leave."

A knock on the door had Kara reaching for her gun. "Stay," she commanded Riley.

Kara looked through the peephole. She was shocked to see Ryder Kim standing there.

She opened the door and hugged him. "Ryder." She didn't want to let him go, and when he hugged her back, she almost cried.

Movement behind him had her reaching for her gun again, then she saw Catherine. She blinked. Nothing could have surprised her more.

Catherine came in with Ryder and closed the door. "All hands on deck," she said, looking Kara directly in the eye.

For Matt. She was here for Matt, and that made Kara feel better. Catherine would never like her, and Kara mostly didn't care, but maybe she would finally accept her.

Catherine smiled at Riley. "It's good to meet you in person, Riley," she said. "Your art is an amazing gift."

Riley didn't say anything.

"This is Dr. Catherine Jones," Kara said. "And our analyst, Ryder Kim." She said to the new arrivals, "Sloane will be back in the morning. Jim is going to continue working the evidence out in Colorado Springs."

"I read his report," Catherine said. "It's valuable information."

Ryder said, "I was only in the way at the lab. Even I didn't understand half of what the cyber team was doing. I can do more here, helping our team."

Michael knocked, then entered the room. He had showered and changed and looked refreshed, though he'd slept only four hours.

He was just as surprised to see Catherine and Ryder as Kara. "Kara, you need to get a couple hours downtime if we're going to find Matt tomorrow."

She stared at him. "You think I can sleep?"

"It's after two in the morning. I promise to get you if we learn anything."

The smart thing was to sleep.

Ryder said, "I'll hold him to it."

"Fine." She turned to Riley. "You're in good hands." Then she went into the adjoining room and collapsed onto the bed without taking her clothes off.

She slept and dreamt of Matt.

43

South Fork, Colorado

Kara woke up as soon as someone laid a hand on her shoulder.

It was Michael. "We found Havenwood."

She jumped up, then wobbled on her feet.

"Go splash water on your face, we still don't have Tony on the line."

She glanced at the clock: 4:45 a.m. Two and a half hours was better than nothing.

She took Michael's advice and ran cold water over her face, brushed her teeth, straightened her clothes. She stepped out just as Dean Montero came into the room. The space had become crowded, even though Ryder must have spent the time since he arrived reorganizing the workspace. There was even fresh fruit and coffee on the small bar. She grabbed a banana and poured coffee.

Riley was asleep on the couch—or pretending to sleep. Kara let her be.

Catherine was sitting at the computer typing, Ryder was putting up a map on the wall.

"Where is he?" Kara asked Ryder.

Ryder pointed to a speck in the middle of nowhere. "They're in the San Juan National Forest on over a thousand acres of land grandfathered in as private property more than a hundred years ago. It can't be sold, but the heirs can keep it in perpetuity. It's north of Durango, south of Telluride, west of state route 550, in a valley that has only one road in and out, and the road on their property isn't maintained by any government agency."

"How far away?"

"Two-hour drive to Durango, but we can take a plane there in half that. Then we don't know how long the drive will take—road conditions aren't ideal, but the west side of the state didn't see much snowfall during the last week. Talking to people on the ground there, they estimate two hours, and a four-wheel drive will be necessary. They also suggested snowmobiles or snow ATVs, but if Anton and his people drove in and out, the road should be passable."

Kara wanted to leave now, but she took in a breath. "Okay."

Tony's voice came over the computer. "I just read the report from our cyber unit and am looking at a satellite map of Havenwood now. Damn. It's really deep in there."

"Yes, sir," Ryder said, "but I've reached out to the forest ranger station in the area and the lead ranger knows the place. He goes out and checks on them once, twice a year. Has never had a problem, usually just gives advice for cutting back trees near the cabins, or tells them if there are physical dangers like the road closing. He's currently checking on road status and will meet up with us when we get there."

"Excellent," Tony said. "Dean, what's your plan?"

"Havenwood is going to reach out to us this morning. I want to be as close to their location as possible when they do that," Dean said. "My guess is they won't have Matt with them. They'll expect a trap and use him as leverage. They'll want to see Riley. If they don't, or if they think we're playing games, I can't honestly tell you what they will do."

"Why would they kill him?" Catherine asked. "They must know if they kill a federal agent they will lose their home. According to Riley, everything they did was to protect Havenwood."

"Then why take him in the first place?" Dean said. "It makes no sense, based on Calliope's psychology and what Riley remembers, that she would bring not only a stranger, but a man in authority into her camp."

"She didn't," Riley said without opening her eyes. "If he's there, she didn't know they were bringing him."

Catherine looked like she didn't believe her, but Kara wanted her to keep talking.

Riley sat up, rubbed her eyes.

"Who would defy her?" Catherine said.

"I don't know. Anton, maybe. I don't know who else she sent. They want me, they know I'm alive, and maybe that twisted my mother up into doing something reckless, but she wouldn't bring Matt to Havenwood."

"Maybe he's not there," Kara said. "Could they have taken him to another place?"

No one said anything.

"Until they call, we won't know," Dean said. "But," he continued slowly, collecting his thoughts, "I think he's there. I have rewatched every interview we had with Riley, read the transcripts, looked at the satellite images, and I don't think they have any other place to go. There's a better than even chance that he's there. We'll ask for proof of life when they call."

"How will they reach out?" Michael said. "Havenwood is remote, they couldn't have cell reception."

Riley said, "I drew you the map. They have an office. It used to be open to everyone, but my mother stopped that after

Athena died. There is a computer and she has a cell phone with a hotspot. It's slow, but it works."

Everyone turned to her simultaneously. She rubbed her eyes. "It's marked 'the Office' on my map. It's the building closest to the road, but sort of on a little hill. It's the only place someone can get and receive calls. Cell phones don't work anywhere else in the valley. We kept them charged in the Office to use at fairs."

"So," Michael said, "they can keep Matt in Havenwood and someone will be able to communicate with Calliope and the others."

Dean said, "If they believe we'll make the trade, they plan to take Riley, then call in and have Matt taken from Havenwood and left somewhere remote. The hitch in my plan is that they could already have taken him elsewhere."

"They're going to kill him," Riley said, voicing Kara's greatest fear.

"We don't know that," Catherine said.

"Yes, I do know that," Riley said firmly. "You weren't there when Todd and Sheila came to Havenwood. I was little, but I saw what that did to my mother, to the others. Their actions shocked everyone, reinforced their fear of the Outside. Created an underlying hatred of strangers, born of that fear. I still miss the serenity of Havenwood and I know the darkness that lives beneath. No one leaves. They killed people who tried to leave. And now they're hunting down those of us who escaped. You have to go in before they call. You have to find him and save him."

"The problem, Riley," Dean said with kindness, "is that a show of force will put innocent people in jeopardy. There are children in Havenwood."

"I will not have another Ruby Ridge or Waco, not on my watch," Tony said firmly. "Some of the smartest people I know are in that hotel room—start thinking."

No one spoke for a minute, then Ryder said, "Can we assume they don't know that we found Havenwood?"

Dean said, "They've felt safe for a long time, but they know we have Riley, and they know that we talked to Andrew."

"They've been in South Fork for days," Kara said. "They poisoned Andrew and know that he was unconscious. They might think he's dead or in a coma. And since that attack, they haven't seen us near Havenwood, which would reason that he didn't tell us how to get there. So, Ryder, if we do assume that, what are you thinking?"

"Go in quietly and get Matt."

"I like that idea," Kara said immediately.

"What about the people suspected of murder?" Catherine said. "We can't walk away and let the status quo remain."

"Getting Matt out is our first priority," Tony said. "Then, we start negotiations. We have five people on camera attacking Matt and Michael in their car. Those are the five people we are investigating. There is evidence at the crime scenes, we need their prints and DNA to compare."

"It won't work," Riley said. Kara had to give her credit for contradicting the boss. "My mother will not negotiate."

"We'll need to find a way to get the children out of Havenwood," Dean said. "If we can do that, then we can go in and execute a search warrant."

Unspoken was that people might die if they resisted.

"Matt first," Tony said. "He may have insight when we get him out. What is your plan to retrieve him?"

Ryder spoke again. "Split the team in two—half goes to a staging spot as close to Havenwood as possible, but without alerting anyone in Havenwood that you're there. If they call, we route the call to where we're staged. But the other half of the team goes quietly into Havenwood."

"What about the cameras?" Michael said.

"They are only on the gate," Ryder said. "Thalia got people

out through the north, which is typically impassable in winter and early spring. But that region had a mild winter which helps us now. I looked at the terrain and we can go in from the north. We should also find a way to disable the cameras. I don't think the technology is state-of-the-art, and they wouldn't have consistent Wi-Fi to stream video. My guess is that the cameras are either hardwired in, which means they have a cord we can cut, or they are connected to Wi-Fi and there's a repeater, but they would be prone to going out, so a glitch isn't going to alert them that we're on-site."

"We still don't know where Matt is on the compound," Kara said.

"Havenwood has a prison," Riley said. "It's our old food storage cellar, which is partly underground to keep produce cold. That's the most likely place."

Catherine nodded. "I see that on your map."

Tony asked, "Dean, what are the odds that Matt is in that prison?"

"Better than even. They wouldn't want to give him free rein, so he is likely restrained, and that would be the logical place."

"Put together the plan, pick the two teams, and go," Tony said. "You have an arrest warrant for the five people we have identified from hotel surveillance, and a search warrant for the property, but it's your choice whether to execute it. You know what to look for—anything that connects Havenwood to these murders, including red poppies, burlap, the fungus that Jim found on one of the victims, marijuana, the murder weapon. Also any computers or records. Ideally, you won't use the documents until after Matt is safe and we bring in the AUSA to assist. The warrants are only if you need them, understand?"

Everyone nodded.

Tony looked stern over the computer. "I see a hundred ways this can go wrong, let's do it right."

"What about my mother?" Riley asked in the background.

Brave girl. Tony Greer was on his full authority rant, and she was challenging him, in a way. Kara was beginning to *really* like her.

"What crime has she committed that we have evidence for?" Tony asked, his voice just a fraction softer. "Not a crime that you suspect her of committing, but a crime you have firsthand knowledge that she committed and will swear to under oath in a court of law?"

Riley glanced at Kara and Kara nodded. "I—I have firsthand knowledge that she let Donovan's younger brother die. She ordered Anton and Evan to dig a pit—I was there when she told them to do it—and when Donovan's brother, James, fell into it, she wouldn't let anyone go help him. She told me that bad boys and girls must be punished."

The room was silent.

"She runs Havenwood," Riley continued. "And you're right, I don't know firsthand most of what she did. I can't prove she killed my grandmother—her own mother. But I think she poisoned her. I can't prove that she killed William, Thalia's dad, but I'm positive she did—or ordered someone to do it. She was growing, cultivating, and selling hundreds of pounds of marijuana every year. But everyone at Havenwood is part of that. So you'd have to arrest everyone. I can't prove she ordered someone to kill Robert or Jane or anyone else. But Thalia was tortured there before they killed her. I heard you, Kara, when you were on the phone. And wouldn't there be evidence of that?"

Tony considered this. "I will leave all decisions to the team on the ground. Our number one priority is to extract Matt. Period. The warrant is to protect us, but we can return with it once we have Matt and know how many people are on-site, how many are children, and the exact layout."

"We'll have the assistance of the Forest Service," Ryder said. "That will save us time."

"We need to get this done before Havenwood calls us," Dean said. "If they think we're stalling, they may act rashly."

Like they haven't already acted rashly by kidnapping Matt? Kara thought.

"I need to go," Riley said.

"We're not putting you in harm's way," Dean said.

"It's my choice. I'm not under arrest, right? This is *my mother.* I know her better than anyone here. I also know Havenwood better than anyone here."

"It's too dangerous," Kara said. "You will stay with the staging team."

Tony cleared his throat.

"What? We need to leave *now,*" Kara said. "We can't put Riley, a civilian, into the field."

"No," Dean concurred, "but she's right that she knows more about this community than anyone, and we need to tap her resources."

Kara hadn't kept Riley safe for the last few days only to put her head on the chopping block.

"Dean," Tony continued, "I need to talk to the director and meet with the judge. You'll have your warrants shortly. You're in charge of this operation. I expect all of you to give Dean the same respect as Matt."

He signed off and Kara asked again, "So when do we leave?"

Dean looked uncomfortable. "I think you should be on the team in the staging area."

"No."

Catherine cleared her throat.

"No," she repeated with a glance toward Catherine. She couldn't read her, but the woman had been a thorn in Kara's side since they first met. "You're in charge, Dean, you know how to deal with these people, but Michael and I have been partners for a year. We work well together. I trust him explicitly. You don't know me or my past, but it's not easy to earn my trust. And I know you're going to assign Michael to Havenwood."

"Riley is most comfortable with you, Kara," Dean said.

"I'm okay," Riley said. "I'll do whatever you tell me to do."

Dean ran a hand through his hair. "I guess I'm outvoted," he mumbled. "Okay. Ryder, have the Forest Service identify the best staging area closest to Havenwood, and ensure that the fire road on the north side of the valley is clear, and what vehicles we can take and to what point. That's how we're going to get in. Notify FBI SWAT in Denver and get a team together just in case we need them. We need a plane to Durango and transportation to the staging spot, then we'll split up and find Matt. Let's do this before they make contact."

Kara desperately wanted to get going. Ryder sensed her frustration and put his hand on her arm and said to the group, "Our charter flight leaves in fifty minutes, at dawn. The airstrip is ten minutes away. I need to coordinate SWAT and the Forest Service, if you'll excuse me."

He left the room and Kara realized she was risking her chance to go on the away team if she showed her impatience. She needed to be calm, professional, and stop thinking about what Matt might be suffering.

The plane wouldn't leave any faster if she pushed.

Jim's words about how Thalia had been restrained and malnourished haunted her. Matt had only been gone for twelve hours. He was strong, but he'd been injured during the attack. Was he kept in the same prison that Thalia had been in?

"We know from Riley that two people who left Havenwood returned with ill intent," Catherine said. "They were shot and killed and since then, Calliope has shunned all strangers and stopped people from leaving. This is going to be a dangerous assignment. The residents have lived in isolation for years, some their entire lives. This life, this place, is all they know. They will feel threatened if the authorities come in, even without a show of force. I don't know what weapons they have, but we know at least two of them have guns, based on Michael's statement about what happened yesterday, and they are proficient with knives. You all must be cautious."

Catherine paused, as she often did when putting her thoughts together. "Calliope will lie to protect herself," Catherine continued. "She will not leave willingly. You'll have to make the decision whether to forcibly extract her, and that will be problematic because her people have been trained to defend her as much as Havenwood. If you can find a way to take her quietly, that would be ideal."

"Our number one goal," Dean said, "is to retrieve Matt and protect the children. We don't want bloodshed. Catherine, I know children can be trained from an early age to be violent, so my goal is to restrain and search them, get them out of harm's way."

"They're not violent," Riley said before Catherine could answer. "My childhood was wonderful."

"Be that as it may," Dean said, "you've been gone for nearly four years."

"The people of Havenwood are there because they don't like the violent and uncertain world. They want something simpler," Riley said. "Think the Amish, but with generators and marijuana. It's not an easy life, but it's comfortable. I can't see anyone training the kids to behave in a violent fashion. If anything, they have been sheltered—though they know how to skin a rabbit and kill a chicken. Because that's food, and we thank the earth for providing for our nourishment and health."

She was emphatic about that, and Kara had to consider she was either clouded in her judgment, or—maybe—she was right.

"But," Catherine said, speaking mostly to Riley, "your mother instills loyalty, doesn't she?"

Riley nodded.

"And we believe your mother ordered the murders of everyone who left. The children may not be involved, but they may not think there's anything wrong with punishing those who are perceived as hurting their community. So go in cautiously, Dean. Be prepared for anything."

"I need to go," Riley said.

"You'll be in the staging area, protected," Dean said.

"I need to go to Havenwood. When they see me, they'll listen. They all think I'm dead. Not my mother anymore, but I don't think she would tell the town that I'm alive. That would undermine their confidence in her. If they see me with their own eyes, I might be able to convince them to turn on Calliope. If she has no one but her inner circle, I think you can resolve this peacefully. At least, as peacefully as possible."

"You're not going to Havenwood," Dean said. "It's not safe."

Kara looked at Riley. Someone was going to have to watch her—Kara recognized the girl's stubborn streak because she had one of her own.

Fifteen minutes later, Kara met Dean in the lobby. The kitchen was still closed but the staff had put out coffee and pastries for the FBI. He was drinking coffee and staring at the dark outside. He'd texted her to come down and talk to him.

"You wanted to see me," Kara said.

"I hadn't wanted you to go to Havenwood because it's clear to me that there's something between you and Agent Costa and that might put you in a compromised position."

"Have we acted in any way unprofessional?"

"No. I wouldn't have guessed except for Riley."

"Her drawing."

He nodded.

"Matt and I have a personal relationship," she said, "and it has never gotten in the way of our work. The team knows about it, we don't discuss it because it's none of their business, but they deserved to know so if we cross a line, they'll call us on it. We haven't. Tony knows because he's the boss, and I guess there are FBI rules that relationships are accepted as long as it's known."

Dean smiled slightly, and Kara continued.

"It started before we worked together on the MRT and it is what it is. I want to go because Michael and I are partners. Matt and I too, but Matt is the boss and Michael and I have worked together more in the field. I wasn't lying—I trust him. Matt trusts him. And Michael is having a difficult time right now because he was there when Matt was taken. I know him—he's running through every scenario in his head to figure out what he did wrong. I need to be there for him, and yes, if Matt is injured, I need to be there for him, too. But mostly, I'm a good cop. I may not be FBI, I may not have a psych degree, but I know people. I will be valuable on the team."

He nodded. "You don't need a psych degree to understand people. I read your file when I couldn't sleep. You *are* a good cop. But you also take risks."

"Doesn't every cop?"

"No."

"I don't take unnecessary risks." She got up and said, "I'll meet you upstairs." As she left the lobby, she saw Ryder crossing the space with Sloane. Sloane gave her a hug and said, "You good? Michael?"

Kara nodded. "Thanks. I'm glad you're here."

"I need to brief Agent Montero," Ryder said. "We have some new information and it might change our plans."

44

Havenwood

Matt dozed on and off through the night, unsettled by the complete silence. He'd been camping before, mostly when he was younger, but it wasn't a regular occurrence in the Costa household. They usually spent their vacations—rare as they were—at the beach or going fishing before his dad died. The ocean was never silent, and the stillness here was eerie. He heard the occasional coyote, and before dawn he heard the squawk of birds closer to the village. But mostly, nothing. There was not even a wind to rattle the windows or trees.

Someone unlocked his door at 5:45 a.m., according to his watch—the one thing they didn't take from him. It was Anton.

"Breakfast."

He stood in the doorway, filling the narrow frame with his bulk.

Matt used the washroom, splashed water on his face, and put

on his shoes and jacket, since he'd slept in his clothes. Anton just stared at him.

Matt's head pounded from the concussion he was certain he had, but his vision had cleared and the lump on the back of his skull had gone down by half. But it was still tender to the touch. He felt cuts on his face, and one that bled onto the pillow kept opening up.

Anton led Matt downstairs to where Calliope sat at a large dining room table. Anton was one of four men in the room and Matt wondered if they were all Calliope's partners. Matt recognized Garrett, and the other two he had seen last night, Evan and Marcus. The table was full of food that smelled just as amazing as the dinner before.

Evan looked like he hadn't slept for days. He seemed ill.

"Sit, Mathias," Calliope said and motioned to the seat next to her. "Today is a big day. My daughter is coming home." She smiled and waited for him to sit.

He didn't.

Anton pushed him into the seat when Calliope scowled.

"It's going to be a long day. I suggest you eat, because this is the only food you're going to get."

He ate. He needed to be prepared for whenever his team acted—and he was certain they had a plan. He wished he had some idea what they were going to do, but he didn't have the information they had. Had they found Havenwood? Were they coming here? Or were they going to wait for the exchange and try to mitigate casualties?

"Marcus, is Riley's room ready for her?"

"Yes, just the way she likes it. Aired out and clean, and I put fresh flowers from the greenhouse."

"Thank you, darling." Calliope beamed. "You can thank Marcus for the meal, Mathias. He's an amazing cook. The ham is from our own stock, the eggs from our chickens, the bread made at our bakery—don't look so surprised, we have one house dedicated to baking. Everything we serve is fresh. Even in the winter when we're snowed in for months, we have fresh vegetables, meat, water. Havenwood is paradise."

Matt glanced at Marcus. He was missing his pinky finger. Just like the woman Matt saw last night.

Coincidence? Maybe. But it was creepy.

He was still trying to gauge the relationships and what was really going on here—because this was a woman who ordered the murder of several people. He would find it hard to believe that Anton and the others were killing without her knowledge.

"So, Calliope," he said conversationally, "what happens when the FBI refuses to cooperate?"

"It won't matter. Riley will return of her own free will."

"Riley knows that you had her best friend killed."

"I have no idea what you're talking about."

"You know Jane is dead."

When Matt said it, he saw Evan flinch. Interesting. Evan... Timmy's uncle. Timmy was the boy who was mauled by a mountain lion, and Jane's boyfriend. The boy in the picture in her box.

He wondered if Evan was angry or guilty about Jane's murder. He looked like he was struggling.

"I'm sorry to hear that," Calliope said. "Jane was a sweet girl, and the world outside Havenwood is a violent place."

"And she knows you had Robert, one of her fathers, killed."

"Robert has been dead for eleven years," she said with an undercurrent of venom. "At least to me."

Her jaw had tightened and she was getting angry. Because the FBI had figured out the connection? Because she was just now realizing she wasn't going to get away with murder? He didn't know.

"If you think—" Matt began, and Calliope cut him off.

"Anton, get him out of here. Back to prison."

Matt was pulled roughly to his feet.

"Don't kill him, not yet," Calliope said. "But make sure he can't get out."

45

Outside Havenwood

Catherine wasn't completely comfortable with the plan Dean settled on, and she suspected that Kara had intervened and convinced him to do something more risky than necessary. Yet... Catherine was as worried about Matt as Kara was, and while she didn't like the cop, she had grown to respect her instincts. Catherine didn't think Dean could be swayed to go against his best judgment and experience, so maybe this was the best option.

Catherine, Ryder and Riley were in a ranger's cabin three miles off the highway. The cabin was accessed from the same road that eventually led to Havenwood, but that was five miles down an unmaintained road.

Ryder was monitoring communications, while Catherine was protecting Riley. She might be a psychiatrist, but she was also a trained FBI agent, something she thought Kara often forgot.

The day was cold though the sky was clear. While the ranger

station was three miles as the crow flies from the valley of Havenwood, it was a more than five-mile trek down. The first half of the road was maintained by the Forest Service: it was paved though not generally plowed. The ranger had gone down to ensure there were no obstacles and reported that the road had been used recently, but not today.

The second half of the road was property of Havenwood, blocked by a gate with cameras. Ryder was analyzing the cameras now using a drone.

George Stewart from the Denver office, who'd been their local agent from the beginning of the case, was outside under a heated tent with Denver SWAT. They were on standby and the goal was not to use them. If necessary, they would access Havenwood by the narrow main road, cut the chain to the gate once cameras were down. But the road was too narrow for tactical trucks. The SUVs would work, but they would have to drive slow because of the sharp turns in the road. It would be nearly impossible to traverse the road at night.

The rest of the team was headed down the fire road on the northern edge of Havenwood. Even though Riley said no one in Havenwood knew about the cabin she and Thalia had used as a way station, that was nearly four years ago. It could now be guarded. It could be occupied. They didn't know what they would face.

Catherine agreed with Dean's assessment that when the meet was scheduled, Calliope would dispatch several people—likely Anton and Ginger, who were involved in Matt's abduction—to ensure that there was no trap. They also concurred that they might send the FBI on a scavenger hunt, to go from place to place to ensure no one was following them.

Catherine had also warned Riley that Calliope might want to talk to her. Riley seemed to be okay with talking to her mother, but there was a lot of history between them and family was always complicated. Catherine knew that from experience.

But Catherine wouldn't allow Calliope to talk to her daughter until she had proof that Matt was alive.

She glanced at Riley. The young woman was sitting in the corner sketching, her legs crossed in front of her. She seemed oddly at peace.

"A call is coming in from the hotel in South Fork," Ryder said. He answered, then said to Catherine, "It's the security chief. A caller has asked to speak with the FBI."

They had arranged with the lodge in South Fork to conference any call into the mobile unit set up at the rangers' station.

"Put the call through," Catherine said.

She glanced at Riley. The girl was nervous, but she was holding her own, and that impressed Catherine. She motioned for the room to be quiet, then nodded to Ryder to put the call on speaker.

"This is senior special agent Catherine Jones. To whom am I speaking?"

"Catherine," a female voice purred, "this is Calliope, of Havenwood. How are you?"

"I would be better if my colleague was with us."

"Right to the point, aren't you?"

"I've always felt it was best to speak succinctly."

"This entire affair has been a misunderstanding. I would like my family together again. Before I tell you where you can find Mathias, I need to speak to my daughter."

"I can arrange that," Catherine said, "but while you tell me that Mathias is well, I need to hear his voice and confirm his health."

"That will not happen," Calliope said, "until I know my daughter is with you."

Catherine didn't want to do it, but she wasn't actually trading Riley. And Catherine needed to draw out the call to give her team time to get into position and down to the valley.

"Is Mathias there with you?" Catherine said. Since Calliope was using Matt's full name—likely because she'd seen it on his identification—Catherine used it.

"No. But I can get to him in two shakes of a lamb's tail. Riley. Please, Agent Jones."

Catherine motioned to Riley. She hesitated, pale, hands shaking. Riley hadn't spoken of physical abuse, but she was scared. This reaction was difficult to fake.

"It's me," Riley said, her voice a whisper.

"Speak up, Riley."

"What do you want from me?" Riley said.

"Your love and loyalty, as always. You betrayed me—you pretended to die. There is a grave with your name on it."

Was that a threat? Catherine suspected it was, and she wanted to end this call, but Riley didn't give up the phone.

"I had to," Riley said. "How did you find out?"

"Evan saw you, sweetheart. He didn't believe at first, but he saw you and promised to bring you home to us. I have missed you so much."

"I miss Havenwood," Riley said.

"I knew you would. You'll be back home soon."

"I don't miss you."

"You have been tainted by the Outside. Once you return, you'll never want to leave again."

"You're twisted, pretending you're a kind benefactor," Riley snapped, her voice stronger than before. "You are a killer. You manipulate and brainwash people to do things they would never do if they just thought about it!"

Catherine motioned for her to stop. This wasn't going to help Matt.

"I hate you," Riley said to her mother.

"I love you," Calliope said. "I've always loved you."

"You only love yourself."

"Catherine," Calliope said, her voice sharp. "Can you assure me that you will deliver my daughter to the destination of my choosing?"

"If Matt is there."

"No. I don't trust you, and I clearly shouldn't trust my daughter either. In fact, Riley, if you fight me on this, you know what will happen. One. By. One."

"I hate you," Riley repeated, but her voice cracked.

As if Riley hadn't spoken, Calliope said, "Catherine, you and you alone will fly with Riley to the Telluride Regional Airport. When you arrive, my people will bring Riley home and give you the location of your colleague once they have determined it's not a trap. It's as simple as that. You have three hours from now."

"I need proof of life—" Catherine began, but Calliope had already cut off the call.

Catherine set her watch to countdown.

"I'm sorry. I just—I heard her voice and everything came flooding back."

"It's my fault for letting you talk to her before I had proof of life." Catherine had made a mistake. She rarely made mistakes. But this one might cost Matt his life.

Or he was already dead. Her stomach twisted in pain.

"What will happen?" Catherine asked. "She said if you fight her, you know what will happen."

"One by one," Riley whispered.

"What does that mean?"

"She'll start cutting off people's fingers. She did it once before. Seven people lost one of their fingers before I gave in."

"Gave in to what? What did she want you to do that necessitated torturing others?"

Riley's eyes teared.

"You can tell me, Riley. I'm not going to think badly about you because of anything that happened in your childhood."

"I…I had to kill…my favorite horse."

"Was it injured?"

Riley shook her head. "I was riding in the field and went to the creek, which is our western boundary—I don't know what the property line is, just that we were not allowed to cross the creek. Biscuit was grazing while I drew and he got spooked—

I think a snake, though I didn't see it. He ran across the creek and I went after him. He stopped at some boulders. I soothed him, but he was agitated and we got back late."

She paused, looked at her hands. "The next day, my mother told me to put him down because I was irresponsible. I refused. She then lined up twenty people in the barn and had them put their hands on the rail. I didn't know what she was going to do. She told me if I didn't put my horse down, they would lose a finger. I didn't believe her until the first finger fell. But I thought someone would stop her. Even after they saw what she was doing, they kept their hands there, on the railing, waiting. As if they accepted the punishment and blamed me. They stared at me. Accused me. And after the seventh finger fell I screamed I would do it.

"My mother gave me a revolver. She put one bullet in it. She told me the shot had better be a good one or Biscuit would suffer, because I wasn't going to get another bullet. And if I missed? She would cut off the next seven fingers."

Catherine wanted to pull this poor girl into her arms and console her as the tears fell.

"I...I had been with my grandmother once when she had to put down an old horse who was sick. I knew what to do. But Biscuit wasn't sick, and he wasn't hurt, and I wanted to put the bullet in my mother's head instead of the horse's. But I didn't. I killed him. And I know that the people in Havenwood put their hands out for my mother to mutilate, but blamed me for what she did. It will happen again."

Riley stood, then said, "I'm going. She will hurt Agent Costa and others if I don't."

"Just—hold it. We have a plan. It's a good plan, we need to stick to it. She gave us a time. Three hours. We have three hours to save Matt."

"You think he's still alive?" Riley said. "I hope he is, but he's an outsider."

Catherine called Dean Montero and told him what she'd

learned. She glanced up when Riley walked across the cabin and went into the bathroom, wiping the tears from her face.

Catherine feared Riley was right. She said, "I don't know if we can wait, Dean. They're not going to give Matt back. Calliope is sociopathic and manipulative, a narcissist. If we don't turn Riley over in three hours, they will kill him if he's not already dead."

"We're in position, we'll be going in shortly."

"Be safe." She ended the call.

Riley was still in the bathroom. Catherine said to Ryder, "You holding up?"

"Yes, ma'am."

"You don't have to be formal with me, Ryder." She had noticed the way Kara had elicited respect from the team in how they communicated with each other. Ryder was formal with everyone, but not Kara. Originally, Catherine thought it was because he didn't respect her. On the contrary, he liked her. They were friends, and Catherine didn't think she would ever understand it. Kara was antithetical to the structure that Ryder thrived in.

When he only nodded, she said, "Alert George and the SWAT team that the plan is a go." They had lookouts camouflaged at several key spots along the route from the Havenwood property line to the highway road. They would alert the team when anyone left.

She walked over to the bathroom and knocked on the door. "Riley, are you okay? Do you need anything?"

Silence.

She tried the door.

Locked.

For a second she feared Riley harmed herself. But before she forced the door open, she knew the truth.

Riley had left through the window.

46

Outside Havenwood

Riley liked Catherine and hadn't wanted to deceive her, but Riley wanted no more deaths on her conscience.

She trusted that the FBI had a plan, but when Calliope was forced into a corner, she acted irrationally. That put Agent Costa in danger. How could she explain it to everyone?

There was only one way to end Calliope's control over all those people. One way to stop more innocent people from dying. For her aunt, for her grandmother, for Jane and Robert and the others.

Riley had to kill her.

The realization had come to her slowly after she learned her mother had Agent Costa kidnapped and used her aunt's dead body as the messenger. Maybe Calliope wanted a showdown. Maybe she wanted everyone to die defending Havenwood. But Havenwood wouldn't be at risk and no one would be in danger if Calliope hadn't turned what was beautiful and pure into an evil, ugly cult with her at the center.

For all the psychology classes she'd taken, and listening to Dean and Catherine talk, Riley still didn't understand what motivated her mother. Yes, she understood her need to protect what was hers. What happened to Glen and Annie, losing the baby, the people who left and came back to do them harm. But her mother had been not completely right in the head even before that. She was beautiful and evil, hot and cold, cruel and sadistic.

But she would never leave Havenwood because at the heart of everything, Calliope was terrified. Whether because of watching the murder of her father or because she saw Havenwood as her only sanctuary, Calliope was terrified to leave.

Riley understood fear. And she would use it to her advantage.

Riley was scared, but not like before. Because there was a greater good to be had.

Liberating Havenwood.

It was time to make a stand. It was time to tell her mother that nothing—*nothing* she could do to her or anyone else would send Riley down the same dark path.

Riley didn't want to kill her mother, but there was no doubt in her mind that Calliope would force her to.

Just like she forced Riley to kill her horse.

Riley hadn't known where Havenwood was in the state of Colorado, but now that she was on the edge of paradise, she remembered every inch of the land she'd been born on.

And she ran as fast as she dared down the mountain.

47

North of Havenwood

The cabin was exactly where Riley said it would be.

Forest ranger Toby Strong had led the four of them—Kara, Michael, Sloane, and Dean—along the fire road and down a narrow trail to the cabin. Though they were dressed for the cold, Kara was still freezing by the time they arrived. The sun was up, the sky was blue, the mountain was beautiful, but the cold seeped into her bones, reminding her of her years with her grams—when running around in the cold didn't bother her nearly as much.

Toby was an older ranger, he had to be near sixty, but he was sure-footed and in good shape. He knew Havenwood, had met several of the people, including Thalia years ago, but mostly the people kept to themselves. "I didn't know they hurt anyone. The few times I've been down to the valley, they were hospitable and friendly."

Kara was surprised they tolerated the stranger, but maybe they understood that if something happened to the forest ranger, another would replace him. And another. They were legally on the land, so perhaps they didn't fear him.

Dean was talking to Catherine for a second time, but Kara was studying the map with Michael and Sloane. Michael said quietly to Sloane, "Are you good partnering with Dean?"

She nodded.

"I know it's a lot of pressure, considering he's not a field agent."

"I got him," she said. "In the Marines I was tasked with babysitting journalists and politicians—I can keep him alive."

Michael cracked a smile, the first since Matt was kidnapped.

"Then it's you and me, KQ," he said to Kara.

Dean came back into the cabin. "Riley snuck out the bathroom window. Catherine thinks she believes her mother will kill Matt if she senses a trap. She blames herself. Catherine said there's a lot more to unpack in Riley's past, things she didn't share before, but that there were hints in her art. So we now have Matt as our priority, and finding Riley before she does anything she can't come back from."

Damn! Kara thought Riley trusted them. They'd been together most of the week, and Kara saw Riley relax, listen, talk. Why run now? What had changed?

"The plan is still the same," Dean said. "We don't leave this cabin until SWAT is in position. They need thirty minutes. They'll come in on my call. I'm hoping it doesn't come to that."

"We need to go in now," Kara said. "Riley knows this mountain. She'll be in Havenwood before us, and that means one more hostage for Calliope, and no reason to keep Matt alive."

Dean looked indecisive. Not a good look on their team leader.

"I'll find Riley," Kara said. "You rescue Matt."

Saying it pained her, but it was their best option.

"Riley will listen to me. I'm small, fast, good on my feet. I've studied these maps over and over." To make her point, she drew attention to the map she and Michael had been looking at most recently. "Here," she said, "is the forest station. Here—" she dragged her finger down the road "—is Havenwood. Riley isn't going to walk on the road, but she has to stay close to it because if she goes too far south, it's too steep, and too far north is out of the way. So I think she'll stick low through here..." As she spoke she looked at the area. "Toby, what's this here?"

"It's a small creek. Most of it is still frozen over."

"It runs along the road?"

He nodded.

"And it lets out here, into a pond, then another stream—here—runs to the lake, correct?"

"Yep," Toby said. "I've been down to Havenwood a few times, so I know exactly what you're thinking. It's more a wide spot in the creek than a pond. It's on the northeastern side of the community. In late spring, the pond overflows and runs down to the lake, but it's still too cold for that."

"That's where she's going. And she's going to confront her mother, or create a distraction so we can reach Matt. We need to act now, not later."

No one said anything. They were all watching Dean. Why couldn't he make a decision?

Dean turned to Toby. "This could be dangerous, so it's your choice. Can you show Kara the way down without being seen by anyone in the community?"

"I should be able to do that. Not a problem."

"Okay. Kara—I'm letting you do this against my better judgment."

"Just find Matt. I'll get Riley to safety." *If I can*, she thought.

"Go before I change my mind."

48

Outside Havenwood

Catherine listened to the communications coming from the SWAT team checkpoints along the road. Two trucks were coming up the road, a white pickup with a camper shell and an open-bed darker pickup.

As the trucks passed each agent, additional details were relayed, and the vehicles came closer. Two people, a man and woman, in each truck. When they hit the paved road that led to the highway, they wouldn't be able to see the rangers' station or the many vehicles and tactical truck that had taken over the area. They also couldn't see what was on the other side of a sharp curve in the road.

George said over the comm, "ETA, ten minutes."

At first confirmation of the vehicles, SWAT had driven a Humvee onto the narrow road on the other side of the curve. When the trucks passed the ranger station hidden among the trees, another vehicle would drive onto the road and stop, to prevent them from backtracking.

Catherine, as a trained hostage negotiator, would attempt to convince the four people to stand down. She joined George outside, pulling her jacket tight around her against the cold, still air. They headed down the path to the road, then around the bend to where the SWAT leader waited with his Humvee and three trained tactical agents.

She was tense but calm. Hostage negotiation was a delicate conversation, and required finesse and experience. With a cult like this, Catherine didn't know what to expect. They didn't have enough information about the group. Would they surrender? Attempt suicide by cop? Delay the inevitable?

Cell phones were unreliable here, but they could have radios. Catherine assumed that when they were stopped, at the first sign that something was wrong they would have a way to alert Calliope and Havenwood. That would give Dean's team limited time to rescue Matt. It was a delicate balancing act, and she feared she might make a tactical mistake that would cause Matt his life.

She feared he was already dead.

The realization that life was too short to hold grudges hit her. She was forty-two, a trained forensic psychiatrist, a mother, a wife. She had lost her sister and while Matt had nothing to do with Beth's murder, she had held a grudge against him because he hadn't loved Beth. Catherine had wanted Matt as part of their family, and thought brother-in-law was perfect. They were friends, they would be family.

She knew one reason she didn't like Kara was because Matt loved her like he didn't love Beth. Petty, childish, she saw now. Kara was rough around the edges, borderline violent, with a highly unusual upbringing. Her parents were criminals, her childhood filled with crime. How could she even compare to Catherine's sweet, educated, beautiful, kind sister?

But it shouldn't matter, Catherine realized. She'd kept a barrier between her and Matt for the last two years, first after Beth's death because of her grief and pain, then after Matt started sleeping with Kara, out of anger and frustration.

It was Matt's life. And Catherine didn't want anything to happen to him without her telling him she was, truly, sorry for how she'd treated him of late. Even at dinner the other night—was it really less than a week ago?—she'd made snide comments about Kara. And he had ignored her.

She realized she should be apologizing to Kara, that Matt would appreciate that more.

Catherine hoped she'd have an opportunity. She didn't have many friends; why did she think she could abuse those she had?

"You good, doc?" the SWAT leader asked.

She dismissed her contemplation.

"Good."

"Stay behind me. You're the negotiator. You wearing a vest?"

She nodded.

He listened to his earpiece, then said, "Rear block in place. Three. Two. One."

The first truck came into view. It stopped almost immediately when the driver saw the Humvee, the second truck right behind it. They were fifty feet away.

Silence, except for idling motors and Catherine's racing heart.

She willed it to slow. She signaled on her radio to Dean—three short clicks—that the trucks had been stopped.

He was supposed to signal with two long clicks in acknowledgment.

She got nothing.

Dean, Michael, and Sloane moved through the trees toward the eastern side of the Havenwood compound. They had given Kara and Toby a fifteen-minute head start.

When they were closer to the camp, he turned his radio down

to silent. The air was too still, the morning too quiet. One unusual sound and the people of Havenwood would hear them.

He should have anticipated Riley's actions. In hindsight, all the signs were there. Her fear of authorities. Her willingness to help. The drawings of her mother—the only drawings that showed something that wasn't there. Everything else she drew was true to life—the other people, the animals, the nature. Trees were trees, flowers were flowers. But her mother was both mother and goddess, beautiful and evil. Medusa was a legendary villain in Greek mythology. That and that alone should have signaled to both Dean and Catherine that Riley might be compelled to face her mother.

Riley had insisted on coming with them. Had she planned this the entire time? He thought back…it was after Ryder Kim came in with the news of working with the forest rangers in the area. Toby Strong said he'd been in the valley, that he knew several of the people. She knew if she got closer to Havenwood, she might have a chance to slip away from them.

What was her plan? To warn her mother? He didn't think so. After everything that happened to her, to her friends, he thought it more likely that she would either confront or kill Calliope.

Either one was a problem for them, but killing her mother was something she couldn't come back from.

Especially if it was premeditated.

Dean understood cult mentality, but only after the fact. He had studied cults in history, could dissect them. He'd negotiated successfully to end standoffs three times, unsuccessfully once with a small doomsday group in Idaho. Five people had died that day.

He'd interviewed cult survivors and the one thing they had in common was the strong need to belong to something bigger than themselves. Many had faced tragedy, or had low self-esteem, or felt like outliers in society. But they all craved belonging, a community, a common, shared existence with other human beings.

Cult leaders preyed on the very human need for community, and through psychology and manipulation and often brainwashing, changed perception of right and wrong, good and evil, to conform to the needs and desires of the cult.

Every time Riley spoke of Havenwood, she recalled what it had been before her grandmother's death. She spoke with affection and longing of a place that no longer existed—a place she felt her mother had destroyed. At the time, she could do nothing to stop it—she was a child. Now she was an adult with nearly four years in the "real" world to learn how to fight back.

Dean picked up his pace. Michael looked at him, mouthed, *What?*

Dean shook his head. He couldn't explain what he'd been thinking, or how he had missed the signs. All he knew was he didn't want Riley Pierce to go down a dark road from which she might never recover.

Toby Strong was a tall, lean, fit ranger who maintained a steady pace through the thin layer of snow that covered the ground. At first he chatted, saying it was good the last storm hadn't hit western Colorado because then they wouldn't be able to do this. There were places where the snow had melted, places where it was thinner than others. Kara tripped a few times, fell once, but Toby simply helped her up and they continued on their way.

Fifteen minutes later he stopped chattering, and five minutes after that, as they stood in the middle of trees with the sense of something vast beyond—something Kara couldn't see—he whispered, "We're on the edge of the valley floor. Listen."

She did. She heard faint voices and sheep baaing. The far, distant sound of a handsaw echoing in the valley. No shouts, no panic, people weren't hiding inside or running away. It was… normal.

Were they wrong? Was Matt not here? Had they already killed him, thinking they'd bring Riley to a meeting place?

"Where to?" she whispered.

He motioned to the left. "Follow my footsteps."

She did as he told her. A hundred yards later, she saw a recently used gravel road, a strip of gray snow in the middle and banks of white snow on the sides. The road led into the mountains. Directly across, on an elevated plateau, was a building. The Office that Riley mentioned?

She looked around. There were cabins she could see, but no people nearby.

She saw a building near the Office that could have been the underground food storage that was turned into a jail. Matt could be there now. She itched to look.

But that wasn't her job.

She tore her eyes away from it. She trusted Michael. He would save Matt.

"Where would Riley come from?" Kara asked.

He gestured to the other side of the Office. There was a field of snow. She didn't know what he was pointing to.

"That wide spot there, at the base of the cliff? That's the pond. On the other side it's not as steep, and that's the easiest way to come down from the road, cutting across behind the building."

"We need to get to that building without being seen."

He considered that, said, "Follow me."

She did. He hadn't steered her wrong yet. They walked along the edge of the road, on the other side of the bank of snow. Her legs sank deeper into the snow, over the top of her boots. She was cold and uncomfortable and couldn't wait for hot coffee and a hotter shower.

The road curved just a bit about a hundred feet up, and that's where Toby crossed it. He climbed up the embankment, then reached out and helped her up.

They were at the back of the cabin. She immediately ran up to the wall, put her back to it, hoping no one was inside and had seen them. There was a path that wrapped around three sides of the building. The fourth side was too narrow. She peered cautiously into one of the windows.

The one-room building was empty of people, but had several desks, filing cabinets, phones, and two computers. An old couch and table filled the rest of the space.

And she saw Matt's gun, pocketknife, and badge on a table.

She motioned to Toby that she was going in. The door was locked. Probably to keep anyone who didn't have Calliope's approval from communicating with the outside world. But it was a flimsy lock, and she easily broke it with the butt of her gun, the *crack!* of metal on metal surprisingly loud.

She slowly entered.

A quick look told her this was a treasure trove of evidence. On a clipboard next to the computer was a list of names and addresses—including every murder victim. Why would Calliope keep this out in the open? Did they not think they'd be caught?

Clearly not. Killers rarely thought they'd be caught.

She said to Toby, "I need you to stay here and secure this building." She pocketed Matt's badge and knife and handed Toby his gun. She had two of her own. "You good?"

"Yes, ma'am."

Ma'am. She almost smiled.

She was about to leave when she heard a radio beep.

"Feds are here. Repeat feds are here," a crackly voice came through.

Dammit. Were Anton and the others alerting Calliope right now? Did she have another radio? Would she hear the warning?

"Dean, it's Kara. Over," she said into her own radio that was set to Dean's channel.

No response.

"Dean, they know we're here. Proceed with caution."

No response.

Dammit!

"I have to go," she said to Toby. "Stay safe, keep this place locked down. We need this evidence."

"Roger that. Be careful."

Kara went back outside and almost immediately saw footprints in the snow.

Two sets went down a path that led to stairs built into the cliff.

The other, single set went perpendicular, toward the far side of the pond, as Toby had indicated.

Riley.

Kara followed her path.

Catherine sensed something was wrong as the four Havenwood residents stayed in the trucks.

The SWAT leader said, "Exit your vehicles with your hands visible. Leave any weapons inside."

They didn't move. The lead driver—Anton, Catherine determined—was talking to the passenger, Ginger. Ginger had a daughter. Would she risk leaving her daughter motherless to fight the police? Catherine prayed it wouldn't come to that.

Then Anton was just talking. On the radio? A cell phone? What was going on?

He drank from a thermos, looked at his watch. What were they waiting for?

"His name is Anton, no known last name," Catherine told the team leader. "He's wanted for questioning in a murder investigation. Ginger is the passenger, and she's wanted for suspicion of attempted murder. I don't know who the other two people in the second vehicle are."

The leader shouted, "Anton, Ginger, it's over. Please step out of the truck, hands visible, no weapons."

They sat there drinking from their thermos. Back and forth, sharing.

"May I?" she said and took the bullhorn. She set it on the lowest setting, but it still sounded loud. "I'm Catherine Jones. I spoke with Calliope earlier. We don't want anyone to get hurt. We're not here to shut down Havenwood. We just want to talk."

They didn't respond.

"Do you have the FBI agent in the back of the truck? Can we please discuss this? We can't have a conversation standing out here in the cold. Let's go to the ranger station. It's warm there. We'll just talk."

They were talking to each other. Catherine couldn't see the two in the rear truck, but SWAT would have eyes on them.

The driver's door opened and Anton stepped out, hands up. Ginger did the same thing.

She sighed in relief.

Her relief was only temporary.

As the two followed orders to turn around and put their hands on their head, Ginger faltered. She fell to the ground. A moment later, Anton stumbled, as well.

Catherine, ignoring the shouts of SWAT to stop, ran over to the fallen couple. They were frothing at the mouth, their skin was splotchy, and their eyes unfocused.

"We need a medic! They're poisoned."

They poisoned themselves.

Suicide.

She immediately ran back to the ranger station and got on the radio. "Dean, Dean! Anton and Ginger committed suicide. You have to stop them—I think there's a mass suicide in progress. Dean!"

There was no answer.

49

Havenwood

Dean could hear everything Kara, then Catherine, said through his earpiece, but he didn't dare respond.

He and Sloane were standing on the far side of the barn. There was something going on inside, but he couldn't see what. Michael was headed to the building Riley had identified as the prison.

The valley was open and wide; there were trees all along the eastern edge, and the cabins had been built among them, but here where the barn, warehouse, greenhouse, and storage stood was right in the open.

Mass suicide? Nothing Riley had told them about Havenwood said that they were suicidal. They weren't a doomsday cult. They weren't a religious cult. They were a personality cult built on a cooperative lifestyle that saw themselves detached from the outside world. Would that detachment equal a death agreement? Dean didn't know.

That he didn't know bothered him.

★ ★ ★

Matt heard a rattling of the lock. He braced himself, then he heard a familiar voice.

"Matt, you here?"

"Michael?"

His friend and colleague came down the stairs.

"I knew you'd find me," Matt said.

"It was a team effort. Are you injured?"

"I can walk," Matt said, "but I'm chained. I don't know where the key is."

"I don't need a key. Just a better light."

Michael turned on his flashlight, held it between his teeth, and worked on picking Matt's locks.

"What's happening out there?"

"Catherine is negotiating with four of Calliope's people on the road who were sent, we believe, to find Riley. Calliope refused to give proof of life, and then Riley ran away through a window."

"Did you find her?"

"She's here somewhere. Kara is tracking her. Dean and Sloane are in position behind the barn. It'll take SWAT nearly thirty minutes to get down the road. But Tony doesn't want SWAT action unless there's no other option. Too many children."

"Good call. Catherine hates it when I say this, but Calliope has a screw loose. I'm worried about these people. They looked both content and scared, as if they are content living in fear. It's weird."

"Hold on." Michael stopped working for a moment, was listening. "Dammit. Catherine said Anton, Ginger, and two others committed suicide rather than be taken into custody."

"Get me out of these," Matt said, fearing for the lives of everyone in Havenwood.

Suddenly, the chains fell to the floor. Michael handed Matt his backup piece and spoke into his comm. "Agent Costa is okay. He's with me." Michael looked at him pointedly. "You look like shit."

"I'm sore and need a hot shower, but I'm okay. I have your back."

★★★

Kara saw Riley exit a cabin on the edge of the community. By the looks of it, it had been her grandmother's—she could tell by the tree in the front, the way the trunk twisted, just like in Riley's drawings.

"Riley," Kara said quietly.

She turned, eyes wide. "Go."

"We have a plan and you're blowing it."

"You don't understand. My mother will hurt people."

"We have Anton, Ginger, and two others in custody," Kara said. She didn't tell her that they all tried to kill themselves. Kara didn't know if they were dead or alive, but sensed that if Riley knew they might die, she would be even more furious.

Riley shook her head and started walking toward a barn on the opposite side of a cleared-out area with a giant redwood in the center of the small community. Kara needed to get Riley away from the situation.

"Your grandmother wouldn't want this," Kara said.

Riley stopped, whirled around. "My grandmother created heaven and my mother created hell. I will stop it today."

That's when Kara saw Michael and Matt coming from the food storage. She was so relieved, so happy, that she smiled like a loon. "Riley," she said. "Look."

Riley watched Matt and Michael approach them. She stared at Matt. "You're not dead. I thought for sure she had killed you."

"She planned to, but I think she's hedging her bets."

"Something's going on in the barn," Michael said. "Dean needs backup."

Kara held Matt's eye for another beat. In that moment, she silently said all she wanted to say. And it was as if he read her mind.

I love you. Don't scare me again.

He smiled at her and mouthed, *I love you, too.*

A woman came out of one of the cabins holding a tray. She stared at Riley. "Riley? *Riley?* Is that you?"

Great, Kara thought. So much for stealth.

The barn doors opened. Calliope stood there. In person, Kara was stunned at how accurate Riley's drawing had been. It was as if her mother had posed for her.

"I knew you would come home," Calliope said loudly, her arms spread wide. "My beautiful, sweet girl." She scowled at Kara. "Go away."

"Not going to happen," Kara said. "Where Riley goes, I go."

Calliope stared at Matt and Michael, frowned. She opened her mouth to speak, but Riley interrupted her.

"You have destroyed Havenwood, Mother. I won't let you hurt anyone else."

"You are my *daughter.* You left me. But you came back, just like I knew you would."

"I came back to stop you." Riley raised her voice. "Havenwood! You know I speak the truth! Calliope has kept you in prison long enough. You are now free to come and go as you please."

Calliope scowled. "That is not how this works. You know better."

"You're scared, Mother. You must be terrified that you kidnapped a federal agent, which will bring the wrath of the government down here to our valley."

They had drawn a crowd and Kara couldn't tell whether these people sided with Riley or with Calliope. She couldn't keep her eyes on all of them at once. Slowly, she, Matt, and Michael shifted so their backs were to the giant tree so no one could get them from behind. But still, they were sitting ducks. The entire village seemed to come out of the cabins, the greenhouse, the paths.

The barn doors opened again and two men went immediately to Calliope's side.

"It wasn't my decision," Calliope said. "It was a mistake. But I adapted. I've always adapted when other people screw everything up. My mother, my sister, my father—all dead because they screwed up!"

A gunshot rang out and Kara pushed Riley to the ground, gun in hand.

"Shut up!" A blond man held a .45. He had come not from the barn, but from a path behind it. He was only twenty feet from the group, and he didn't look well. Riley had drawn him, but Kara didn't remember his name until she said it.

"Evan," Riley whispered.

Matt was only a few feet behind Kara and Riley. He motioned for Kara to stay down. He and Michael sidestepped so they were partly obscured by the giant tree.

"Everyone, do not drink anything in that barn!" Evan shouted. "Calliope poisoned the tea. She would rather everyone die than admit she destroyed Havenwood."

Murmurs in the group.

"Liar," Calliope said, her face red with anger. "Traitor!"

"It's the truth," Evan said. "I killed Jane. I *killed* her. I didn't want to, but I did for you, Calliope. I lost everything and everyone I loved. You twisted my grief and I didn't see the truth until now. You are the killer."

He turned to the group. Out of the corner of his eye, Matt saw Dean and Sloane behind the barn, eyes on the situation. No one had a clear shot of Evan. People or trees were in the line of fire. Dean was trying to maneuver to get to a better position.

"She killed Athena," Evan said. "You all remember Athena, everyone loved her. I heard Anton and Calliope discussing her death. They *killed* her. And so many others. Anyone who wanted to leave. And you know it! You all know it and do *nothing*."

Riley slowly rose. Kara tried to pull her back down, but Riley sidestepped Kara to get out of her reach.

"Evan is right," Riley said. She walked over to a bench and climbed on it so she could be heard. It also made her a damn target. "Calliope ordered the deaths of people we all loved. I left here nearly four years ago with Jane. Two weeks ago, Calliope killed her. She used Evan—" her voice cracked, but she didn't look at him "—but it was her decision. Calliope told you that Thalia killed Robert, my father. Thalia didn't kill him. Robert left of his own free will. He was living in Virginia until Calliope had him killed two weeks ago."

"He stole from us!" Calliope said. "What is the punishment for thievery?" she asked the assembled group.

No one responded, though there was some whispering among the people.

"Don't make this any more difficult than it needs to be," Dean said as he slowly approached Calliope. "Evan," he said, "put the gun down."

"No," Evan said. "She can't get away with this."

"She won't," Dean said. "Everyone, stay where you are, hands where we can see them. No one needs to get hurt."

His voice was calm, clear, in control.

"I'm not leaving," Calliope screamed. "You can't take me!"

She sounded panicked. Gone was her control, her confidence. Fear etched her face.

A gunshot rang out. Calliope fell to the ground, blood spreading across her chest.

Evan dropped the gun he held and fell to his knees. "I'm sorry, Riley. I'm so, so sorry."

50

Havenwood

Kara sat on the couch in Athena's old house and drank a full bottle of water that Michael handed her. She was exhausted—physically, emotionally. Matt was in the adjoining room being checked over by a SWAT medic.

Ryder sat in the corner looking relaxed for the first time in days. He had been working communications for the last several hours, but was taking a much-needed break. She was glad he was here now.

Michael sat across from her. "It's over," he said, drinking his own water.

For them, but not for Riley and the others. Evan had been taken into custody and would be on suicide watch for the time being. Dean and Sloane were coordinating interviews with all Havenwood residents with the assistance of Denver FBI. They were using the barn to do it, after clearing all food and drink from the area. They still didn't know if Evan was lying that Calliope had poisoned their tea, but Kara thought not.

The woman had been half senseless with fear. She would rather have killed everyone she knew than leave Havenwood. Would she have killed herself, as well?

Riley was assisting Dean with the interviews, because no one would talk to the FBI without her present. They could have asked for lawyers, but no one did, even after being read their rights. It was odd, and something Kara would be thinking about for a long time. But it seemed most of the people in Havenwood were thrilled that Riley was alive. It would take days, maybe longer, to sift through everything here in Havenwood.

But Kara wanted to go home.

Matt came out of the room and the SWAT medic left. He had a bandage around his left wrist and the cuts on his face had been cleaned and taped. He looked as tired as she felt.

Michael handed him a water bottle, and Matt took it and sat on the couch next to Kara. He kissed her.

"Promise, I won't do it again in front of Michael, but I had to."

She kissed him back. "Ditto."

At that moment Catherine walked in. Great, Kara thought. She'd probably write them up for inappropriate display of affection while on duty.

Matt put his arm around Kara, as if sensing her thoughts, and pulled her to him.

"How are the interviews going?" he asked.

"It's a process," Catherine said. "Riley is doing surprisingly well. She's stronger than I thought."

Kara nodded. She knew there was a spine of steel under the fear. She was glad she was right.

Catherine sat on a chair. "Dean, Sloane, myself, and a couple Denver agents are going to stay here overnight to finish the interviews and search. The searches may take a few days longer because of the unmarked graveyard on the far south end of the property. Riley will lead us to it in the morning. There's a lot to sort through. It's going to take time."

"Do you need me to stay, as well?" Ryder asked.

Normally, Ryder would do anything that was asked of him, but Kara sensed in his tone that he wanted to leave.

"No, you need downtime. We all do."

"I'll book us on a flight out of Durango first thing in the morning," Ryder said. "I made hotel reservations, and arranged with one of the Denver agents to drive us."

"Thank you," Matt said. "I owe you."

"No, sir, you really don't. I'm glad you're not seriously injured."

Catherine cleared her throat. "Kara, I owe you an apology."

Kara couldn't keep the surprise off her face. Not only because Catherine was apologizing to her, but because she was doing it in front of Matt and the others.

Kara shrugged. "I doubt it."

"I allowed my personal feelings to interfere with my professional responsibilities. You are a very good cop. You see and understand a lot more than I gave you credit for, because I—" she cleared her throat "—I didn't like that you were in a relationship with Matt. That's my personal issue, not yours. You haven't done anything to make me or anyone believe your relationship has put any case in jeopardy. So, I am sorry."

Kara didn't know how to respond. Matt didn't say anything. Accepting the apology was solely up to her.

She didn't want to, because sometimes Catherine intentionally made her feel inferior. But that was Kara letting Catherine make her feel less than. Now, with the apology, Kara hoped that would change. And if it didn't...maybe she'd just call her on it.

"Accepted," she said.

Catherine visibly relaxed. "Thank you." She stood and said, "Have a safe trip home. I'll see you in a few days."

When she left, Kara said, "Wow. I didn't expect that."

"It was a long time coming," Matt said.

"Agreed," Michael said. "Though maybe now you can stop deliberately baiting her."

"Maybe," Kara said with a half smile. "But sometimes, it's fun to pull her chain."

TWO WEEKS LATER

51

Havenwood

Riley stood in the center of Havenwood and felt for the first time since her grandma died that she was home.

It was an odd feeling. She'd been raised here, and then there had been violence and sorrow.

But there had also been good.

She remembered learning about edible plants from her grandmother. About how to bake bread from Aunt Thalia. About carpentry from William and animals from Andrew. She remembered the harsh winters and beautiful summers. How she tried and failed a hundred times to quilt, and marveled at Tess's swift, sure fingers as she created clothes from cloth.

Havenwood was not the world, but it was *a* world, and her past wasn't all bad.

Now Havenwood was hers.

Ryder Kim had told her that her grandfather William had left a will giving the land to her if Thalia was deceased. That alone wouldn't have guaranteed the transfer, but the original deed was clear: descendants of Thaddeus Riley, William's grandfather, could stay on the land. William had legally adopted Calliope, something Riley hadn't known. Because the adoption was legal, Riley was his legal granddaughter and one of his descendants.

In fact, his only descendant. The last heir because William's brother had signed over all rights to Havenwood long ago.

When Riley died, if she had no children, the land would be deeded back to the government, unless she signed away her rights to them before then.

She couldn't imagine doing that.

There was so much to do. Half the people of Havenwood had left, walked away disillusioned after learning the truth. Several had been arrested—including Garrett, Abby, and Evan. Some were dead. Anton had survived his suicide attempt and was now in jail awaiting his trial, but Ginger, Marcos, and Karin all died from the poison. Riley didn't know if she could trust any who remained, but how could she send them off into a world they knew nothing about?

She was in limbo, but she had ideas. So many ideas. She shared her thoughts with the remaining residents, and most supported her.

Matt and Kara came to visit. They told her they had to wrap up some legal details in Colorado, but Riley sensed they came to make sure she was okay.

They drove down in a four-wheel-drive rental car. No one tried to stop them because Riley had taken the gate down. Havenwood was open now, and people could come and go as they pleased.

Riley greeted them with Banjo, the Saint Bernard, at her side. She'd moved into her grandmother's cottage; she would never live in her mother's house. She couldn't even cross the threshold. Maybe someday she could face the demons between those walls; not today.

She'd considered taking the entire building apart.

"I'm glad you came," Riley said to Matt and Kara. She smiled and it felt genuine. She'd smiled a lot lately, more than she had in years.

In fact, she didn't think she had smiled much since her grandmother died.

"We're flying out tonight, wanted to check on you, make sure everything was okay," Matt said. He looked around, skeptical.

"I'm good," she said, and meant it. "Most people left, but some stayed. Enough, I think. We have a lot of work to do."

She motioned for them to walk with her and she told them how Ryder had helped her find a lawyer to make sure she didn't lose the property. Because part of the land had been used for growing and selling illegal marijuana, the government could have come in and kicked everyone off. But because Riley hadn't participated in it, and was shutting down the operation and allowing inspections and fully cooperating with the authorities, the lawyer was confident she could retain the land.

"And you've been working with Agent Stewart, right?" Matt said. One of the agreements Riley had made was to be available for questions. George Stewart with the Denver FBI office was her assigned contact.

"Yes," Riley said. "He was here the other day, told me what was going on in the process. He's very kind." She paused, bit her lip. "I've been giving something a lot of thought." Saying this out loud was awkward.

"What?" Kara asked.

"I'm going to turn Havenwood into an artist retreat. We have to earn money to survive, pay taxes, all that stuff. So from April through September, we'll open cabins to writers and painters and creators of all sorts. They can stay for a week, month, all summer. They'll pay for it, and help run the place."

"That's a great idea," Kara said.

Riley beamed. "Yeah, I think so. It's just such a change. We have to get the word out, but I think it'll work. I really do."

Matt and Kara stayed for lunch, then they said their goodbyes and left.

Riley walked around, Banjo by her side, seeing all the possibilities. Yes, a retreat was a great idea.

She headed back to her cottage and sat on the bench, watched the community go about their business.

There were forty-two people left. And a few more were going to leave, she knew. Probably by the end of the summer, before the snow would change the way they lived. But that was okay.

She would make Havenwood work, in a way her grandmother would be proud.

Kara leaned her head on Matt's shoulder as they flew not to DC, but to Miami. They had a three-day weekend and he was going to make the most of it.

Matt had convinced her to meet his brother and family. He didn't know if she agreed because of everything that happened two weeks ago, or if she really wanted to. Maybe he didn't care.

Maybe he cared a little.

He played with her fingers, wondering what she was thinking.

"When do you close escrow on your house?" he asked.

"May 15." She sighed. "I'm going to miss Quantico."

"You don't mean that."

"It was free." She grinned at him, kissed him. "I'm looking forward to making the house my own. I loved my condo in Santa Monica because it was mine, something I bought all by myself. But I never did anything to it. I was hardly there."

"With our schedules, I doubt we'll be spending much time in either of our houses."

She laughed. "True. But, when I'm home, I want it to be mine. I want it to be personal, special."

"I understand that."

"Okay, Matt, spill. What's bugging you?"

"Are you okay with meeting my brother and his family?"

She didn't say anything.

"Kara?"

"I'm nervous. I know they are important to you, and I just… I don't know, I don't do family events well. And it's your niece's baptism. Right? Baptism?"

He smiled. "Yes. She was born right before Christmas and is adorable. Baptism is probably the mellowest of Catholic traditions. And then there's a party with lots of people, but they're good people. You'll like most of them. But tonight, it's just you and me on the beach."

"Isn't that a drink?"

"That's sex on the beach."

"Right."

She nipped his lip and he kissed her. "You drive me crazy. Don't stop."

"I won't." She leaned into him. "You think Riley is going to be okay?"

"She seemed…at peace. Yeah, I think she will be okay."

"Good."

Kara, who never slept on planes, fell to sleep. Matt looked at her, kissed her hair, reached for her hand, and closed his eyes.

They were exactly where they were supposed to be.

★ ★ ★ ★ ★